fin

a story of love and hope

gamal c williams

ISBN: 978-1-7355247-0-2

fin: a story of love and hope

by Gamal C. Williams

Published by Rae Legacy Publishing

Cover designed by Gamal C. Williams and Mario Webley

Reviews for fin: a story of love and hope

"...the first book I read in a long time where I couldn't put it down...I laughed, cried, and shared moments with each character. You know it's an amazing story when the author can cause you to cry. This was my first time reading a book from Gamal Williams, and I hope to read more in the future."

Leslie Crawford, CEO, Exposed Books Publishing

"Fin is an absolute real and vibrant read. Gamal C. Williams is an extraordinary and brilliant writer who knows how to bring the realness of street life, loyalty, and betrayal to life. The creative writing of each story leaves the reader wanting more. Fin is a true, non-stop, emotional read that really devours the reader and propels them into a different world."

Courtney Kittrell, Author of *Unapologetically Favored* and *Wake Up. Turn Up. Bless Up. Beautiful Inspiration For Her*

"Fin is a page turning, emotion evoking tale about a young man's life and the love that tethers him. A deep read into the hearts and minds of those connected to him on his journey. Fin isn't an extraordinary love story. This book is a magnificent look into what the word truly means, at the core. You think you know love, and then you read Fin."

Amber Hightower, Poet, Artist

"With the mastery in his storytelling, it is difficult to believe this is Mr. Williams' debut novel. ...It is a gritty, touching, and smart... It grips the reader from the start and makes you want to know more about the characters. ...The book does not shy away from tense and uncomfortable situations; however, it deals with them in a way the reader can understand. It is significant to note, because it is rare, I was able to experience a range of emotions from crying to uplifted."

-Tamara S.

For

JJ, Poppa, Man Man, Mega, Livy,

Mike, Cookie Girl, DJ, Buddha Boo, Bri Bri,

Tez, Old Lady, Rockhead, Dee Dee,

Lysie, Koopa, Nani, Gabby Baby,

Tuck Tuck, Gracie, Lizzy, Kyra, Liyah, Yoke Yoke,

Choco, Holla Baby, and Crunk Juice

It's never too late or too soon to make your dreams a reality.

May all your dreams come true. I love you.

...and for Nook and TiTi

We love and miss you every single day.

table of contents

cori

epilogue

acknowledgments

To Sasha Ridley and Rae Legacy Publishing. This project wouldn't exist if not for your encouragement, guidance, and sound advice. What once was a literal dream turned into a dream, I never thought I would or could dream. You made that dream a reality. I am forever in your debt.

To Brian Marsh. Cuzzo, I can't begin telling you what your guidance and expertise meant not only to my writing, but to helping me define my voice. Love you, Cuz. Thank you!

To my Navy and Marine Corps family. Your camaraderie has been a blessing to my soul. Thank you for all of the laughs, the cries, the shared joy and anguish. No matter what, we always did it together and succeeded. My success was only because of yours.

To my friends and family that endured my long ramblings on social media. It's because of your encouragement that I began to believe that I *could* be a writer. Thank you.

To my mama aka my Pretty Lady. You mean the world to me. I love you to the moon and back again.

I'll save all the really mushy stuff for those special people...you know who you are. Leave this page blank. When I see you, I'll write what my heart wants to tell you.

prologue

the note

"Ok, class. Let's put our things away so we can get ready to go."

As Mrs. Graves gave direction to her second grade Olde Park Elementary School class it caused excitement in the twenty-two seven and eight-year olds. Not for Fin, however. His heart dropped. The shuffling of chairs against the linoleum floor, papers rustling and crinkling as they were stuffed into desks, bookbags, and cubby holes, and the escalating voices of the second-grade class began to grow into a dull roar. The normally energetic, sociable, and extremely intelligent Fin was melancholy. The seven-year-old didn't really say much to his classmates. He didn't joke with Khalil about how much Khalil's favorite football team, the Mustangs, sucked. He didn't smile extra hard at Franschel, his secret crush. He didn't even ask Mycheal if he saw last night's episode of their favorite anime, Lucumi Warriors. Today, his mind was on the finality of the moment.

Mrs. Graves taught the gifted second grade class at Olde Park Elementary School in the Valebrook section of Norfolk, Virginia. Fin

xiii

was her top student. His teacher marveled at how fast he grasped concepts. Sometimes Mrs. Graves would ask him to help other kids with their reading and math assignments. He loved to do it too, save for when it was Russy that needed the help. He got along with everyone in his class, everyone except for Russy aka Russell McDavid. Russy was the second tallest kid in the class after Fin and seemed to think that by challenging Fin, he would either grow an inch or two or Fin would somehow shrink. Whenever Russy would realize that his daily "Ways to Challenge Fin" list wasn't going to be checked off, he would move on to a smaller kid, prompting Fin to step in. His mother would often tell him that his need to protect those smaller than him was a trait he got from his father. Every day there was something between the two of them, pushing in line, shoving on the playground, Russy throwing things. The cardinal sin though was Russy talking about Fin's dad. That usually resulted in a fight. Things had gotten worse between Fin and Russy recently. Mrs. Graves decided to place them as far away from each other in class as possible. She placed Fin in the back right and Russy in the front left. Fin was glad Mrs. Graves assigned their seats that way so Russy couldn't throw an unexpected paper ball at the back of his head. *Mama said hate is a strong word and we must not hate people. Maybe I'll ask her that if I hate just one person, maybe God will forgive me.* He quickly realized that conversation wouldn't go over so well. *I'll just hate him in my head. Mama doesn't have to know.*

School would be letting out soon and he was dreading it. After an earlier scuffle with Russy during lunch, Mrs. Graves informed both boys they would be receiving notes home. *Maybe she won't be too mad at me. I mean, I was sticking up for someone. Mama said I have to know how much bigger and stronger I am than other kids and I should never be a bully. I guess Russy's Mama never told him that.* He knew his mama was *not* going to like it, but that wasn't what had him down. Today was his last day. Though Fin never told anyone that they would be leaving soon, his angst about his family's impending move left him angrier than normal and with a very short temper. In a few minutes, the dismissal bell would ring and his time at Olde Park Elementary would be over.

Whenever Fin was down, he would get really quiet like his father would. It was usually in those moments his mother would grab his face, look him in the eyes, smile and say *"What could be troubling that loving heart?"* to which Fin would shrug. *"Well, whenever you're ready to talk, I am here. You will never be alone in this world."* He would normally look up at her, then fling his arms around her waist, bury his face in her belly and cry a bit. It was the safety in that space that allowed him this release. She would rub his back for as long as he needed. Fin loved his mama. Mrs. Graves took a break from corralling her rambunctious group of children and focused her attention on Fin as she made her way back to the front of the class.

"Okay class, we should be getting into our seats for the announcements. Fin, can you come to the front."

He knew this was it. It was time to get his note, one last little kick in the behind on his way out the door. Last time Mrs. Graves sent a note home he was on punishment for a week and missed Lucumi Warriors! He hoped she would show him some mercy. He slowly navigated through the aisle of desks, stepping over bookbags and lunch boxes resting next to his classmates. He finally made it to the front and planted himself, head hanging low, adjacent to Mrs. Graves' desk just as she finished scribbling something on a piece of paper. She then folded it, slid her wooden chair on the linoleum, causing a loud screeching sound and rose to greet him. She placed her arm around his shoulder.

"Class today is Fin's last day with us. Fin and his family are leaving the area. Let's say goodbye to him and let him know how much we will miss him."

fin

the note

WOOOOOOWWWW *Mrs. Graves! You gonna embarrass me and send a note home to my Mama??* The class let out a collective, sorrowful sigh. Mrs. Graves even became emotional. She genuinely loved Fin, his protective nature, his inquisitive mind, his playful yet respectful demeanor.

"Fin, we are all definitely gonna miss you! I can't wait to hear about the great things you're going to do in the future!"

Mrs. Graves gathered herself, hugged him and handed him the note. He accepted the note and slowly made his way back to his desk, plopping down into his chair. His classmates stared at him as he walked. He felt like he had a big booger on his forehead the way everyone stared. *Embarrassed in front of the class and a note.* Just then, Principal McMichaels came over the loudspeaker in his normally loud and enthusiastic voice. It was time for the afternoon announcements, the signal that school was about to be over.

"GOOOODDDD AFTERRRRRNOOOOON OLDE PARK PIRATES! What a *great day* we had today! I want to take this time to say........."

Fin tuned him out. He didn't want to listen. He didn't want to hear about tomorrow or the rest of the week or anything. He wasn't going to be there. In his head, he was screaming.

I DON'T WANT TO GO!

I DON'T WANT TO LEAVE!

THIS ISN'T FAIR!

MY FRIENDS ARE HERE!

GRANDMA IS HERE!

WHY DO WE HAVE TO MOVE?!!

WHY CAN'T I JUS..............

fin

the note

RRRRRRIIIIIIIIIIIIIIIIIIIIIIIIIIIIIIINNNNNNNNNNNNNNNNNNNGGGGGG!!

It was over. He had a knot in his stomach. While everyone else raced to the door, he sat there, not wanting to leave. Mrs. Graves watched him sulk from the door threshold, her heartbreaking knowing he would no longer be in her life. As he fought back tears, he looked up and saw her watching him. He stood from his chair, grabbed his bag, reluctantly snatched the note off his desk, and slowly made his way to the door. As he passed by her, she placed her hand on his back. He stopped, looked up at her, then hugged her. He could hear her sniffling, trying to hold back tears. He looked up at her again and she smiled at him. Then, he exited into the hallway as his classmates all screamed "BYYYEEEEE FINNNN!" Even Russy said goodbye.

"Bye Fin," Russy said, his head down. Fin almost didn't know what to say.

"Bye."

He would normally ride the school bus to his grandmother's house but today his mother was picking him up. As he walked down the hallway for the last time, he looked at the kids scurrying off to meet parents or get on to the school bus. He saw some standing in line to grab a quick drink of water before leaving. He looked at the cinder block walls covered in other children's artwork. The hallway was loud, but to him, it sounded amazing. It was a sound he knew he would miss. When he reached the doors leading to the parking circle for parent pick up, he wished the hall was longer. It was a warm day, though the sun wasn't really shining. Children rushed by him, on their way to their destinations, crossing in front and behind him in random zig-zag patterns. He dropped his head and made his way through the door. Just then, through all the noise, he heard a familiar, soothing

fin

the note

voice. Even though he was mad at her, it was the voice of the only person he wanted to be with, his mama.

"FIIIIIINNNNNNNN!"

part one

fin

chapter one

a night at brown's

Studying for a test on the principles of data science was not how Fin wanted to spend his Friday night. Cori would be there soon to pick him up from work, but instead of curling up on their small couch and watching TV, his nose was going to be in this massive text. Brown's Stop-N-Go was usually empty on late nights but it was oddly empty for a Friday. Fin welcomed it though. The quiet allowed him to focus on his studies.

Ding-a-ling!

The chime from the bell on the back of the glass door, alerted Fin that a patron was entering the store. He looked up to see his relief, Paulie. Paulie was an old, heavy set Black man that reminded him of a church deacon. Fin watched him as he navigated his rotund frame carefully through the threshold of the door.

"Nose always up in them books."

a night at brown's

"I'm not tryna work here the rest of my life."

"Ain't nothin' wrong with a simple life, nah. Good pay for good work. Whatcha studyin' tonight?"

"Data Science."

"That's like chromosomes and what not, right?"

Fin chuckled at the old man's ignorance.

"Not the science of DNA, *data* science.   It bridges mathematics, programming and business analytics."

"Ana-what?"

"Analytics. It's the... Its computer stuff. It's for computers."

Fin looked at Paulie from behind the counter with a huge smile on his face as Paulie began to rant and rave about technology and his disdain for it.

"There you go, tryna talk all fancy. I don't know nothin' 'bout computers, no way. Hell, I need my grandbabies to work this damn phone my daughter got me. Everythang is just too damn complicated. Tried to take one of them self-pictures and all I got was my damn nostrils! A phone just needs to be a phone."

"Self-pictures? You mean a *selfie*?"

"A selfie, a melfie, a whatever y'all youngins call 'em. You know what I meant!"

Fin's smile grew bigger.   Paulie noticed Fin's apparent enjoyment at his expense and didn't take to kindly to it.

"Oh, that's funny to you?"

fin

a night at brown's

Fin couldn't hold it in any longer and talked through his laughter. "I don't want no trouble, Paulie. Here, gimme your phone."

"I don't need yo' laughin' ass givin' me no pity! I'mma step outside and smoke me one."

"Cool."

Brown's Stop-N-Go rested in the Clinton Hill section of Norfolk, near downtown, but not the good part of it. The delineation between one side of the tracks and the other was stark. Where the office buildings, chic gastro pubs, restaurants, sports arena and the shopping district ended, began a neighborhood rife with low-income housing, liquor stores, homeless shelters, and industrial plants. Brown's was the last business at the end of a strip mall that had seen better days. The four gas pumps in front of Brown's were old and only three of them functioned properly. The awning overhead flickered intermittently like the fluorescent lighting of a bug zapper, often going dark for long periods of time before flicking back on without warning. At night, the customers that frequented Brown's would hang out in front of the store, sharing their stories over cold beer and cigarettes, the smell of spilled alcohol on hot days would mark their past night's fellowship. Tonight, wasn't one of those nights, however. Fin wondered where the outside regulars were, the "Corner Boys" as he jokingly referred to them as. He reasoned they must've found a warmer location to enjoy their evening drinks on this cool, early-fall evening.

Fin grew up in nearby Valebrook, a predominately Black neighborhood of Norfolk. Valebrook was an area of poor, yet hard working folk, much like those that inhabited the section of Clinton Hill. While there are plenty of good people in these areas, there is also an element that has resorted to other means to survive. He had friends who are third and fourth generation gangsters that are friends with

5

third and fourth generation construction workers, garbage men, and postal workers. In neighborhoods like Valebrook and Clinton Hill, people tended to accept their lot in life, and lived it to the fullest. That ideology, that acceptance of a lesser life, he couldn't understand. It wasn't how he was raised.

Cori, the love of his life, was his one constant. In Cori, he found focus, motivation and a renewed sense of purpose. She, however, didn't exactly approve of him working at Brown's, due to the dangerous neighborhood it was in. He had grown comfortable at Brown's and enjoyed the solitude of the late shift. She thought he could find a job in his field, in a safer environment, but was resigned to the fact that he could be stubborn and wasn't going to budge. She finally relented and told him, if he was going to stay, he might as well practice his craft there. Fin took it to heart and installed a video-monitoring security system, developed an algorithm that anticipated future inventory requirements, and installed a server which he remotely backed up off-site. She always had a way of convincing him he could do more, and that he could be better than what he was. It's been a year since they first met in their College Algebra class, a chance meeting on his first day back after a long hiatus from school. He would often daydream, recalling the first time he saw her, and he still felt the same way he felt about her after seeing her for the first time.

His friend had just dropped him off on campus, and Fin rushed to the registrar's office. Luckily, that day was the last day of registration, a fact his boy pointed out to him. The registrar told him that one of the classes he signed up for just started ten minutes ago, and if he hurried, he wouldn't miss so much of the class that the professor would turn him away. Fin ran across the quad towards the Learning Center, up two flights of stairs, then down the hallway, looking up at the classroom numbers above the door and comparing them to his schedule. *Was it 3123? 3124? No, 3126.* He was confused by where his class was, then he heard a distant voice posing a question.

"So, what if we change the function of *f*?"

That must be the professor. Only they talk that loud. He followed the sound of the echoing voice easily, as the hallway was extremely quiet and empty. He swung the door open, causing all the students to turn and stare at him. He hated to be the center of attention, and a rush of embarrassment washed over him. The professor looked visibly disturbed by the interruption.

"Can I help you?"

"Ummmm, yes. I just registered for this class."

"Get a syllabus and student information sheet off the back table and grab..." said the professor, pausing as he scanned the room, "...there seems to be only one seat. Just take that one."

As the rest of the class turned around and refocused on either the whiteboard or their laptops, Fin blindly walked over to the table. His eyes remained on the front of the class. He barely grabbed the sheets correctly as his focus was on one thing: Cori. Cori sat in the front left-center of the fluorescent lit classroom, filled with tables that seated two though many had three or even four eager students huddled around them. He grabbed a few of the papers off of the desk, and sat in the back right, never taking his eyes off her. He was smitten just by her profile alone. Her curly, rusty brown afro with blonde-orange tips nestled throughout, seemed like a crown on her head, and almost glowed next to her deep brown skin, which was the color of healthy soil. She wiggled her pencil in her right hand, close to her ear, as she intently listened to the professor. She was wearing a green turtleneck, jeans, and no makeup. Fin wasn't sure if her bare face was a conscious choice of confidence and security, or the hasty decision of a rushed college student, a feeling he remembered all too well.

fin

a night at brown's

Normally, he would be in a more prominent location than back right, under the air conditioner supply vent where he could see her better, but that's what happens when you pick a class up late; his indecision left him with no decision at all.

BZZZZZZZZZZZZ! BZZZZZZZZZZZZ!

For a cellphone, he thought that vibrate feature sure was loud! Cori, realizing it was her phone, turned over her right shoulder to silence it, and when she did, he knew her makeup-less face was no mistake. Her full lips pursed in frustration as she examined the identity of the caller. Her deep brown eyes rolled as she returned the phone to her purse hanging off the chair. *Even angry she is gorgeous!* As she turned her head to refocus on the lesson, their eyes met, and he felt sparks. Cori, however, seemed to overlook the exchange as if nothing happened. Fin could barely take his mind off her until he realized an actual question was being posed to the class.

"So, if f times x equals the square root of seven minus x, which of the following would be the domain of this function?"

Cori's hand shot up

"Ms. Porter."

"Negative infinity and seven."

"Good. Now what happens if..."

The sound of the professor's voice trailed off for him. The rest of the forty-five-minute class was a blur. He realized he spent most of it staring at Cori, and thinking of what her kiss felt like, her smell, her warmth, her conversation. When the professor released the class, anxious and embarrassed, he popped up, grabbed his laptop, bag and cellphone then raced out the door. He often felt tongue tied when it came to women, so though he wanted the answers to all of his questions, he left. He made his way down the hall, his mind still on Cori, but he got no more than a few feet down the hallway before realizing he forgot something.

FUCK! He was in such a rush to leave the class, he realized he had left his lunch bag sitting on the floor. It wasn't the meal in the bag, it was the bag itself. It was once his father's. As he stopped, he raised his frustrated head to the sky, then he heard a voice.

"You know, if only you were focused on *you* during class, you might've remembered this."

He spun around. There she was, standing there with his gray lunch bag dangling from her two outstretched fingers. She had a smile that conveyed confidence and an eagerness in her eyes. She was taller than he thought she would be, but even more beautiful up close. As she stood there in anticipation, waiting for him to respond, her engaging smile began to dissipate. His blank stare was not the response she thought she would receive.

"Stare at me all during class, rush out without saying anything to me, and now zero gratitude and a blank stare?"

Her subtle country drawl snuck in in that brief moment. There was a sass in her voice, which later on, he would discover is her way to get a response. It was then that he realized that she was aware he had been gawking at her. His heart began to beat faster.

"Oh! Umm, my bad. Thanks. Thanks a lot. Can't believe I left it!"

His response elicited the same pursed mouth as her unexpected phone call did.

"Mmmm-hmmmm."

fin

a night at brown's

He was completely tongue-tied. *Tell her how beautiful she is! No, she probably gets that all the time.* His mind was in a state of contention; part of him wanted to speak, the other was gripped in the fear that he would say the wrong thing. *Say something! Anything, stupid!* She waited patiently, but her eagerness quickly turned to utter disappointment. She figured he either wasn't interested or had a girlfriend. Her shoulders slumped a bit, the corner of her mouth turned down and her eyes grew sad. She decided to end the awkward situation.

"Sooooo, I'm going to go. I have a tutoring session to get to but ummmm, I'll see you around I guess."

"Wait. I'm sorry. It's just..."

Fin searched for the words, but nothing seemed right or felt good enough to impress her. She decided to give him one more shot, one more attempt to engage with her the way she wanted to engage with him. Her forward nature went on full display.

"Would you like to have a late lunch with me? How about you meet me here around four thirty? I should be done with my tutoring session by then."

She wanted to spend time with him more than anything. *C'mon, dude. Say yes!* Fin was surprised by her forwardness. His face frowned and his voice elevated.

"Really?"

"You know what..."

She threw her hand up and turned to walk away. He grabbed her outstretched hand, causing her to stop and look over her shoulder.

"Yes. I'll have lunch with you."

a night at brown's

For the first time, she heard a confidence in his voice. She turned to look at him. She liked his eyes, they seemed kind, yet sorrowful. As he held her hand, his thumb gently rubbed the back of it. Whatever he was trying to say but couldn't, his touch said loud and clear. She looked down at her hand in his soft embrace, then up at him and exhaled.

"Cori. Cori Porter."

"Fin. People call me Fin, but my real name is..."

"James Finley."

"Wait. You know my...how did you know..."

"I'll tell you at four thirty. Right here. Don't be late."

His face was in conflict, his brow frowned from confusion while his mouth smiled from surprise.

"Yeah, I'll meet you here. I'll meet you wherever you want me to."

She took a few steps backward, slowly pulling away, their hands clasped until distance pulled them apart. She smiled, biting her lip. Now *she* was the nervous one. She quickly turned and walked away. She needed a moment to regain her cool. He stood there, admiring the way her shapely figure moved. When he finally decided to turn and go, he didn't make it three steps before he heard her voice call to him from down the hall. It sounded like the melody to his new favorite song. He turned back to see her one last time.

"Four thirty, Mr. Finley!"

Her last words as she looked back at him, still smiling, her face glowing from forty feet away, and then she was gone. They shared lunch that day at four thirty, talked for what seemed like hours about

a night at brown's

everything, and then had dinner that night at a local diner not too far from campus. From that day forward, schedule permitting, the couple hadn't missed a lunch or dinner together. That was a year ago, and Fin often reflects on that day; her energy, her smile, her willingness to see him in that moment, is what kept him going on nights like this. The convenience store sat four blocks away from the apartment they shared. It was a small studio close to campus, around the corner from that diner, which was now their favorite. Cori worked at Norfolk General Hospital in the cafeteria. On nights when he doesn't work, he takes their white 2008 Caprice up to the hospital, and they have a meal there. Afterwards, he liked to sit in the cafeteria doing homework until she got off. Tonight, they were both working, so she had the car. On nights when they both worked, it wasn't too far for him to walk home if need be and he damn sure wasn't letting her catch a bus or cab. On those nights, she would pick him up once she got off, then they'd either head home, or to the diner for a late dinner.

It was 10:37pm, which meant that Cori would be there any minute. While Paulie stood out front, smoking his last cigarette of the night, Fin counted out the register. Paulie dropped the cigarette butt on the ground, extinguishing it with his heel.

Ding-a-ling!

"Count right?"

"Of course, it is. Only made about fifty bucks tonight."

"Aight youngin', I got it. Go on and get ready for that fine lil' gal you got coming." Paulie let out a belly laugh.

"Man, what I tell you about talking about my girl, Bruh!"

Paulie was wont to make slick comments about Cori's appearance and shape, mostly to get under Fin's skin. Cori liked to use that bit of information against him too and would often reply to his refusal to do something for her with, "I betchu Paulie would do it for me." He almost never told her no, though she couldn't resist the chance to poke fun at him.

"Man, calm yo' ass down! I swear you youngins sensitive boutcha lil' girlfriends. Man, back in the day..."

"Look, Bruh. I done told you about that back in the day stuff too! Nobody trying to hear all that, man. Now slump yo' big ass back behind this register!" Fin liked giving Paulie just as much grief as Paulie gave him.

"Oh, so we just gonna talk about my weight? You know I got the sugar!"

As if he didn't just allude to his weight being caused by diabetes, Paulie snatched a cake from the pastry rack, opened it and shoved it into his mouth.

"That's the problem, man. Yo' ass got *too much* damn sugar! All them damn pies and cakes you stuff in your mouth!"

"Yeah, well I know you better take this damn trash and these books as you leave. Look like the damn Library of Congress back here!"

Fin glanced at his watch. 10:41pm. He knew he had better hurry. He gathered his "library" and school materials, placed them in his bag, and brushed by Paulie, giving him a gentle nudge in jest with his forearm as he passed. Paulie lumbered passed him as if it was nothing, he always seemed to move as if he had just woken up.

"Don't forget that trash either!"

Paulie said the same thing every night, as if Fin *ever* did. Fin didn't respond though; his mind was on Cori. He grabbed the trash out of the bin behind the counter, threw his bookbag over his shoulder, slid his cellphone into his back pocket, and headed out.

fin

a night at brown's

"Nite, Paulie. Be safe."

"You too, youngin'!"

Though they gave each other a rash of shit, Paulie was fond of Fin. He saw his potential and drive, and more importantly, he saw the way Fin and Cori loved each other. He was rooting for them to succeed. Fin walked through the back aisle, which was stocked full of house cleaning products, car automotive supplies to his right, and a row of coolers with beer, milk and sodas to his left. He always lamented there weren't more fresh juices and water in Brown's, but he figured old man Brown knew what would make money, and that is all he would stock. As he passed the few selections of water, he opened the cooler and grabbed a cold one, and shouted back at Paulie.

"I'm snagging a water. Take care of that for me."

"Man, whatchu think this is?!"

Paulie's grumblings became more inaudible as he moved towards the back door. Fin chuckled. He swung the back door open and felt a slight chill. It was unusually cool on this late September night and he wondered if Cori remembered her sweater. He was glad he got the car's heater fixed a few months back, despite her objections. "Baby, we don't have the money to fix that right now. Besides, it's April, and summer will be here soon. We can put that off for later," he remembered her objecting. *I'll bet tonight, she'll be glad I convinced her.* He set his bag and recently acquired water on the ground, then walked over to the dumpster. He looked at his cellphone and noted the time was now 10:42. He looked to his left and saw a Norfolk Police car turn into the parking lot, and pull around front. He rarely interacted with the police officers that came in for their nightly coffee and snacks, but was pretty cool with one in particular. He was usually gone by the time the night patrol arrived. Moments before the police entered the Brown's parking lot, Paulie, still mad that Fin took that

fin

a night at brown's

water knowing that his register may come up short, slammed the register drawer closed after he added a dollar seventy-three to the count, two dollars short of its actual price.

"Be damned if I pay for that expensive ass water he be drinking."

Ding-a-ling!

Paulie looked up to greet the late-night customer only to see the barrel of a Walter Creed 9mm Luger semi-automatic pistol staring back at him. Paulie didn't know much in this world, but he knew his guns. Even in this moment of dread, his mind fell back to one of the things he knew.

"YOU KNOW WHAT THIS IS, MOTHERFUCKER! LET'S GO FO' I BLAST YO' FAT ASS!"

Paulie was visibly rattled. "Take it easy now, youngin'. Nobody needs to get hurt. I'll get you yo' mon..."

CRACK!

The flash of pain and light and the metallic sound against bone and flesh let Paulie know he had been hit in the face with the gun and not shot. *Fucker moves fast!* His mind was in a tailspin.

"SHUT THE FUCK UP, AND HAND THAT MONEY OVER! SAY ONE MORE WORD AN' I'MMA SHOW YOU WHAT'S INSIDE THIS FUCKING BARREL!"

Then Paulie heard the other voice. "HURRY THE FUCK UP!"

As he regained his senses, Paulie realized there were *two* robbers and not one, a detail he understandably missed after his initial meeting with "Mr. Luger". It bothered him that in the moment, he couldn't even recall what the man pointing the gun at him looked like.

a night at brown's

He had once been robbed at gunpoint in the street. In that instance, a man walked up on him and drew a pistol. He never forgot what the man looked like, and that was some ten or eleven years ago. However, one's brain tends to focus on the immediate threat, and when a 9mm semi-automatic pistol is less than two centimeters from your face, your vision tends to hone in on that dark barrel. His vision wouldn't have been so narrow, once upon a time. In his heyday, he would have dropped both of these would-be gangsters. That was years ago, however. Now, all he saw was the gun. At that close proximity, the barrel looked like a tunnel he could walk into. He gathered himself from the hit, though his ears and head were still ringing, and hit the drawer eject button on the register. The sound of the drawer hitting the mechanical stop caused the second robber to look over at him, and for a moment, they locked eyes through the robber's knit ski mask. The moment caused the gunman to grow impatient, fearful of being caught.

"ALL THAT SHIT! HURRY THE FUCK UP!"

As the gunman waved the gun towards the register drawer, Paulie's mind began taking mental pictures. He was a thin, muscular man, with a long-sleeved white shirt that clung to his frame. Though his ski-mask hid his face, his mustache and part of his beard protruded from the opening for his mouth. Towards the back of his head, Paulie noticed what appeared to be dreadlocks hanging from underneath the ski-mask. He wore leather gloves that exposed his wrist and what looked like some sort of tattoo. *Bullets surrounded in words. THREE ...THE...* He couldn't make out the rest. *I'mma remember that shit! Mafucka try and rob me!* Suddenly, something spooked the second robber.

"OH FUCK! THE COPS IS OUTSIDE!"

He had just seen the police cruiser that Fin saw moments earlier, pull in and park about four spots down from the door. From

a night at brown's

the police's vantage point, they couldn't see inside the store, as their view was blocked by the ice freezer and video disc dispensary machine outside. The gunman pressed the gun into the top of Paulie's head.

"WHERE'S THE BACK DOOR?!"

Paulie began to play the scenario out in his head. *Get these stupid mafuckas they money and get them the hell out of here!* He motioned with his head where the back exit was and handed over the money.

"It's right through there, son. Now, you don't have to do this."

"I AIN'T YA' FUCKING SON!"

"Calm down, nah. I ain't mean no harm. You ain't gotta do this."

The gunman grew increasingly agitated. What Paulie meant as calm reasoning, the gunman took as condescending and disrespectful.

"You know what?"

In that split second, Paulie knew what would happen next. He saw the gunman's eyes squint; his lips curl up into what he could only imagine was a snarl. As the gunman opened his mouth to speak, Paulie knew there was no escape. He closed his eyes.

"FUCK YOU!"

BANG!! BANG!!

The bullets tore through Paulie's skull and upper torso. His lifeless, rotund body hit the floor behind the register with a thud. The second robber was terrified. He panicked.

"OH SHIT!"

fin

a night at brown's

The second robber darted out of the front door, heading away from the parked police cruiser. The gunman paused for a moment and stared at Paulie's body before sprinting to the back of the store, turning down the same aisle Fin had just travelled, knocking merchandise off the shelves in his panic to escape.

Fin had just closed the lid on the dumpster. *Those two shots were really fucking close! What the fuck is going on now? Babe was right. I need to get out here.* Fin wanted to go check on Paulie, but first, he needed to warn his love. He reached into his back pocket to grab his cell to call Cori to tell her to stay away, and to either go back to the hospital or to her parents' house and wait for him to call.

When the shots rang out, the two officers were seconds away from exiting the vehicle. Now, they were instantly on alert. The squeal of the tires as the police cruiser pulled off could be heard all the way around back. The senior officer hit the siren and lights on the police cruiser. He shouted into the car's police radio as he engaged the car's gears into reverse and started to pursue.

"I GOT SHOTS FIRED AT BROWN'S STOP-N-GO ON THE CORNER OF EAST PRINCESS ANNE AND BALLENTINE. MALE SUSPECT HEADING NORTH, BLACK, WEARING DARK BLUE PANTS, WHITE SHOES AND A DARK HOODED SWEATSHIRT."

The officer's partner, a rookie pumped with fear and adrenaline by the shots, had only been on the force for about a year. He was new to nighttime patrol duty. His heart was racing, and he almost wanted to cry. He had never responded to an active shooter before, let alone one so close. As the car pulled off in pursuit, the young officer glanced into Brown's and saw the gunman escaping through the back. *Oh my God! I can take that asshole!*

fin

a night at brown's

"STOP THE CAR, CARL! THERE'S ANOTHER ONE IN THE STORE HEADING AROUND BACK!"

The young officer's scream caused his partner to slam the breaks on the cruiser. Once at a complete stop, and to the utter shock of the senior officer, the rookie officer jumped out, drew his weapon and headed around back. He took off towards the alley behind Brown's, shouting behind him as he did.

"HE'S HEADING AROUND BACK!"

The officer driving became instantly infuriated with his young partner's hubris.

"GOD DAMMIT!!!! GET BACK IN THE CAR!!!"

The rookie officer didn't listen. He kept running around back, charged on adrenaline and panic.

"FUCKING ROOKIES!!" he screamed before shouting into his radio. "SECOND SUSPECT IN PURSUIT BY OFFICER...."

Fin unlocked his phone to call Cori and had just pushed the icon with her face when the sound of the back door bursting open startled him. The gunman ran out in a frenzy. They collided, knocking Fin to the ground and sending his phone flying.

"MOVE, MOTHERFUCKER!"

The gunman darted away, heading towards the park across the street. Fin was confused and thoroughly scared. He was sure of one thing; that shot he heard was for Paulie. He started to go check on Paulie but thought better of it. Panicked, he frantically looked for his cellphone. He needed to make sure Cori would remain safe. He reached down, and found his phone, its glass face shattered, and

19

fin

a night at brown's

pushed the icon with her dark chocolate face. The red and blue lights from the police cruiser momentarily lit the dark alley behind Brown's Stop-N-Go the way Christmas lights illuminate a hallway from a distant room. He listened urgently to the dial tone and eventual connection.

RIIIINNNNGGGG!!!

His phone was on speaker. The sound echoed behind the empty building and into the night air. The world went silent for him, save for the ring of Cori's phone on the other end.

"FREEZE! SHOW ME YOUR HANDS!"

Fin didn't hear the officer. He had tuned everything out. His mind was laser focused on the love of his life, the same way it was that day in algebra class. Danger hung in the air. He felt his body shaking.

RIIIINNNNGGGG!!!

With his trembling thumb, he took the phone off of speaker mode and then drew it closer to his ear.

RIIIINNNNGGGG!!!

BANG!

The first bullet tore through his left arm, his cellphone thrown once again.

BANG!

The second hit him in the stomach.

"SHOTS FIRED!! I HAVE SHOTS FIRED! SUSPECT DOWN BEHIND SHOP-N-GO ON EAST PRINCESS AND BALLENTINE! REQUEST EMT ON SCENE AND A SUPERVISOR!"

fin

a night at brown's

Fin slumped down as he gazed at the silhouette of the officer approaching; he could still see the officer's gun pointing at him. Fin's body eventually forced him to lay down on the warm, dirty ground adjacent to the dumpster. He stared up at the dark sky in disbelief of the moment, a feeling at war with his sorrowful acceptance of it. He could see the stars peeking from behind sporadic clouds despite the glow of the streetlamps. Oddly, he had an acute awareness of all the sensations of his body; the denim rubbing against the tops of his thighs and back of his calves as his legs kicked involuntarily; the dry sting of thirst in his throat that felt as if he swallowed a spoon full of sand; the pungent odor of trash and urine burning his nostrils; the hard ground against his head as he lost the energy to lift it, his hair offering little cushion; the tightness of his sneakers on his feet. The burn in his lower abdomen wasn't nearly as annoying as the flow of blood that now ran down his left side towards his back, pooling beneath him. It tickled and he hated that sensation. He began to sweat. Yet through all of this, these warring sensations read by the rapid firing synapses in his brain, his thoughts kept going back to one thing: Cori. *She is gonna go crazy when she sees this.* He could hear her screaming "GET UP FIN!" like she did most mornings to waken him. His heart was breaking for her. The young officer approached Fin as he laid on the ground, gasping for air. The officer side stepped the glow from the orange, fluorescent streetlamp to cast light onto Fin's face.

"NORFOLK POLICE DEPARTMENT! SHOW ME YOUR HANDS!"

BZZZZZZZZZZZZ! BZZZZZZZZZZZZ!

Fin's phone was ringing but he couldn't see where it had flown. *Cori...* He coughed. The metallic savor of blood rose from his throat. As he stared up at what he now accepted would be his final night sky, a face slowly appeared from overtop of his head. He thought the sound of the officer's radio was unnecessarily loud. The wind roared hard causing the sound from the rustle of trees to echo. The officer's service weapon, which was initially trained on Fin's shadowed body, slowly lowered as the light revealed the damage he had done. Fin reached for the sound of the phone.

BZZZZZZZZZZZZ! BZZZZZZZZZZZZ!

"oh my God......" the young officer whispered.

BZZZZZZZZZZZZ! BZZZZZZZZZZZZ!

As Fin struggled for air, he desperately reached out for what the officer now saw was a cellphone. As the officer drew closer, Fin stared up at the young officer's face in horror and confusion. Though upside down, the glow now cast its truth on the officer's face as well. He could make out the face clearly, then intermittently. Fin felt himself fading. Tears began to stroll down the sides of his face, settling in each ear, his heartbreaking slowly as they traveled. All he could think about was his love. The young officer's hands began to tremble, his eyes welling up.

"No.......no.......noooooooooooo.........."

Fin looked at him, his face now awash in hurt, shock and sadness.

"I was just trying to call Cori.."

chapter two

leaving bro bro

Fin was born to loving parents. James "Big Fin" Finley was a twenty-five-year Master Chief in the Navy. Rose Finley was Head of Foreign Relations for a major Japanese computer component manufacturer. They weren't always this accomplished. Big Fin met Rose in his tenth year in the Navy, while he was stationed in Norfolk. Born in Miami, Florida, he enlisted in 1980 as a result of the Overtown Riots and had a rather tumultuous start to his Naval career. In 1990, in between his second and third duty stations, Big Fin decided to go back to college to finally get his degree, a promise he made to his father years before. In his sophomore year at Old Dominance University, Big Fin took an Introduction to Public Policy course, an intentional choice that would lead to his first encounter with Rose. He had seen her around campus, but never found the right moment to approach her. During a conversation with a fellow student, he discovered Rose was a Graduate Assistant and would often grade assignments for the professors. The decision to enroll in the Public Policy class was made easy. On the first graded assignment, Big Fin *leaving bro bro*

received a B plus on an assignment that he was positive warranted no better than a C. No matter, he decided to use this as an opportunity to talk to Rose. His plan was to march into the Teacher Assistant's office, feign disdain for his grade and demand she explain why he didn't get an A. He knew Rose had graded the paper by the handwriting. Most men had handwriting that resembled chicken scratch, like a rushed doctor. The handwriting on his paper had a flow to it that was effortless. This was Rose. He walked over to the main building, paper in hand, his mind rehearsing what he would say. His hands were moist, and his heart was racing. As he ascended the steps to the old stone building, his mouth began to water. *Get it together, James.* The Teacher's Assistant office was at the end of a long hallway, lined with blue and gray carpet squares arranged in a checkerboard pattern. His nervousness turned his normally long stride into short, choppy steps, landing his feet in every square. He arrived outside the office, took a deep breath, then opened the door.

The Teacher's Assistant's office was full of cubicles with graduate and early graduate students busy at work. Some had textbooks open on cluttered desks, studying for upcoming exams, while others were typing at feverish paces that he only wished he could replicate. His tall frame allowed him to survey the office, looking over the short cubicle walls, as he scanned for Rose. He spotted her in the corner, head down, a red pen in her hand as she harshly graded papers. He began to fidget with his watch and rubbed his wrist as his mind contemplated what he would say. People in the room began to notice the six-foot-four, two-hundred and forty-pound Big Fin, their eyes raising up to greet him, wondering why he was there. The student at the cubicle closest to the door decided to offer him assistance.

"Are you looking for someone?"

fin

leaving bro bro

He ignored the woman's question and walked straight to Rose's cubicle. He cleared his throat hoping to get her attention. She never looked up. *Well, here it goes...*

"Excuse me."

Rose glanced up to see who was addressing her before returning her gaze to her work. *Jesus, this man is fine!* She composed herself and tried to act unfazed.

"Can I help you?"

Rose had seen him around campus, as he did her. She thought he was astonishingly handsome. She noticed how he walked around with a commanding presence, not one of cockiness or arrogance, but of confidence like he could tackle any obstacle thrown his way. She saw how people often moved quickly out of his way, intimidated by his size. One day, she saw him in uniform, and she was instantly infatuated by him. She also noted how women fawned over him and decided she would get *him* to approach *her*. Imagine her surprise when one of his papers landed on her desk. She was a little disappointed by how little effort he put into the paper, however. Big Fin extended the paper towards her with a feigned confidence he knew the paper didn't deserve.

"Yes, I would like to talk about my grade on this paper?"

Rose looked at the paper, now inches from her face, looked up at him for a moment then accepted it from him. She wasn't going to clue him in that she knew his paper very well, so she acted as if she needed to look at it to jog her memory. When he saw her light brown eyes at such an intimate distance, he lost a bit of his bravado. *This woman is even finer up close!* Rose often felt offended when people questioned her grading criteria, but never seemed to question Professor Quinton's. This was the first time Big Fin would get a taste of the future Mrs. Rose Finley's squinted stare.

25

fin

leaving bro bro

"What's the problem?"

"I laid out some pretty good points in that paper. A B-plus?? Really?"

"You did, and you got a pretty good grade on it too."

She handed the paper back to him. Big Fin wasn't ready for that. He expected her to explain her reasoning, instead she turned his weak argument on its head by equating his grade to the work submitted, pretty good. He knew he had only worked on the paper for no more than three hours, but he was committed to the ruse.

"That paper deserved an A! You know how hard I worked on it?!"

"First of all, what you're *not* going to do is come up in here, interrupt *my* classwork and raise your voice. Second, while your paper was as you say 'pretty good'..."

Rose used air quotes for that part. She wasn't about to have some upstart, sophomore, military guy tell her what's what, no matter how handsome she thought he was.

"...it was rather simplistic in its position. I mean who lays out a position by starting 'It's like my momma always said'? Lastly..."

Big Fin knew he needed to stave off drowning on that small little dingey she now had him marooned on.

"Wait, wait, wait. Maybe we got off on the wrong foot here."

"*You think?!*"

"Look, I'm sorry. It was a stupid idea for me to come in here like this."

"Now *that* is an excellent point, Mr. Finley! A plus!"

"Can I make it up to you? Coffee maybe?"

fin

leaving bro bro

She let out a laugh as she laid her pen down and looked up at him.

"I almost wished I didn't want to. You aren't very observant, Mr. Finley."

"Wait - huh?"

She grabbed the six-page paper out of his large hand, turned it over and shoved it back at him. On the back was a note that read:

If you want to know how to improve this paper, call me! 757-555-0092 :)

He chuckled in amusement and embarrassment. She had already grabbed her purse and walked by him while he read.

"Are you coming? Or do I need to drop that paper to a C?"

She stood, waiting for him by the exit door, with a smile that melted him as only she could. The triumphant look on her face spoke to him: _"I won, get used to it!"_ He grinned.

"Yes, I am definitely coming."

He fell for her right then and there. Coffee led to dinner, which led to a second dinner, which led to them moving in, then marriage, then the one true love they shared, Fin. Big Fin would do anything for this amazing woman. He actually entertained leaving the military so that she could pursue her dreams, dreams and ambitions that far exceeded his. Rose, never wanting him to give up on his "other" love and family, the Navy, convinced him she could still succeed without such a sacrifice. Their compromise? Japan. When the opportunity to work as Head of Foreign Relations in Japan arose, he negotiated orders to Naval Air Station Iwakuni so that they both could be the best versions of themselves both personally and professionally. He never wanted her to put her dreams on hold, not when he had the chance to help her realize them. The Finleys left Norfolk when Fin was eight, but now, six years later, it was time to return back to the States, back to Norfolk.

Leaving Iwakuni was something Fin wanted no part of, however. *Can't believe we gotta go!* was the prevailing thought running around in fourteen-year-old Fin's head as he sat brooding in the corner in the backyard full of people. The large backyard was that of one of his father's fellow Chiefs. It was framed by a high, wooden fence, with cherry blossom trees on one side that shaded half of the yard. The lush green grass was cut low with irregular sized pavers that offered paths to a stone planter with a variety of flowers to the left and a small seating area to the right. White, plastic chairs were grouped together throughout the back yard, filled with adults as small children ran around in play. Big Fin had just been promoted to the rank of Command Master Chief, the highest Enlisted rank within a Naval command. Fin, or Lil' Fin as he was known to his father's comrades, was happy for his father's promotion, but inside, he was secretly wishing it didn't happen. Big Fin's promotion meant that he was to be assigned to a new duty station. The party was their going away party, known in the Navy as a Hail and Bail. The Hail (for welcoming newly arrived Sailors and their families) and Bail (a chance to say goodbye to those executing new orders) was comprised of many of the Senior Enlisted and Officers at the command, Strike Fighter Squadron One Three One, The Wildcats. The Wildcats were an attack fighter squadron comprised of F/A-18 fighter jets, the Navy's most lethal attack aircraft. Over the six years that the Finleys lived in Japan, Big Fin was a part of the Wildcats for the last three and completed combat deployments in each of them. When men and women spend long periods of time away from their families, putting themselves in harm's way, long-lasting bonds are formed and no command wants to see their fellow Sailors leave, especially when that Sailor is as revered and respected as Big Fin was.

fin

leaving bro bro

So, while everyone celebrated and reminisced, Fin felt out of place. He wasn't in a celebratory mood. He was normally pretty reserved, but his lack of enthusiasm stood out amongst the smiling faces. Fin had always been the tallest kid in all his classes, yet amidst the crowd of adults, his height stood out even more. The ages of the children in attendance were from eighteen years down to three months, and Fin towered over all of them. Though he was only fourteen, if you didn't know any better, one could easily mistake him for one of the Junior Officers in attendance, many of them pilots. There were numerous families there: The Millers and their son Tristan who he was in class with, the Carters and their three children (they lived next door to the Finleys), even a new family that he had never seen before. He thought their daughter was cute, but he couldn't concern himself with her. Everyone was there except his best friend, Curt.

There was a cool breeze blowing through the backyard, providing relief from the warm temperature. Fin watched the small children running around, his father's comrades conversing, laughing as they swapped sea stories and fond memories, Their spouses, men and women alike, were sharing their own personal adventures of dealing with children while their spouses were deployed. Fin sat in the corner lamenting his departure from a country he had grown to love. Japan was a world of wonder for him, a far cry from the inner-city life of Norfolk. The vast, scaling mountains with trees a color of green he had never seen before. The fresh air, that smelled rich with lotus blossoms, peonies, irises and baby blues, once you left the city. The old fifteenth and sixteenth century buildings still standing, spared the destruction of war, that allowed him to envision himself as a Samurai. The gaming culture, the anime, the food, in fact, there was nothing about Japan that he didn't love. As he sat in the corner, Rose decided to approach him to try and get him out of his funk.

"Fin, are you hungry?"

fin

leaving bro bro

"Naaaa, Mama. I'm good."

"*Naaaa?*"

"No, Mama. I'm not hungry."

Rose sat down next to her son in an empty chair.

"Baby, I know you don't want to go. I know you'll miss your friends, but your father is needed elsewhere. This is a big promotion for him, baby. Can't you *try* and be a little more cheerful?"

He shrugged his shoulders. "I get it, Mama. It's just...why can't Dad go to Virginia and leave us here? He deploys all the time, and we don't go! You have a great job! We can stay!!"

"Fin, that's not fair. Yes, your dad does deploy a lot and I know you hate it, but we are a family. Where he goes, we go. Could you imagine not seeing your dad for three years?" Again, Fin shrugged. She reached over and grabbed his chin to lift his head.

"Look at me, baby. You...*we* are going to be just fine. We will adapt to wherever we go, and we will do it as a *family*. Besides, Grandma and Grandpa are so excited to see you."

Rose emphasized the word "family." Her normally soft, sleepy eyes squinted a bit as she said it. That was Rose Finley's code for *"Tighten up. We are at your dad's function and we will put on a good front for him because we are family."* Fin loved his mama and knew enough that whenever she said something and squinted like that, it meant that was the last time she was going to say it this nicely, and he had better fix his attitude. Thankfully, a new arrival saved Fin from the rest of that rather uncomfortable conversation. Shouts of "SIR!" and "BIG CURT!" rang out from across the open backyard which signaled the arrival of Commander and Mrs. Davis, and Curt.

"Go on. Go talk to your boy."

fin

leaving bro bro

"Love you, Mama."

He rose and kissed her on her forehead. Rose smiled as he walked across the backyard, then shot Big Fin a look as if to say, *That's your son.* Big Fin, who had been watching his wife and son, smiled and silently mouthed, *I know.* Of all the things Fin would miss about Japan, the one thing he would miss more than anything else was his best friend Curt. Curt's father, Commander Curtis "Big Curt" Davis, was the Executive Officer at another command at Navy Base Iwakuni. Fin and Curt met six years prior at a similar command organized function like the one they were at today and the two formed a fast friendship. The boys found themselves together most of the time; if they weren't passing notes in school, laughing in the bleachers during gym, or off in a corner talking during lunch, they were on the phone texting, talking or tinkering around with their burgeoning interest in computer programming. The two fourteen-year-olds were inseparable and Curt's father labeled them "The Lils" as both Curt and Fin were often called Lil' Curt and Lil' Fin.

Curt was a short, pudgy little guy with a quick wit and even faster intellect. He had round cheeks that revealed double dimples whenever he smiled. Though a good seven inches shorter than Fin, he more than held his own. He was initially very quiet at school, but once he met Fin, his personality flourished. His mouth and penchant for ill-timed jokes would often lead to someone wanting to pick on him. Fin's swift arrival however usually squashed any aggression his way. Besides computer coding, the boys shared another love: sneakers. They were avid sneakerheads and loved trying to make each other jealous with their latest prized, often rare acquisitions. Fin looked down at Curt's sneakers. *This dude is trying to show me up, I see.*

"Oh, so you just gonna bring out the showstoppers as I go, huh?"

Curt smiled as he modeled his Air Jordan 8 Retro SE's.

leaving bro bro

"What? These old things? You know, I'm not one to try and show out or anything so I just threw something on. Nothing special."

The two looked at each other, as wry grins crept over both of their faces. They then burst out in laughter.

"Ain't like you wearing some bo-bo's!"

Bo-bo's was their term for cheap, off-brand sneakers. Fin was wearing a pair of Air Jordan 1 High OG's, the Travis Scott edition.

"Well, I knew yo' ass would come up in here trying to show out on my last day."

Those last words, "last day," stung for both of them. The two boys began to walk to a pair of empty chairs in the corner of the backyard, away from the crowd. Curt's face fell somber, his joyous smile slowly evaporating.

"I can't believe you're leaving, man."

"I know, man. Six years, Bro Bro."

"We had a good run, though. Who's gonna keep my sneaker game sharp? These fools on this base don't know kicks like you."

"Bro, you're in Japan. They always have fire kicks out here."

"I know, but the challenge of getting them first and leaving your mouth open like a hungry baby looking for a tit was half the fun!"

"HA! What's the other half?"

"Knowing yo' ass ain't never gonna get no tit!"

Again, they burst out into laughter. The two young boys continued throwing jabs at each other; Fin commenting on Curt's weight, Curt commenting on Fin's boat-sized feet. They laughed knowing they both wanted to cry, unsure if the two would ever see each other again. Their expressions of love for each other were interrupted though as the Commanding Officer of Big Fin's command began to speak.

"Master Chief, can you come over here please? Rose, Lil' Fin, please come join us as well."

The party all paused and faced the Commanding Officer. Big Fin, all six-foot-four of him, presented a huge smile as he set his cold beer wrapped in a coozi with the command's crest on it down. He was a proud, powerful man with a commanding presence. His arms looked as if they had been carved from solid oak. His bright smile often put people, intimidated by his size, at ease. As he moved towards the Commanding Officer, he grabbed Rose's hand. Rose paused ever so subtly to look at Fin who had yet to get up from where he and Curt had sat down. She gave a slight little head nod and a squint of her eyes, again Rose Finley code for *"If you don't get yo' ass out that chaaaaiiirrrr..."* She never broke her smile. Big Fin stopped his stride as Rose Finley "Rose Finley-ed" the situation.

Rose was a strikingly beautiful woman. Her thick, brown hair was wrapped in a bun displaying her long, beautiful neck. Her light brown eyes almost glowed against her brown sugar complexion. Her taut waist, which she spent many a day in the gym to maintain, only made her full bosom and ample bottom all-the-more alluring in the green sun dress she wore. Her beauty was her secondary feature. Wielding dual master's degrees in Psychology and Politics, her mind was a true force and many a person learned to tread lightly in the deep waters of her conversation lest they drown. She always carried herself with an ease and self-assurance one would expect in a woman of her caliber.

"Time for the dog and pony show," Curt mumbled as Fin rose from his chair.

fin

leaving bro bro

Mrs. Davis gave Curt a slight pop in the back of the head. He didn't realize she was so close. Fin looked at Curt, pointed and feigned laughter as he left Curt to join Big Fin and Rose, only to have Rose snatch his hand and pull him towards the front with his father. A slight chuckle passed through the crowd. Once in front of the party, Fin's biggest dread was occurring. He hated being the center of attention and now his anxiety was through the roof. Though six feet in height, he felt so small in these moments.

"Master Chief, I can't tell you how much we are going to miss you around here. Your impact not just on our mission, but on the lives of all of the Sailors, Officers and fellow Chiefs cannot be put into words."

Rose had her arm wrapped around Big Fin's bulging bicep. She looked up at the love of her life with such pride and admiration it seemed her smile might extend pass her cheeks and fall off her face. Fin always loved the way his parents looked at each other, the way they fed each other energy and love, that without one, the other wouldn't survive. He'd always hoped that one day, someone would look at him that way. The Commanding Officer continued:

"Now anyone that has gotten to know Master Chief knows that he gets all his smarts, all his confidence, all his sound and sage advice, from Rose."

Everyone laughed out loud. Even Fin smiled at that one.

"Rose, thank you for supporting *not only* Master Chief, but for being a mother and friend to all of us. You know, in our business, often it's the service member that is lauded by the outside world for all of the sacrifices they make, but it is only those that serve that know the true heart and spirit of our fighting forces are those that support us. *You* have been just as valued and important member of our family as Big Fin here."

fin

leaving bro bro

Fin loved seeing his Mama smile the way she was in this moment. Big Fin gently pulled his arm from her grip, turned and faced her and began clapping. Everyone stood, if they weren't already standing, and joined in on the appreciative gesture. The ever-composed Rose broke character and began to shed a tear, giggling and trying to say thank you as she did, but couldn't. Fin put his arm around his mama. It is a rare moment when a son gets to be his mother's comfort and he wasn't going to let this one pass him by. As the claps died down, the Commanding Officer turned to Fin.

"Lil' Fin, you are one lucky young man to have two such amazing parents as these. I know that with these two in your corner, there is nothing you will not be able to accomplish!"

"EXCEPT GET A GIRL TO LIKE HIM!" a voice screamed from the back.

Everyone burst out into laughter. Fin looked at a laughing Curt. *Really dude?* Mrs. Davis' pinch on the back of Curt's pudgy arm and his subsequent yelp gave Fin a vengeful chuckle.

"Well, I don't want to get too sentimental as I know the Finley's have to leave and finish packing up. Master Chief, I just wanted to thank you, Rose and Lil' Fin for everything and bid you all the traditional, Fair Winds and Following Seas."

The Commanding Officer then turned to the party and led them in the command cheer:

"ONE TEAM! ONE FIGHT!"

"WILDCATS!" the party shouted before bursting out into applause and approaching the Finleys to shake hands, exchange hugs and say goodbyes. Fin shook a few hands before slowly making his way back to where Curt was. Curt, already standing at this point, knew this was it. He slowly met him in the center of the backyard. Curt's

35

parents joined Curt to say their goodbye to Fin. Mrs. Davis hugged him.

"We're gonna miss you."

"Take care of yourself, Lil' Fin," said Commander Davis with a pat to Fin's back.

The two boys were now alone as the rest of the party were engaging with Fin's parents. There are no guarantees in military life. Friends and members who you serve with once, may never be seen again. This unfortunate truth was especially hard on their families. Curt still hadn't grappled with it.

"So, this is it, huh?"

"Looks like it."

Curt extended his closed fist. "Well...aight then."

Fin fist bumped him back. "Okay."

Neither boy wanted to say the word "goodbye."

Curt smiled and poked his chubby chest out. "Get at me on MySpace!"

Fin smirked. "Like you be on the MySpace!"

"Bro Bro, I got followers! I'm what you would call a social influencer and what not!"

"Who you influencing? Yo' Mama?"

"Might even influence *yo'* Mama, wit' her fi...."

"Watch ya' mouth, boy!" They laughed again, stared at each other, then embraced.

fin

leaving bro bro

"I'm gonna miss you, Bro Bro."

"I'm gonna miss *you*, Bro Bro! I'm gonna miss all of this."

Fin gave one last squeeze then let go. He turned and walked away, navigating the crowd to get to his father. Big Fin knew Rose was right; this was his son. He realized his boy didn't handle goodbyes well. They shared that trait.

"Dad, can I get the keys?"

"You ok, son?"

"Yeah, I'm just ready to go."

Big Fin retrieved the keys from his pocket. "Okay. Go wait in the car. Your mother and I will be there in a second."

Rose glanced at Fin as he walked out, her heart aching for her big baby. Fin turned and looked back to find Curt hadn't moved from where he left him in the middle of the backyard. He had been waiting for Fin to turn to see him again. Curt nodded and smiled. Fin nodded and smiled. Curt then dropped his head and turned to go sit, disappearing amongst the partygoers. Fin dropped his head, walked to the side gate of the fence leading to the front and left the party. A tear rolled down his cheek. They never saw each other again.

chapter three

eastwood high

Fin was glad the long journey back to the States was over. The Finleys left Japan, landed in Hawaii, then San Diego, Chicago, and Philadelphia before finally arriving back in Norfolk, Virginia after thirty hours of travelling. Norfolk is where Rose was born and raised and while Fin would sorely miss Japan, and Curt, he took solace in seeing his grandparents. Their belongings wouldn't arrive from Japan for another two weeks, so they were staying with Rose's parents, Odella and Patrick Murphy.

Patrick and Odella lived in one of three small smatterings of single-family homes in Valebrook. They bought their house in nineteen fifty-two, one of the first to purchase in the then new constructions being built and open to Black buyers. Patrick Murphy was proud of his accomplishment, the first man in his family to own his own home outright. Over the years, as the once residential area of Valebrook was rezoned and repurposed by the city due to overcrowding, Patrick and Odella watched Valebrook get completely disregarded. Nevertheless, this was their home, and they were not leaving it. They raised their only child in that home, worked forty-seven years to pay it off, and had no intentions of ever leaving. Fin couldn't wait to get to his grandparents' house. He looked forward to watching football and BBQing with his grandpa. Patrick Murphy was a renowned "BBQ-ologist" as he liked to say. As far as Fin was concerned, when that man married ribs with seasoning and smoking wood, if God Himself was about to bring the rapture, he would pause midway to grab a slab of his grandpa's ribs. Odella was the matriarch of the Murphy clan in every sense of the word. Grandpa ran all outdoors, but in the four-bedroom house they had lived in for over forty years, Odella ruled. As Big Fin, Rose and Fin arrived at the house, Patrick and Odella were already outside waiting on them. Odella embraced her only grandson and greeted him with her sweet, southern drawl as he stepped onto the porch.

"Boy, look how *big* you done got, Fin!! Ain't Lil' Fin, no mo'!"

Patrick smiled. "What y'all feeding this boy, James?"

"More like, how do we stop him from eating."

"Well, y'all come on in here and get some supper."

When Odella Murphy said come eat, there wasn't really an option other than going to wash your hands and preparing your palette for one of the best meals you had ever eaten, at least Fin thought so. Rose was many things, and could hold her own in the kitchen, but being as good of a cook like his grandma wasn't one of them. Luckily, Fin had been looking forward to this meal. The family sat and talked and laughed. The comfort of knowing that Big Fin, Rose and Fin were home for good replaced the unspoken anxiety that the last six years of cross-continental visits always had. There was an ease and relief in their kinship in this moment as they knew there would be many, many more. Patrick sat back in his chair, his large stomach full of Odella's cooking and wiped the crumbs from the last piece of cornbread out of his beard. He looked at his grandson that had grown so much since last he saw him.

"So, Fin. You ready for school?"

"I guess, Sir."

Big Fin swallowed his last fork full of his dinner then dropped his fork onto his plate.

"Well, he better be. He starts tomorrow."

Odella was surprised that Big Fin and Rose were rushing Fin into school so soon.

"Tomorrow, James? Don'tcha think that's a bit too fast? Y'all not gonna let this boy rest a bit?"

Yeah, Dad! Y'all not gonna let THIS boy rest??! He dared not ask it out loud, but his face said it all.

"Fin was still in school when we left Japan, Mama. We need to get him acclimated and back in school as soon as possible."

"Yes, Mama. Our big baby will be alright," Rose said as she looked first at Odella then at Fin while rubbing his back.

"Well. That's y'all son. Y'all know best."

"That boy gonna be just fine, Odella. Let them raise their son. He ain't no baby no mo'. That's a grown man right there."

"Well, he sho' eat like one, that's for sho'. You still hungry, baby?"

"No, Ma'am."

Fin felt too uncomfortable to eat any longer. He hated adults talking about him as if he wasn't there or couldn't comprehend what was being said.

"May I be excused, Grandma? I'mma go get my bag and take a shower."

"Sure, baby," Odella said causing Fin to rise. "Just make sure that trash is taken out before you do."

"Yes, Ma'am."

Fin quickly realized he was back alright. He complied with his Grandma's wishes. He washed his plate and helped clear down the table as Big Fin and Patrick walked out to the back porch to enjoy a cigar and some moonshine Patrick had recently got from a friend. Fin took out the trash, kissed Odella and Rose, said his goodnights, then set off to get ready for bed. Having resigned to the inevitable, he thought he might as well be rested for his first day back in an American school. The next morning, Fin arose to the glorious smells of fresh biscuits, eggs, locally made sausages and grits. Even the coffee brewing smelled good. *I hope Mama is taking notes!* He sleepily sloughed off to the bathroom. After getting himself ready for the day, and eating Odella's delicious cooking, Rose came into the kitchen and let him know his father was waiting for him in the car.

"Have a good day, baby," said Rose as she kissed his cheek.

"Love you, Mama."

"Bye, Grandma."

"Bye, baby."

Fin walked to the car, got in and they pulled off. Big Fin loved sports radio so that was the only words heard in his grandparents' car as they drove to Eastwood High School, not too far from Olde Park Elementary. As they pulled up to the school, Fin marveled at all of the children wearing regular clothes, a stark contrast to the uniform he had been accustomed to wearing his last six years in Japan. It was also a lot louder than Japan, the students seemed to be in a frenzy on that dry October day. His mind drifted off. He didn't want to be there. He wanted to be back in Japan.

"You ready for this?"

"I guess."

"Fin, I know this will be an adjustment. You have spent the last six years not just at a different school, but in a different country. There will be an adjustment period, no doubt. But you are a *Finley*, and Finleys don't back down to a challenge..."

"...we take it head on," Fin finished his father's rallying cry. He had heard it a hundred times or more. Big Fin opened his door.

"C'mon. Let's get you registered."

Fin welcomed the fresh air the door opening provided. Patrick Murphy didn't believe in air conditioning thus, when the freon ran out, he never replaced it and the electric motor that drove the automatic windows in the car died, which posed a problem because he thought it smelled like "old people." He jumped out of the car, slung his bookbag on his shoulder and met up with Big Fin on the other side. They walked across the parking lot, evading slow moving vehicles, fast moving students and school administrators that never moved as if planted in their spots, attempting to direct traffic.

Eastwood High was a predominately Black school with a sprinkling of white, Hispanic and Asian students here and there. While considered a low-income school, the school's innovative approach to education was renowned throughout the city. Imagine Fin's surprise when they not only had a computer coding course, but a sign in the hallway promoting the computer coding club afterschool! Big Fin and Fin entered into the main office; Fin sat in a chair while Big Fin talked with one of the many secretaries about his enrollment. The office was a bright, spacious room with tall windows that seemed to run from floor to ceiling. Even with all of this natural light, the eight banks of florescent lights seemed to overpower the sun. There were four desks in the center that were arranged as if they intended to put cubicle walling up around them but never got around to it. On either side of the desk arrangement were three doors with the Principal, Assistant Principals of Instruction and Twelfth grade on one side, the other three grade's Assistant Principal's offices on the other. The walls were littered with announcements, anti-drug posters, Eastwood citizenship policies and other various displays.

Fin sat in a wooden chair that had years' worth of graffiti carved into the arm rests. His seat was one of six that sat in between the two doors accessing the office. He traced the carvings of students past with his finger. He was so focused on these markings, he hardly noticed the small, frail boy that sat at the other end of the chairs. A loud, butter smooth voice snapped Fin out of his trance. He looked up to see his dad and the secretary looking down at him as he sat.

"Mr. Finley. Here is your schedule."

"You're all set, buddy."

"Your next class starts in about ten minutes, so you'll have time to get a locker. Do you have a lock?"

"No, Ma'am."

"Stand up, son," Big Fin instructed in a reminding yet scolding tone.

Fin popped tall. The secretary extended his schedule to him.

"If you don't, just pick a locker and report back to the office to let us know which one you have chosen."

He paid particular attention to how she annunciated all of her words. He had never heard a person with such a distinct Norfolk accent speak so eloquently.

"Yes, Ma'am. Where should I..."

"Mrs. Baker..."

Fin snapped his head around to see where the voice was coming from. It was the small, frail boy sitting in the chair at the end of the row of wooden seats. Justin seemed a bit disheveled, as if he had a rough night of drinking and rolled out of bed just in time for school. His clothes were clean but noticeably worn and out of fashion, and his sneakers were definitely what he and Curt would call Bo-Bo's. His black, stringy hair was slicked back and shaved on the sides as if styled by the hairdresser of a teenage boy band. His pale skin only highlighted the brown freckles on his face and his eyes seemed tired. He thought the boy seemed rather desperate. The secretary looked over and addressed him.

"Yes, Justin?"

"There is a locker not too far from mine over by the English corridor. I can take him there." His voice seemed drenched in a need for approval and acceptance.

"Thank you, Justin. Way to make a new War Eagle feel at home in the nest!"

"What do you say, Fin?"

"Thanks, man. Fin." He extended his open hand.

Justin sprung out of his chair the way water jumps on a hot griddle. He offered Fin a fist bump, to which Fin reciprocated.

"Justin. Well, Mrs. Baker already said that but Justin Bell,"

Big Fin was happy Fin already had a friend. "Alright, son. I'll see you tonight?"

Fin nodded. "Later, Dad."

The two boys walked out of the door closest to Justin and into the hallway which, save for a few students, the school police officer and a janitor passing by, was completely empty. As they spoke, their voices echoed a bit.

"So, where you coming in from?"

"Japan."

"Oh shit! Japan?!?! So, you're a military brat, huh?"

Fin hated that term, military brat.

"My dad was stationed there for like six years."

"Six years in Japan?? That's pretty dope."

"Yeah, Japan was pretty cool."

"I bet your glad to be back though, huh?"

Justin was looking for common ground, something they could connect on. Fin thought Justin seemed pretty sad, almost pathetic, and he didn't want to reciprocate. But when Justin adjusted his bookbag on his small wiry frame, Fin noticed a bruise on his bicep peeking out from underneath his faded polo style shirt.

"What happened to your arm?"

Fin was both curious and worried about Justin's response. Justin quickly looked down at his arm and pulled his short sleeve down to hide the black and blue bruise the size of a playing card. Fin wondered what could have hit his garden hose thin arms that hard and not broken it.

"Oh, that?"

Justin attempted to downplay the severity of the bruise with his casual yet nervous tone. Fin could visibly see his mind scrambling for an excuse.

"That was from gym. Fell against the bleachers."

Fin noticed a bruise on his neck as well. "You hit your neck too?"

"Damn, Bro! What are you the police or something?"

He realized he had pushed too far. He had seen someone push back like that before. It happened when he first met Curt, though in that situation, Curt was sensitive about his weight. *This* was different. This wasn't someone being called fat. He thought Justin would learn to tolerate, if not overcome, jabs about his frail build. The way Justin became defensive bothered Fin. He attempted to deescalate the conversation.

"Sorry, man. I was just asking. Look, I know I'm new here and all, but if someone is fucking with you, I got you. Cool?"

This time, Fin extended his fist to Justin to meet him on his common ground.

"Naaaa, we good. And I'm not some kinda punk. I can hold my own."

Justin reluctantly returned Fin's fist bump gesture. In the brief few minutes since they met, Justin had grown on him a bit. *He is a prideful little guy.* Justin began to slow his pace down as he spotted an available locker. He pointed at it.

"There you go. I'm right over there. What class you got next?" he asked as he looked overtop at Fin's schedule.

"Math. Mr. Ferguson."

"Oh, he is cool man. You coulda got Mrs. LeRoche. She's a bitch!"

Fin smirked at the comment.

"Catch me at lunch, Bro."

"Sure. Bro."

When lunch came around, Fin made his way through the lunch line pretty fast. He didn't have much of an appetite, though. He was far too anxious to eat. While he was the tallest kid in all of his classes in Japan, here he was average at best. He enjoyed not sticking out like a sore thumb on that front, but word must've spread pretty fast that he was the "new kid" in the building by the amount of stares he was receiving. As he turned to locate a seat, he felt a tap on his shoulder. It was Justin and Fin could tell he had been anxiously awaiting his arrival.

"What up, Bro? See you made it through your first morning ok."

"I guess."

Justin looked down at his tray. "It's wing day, Bro!! You didn't get the wings?"

"Didn't know that was a requirement."

"Brooooooooo! You gotta get the wings!" He turned to the lunch lady. "Mrs. Lincoln! Hook my man up with the wings, yo!"

Someone shouted from behind Fin.

"SHUT YO' BITCH ASS UP!"

Fin snapped his head around. Justin froze for a second, mustered up some courage and prepared for the confrontation.

"FUCK YOU, LATRELL!"

The whole cafeteria let out a collective "Oooooooooooo" to signal the disrespect shown to LaTrell. Fin's head was on a swivel. LaTrell didn't take too kindly to such public disrespect. He angrily stood from the cafeteria table, about four feet from where Fin and Justin were standing, shoving his lunch tray away from him as he did. He wasn't as tall as Fin, but he easily had him by fifty pounds of young,

48

wiry muscle. He slung the eight-inch dreads hanging in his face to the back of his head and addressed Justin.

"Fuck you say, lil' bitch?"

Two other boys rose with LaTrell, each just as muscular, each looking just as menacing. It was as if they fed off of each other's teenage angst and aggression. Justin puffed his chest out to save face.

"So, we gonna do this again? Fuck it! But y'all gonna feel it this time!"

Again? Fin hated bullies. This obviously wasn't the first time Justin has had to tangle with LaTrell and company. As the boys approached Justin, Fin slowly slid in their paths and looked LaTrell square in his eyes. LaTrell paused, his hesitation told Fin all he needed to know. He had seen his type before, seen them all his life. The type to be big and bad for a crowd and when they had numbers at their back, but call them out, make them prove their bravado wasn't more than just talk and they usually wither. LaTrell just withered. Now it was LaTrell's turn to fill his chest full of air.

"Oh, we got a problem here?"

Fin said nothing. He just stared at him. LaTrell stared back for a few seconds, his testosterone levels draining right before Fin's eyes like water going down a drain. LaTrell realized he had met his match. Fin let out a sly smile. His stare, Rose's stare, is one of many traits he inherited from her. He looked at the two boys behind LaTrell, they too draining out. LaTrell leaned to the side to threaten Justin.

"I'mma see you soon, lil'..."

Fin tilted his head right in between them, cutting his sentence short, and stared deep into his soul. His eyes squinted, an aggressive scowl on his face. LaTrell was defeated. He began to retreat, tapping one of the boys behind him with the back of his hand.

"Yeah. I'mma see you *and* that lil' bitch real soon. Don't worry, we gonna see they asses real soon."

Fin continued staring at him as LaTrell slowly backed away until he accepted defeat, turned and left the cafeteria. Fin dropped his head then looked around. *Day one, and already some bullshit!* Justin stood there in shock. Suddenly, there was a deep, bellowing laugh that could be heard throughout the silent cafeteria and elicited soft murmurs.

"BWAHAHAHAHAHAHA!"

What now? Fin looked over his shoulder and saw another student laughing before returning to eating his wings. The boy looked like he should be working at the school, not attending it. He didn't know exactly how tall the boy was, but there was no doubt the laughing student was bigger than him. The boy was seated at a table that could easily have sat eight to ten students, yet this table was empty save for the boy and another similarly large "student." The other student was looking over his shoulder at him, looking him up and down before staring into his eyes momentarily then turning to finish his meal. In that moment, Justin found his voice again.

"No worries, Bro. You can have some of mine."

What little appetite he may have had was now gone. Fin spotted an empty table in the back of the cafeteria. Justin followed him like a scolded puppy. The laughing student paused in his chicken wing feast and watched Fin as they passed. Justin looked at the student and was met with a snarl in return. When they reached the safety of their isolated cafeteria table, Justin wanted to show his appreciation.

"Thanks, Bro."

"Don't mention it. We're good."

The rest of the day went without incident. Fin learned his classroom locations and teacher's names, received his textbooks, and tried to get into the rhythm of his schedule. When the final bell of the day rang, he just wanted to get back to his grandparents' house. As he slowly traversed the hallways at Eastwood High, heading towards the main entrance, he had a moment to reflect on Japan. *Wonder what Curt is doing right now? He isn't gonna believe today when I tell him!* After wading through the sea of students, hurrying to get home, find friends or high school sweethearts, he was relieved to finally get outside. His relief was short lived, however. A smiling Justin was waiting for him. He had the sudden realization that he was going to have to be Justin's friend, whether he liked it or not. Justin needed a friend.

"Yo! How you getting home? You ride the bus?"

"Naaaa. Think I'mma walk. Get some air."

"I live over on Cresthill. Where you at?"

"Dorian."

"Bro, that's like three blocks away."

As they walked down the cement steps leading to the sidewalk on the other side of the black, wrought-iron gate surrounding Eastwood High, he thought maybe he should've lied about where he lived. Last thing he wanted was the small, wiry, little white boy always around him like some lost puppy. He started down towards Dorian, then realized Justin had invited himself to his tranquil, mind-clearing walk. They had walked no more than twenty feet when they heard a voice.

"You got heart, Captain Save-a-Hoe."

Fin turned and met the voice eye to eye. "What?"

It was the laughing kid from the lunch table eating chicken wings. His initial assessment was right; this kid was HUGE! Every bit of six-foot three, and his muscles had muscles. He wore a plain white t-shirt, blue jeans and a pair of ultra-rare Nike Air Force One Low "PLAYSTATION" additions. He stood there, arms folded, leaning against a dark blue, candy painted Cadillac DeVille. *Nice kicks! Car too!*

"You got balls." The student turned his attention to Justin, snarling at him once again. "Fuck you standing tall for this lil' mafucka for?"

"I just don't like punk fucking bullies, is all."

The student motioned his head to the car he was leaning on. "Hop in."

"Naaaa, I'm good."

"Yeah we're goo..."

The student cut Justin's sentence short. "Who the *fuck* was talking to you?"

Fin glared back at him with the same intensity he did LaTrell. This pleased the student. He raised up out of his leaning position and approached Fin and extended his hand.

"So, it wasn't just a show. Stacks."

"Fin."

"Aight, Fin. Take a ride with me. Both of you. I'll drop you home."

Fin looked back at Justin and motioned his head towards the car to which Justin happily obliged. Fin didn't know exactly why he was getting in the car, but that ride would forever change his life.

chapter four

brevoit

As Fin entered the car, he noticed a large duffle bag across the back seat.   Justin slung the back-passenger seat door open and went to move the bag; Stacks was having none of it.

"Don't touch that bag, white boy."

His calm yet threatening tone unnerved and perplexed Justin.

"Where am I supposed to sit?"

"You can sit on the fuckin' roof, for all I care! You only getting this ride because I know Mr. Fin here would have it no other way."

Stacks was bothered by Justin's presence, if not his very existence. Fin wanted to get going and gave Stacks a look that said *C'mon man, cut him some slack.* Stacks laughed and shook his head, then he got out of the car, walked around back and then over to the door Justin stood in front of and stared at him. Justin got the message and jumped out of the way. Stacks stared a moment longer for emphasis, then grabbed the bag, popped the trunk and tossed it in with a loud THUD! The sound startled Fin. *Whatever was in that bag sure was heavy.* Stacks made his way to the front door, never removing his eyes from Justin, who stared back not out of a sense of challenging, but out of sheer fear, like an antelope ever watchful for the lion's pounce. Stacks got in the car and started it up, the smooth purr of the engine only drowned out by the heavy bass from the radio. He glanced in his rearview mirror as they started to drive and fixed his eyes on Justin.

"Where you stay at, white boy?"

"Justin," snapped Fin.

"What?"

"His name is Justin."

"Oh, *pardon me.* Where you stay at, White Boy Justin?"

Fin just shook his head and snickered. Justin was still frozen, however.

"SPEAK, WHITE BOY...Justin."

"Oh, uhhhh...Cresthill. Cresthill and Tenth."

"Huh! I knew you lived in the hood but you right in the mix. How you feel about living around all of us?"

Fin thought this was a trap for Justin. If he tried to sound tough, tried to sound "down," Stacks might throw him out the car. If he trivialized the question, brushed it off, Stacks might throw him out the car while it was still moving. Surprisingly, Justin did neither.

"I don't even know anything else, man. Been here as far back as I could remember. I know I ain't black, but I *am* Valebrook."

fin

brevoit

Stacks looked in the rearview mirror at Justin. Fin turned around and looked over the seat. Then Fin and Stacks both looked at each other and burst out laughing.

"Aight, Mr. Valebrook. This is your stop."

Stacks had stopped on the corner of Cresthill and Tenth. Justin grabbed his bookbag from off the floor in between his legs, opened the car door and then closed it with the utmost of care.

"Thanks for the ride."

Stacks didn't reply. His eyes remained looking forward. Fin realized he had no intention of acknowledging Justin.

"Later, Justin," said Fin.

Stacks slammed on the gas and as the car squealed away, he leaned his head out the window.

"Valebrook!"

Fin looked at Justin in the side mirror. Justin dropped his head as they rode off, slung his bag onto his shoulder and turned down Cresthill. Fin had an unexplained fondness for Justin, he couldn't quite put his finger on why though. Maybe it was the fact he was bullied. Maybe it was he knew the feeling of being an outsider in a foreign environment, much like how he felt when he first got to Japan. He knew right then and there Justin was going to be in his life for a while. Stacks must have been reading Fin's body language.

"Them weak attachments are dangerous, man. That lil' mafucka ain't got no place around here."

"We all got a place, and if not, we learn how to make a place for ourselves."

fin

brevoit

"Philosophical ass mafucka, huh? Well look Socrates, we need to make a stop before I drop you home."

"Why you doing this?"

"Doing what? Making a stop, or dropping you home?"

"Man, I give two shits about why you stopping. Why you want me to ride with you?"

"'Cause, despite your affinity for lost and wayward white boys named *Justin*, you got heart. I fucks with that."

Fin looked at him hard. He misjudged his intelligence. Though he carried himself like a common street thug, the common street thug doesn't casually drop Socrates in conversation. This intrigued him.

"You read Socrates?"

Stacks just smiled and kept driving.

"I'll make that stop a little later. I'mma take you around the way."

In Valebrook, it felt as if housing projects outnumbered the single-family homes. Valebrook was indicative of many poor, Black neighborhoods scattered throughout the country. Decades of unfair housing practices restricted where Blacks could live, often forcing them to or keeping them in areas near industrial zones. While more affluent White areas were brimming with single family homes and little commercial buildings and even less of an industrial footprint, Black neighborhoods were often where garages, landfills, incinerators, liquor stores, and any other business deemed less than reputable were located. Couple intentionally segregated housing projects, the decades long practice of stonewalling would-be Black buyers from purchasing homes in all-White neighborhoods, and banks refusing to grant loans for home improvement or repair to Black homeowners in

fin

brevoit

Black neighborhoods, and you have the makings of the Black ghetto. Of all the ghettos in Norfolk, Valebrook was one of the toughest places to live. Not due to violence or drugs that plagued many ghettos, but for the bleak outlook its unrepaired roads, dilapidated housing, high unemployment, and lack of community services created. It imbued a sense of malaise that engulfed the Valebrook residents. It's one beacon of hope was Eastwood High School, whose teachers found innovative and new-age ways to reach the students, trying to fix Valebrook's problems from within. Fin had never really seen Valebrook as bleak before he left for Japan. To the young Fin, Valebrook was just home as he had no other point of reference. Now that he has returned a more mature, more educated, and more worldly young man, its desolate nature disheartened him. Stacks lived in the Brevoit Homes, one of the many low-income housing projects in Norfolk. The Brevoit Homes was by far its most notorious.

Stacks pulled up in front of one of the eight brick buildings that comprised the Brevoit Homes. The old tenement homes had ten single-family dwellings in each of its eight buildings. The buildings were broken up into two squares of four buildings each with a large, open courtyard that had long stopped being upkept by the city. Though the sun shined brightly, there seemed to be a dark cloud over the Brevoit projects; a heaviness that was palpable. Stacks turned the car off, exited the vehicle and looked at Fin still sitting in the car, taking in the scenery. Fin was a bit wary about the situation. *My first day back and I damn near got into a fight, now I'm up in Brevoit.* The ever-observant Stacks picked up un his uneasiness.

"Ain't nobody gonna fuck with you, Socrates."

"You just gonna leave the car like this? Windows down?"

Stacks paused and stared at him. He knew that in Brevoit, no one dared disrespect him. He was a Morton.

57

fin

brevoit

"Ain't nobody fucking with my car around here either."

Fin reluctantly got out of the car, looking around his surroundings. What surprised Stacks was, *how* Fin looked around. Not as if he were prey in the lion's den, but as if he was the lion. They walked up the small grassy hill to the cement walkway that wrapped around each block of homes. As they did, it seemed Stacks' arrival was an event worthy of note. Calls of either "Stacks!" or "What up, Stacks!" rang out as they cut diagonally across the weed filled grass. Stacks either nodded or threw up a passing hand gesture to acknowledge them. Fin figured out which home they were walking to by the intense stare being thrown their way. A young man dressed in gray shorts, gray t-shirt and a pair of gray Nike Air Max sneakers. It was the boy Stacks ate wings with during lunch.

"What up, Gray?"

Gray Boy never looked at Stacks but kept his gaze fixed on Fin.

"We bringin' nobodies home now?"

"Stall him out, man. Fin's good."

Fin approached Gray Boy and extended his hand. "Fin."

Gray Boy didn't reciprocate. Stacks watched the exchange as he approached the front door.

"Who in there?"

"Ya' pops and Shan," Gray Boy replied, his eyes still fixed on Fin.

Gray Boy never accepted Fin's handshake proposal. Fin lowered his hand then began to follow Stacks into the Morton home. *Fuck you then!*

"Hmmph!"

58

fin

brevoit

Gray Boy stood up at the sound, and blocked Fin's passing.

"You tough with bitch ass LaTrell. Think you gonna punk me like that?"

Fin just stared right back in his eyes. Gray Boy was just as tall as Fin and slightly heavier, but to Fin, it didn't matter. He never backed down from a fight, and never felt scared or anxious. In these moments he felt focused, his senses on alert. He felt the wind whip in between them. He heard the sounds of talking coming from the now open door. Stacks doubled back having realized that Fin wasn't behind him. Stacks stood in the open threshold of the door. Suddenly, a voice screamed from inside the house, causing all three boys to look inside the dimly lit room.

"CLOSE THAT FUCKING DOOR!"

Stacks grabbed Gray Boy's shoulder from behind.

"I said, he's good."

Gray Boy backed away allowing Fin to pass. They never broke their staring match until Fin finally turned to step up in through the threshold. As the door closed behind him, Fin tapped Stacks.

"Fuck is his problem?"

"Gray Boy is doing what he does best."

"What? Stare passionately at mafuckas?"

"Naaaa. Know who everyone is. He don't know you."

"Who the fuck is this?"

Now Fin knew who yelled for the door to be closed. They were in the front part of a large living room. To his left was a room that should have been a dining room, but it was sparsely decorated with an

59

old sofa chair with worn upholstery and a small coffee table. The living room had a sectional couch in the corner, with one side butted up against a wall adjacent to the dining room, the other part was against a small wall below a large opening that gave view of the kitchen. To his right was a hallway that Fin assumed led to the bedrooms and bathroom. The walls had old photos and a large painted portrait of a dark-skinned woman with an afro on a velvet canvas. There was a small coffee table in front of the sectional covered in magazines, beer cans and a plate that looked like it had recently been used. As he looked towards the back of the living room at the sectional, he noticed two men, one seated and one standing. The man standing looked like what Stacks would look like in five or so years. He had the hard, chiseled muscles of someone that had lifted weights for a long time. By the rough, unsmooth nature of his tattoos, Fin estimated those muscles and tattoos were crafted in prison. Stacks was visibly frustrated.

"Man, shut your drunk ass up!"

The older man grabbed the younger man by the wrist, pulling him back to his seated position.

"Relax, Shan. Your brother felt the need to bring company home."

Fin could tell by the word "need" that his presence wasn't exactly welcomed. The older man stared at Fin. There was a book opened, faced down on his lap. His brow was frowned and his arms spread out over the back of the sectional.

"Now son, I don't know where you from, but 'round here, we introduce ourselves when we come in another man's house."

Fin began walking towards them to introduce himself. As he approached Shan and Coop, Stacks watched. *This kid don't rattle at all.*

fin

brevoit

"Excuse me, Sir. I'm Fin."

Coop looked down at Fin's extended hand then back in his eyes. Shan stood back up, attempting his best to look menacing. Fin ignored him. He knew Coop was the man of the house and the only approval he needed.

"Now I know yo' people ain't name you Fin, nah."

"No, Sir. James. James Finley."

The older man looked at Fin as if he just told him he had wings and could fly.

"James Finley? You any kin to Big James Finley?"

Now Fin had the surprised look. *How does he know my dad? How does dad know anyone that lives in Brevoit?*

"Yes, Sir. That's my dad."

Coop became excited by this revelation.

"I'll be damn! Don't look so shocked, nah. Ya' daddy wasn't always a goodie two shoes, Navy man. Boooyyyyy, me and yo' Daddy had some *good* times!"

Fin jerked his head back. *What does that mean?* Coop shook his head and laughed.

"Ya' even got his mannerisms. You look just like ol' Big Fin. Tell yo' daddy Coop said hello!"

"Ummm...will do, Sir."

Stacks walked past Fin and headed towards the hallway to their right, tapping Fin with the back of his hand on his chest.

"C'mon, Bruh."

fin

brevoit

Fin followed Stacks towards the hallway. Coop went back to reading the book on his lap. Shan stared at him in the same menacing way Gray Boy did moments earlier. Fin turned the corner and saw a long hallway that ran adjacent to the big room they just left. As they approached the first of three rooms, Stacks popped his head in to speak to the young boy sitting on the bed doing schoolwork.

"What up, youngin'?"

The boy jumped up and ran over to them. "What up, Chris?"

Fin looked at Stacks with a slight grin. "Chris?"

Stacks looked at him disapprovingly then turned his gaze back to the young boy. His eyes lit up when he looked at the boy.

"How was school?"

"It was straight."

"Straight, huh? You doing that homework?"

"No, I'm writing a story about nosey big brothers that stay in my business."

He chuckled then ran to his bed, knowing what was about to happen.

"What? You lil' shit!"

Stacks grabbed him from behind, threw him on the bed and began tickling him. They both laughed as he played with his baby brother, before the boy squealed at being tickled.

"LET THAT BOY BE! FINISH THAT HOMEWORK, BOY!"

fin

brevoit

They both collectively rolled their eyes. Stacks let him up then mushed his head causing him to fall over into the bed laughing. Dee pointed at Fin.

"Who is that?"

"Oh, that's Fin. He's cool. Fin, this is my shit talking little brother, Dee."

"What up, lil' man?" Fin extended his hand.

"I ain't little," the boy said seemingly offended, as he slapped Fin's open hand. Stacks rose off of the bed and walked towards the door.

"Get back to that homework, punk. C'mon, Bruh."

"Lata, Dee."

Fin liked the kid. They left Dee's room and headed down the hallway, passing a small bathroom then entering Stacks' room. The room was almost as sparsely decorated as the dining room. There was an unmade twin bed on a metal frame with no headboard, an old wooden dresser with attached mirror that had tons of pictures stuck in between the glass and the wood frame, a pile of sneaker boxes neatly arranged by the closet, and books, lots of books. Books were on the dresser, the bed, and in stacks on the floor that Fin thought looked like a small city of buildings made of great literary works; Baldwin, Angelou, Homer, Hurston, Shakespeare, Plato, Socrates, Haley, Poe, Hughes, and Ellison. Stacks and stacks of books. Then it hit Fin.

"Books. Stacks of books."

Stacks sat down on his bed and gazed out of the small window covered with bars.

"Since I was a kid. One of my dad's people gave me a stack of books when I was a boy, at least that's the story he tells. It became my escape from all of this shit. People think it means money 'cause of who my pops is. But those that know me, know it's because I'm just as comfortable with a book in my hand as I am with a gun."

"What does your dad do?"

Stacks stood up, turned to his mattress and lifted it up. Underneath was an arsenal of weapons; a 9mm, an AR-15, a .357 and assorted boxes of ammunition for each. Fin wondered how in the hell he could even sleep on the bed with all of that underneath.

"This is what he does, what *we* do. Guess you could say that guns are the family business."

"Guns?"

"Going back to my great-granddaddy. He started arming black folk around here during the Reconstruction Era. White folk didn't take to kindly to slaves being freed. He figured if he was free, he was gonna enjoy all the rights and privileges the law allowed."

"Thought they didn't allow black people to own guns? The Slave Codes and all?"

"They didn't, but that didn't stop great-grand. Good thing he did too. Only chance they had to fight back when them feds left the South. Called him Willie Riffle 'cause he kept that rifle with him wherever he went. He ain't give a fuck. Dude was real gangsta, unlike most of these clowns around here."

"So, you come from a line a gun dealers and runners?"

"Yeah, then my granddaddy kept it up during the fifties and sixties, during the Civil Rights Movement and shit. They always talk about the peaceful protesters, they rarely mention the ones that was out there along with 'em, armed to the teeth ready for whatever."

"Damn!"

Fin now knew what was in that large bag Stacks threw in the trunk. He also figured out what that stop they never made must be about. Fin thought that though Stacks was definitely a product of his environment, he was too smart for this, too perceptive, and seemed to have an innate ability to read people and situations. Fin was a bit of a history buff, he often enjoyed listening to his grandpa Patrick tell the stories about growing up in Franklin, Virginia and how bad race relations were during that time. Patrick often told him stories about himself, and some of the other black men escorting members of the movement through their town, ever watchful for the Klan or police. He thought Franklin was so country that stuff liked that only happened there. He was shocked to find out it happened in other places too.

"What happened to him?"

"Same thing that happened to my great-granddaddy; they killed him. Found him lynched, hanging from a tree out near Courtland. My granddaddy was in a 'traffic accident'."

Stacks used air quotes as he said traffic accident.

"Traffic accident?"

"Somehow, he rolled his car into a tree, then into a lake...from the trunk."

"Fuck!"

"After that, my daddy took over the business. He was on fire! Wanted to kill every white person he saw. Ended up doing a stretch in Deerfield 'cause he shot at some white boys riding through here screaming nigger. Came home with new connections and now the Morton family is back doing what we do."

Fin now had a deeper understanding for the hostile greetings when he arrived. When you are four generations deep of Black men that challenge the system (and break the law), spy infiltration is definitely to be expected.

"You just met me. Why you telling me all this, man?"

"'Cause you stand tall no matter what. Most mafuckas, like that punk ass LaTrell, are only tough with a gun or a bunch mafuckas with him. You stared down three dudes with a lunch tray and a white boy that wasn't gonna do shit but run."

"Justin."

"Justin, Jonathan, Jumjum! *I don't give a fuck!* Point is, you got heart. Heart and you don't talk a lot, which means you don't run your mouth, unless you in here correcting me."

Stacks' frustration with being corrected turned into a slight chuckle and he shook his head, then looked out of the window. Fin smirked, then looked down at the book in his hand, Baldwin's *The Fire Next Time*. He looked back over at Stacks as he gazed out of the window. There was a longing on his face, as if the bars on the window symbolized the prison that he was trapped in, the prison of being a Morton. He didn't think he would tell Big Fin about today's meeting. Fin liked Stacks. He liked him a lot.

chapter five

bruises

Things became pretty normal for Fin, after a while. Over the course of the next few months he, Stacks and Justin formed a loose friendship, Fin being the glue that bonded them. They would often laugh at Justin's wit and energy. Outside of school, Fin would take rides with Stacks around Valebrook, either visiting the park to play ball or stopping into their favorite soul food restaurant Alice Rae's. Other days, Fin would walk Justin home, stopping at the store on Tenth for fried fish sandwiches and sodas. He never had any serious run-ins with LaTrell after that first day. Not only did LaTrell and company leave him alone after losing face that day in the cafeteria, but since he had been hanging with Stacks, no one dared approach Fin with anything but respect. This grace even extended to Justin, who given his previous status at Eastwood, was a welcomed reprieve. Though Fin and Stacks didn't always like having Justin around, the collective of boys could only be found as a trio on school grounds, usually during lunch where Justin provided Fin and Stacks comic relief, sometimes with his wit, others as the butt of their jokes. Fin still noticed the

bruises

occasional bruises on Justin's body, however. It seemed a new one would pop up every few days, and since he was now untouchable at school, he deduced they were coming from home. One day in May, as school began its annual wind down to a close, Justin arrived in the cafeteria. Fin hadn't seen him all day. The left side of his normally pale face was black and blue from bruises. Justin didn't join Stacks and Fin at the lunch table like normal. Instead, he kept his head low and walked past them. Stacks couldn't believe the damage to Justin's face as he passed.

"The fuck happened to you, Valebrook??!"

"Valebrook" became the moniker Stacks used now in reference to Justin. Stacks knew that Fin didn't like when he referred to Justin as "white boy." It wasn't that Stacks feared Fin, he respected him and his ability to see the humanity in people. He just didn't get what he saw in Justin. Justin didn't respond to Stacks. He merely shot a quick glance at the table and kept walking and found an empty table in the back of the cafeteria. Stacks looked at Fin confused, shrugged his shoulders and then continued eating. Fin looked over Stacks' shoulder as Justin made his way to solitude. He swung his leg over the bench attached to the lunch table so he could get up. Stacks shook his head.

"Man, let that dude be."

"Be right back."

Stacks knew Fin wasn't going to stop even as he said it. The cafeteria was buzzing with the sounds of teenage angst. As he made his way to the back of the cafeteria, Fin couldn't help but notice that in all of the commotion, the giggling, laughing of young girls, the loud, boisterous calls of boys, the kids looking at their phones, no one had

bruises

even looked at Justin as he passed, not even the teachers patrolling the lunchroom. He arrived at the table and stood near Justin.

"I'm ok, Bro. I just want to be left alone."

"Yo' face saying something different."

"I said, *I'm ok*. Leave it alone."

Stacks looked over his shoulder to see Fin standing over Justin. He couldn't hear what was being said, but saw Justin wasn't responding as he normally would. He gave a disapproving shake of his head before turning back to his meal. Fin became frustrated with Justin. *Who is he protecting?*

"Who did that to you, Bruh?"

Justin remained silent.

"Tell me who…."

"Or *what*? You gonna hit me too?"

Fin was shocked by that response. Though now fifteen, Fin was wise beyond his years. He knew that the way he approached Justin put him on the defensive. He sat down next to him, his back to the table.

"No, man. I'm not gonna hit you. No one else should be either."

"Just leave it alone, Fin. *Please*. You can't fight all my battles for me."

bruises

"Juss, you too young to be having battles. Was it your mother?"

Justin sank his head lower, shaking it no as he did.

"Your dad?" Again, Justin didn't respond.

"Your dad did this. He the one that sends you to school all bruised and shit."

Fin saw a tear fall and blot Justin's jeans a shade darker. He swung around and placed his arm around Justin. Justin shrugged his shoulder, trying to get Fin's long arm off of him. He looked at Fin, his eyes welled up as if he could burst into raw emotion at any moment.

"Just leave me alone, Fin."

Now up close to his face, he could see just how bad Justin was bruised. The mark extended from just above his left eye all the way down to his jawbone. His eye was slightly puffed and pinkish. He wondered why not one school administrator said anything. He wanted to go grab someone and demand they look at Justin's face. Justin must have sensed that's what Fin was thinking.

"You don't understand. No one around here is gonna do anything."

"How do you know that, Juss?"

"You think I haven't told someone? You think the cops ain't been called to my house a bunch of times? I damn near know all these cops by name. That's the problem though, my dad does too. He was a cop before his drinking got him kicked off the force. I was young when it happened. All I know is it got worse after he couldn't be a cop anymore."

Fin sat in disbelief by what he was hearing.

"But the school has to report it."

"You ain't listening, Bro. No one ever listens to me. They have reported it, a bunch of times. I get removed for a few days or my mama and I go to some shelter, but we always end up back there. I always get brought back."

"How the fuck is that possible? They have to act, right? Child services and shit?"

"Sometimes, it ain't what you know, it's *who* you know. That mother fucker knows everybody."

Andrew Bell, a former Norfolk Police Officer, was an alcoholic. Some of his former police comrades thought he was a good cop that just took it too far at times. Others thought he was a menace, a disgrace, a media scandal waiting to happen. He was kicked off the force after numerous complaints of excessive force and substandard performance reviews. The final straw came nine years earlier, when Andrew stopped an older woman for speeding. The elderly lady became agitated and could smell alcohol on Andrew's breath. Andrew was known to keep a pint of scotch or bourbon in his police cruiser. When the woman pointed out the stench of scotch, Andrew became enraged, angrily opened the car door, yanked the woman out and threw her to the ground. The woman screamed in pain and horror as Andrew attempted to cuff her before another passing patrol car stopped and pulled him away from the lady. The woman turned out to be the mother of the newly appointed district attorney. Andrew Bell was placed on immediate administrative leave without pay and fired less than two months later after the review board. The Norfolk Police Department had finally had enough to remove him from the force. They had had enough of *him*.

Andrew now takes odd jobs to make ends meet, but no matter how bad the family's financial straits were, he always found enough money to make his nightly visit to his favorite watering hole, Pullman's Pub, a cop bar located on the other side of town. Though a former and disgraced police officer, he still had friends on the force. Sometimes, they would even drive him home so he wouldn't get behind the wheel in the drunken state he usually left Pullman's in.

Andrew wasn't a large man, standing five foot, ten inches and weighing one hundred and ninety pounds, though some of that weight can be attributed to almost a decade off of the police force. He was a strikingly good-looking man, with a full goatee and short cropped buzz cut. What stood out the most on his physical frame were his hands. Andrew's hands looked as if someone removed the hands of a professional basketball player standing over seven feet and surgically attached them to his body. His hands were an asset to him in high school and college allowing him to grip and throw a football with ease and precision. Had it not been for his small stature, he may have been recruited by a major college football program and had a shot at the pros, a fact that he liked to remind Justin, and his mother Elaine, of a lot in his drunken tirades. It was one such altercation the night previous that led to Justin's bruised face.

"I coulda been a pro, ya know?"

Elaine said nothing. She didn't hear him. She was in a daze, staring off into space.

bruises

"You don't believe it?"

Andrew's slurred speech told Justin he had been drinking all day. With hours down at the shipyard having been cut back and doled out by seniority, of which, Andrew had very little, he had been at Pullman's since three-thirty. Elaine quickly snapped out of her trance. She recognized his drunkenness and tried to placate his ego so as not to get hit.

"I do, honey."

"Coulda been one of the best! But nooooooooooo...you gotta be some sorta Adonis or somethin' to be a pro. Too short they said. Can you believe that shit? ME?!"

"I know, honey."

"You know *what*?! That I am too fucking short?!?! Is that what you're calling me?"

Elaine became terrified. She cringed into the sofa.

"Nooooooo......."

Justin was in his room listening to music. He hated being around his father when he was like this. He never had the volume up too loud though. He needed to hear in case he had to intervene. Back in the living room, Andrew's threatening frame hovered over Elaine.

"You think I'm short? That I'm a failure? Is that what I am to you?"

"No, Andrew. I know they did you wrong. They shoulda gave you a chance."

"Gave me? *GAVE ME?* I earned that fucking chance!"

"I'm sorry.....please don't."

"Don't what? Teach you to mind your fucking....."

SLAP!

"...TONGUE!"

He struck her so forcefully, she fell off the couch and onto the floor, crying. When Justin heard the sound of his mother hitting the floor, he ripped his headphones off and came running.

"STOP FUCKING HITTING HER, YOU PIECE OF SHIT!"

"Shut your stupid ass up! Let them damn black boys pick on you! My son is a *fucking punk!* Ya' wouldn't have made it ten seconds in my day!"

"SO, YOU TAKE IT OUT ON US BECAUSE YOU COULDN'T HACK IT! YOU'RE A DISGRACE!"

Justin knew what would happen next. He knew what words to say to get Andrew to direct all his attention his way. Failure. Shame. Disgrace. Embarrassment. Fired. Alcoholic. Any of those words sent Andrew into a tirade. Sometimes Justin could fend him off, most times not though. This night it was the latter. Andrew's large hand cracked across Justin's face like the sound lightning makes when it strikes. The flash of light and pain matched the sound and made the lightning analogy all-the-more real to him. He dropped to the floor and immediately covered up, a tactic he had mastered over the years. Andrew had removed his belt and swung with a force comparable to a lumberjack chopping a log. Justin knew he needed to cover himself and stay conscious long enough for the drunk, overweight Andrew to tire himself out, then he could make his move. As Andrew's kicks and lashes with the belt began to slow, it presented Justin with the opening he was looking for. His ribs and stomach ached from the kicks. His back and arms stung from the leather's kiss. He knew he had to move and do it now.

As Andrew's arm went up, and his breathing was laboring, Justin sprung to his feet and punched him in the mouth, sending him stumbling backwards and into the end table, knocking the lamp on it to the ground. Elaine, who had been screaming for Andrew to stop brutalizing Justin, screamed frantically at Andrew falling. Before Andrew could regain what little balance alcohol and exhaustion had stripped from him, Justin hit him again. He knew his blows didn't hurt his father, they merely stunned him. He was too frail and lacked the muscle and weight to put true power behind his blows. But in Andrew's state, they had the desired effect. Elaine was curled up on the couch, crying, gripped in fear and shame, her hands wrapped around her knees. Justin ran to the other side of the couch to plead with her for an escape.

"Let's go, Ma!"

Elaine buried her face in between her knees. Justin cried as he knelt down to her, his eyes darting between his terrified mother and drunk father.

"MA!"

"*MA, PLEASE!*"

It was too late. When Elaine raised her head, her eyes tipped Justin off. Andrew had regained his footing and was now behind him. He moved just in the nick of time and narrowly escaped the fist aimed for his head. His evasive move made him leap to his right, undercutting his father's swing, while keeping his balance enough to place his hands on the old, wooden floor. Justin assumed a sprinter's starting position and ran for the front door. He swung the door open and ran like wild dogs were chasing him, sprinting down Cresthill Street. Andrew chased him but stopped on the porch.

"I'M GONNA FUCKIN' *KILL YOU*, BOY!"

Justin didn't care. He didn't turn around. He just kept running. The street was dark save for an occasional bit of luminance from a neighbor's porch light. When he hit Tenth Avenue, his eyes took a moment to adjust to the brightness of the orange glow of the streetlights, beaming headlights from passing cars and fluorescent lights from open store fronts. *He is gonna come looking for me.* His head was ringing, his heart pounding out of his chest and at this point, he was audibly crying. It was only nine-thirty and the sidewalk was still heavy with traffic, people walking to and from work, hanging outside their homes or standing near the corner store, enjoying the late spring night. Many of the people he passed watched in confusion as the little white boy ran through the predominantly Black neighborhood, a sight that was anything but normal in Valebrook.

He made it to a park a few blocks away from a local convenience store and finally slowed down. The park was completely dark and provided cover from anyone that might be looking for him. He found a bench and sat down, his adrenaline still peaking causing him to shake as if he was freezing cold. He laid down on the bench and cried himself to sleep. A few hours later, he awoke to quiet. The once busy street was now still and silent. The damage on his face now more noticeable. His eye was closing and oozed tears. His once ringing headache was now a full-on migraine level event. He sat up to gather himself, then began the journey home. As he slowly made his way back down Tenth Avenue towards Cresthill Street, he saw a digital state lottery sign in a closed storefront that told him it was three twenty-six in the morning.

Justin made it home a few minutes later. He stood in front of 41 Cresthill Street and stared. He saw that no one was up, though his father's car was still there. He only wanted to check on his mother and get his bag for school. He pushed the gate with the broken lock and entered the front yard. He walked down the narrow cement path lined with overgrown, dew covered grass and weeds. He made his way to the side of the house. The paint was peeling off of the wooden siding and visible cracks had formed in the untreated wood. The windows were dirty, many of their screens broken or missing. The weeds on the side of the house were more prominent than those in the front yard. He crept along the side until he was under his bedroom window. It was open. He'd often use this as his primary exit from the house to avoid any accidental contact with his father. He climbed in but had no plans of staying long. He looked around the shabbily furnished room. A dresser, a mattress and box frame on a metal stand, and a small TV nestled on what should have been his nightstand, were the extent of his décor. The walls were bare. He tried taping posters up to hide the cracked paint, but as the paint peeled off from age, the posters came with them. He took his sweaty t-shirt off and threw it on the floor, grabbed a cleaner one that was laying across his bed, dressed himself, grabbed his book bag and jumped back out of the window. He had wanted to check on Elaine, but he thought better of it. *If she is still here, that's on her.*

Justin walked Valebrook for the rest of the morning until school started, though he was too nervous and upset to enter into the building, so he continued to walk. In a neighborhood where he was the minority by a mile, he enjoyed a level of anonymity. Justin figured people must've thought if his family, a white family, was living here,

bruises

they had to be really hard up. He walked in silence, stopping occasionally at bus stops to rest or to enter a store to enjoy a moment of air conditioning and relief from the rising heat outside. By lunch time, hunger, heat and pure exhaustion had gotten the best of him. He slowly made his way to Eastwood High School and slipped in undetected, blending in with the hectic lunch crowd. He kept his head low, grabbed a tray, and accepted whatever food the cafeteria workers placed on it, and found an empty seat. Now he just wanted to eat.

"You sure you okay?"

"No, but I will be."

"Aight, Juss. I'll catch you later."

"Yeah...later."

Fin got up from the table. He felt anger, sympathy and a sense of helplessness. He went to the lunch line and grabbed a tray. He loaded it up with food and took it over to Justin. He looked at Justin one more time before walking away, peeking back over his shoulder to check on him again and again. Justin finally began to eat and he ate ravenously. Fin returned to his table and sat down. Stacks saw the rage on his face.

"Ya' boy aight? He talk shit to the wrong person, I bet."

"Yeah. His father."

"His *daddy* did that shit to him??!?"

"He the one always giving him them bruises."

fin

bruises

Stacks looked over his shoulder at Justin. He stared at him and got angrier by the second. He knew what it felt like to be in a home of abuse, to be in a home where the man that was supposed to protect you hurt you, endangered you. Stacks turned back to Fin and looked down at his plate. Fin had never seen Stacks so despondent.

"You aight?"

"I'mma catch you lata."

Stacks got up and walked out, leaving his tray on the table. Fin picked at his meal then stood to dump his tray. He looked over to see Justin still sitting there, both plates clean, with a glazed-over look in his eyes. Fin shook his head and went to his next class. For the rest of the day, he had very little focus on his schoolwork. His mind was not only on Justin, but now it was on Stacks. *Why'd he act like that then just get up?* Fin was now worried about both of his friends. He knew Justin couldn't take much more, not physically nor mentally. Stacks' reaction, the look Fin saw in his eyes, the way he fell silent at learning Justin's father abused him, triggered something. Worst part was, Fin knew neither would talk about it. He couldn't wait to get home and talk to his father. In moments like this, when he was confused and didn't know what to do, Big Fin was the first and only person he turned to.

The final bell of the day rang, and Fin hurriedly grabbed his stuff and made it out the door, bumping into a few classmates as he did. He wanted to get to Justin's last class. He knew his friend needed someone, anyone, to show that they cared. He started walking down the English hallway and saw Lailah, a pretty, full figured young girl that was in the same class as Justin. Lailah had a bit of a crush on Fin so he knew she would gladly stop and talk to him. She saw him and immediately began smiling and batting her eyes. He was already looking past her and down the hallway, trying to spot Justin.

fin

bruises

"Heeeeeyyyy, Fin."

"Hey, Lailah. You seen Justin?"

Her face scrunched up at his lack of interest in her.

"Why you always hanging out with him?! He's dirty and shit!"

"Yeah, I know. Have you seen him though?"

Lailah sucked her teeth and pursed her lips.

"No, I ain't seen that boy!"

"He wasn't in class?"

"I ain't that boy's Mama!"

"Cool. Thanks."

Lailah sucked her teeth again, rolled her eyes, threw her hand up at him as she brushed by him and walked off. Fin stood in the hallway asking every kid that passed by if they had seen Justin to which they all replied no.

"Damn!"

Fin made his way outside and saw Stacks leaning against his car as usual.

"Where's ya' boy?"

Fin was shocked by Stacks' sudden concern for Justin.

fin

bruises

"I don't know. Been looking for him but I think he skipped his last class."

"Hop in."

Fin was curious as to why Stacks had a sudden interest in Justin. In the five or so months since he and Justin met, Stacks had never once asked where Justin was and truly wanted to know. Most times Stacks' questioning about Justin's whereabouts was to know if he was going to be inconvenienced or not. As they pulled out of the Eastwood parking lot, and turned onto Clinton Avenue, Fin spotted Justin walking amongst the newly released students. He leaned forward and pointed across the street in Justin's direction.

"There he goes!"

Stacks pulled up alongside Justin and honked the horn, startling him.

"Justin..."

Justin stopped walking. Stacks brought the car to a halt. Justin looked over at him. He was expecting Stacks to ridicule him, but he didn't. *He said my name.* Fin looked over at Stacks as well. *No sarcasm? No ridicule? No "White Boy Justin"?* Stacks just spoke his name, said with purpose, then he motioned his head.

"...get in."

chapter six

the sleepover

After a few hours of the boys hanging out, Stacks decided it was time to take Fin and Justin home. He had what he needed. Now, he needed to drop Fin and Justin somewhere then go find Gray Boy. He looked at Justin through the rearview mirror.

"Justin, where do you want me to take you?"

Justin shrugged. "Home, I guess."

"Naaaa," interjected Fin. "Take us to my house."

"*Your* house?!?!" Stacks and Justin said in unison.

"What are y'all - a chorus or somethin'? Yeah! *My* house."

Justin got instantly excited. He leaned forward, placing his hand on Fin's headrest.

"Yo' dad gonna be cool with it?"

fin

the sleepover

Fin shrugged his shoulders

"Yeah, I guess. You ain't going home tonight. Besides, it's Friday. We can hang all night."

"Yeah and that motherfucker will be drinkin' all night anyway."

"Casa de Fin, it is!" said Stacks with a slight chuckle, as he leaned forward to check his side mirror before pulling out.

"I'mma need a toothbrush!"

"My mama keep shit like that. Relax, Bro. I got you."

"Y'all got food? I'm fucking starving!"

Stacks burst into laughter. "Gotchu a lost puppy!"

"WOOF!" barked Justin, causing the three of them to laugh like longtime friends.

After about a ten-minute drive, they arrived in front of Fin's home. Justin hopped out and ran along Stacks' car to get to the driver's side. He approached the open window and extended his hand.

"Thanks, Stacks. I needed today."

Stacks looked down at his hand, then looked up at Justin with a frown, before smiling.

"Everybody needs a break, now and then."

Fin leaned down so he could see Justin through the opposite window.

"Juss, gimme a minute. Need to holla at Stacks."

"Yeah...yeah. I'mma go chill on your porch."

fin

the sleepover

Justin turned around a bit dejected. He felt that though he enjoyed the day, he was still an outsider. *Why they gotta talk behind my back?* He somberly walked over to the gate of Fin's home and noticed the stark contrast of it to his house. Where Fin's front yard was well manicured, full of lush, green grass, bountiful rose bushes and lilies, his front yard bore signs of wonton neglect. Brown patches of dying, under watered grass dotted the lawn. What little flowers his mother attempted to plant, died long ago. He couldn't remember a time his mother worked their garden. The Finley's porch looked recently painted, a bright off-white, to match the railings on which flower planters full of pink, yellow and red flowers that popped against the white. There were two wicker chairs with flowery cushions, and a small wicker table with a round glass top. His porch was weathered with chipped paint everywhere and a solitary old, rocking chair that Andrew sat in to drink his hooch. He walked slowly, taking it all in, wishing his home looked as loved and inviting. Stacks and Fin watched Justin as he headed to the Finley home and when he was out of earshot, Fin asked him the question that had been on his mind since they got in the car.

"Whatchu about to do, Bruh?"

"Best you don't know, Fin."

"Stacks, don't do nothing stupid."

"Chill, Bruh. Just wanna talk wit' the dude. That's it."

"C'mon, man. Why *you* gotta do this?"

Stacks' snapped his head around and looked Fin square in the eye.

"Why you stand up for him wit' LaTrell?"

fin

the sleepover

Fin knew what Stacks was going to say before he said it. He also knew, Stacks had him cornered.

"'Cause I fucking hate bullies."

"Yeah, me too!"

Fin looked at Stacks, who was now looking straight ahead, and knew there was no talking him down. Whatever he was planning to do was going to happen whether Fin liked it or not. He relented, grabbed his book bag from between his legs, opened the car door and extended his hand to Stacks.

"I'll get atchu tomorrow then."

Stacks extended his hand, and they exchanged their customary hand salutation. "Aight."

Fin walked up to his house as Stacks drove off. It was well past eight-thirty, hours later than he should have been home and he was preparing for an earful from Big Fin and Rose. He had been ignoring their texts and phone calls all day. As he ascended the stairs, his heart racing from anxiety in anticipation of the punishment that awaited him just behind his front door, he saw Justin sitting in his father's wicker chair on the porch. His eyes closed and his chin tilted up, a smile began to creep across his face. The scent of fried fish wafted through the air.

"Yoooooooo! Something smells goooooooood!"

Justin's voice obviously carried because before he could get his key in the door, Fin heard the locks being feverishly opened and the door swung open. Big Fin was furious, his face said it all before his voice did.

"BOY, WHERE HAVE YOU BEEN?"

"I...."

fin

the sleepover

"YOU HAD YOUR MOTHER AND I WORRIED HALF TO DEATH!"

"I'm sorry, Dad. It's just...."

Rose was in the kitchen preparing dinner. When she heard the door open and Big Fin's bellowing voice travelling through warm air laced with the aroma of fried fish, she grabbed her dishtowel and made her way to the front door. She wiped her hands feverishly as her dread over Fin's safety turned to relief, then anger.

"FIN! You *know* better than this!"

Justin hopped in behind Fin, landing with a thud as both feet hit the wooden porch simultaneously.

"HI!"

The appearance of Justin caught Rose and Big Fin by complete surprise. As they examined the boy, they realized something was wrong. Fin read his parents' faces. A look of horror and sympathy gripped Rose's gentle face, her soft sleepy eyes screaming at what they saw. Big Fin's face was different, however. His face shifted from sympathy to pensiveness. He knew what Fin wanted and he also knew he would say no. Fin saw that and prayed Rose could work her magic.

"Mama. Dad. This is Justin. He ain't got no place to go."

Rose was taken aback by his use of broken English as much as the proclamation of Justin's living arrangements.

"Ain't got no place to go?!!"

"He doesn't have anywhere to go."

Justin felt his presence wasn't welcomed. The last thing he wanted to do was get Fin into trouble. Rose and Big Fin couldn't stop staring at the bruise on Justin's face, his dirty clothes, or his frail, malnourished body.

the sleepover

"It's ok, Mr. and Mrs. Fin's parents. I was just leaving."

Big Fin suddenly recognized Justin.

"You were the boy that took Fin to get a locker."

"Yes, Sir."

Rose gently tapped Big Fin on his lower back causing him to look over his shoulder at her. She looked at him, her eyes full of pity. He knew that meant they were having a dinner guest. He acquiesced to her unspoken demand.

"Come on in, young man."

Justin brushed by Fin and through the threshold of the door. Fin took a step forward before Big Fin placed his open hand on his chest, halting him in his tracks.

"Not you."

Fin knew he had some explaining to do. Actually, he had a *lot* of explaining to do. Rose placed her arm around Justin to lead him away from the front door.

"And what's your name, honey?"

"Justin, Ma'am. Justin Bell."

"Well, it's a pleasure to meet you, Justin. I'm Mrs. Finley."

Justin looked behind him as Big Fin closed the door, locking eyes with Fin before the door was shut. Not wanting to embarrass his son, Big Fin waited patiently until the door was closed and he reasoned Rose and Justin wouldn't be privy to what he needed to say.

the sleepover

"Why do you have this little white boy at my house at this time of night, looking like he was just on the wrong end of a prize title fight?"

"Dad, Justin…..his……."

Fin's hesitation to reveal his motives caused Big Fin concern.

"What, son?"

"It's his dad. *He* did that to him."

Big Fin looked at the closed door as if he could see through it. Fin looked up at his father, hoping he would understand, hoping he would show him some kindness. Lord knows Justin needed it. Big Fin became somber.

"His father, huh?"

"Yes, sir."

"So, you brought him here? Why?"

"Dad, Justin is cool. His dad just beats on him. He is always showing up to school with bruises and marks, always looks dirty. I couldn't let him go home. Not tonight."

Big Fin pursed his lips and shook his head. He admired his son's compassion. He also knew that Justin couldn't stay there. If his parents called the police looking for him, Command Master Chief James Finley, would have to answer some very difficult questions at work as to why he was housing a minor without his parents' permission.

"He can stay for dinner, then we are taking him home, son."

"But, Dad…."

the sleepover

"Now, Fin. You know we can't keep him here. He isn't some dog you found on the street. That is somebody's child......even if they treat him like he was a dog."

The words tasted sour as Big Fin said them. He knew he needed to do something, not just for Justin, but for his son. This meant a lot to Fin. Whatever Fin had been doing he was willing to risk their wrath for the sake of this boy. Big Fin respected that.

"C'mon, let's go eat. Ya' Mama made fish."

"*Ya'* Mama?"

"Don't push it, boy."

The Finley's table was already set. Justin marveled at how nice the table looked. The matching plates, more silverware than he knew what to do with, the decorative placemats and napkins rolled up in little, wooden rings, the centerpiece of fresh cut roses in the center of the table. As he looked around the living room and dining room, he saw family photos of Big Fin, Rose and Fin through the years, Navy awards presented to Big Fin, college degrees with Rose and Big Fin's name on them. He couldn't help but notice how clean and orderly everything looked. The contemporary sofa and matching loveseat, the soft, patterned floor rug that provided pops of red, brown and blue, the decorative lamps that gave a soft glow and warmth to the room. Justin thought houses like this only existed in magazines, he definitely never thought he'd see anything like this in Valebrook. Justin was almost scared to move lest he break something or dirty it up. Though he felt out of place, his inquisitiveness got the best of him. As he leaned in to look at family photos on the end table, he slowly drug his hand on the plush, suede sofa, even looking up under the lamp shade, Rose sensed his lack of comfort but marveled at his curiosity.

"Fin, show Justin where to wash up for dinner please."

fin

the sleepover

"Yes, Mama. C'mon, Juss. This way."

Justin followed Fin down the Finley's hallway. His eyes could hardly take it all in. Oil paintings, photos, a beautiful rug runner lining the hallway floor. The space seemed as if it was always warm and inviting, not the dark, daunting hallway atmosphere his home offered.

"Dang, Bro! Your house is nice!!"

"Thanks. Here just use a towel from the shelf right there."

They got special towels to wash their hands! He never wanted to leave. After he washed and dried his hands, he took a deep whiff of them. The lavender and chamomile scent soothed him. Fin smirked, washed his hands, then the boys made their way back down the hallway to the dining room. Rose had laid out what Justin thought was a feast. A large platter covered in fried fish, garlic mashed potatoes, a salad of cucumbers and tomatoes seasoned with olive oil, salt and pepper, fresh baked biscuits and a pitcher of fresh lemonade. Justin sat down at the first seat available, Fin's normal seat which made him frown down on him from behind. While Justin's eyes were affixed on the spread in front of him, his mouth salivating, Big Fin looked at Fin and motioned his head for him to sit on the opposite side of the table. Once seated, Rose, Big Fin and Fin held each other's out-stretched hands. Justin needed only grab Rose's hand to his right and Big Fin's to his left to complete the circle. Instead, he stared at the platter of fish. Fin gently kicked his leg underneath the table to get him to wake up.

"Oh! My bad."

The family bowed their heads and closed their eyes. Justin bowed his as well but kept peeking to see if what was happening was real. Big Fin began to pray.

the sleepover

"Heavenly Father, we come before you tonight humbly and with our hearts open. We thank you for this food that will nourish our bodies. We thank you for the gift of friendship that gives us comfort in our times of need. We ask Lord, that you bless those that are hurting, in need of your protection, your guidance, and your wisdom. We ask all of this, in Jesus' name. Amen."

Rose and Fin echoed with "Amen." Justin's head was still down, his eyes were now fully closed. The Finleys all looked at each other in wonder, then at him. Justin was still in prayer. He had never really prayed before, at least not with any expectation of a positive outcome. As a child, he would pray his father would leave and never come home. Those prayers would later morph into prayers that he would simply get a night of peace. In this moment, he was simply thankful for Fin and his family. Thankful for showing him a kindness he rarely was the recipient of. Finally, he looked up and smiled. Then nodded his head with each syllable as he spoke.

"A-men!"

Fin smiled. Rose was starting to understand why her son was fond of him. She glanced over at Big Fin, and from the look in his eyes, she could tell Justin was growing on him as well. She reached for the platter of fish.

"Justin, would you like some fish?"

"Yes! Please!"

"Mama can make some fish, Juss. You're gonna love this."

"It all looks good."

Rose loved the smile on Fin's face as he reassured his friend that this was a meal he would enjoy. She piled Justin's plate with two pieces of fried fish, a heaping spoonful of potatoes, two biscuits and some salad. Big Fin noticed that while he was eager to dive in, he seemed apprehensive to do so. He wondered if Justin felt a sense of euphoria, almost as if he were to touch the food, he would wake up and find it was all a dream.

"Dig in, Justin."

The Finley's quickly saw that Justin needed no further prompting. They sat and watched in amazement as Justin devoured his food, so much so that they barely touched their own. As Justin ate, oblivious to everyone at the table, Big Fin and Rose looked at each other. No words needed to be said. They both realized Justin was an abused child who probably hadn't had a decent meal in weeks. They attempted to make small talk about their respective days, the boys at school, Justin asked questions about the Navy, anything to prolong the dinner and allow Justin to eat as much as he wanted, as much as he needed. Rose needed to talk to her husband, the thought locked in her head wouldn't let her think of anything else.

"James, give me a hand in the kitchen please?"

Big Fin knew what Rose was thinking. He also knew that he had to be firm and say no. Once they were in the seclusion of the kitchen, away from the boys, Rose began to plead her case.

"James. That boy. Who can we call?"

"I don't know, babe. Been thinking on it since he got here."

"We can't send him back to wherever he calls home. Just look at him! I never seen a boy so unloved."

"Rose, you know he can't stay here. He can't."

"You're worrying about the command, aren't you?"

"You know I am. This is putting me in a precarious spot, baby."

fin

the sleepover

She sighed. "I know. But, James, just for tonight. One night is all I'm asking. Can't we give him *one* night of peace and safety?"

"Rose you know…."

"Jaaaaaames…look at him."

Big Fin looked over at Justin, but he didn't need to. He already knew that he was going to give in to her. He just needed to make some calls to his commanding officer and give her a heads up. This was a delicate situation, and he couldn't allow his commanding officer to get exposed because of his actions. He let out a long sigh.

"One night. I just gotta call the Admiral."

She leaned in and placed her hand on his massive chest where his heart was.

"You're a good man, James Finley. It's where your son gets it from."

While Fin and Justin sat and laughed at the table, Fin's plate was clean and Justin's seemed to keep magically materializing pieces of fish or biscuits that must've gotten lost, Rose walked in.

"Justin, would you like to stay the night?"

Fin sat up. He looked at his mother, then into the kitchen where Big Fin was on his cellphone. Fin mouthed "thank you" to his dad. In that moment, his love and admiration for Big Fin grew even more. He knew Rose would give in; it was Big Fin he was worried about. Justin had a rush of relief and excitement. For the first time, his prayers were answered.

"Yes, Ma'am! Can I?"

"Fin baby, get Justin some towels and an old shirt and shorts to sleep in."

94

"Yes, Mama."

Rose wanted to wash Justin's clothes for him. The boys got up and made their way down to Fin's room. Fin grabbed some shorts and a t-shirt from his dresser. He knew Justin would drown in the size of the clothes relative to his body, but it was all he had. Justin grabbed the clothes and went to shower. Rose met him in the hallway. She handed him a towel, washcloth, a disposable toothbrush, and travel sized toiletries.

"Here you go, honey."

Justin was so grateful he wanted to cry. Instead, he chose to hug Rose, wrapping his small, wiry arms around her waist.

"Thank you, Mrs. Fin's mom."

Rose melted on spot. She placed one hand on his head and the other on his back.

"You're welcome, honey. Leave your clothes in the bathroom so I can wash them for you, okay?"

"Yes, Ma'am."

How could anyone mistreat such a sweet child? Justin released Rose, went into the bathroom, smiled at Rose who was struggling not to cry, then closed the door and undressed. Removing his sweatshirt was painful, his body was still sore. He looked at himself in the mirror. His torso, arms and legs were peppered with bruises from the night before. Rose entered Fin's room, kissed him on his forehead and finally acknowledged her son and the evening's events with four simple words:

"God Bless you, baby."

Then she walked out. The moment was too much for her and she needed to get to her bedroom to release the hurt, anger and frustration she was feeling. She sat on the edge of her bed and cried, covering her mouth to muffle the sound. Big Fin entered the room, having finished clearing down the dinner table, and saw her in pain. He walked to the bed and sat down beside her.

"James, how *could* he? Who could be so monstrous?!"

He placed his arm around her, pulling her to him to comfort her.

"Some people don't deserve the blessing of children, baby."

"I just don't understand, James. Why?"

"I don't either, baby, but I talked to the Admiral and she told me do what we needed to do. She will support us no matter what."

"What are we going to do?"

"I don't know yet."

After his shower, Justin went back into Fin's room, leaving his clothes in the bathroom just like Rose asked. Fin had laid out a sleeping bag on the floor to provide him some cushion, two pillows and a fleece blanket.

"That's you, Bro. I'm gonna shower."

"Never been to a sleepover before."

Fin was surprised by that statement, thinking back on his countless sleepovers with Curt. He gathered his night clothes and underwear and went to shower. Justin laid down on the floor, his body clean, his belly full. The serene moment even gave him comfort from his injuries. He looked around Fin's room and became envious. He looked at his desk with the large computer tower and dual monitors, surrounded by notebooks with computer code notes. He looked at his sports trophies, the shining gold men holding basketballs, baseball bats and a tennis racket. *Fin plays tennis??!* He looked at his open closet. It was orderly and had what Justin thought were hundreds of sneakers, all clean and crisp, all rare. His wardrobe all hanging neatly; the shirts in color order, the pants draped perfectly across their hangers below. He saw the pictures of Fin and another boy with glasses, smiling. He hoped one day Fin would have pictures of him up on the walls. He noticed the thirty-two-inch TV, Blu-ray player and game system. *Man, Fin has the life!* Before long, Fin returned to the room and tossed his dirty clothes into the laundry basket in his closet.

"You good?"

"Yeah, Bro. Thanks for letting me crash here."

"No problem. Sucks you gotta go back."

"It ain't so bad when my dad ain't there. My mom is actually pretty funny."

Fin found it admirable that even in a living hell, Justin found something positive in it. It matched his always energetic and jokey personality in school. Fin figured Justin didn't want to be miserable all the time so he grabbed joy whenever and from wherever he could. He flipped the light off and climbed in bed. Justin looked up at him.

"You know Lailah likes you, right?"

Fin chuckled and looked down at Justin. "Yeah, I know."

Justin folded his arms behind his head and looked up at the ceiling.

"Lailah could get it."

"HA! Talk to her then!"

the sleepover

"Man, anyone not named James Finley don't matter. She always talking about you in class. Be asking me 'Fin got a girl?' or 'Who Fin talking to?' I be like girl, obviously not you!"

The boys laughed.

"Get some sleep, Juss. Mama is gonna make breakfast in the morning. Saturday is pancakes."

This revelation was the icing on the cake for Justin and confirmed his earlier thought about Fin's dream life. *Damn! She makes you breakfast, too?*

Justin turned away from Fin, onto his side, and was fast asleep in moments. His body was exhausted. The warm shower, affectionate hug from Rose, and protection of Big Fin eased the soreness of his still bruised body. Mostly though, he was with Fin, and that always made him feel happy and safe. Fin stared at his friend as he laid there. He hoped that for at least one night, he could feel safe, his body nourished, his spirit loved. In that moment, Fin loved Big Fin and Rose even more, not just for what they did for Justin, but that they ensured he never endured such horrors and neglect. It wasn't long before Justin's soft snoring let Fin know that he was asleep. Fin smiled.

"Night, Bro."

chapter seven

big fin

The next morning, just as Fin foretold, Justin arose to the smell of pancakes, bacon and freshly brewed coffee. Justin slowly pulled himself off the sleeping bag, his body still a bit achy and his mind groggy. He noticed Fin wasn't in bed. He grabbed the toothbrush Rose gave him off of Fin's dresser and walked to the bathroom. Big Fin had just exited his bedroom and saw him.

"Good morning, young man."

"Good morning, Sir."

"Them pancakes woke you up too, huh?"

Justin gave a half-sleepy smile. "Yes, Sir."

Big Fin leaned close to him as he passed.

"Well come on and get some, before Fin eats them all up."

99

Justin chuckled and nodded, then entered the bathroom. Once he was all freshened up, he made his way to the breakfast table where Big Fin, Rose and Fin were already eating. Fin was in between bites of syrup-drenched pancakes when Justin entered the room.

"Morning, Juss."

Rose presented a big, beautiful smile. "Good morning, honey. Did you sleep well?"

"Yes, Ma'am."

"I told Fin not to wake you. Figured you'd get up when your body said it was time."

"I don't know about my body, Mrs. Fin's mom, but my stomach said it was time to get up!"

Justin sat down to the table. The Finleys all chuckled. Rose grabbed the plate full of pancakes and offered some to Justin.

"Well, there is plenty to go around."

Rose thought it was cute how Justin referred to her as "Mrs. Fin's Mom". Justin sat down and admired the spread. A platter stacked with fresh, buttermilk pancakes, a pile of turkey bacon, a bowl with freshly sliced strawberries, a pitcher of juice and a small pot of coffee. Justin ate just as ravenously as he did dinner the night before. He wasn't sure when he would enjoy a meal like this again. When breakfast was complete, and he had his fill, Rose informed him that his clothes were in the dryer and she was going to retrieve them for him. Big Fin stood from the table and began to help Fin as he collected the plates.

"I got this. You two boys go on and get dressed. Need to get you home, Justin."

fin

big fin

Justin's joyful mood shifted almost immediately. Fin saw the shift and smiled at Justin as he walked by his chair.

"C'mon, Bro."

Fin grabbed Justin's clothes from Rose who was standing in the threshold of the laundry room, handed them to Justin then they headed to Fin's bedroom. Rose felt guilty as she watched Justin pass, his head down. She felt as if there was more she could do, more she *should* do, but she knew Big Fin was right. Once they were in the privacy of the room, Justin turned to Fin with a glimmer of hope.

"You think I could come back one day? Spend the night again?"

"Yeah, I guess. I don't see why not."

"You're lucky, Fin. Your parents love each other."

Fin wasn't exactly sure the proper response to Justin's observation. He thought any response could be taken as gloating. He already knew that Big Fin and Rose's love was special, and he was the beneficiary of growing up in a loving environment. There was no need to say something that would remind Justin that he wasn't so lucky. Fin felt uncomfortable and remained silent. *Damn, Bro!* The boys dressed, Fin rather fast, Justin slow and drawn out, trying to prolong his time at the Finley home. Fin waited patiently for Justin to finish then the two boys made their way into the living room. Big Fin and Rose were waiting for them, Big Fin with his keys in his hand. Rose had a sorrowful look on her face. She genuinely cared for Justin and feared for whatever hell he was about to return to. She walked over and hugged him, hard and long. She didn't know when the next time he would receive such affection. Even though her grip hurt his bruises, Justin didn't care. He hugged her back just as hard.

fin

big fin

"Thank you, Mrs. Fin's mom."

"You're welcome, honey. And call me Rose, ok?"

"Thank you, Mrs. Rose."

"You make sure you come back and see us, ok?"

Justin didn't want to lie to her, but he knew he had to. He knew he would never be allowed to come back. Even if Elaine said it was okay, it would be just another log for Andrew to throw into his self-pity fireplace. So, he lied.

"I will."

Fin, Justin and Big Fin piled into the family SUV and made their way to Justin's house. They rode in silence as neither Big Fin nor Fin knew exactly what to say. They were both guilt ridden that they had to send Justin back into purgatory. They pulled up in front of Justin's home, Big Fin turned off the engine and looked at Justin through the rearview mirror.

"What's your parents' names, Justin?"

"Andrew and Elaine."

"Is that your dad's pick up in the driveway?"

Justin nodded. Big Fin let out a deep sigh.

"Let's go talk to your folks."

The three got out of the SUV, Big Fin placing his hand on Justin's shoulder. They slowly made their way up the steps to the old, dilapidated porch that was sorely in need of repairs. Years of neglect had eroded the once white porch, leaving only oblong patches of cracked white paint, remnants of its former glory. There were empty beer cans and a tilted bottle of whiskey on the porch floor. Justin held his head down, ashamed of the look of his home. It was only in that moment that Fin realized he had never been there. Justin never invited him over. Knowing what he knows now, he understood why. As he looked at Justin's home, its woeful look only symbolized what he saw in Justin: something that is trying so hard to be beautiful, but lacks the love and care it needed to flourish. Big Fin approached the door, and opened the screen door with the tattered meshing and rang the doorbell. No answer. He rang again. Still, no answer. He opened the screen door and forcefully knocked on the door. This time there was a response from inside the house.

"WHO IS IT?"

Fin felt a knot form in his stomach. Not from the sound of Andrew screaming, but when he saw how Justin winced at the sound of his father's voice.

"Command Master Chief James Finley, Sir. I have your son with me."

Within seconds the lock and deadbolt were disengaged, and the door flung open.

"WHERE THE FUCK HA.........?"

Andrew stopped mid-sentence as his gaze went from Justin to Big Fin. Big Fin was staring down at him. He wore a gray t-shirt embossed with "NAVY" on the front. The letters looked as if they were draped over two mountains the way his shirt gripped his massive chest. His bulging thighs and calves looked like tree trunks. His biceps were the biggest Andrew had ever seen, and working in the police department he had seen quite a few large men. None of them were as impressive or as intimidating as Big Fin. Big Fin, Fin and Justin all looked at Andrew's face. Someone gave him one *hell* of a beating. Big Fin had no idea how he got those bruises, but secretly, he was happy he did. Fin smiled a bit. *Guess Stacks had that conversation with you after all! Good!* Justin saw too, but he dared not show any glee at the sight of Andrew's battered face.

"Mr. Bell, my name is Command Master Chief James Finley. This is my son, Fin. Justin stayed with us last night. Mr. Bell, I am concerned about Justin's safety. He had quite a few bruises on him. You know how they got there?"

"You Navy, right?"

"Yes, I am."

"So, that means you ain't no fucking cop! Whatchu worrying about me and mine for? Thank you for watching him. Git' in this house, boy!"

Justin started to walk forward and was met by Big Fin's large hand in his chest, stopping him in his tracks. Big Fin never took his eyes off of Andrew. His glare was hard and intense, full of disdain and anger. His one free hand reached into his shorts pocket and removed a card. Andrew flinched and quickly tried to regain his composure. One eyebrow on Fin's forehead raised as an evil grin crept across his mouth. *Scared now, ain'tchu?*

"You're right, Sir, I ain't a cop. What I *am* is a concerned father, and when I see a boy that's being abused, I will act. Justin, you take this."

Big Fin transferred the card from his one hand to the hand that was on Justin's chest, doing so in one smooth motion and never taking his eyes off of Andrew. Fin watched Andrew wither; fear gripped him. Fin looked at Big Fin in a way he never had before. He had never seen this Big Fin. Intimidating. Powerful. Terrifying.

big fin

"Son, you call me whenever you need to. Don't matter the time of day. If you get scared, I mean for *any* reason, you call me. I'll drop what I am doing and swing by."

Justin slid the card into his pocket.

"Thank you, Sir."

Andrew dared not object to Justin's acceptance of that card, at least not in front of Big Fin. His pride was severely damaged last night. In this moment, it had been stripped of him completely. After last night, he was terrified. His eyes remained on Big Fin the way one stares at a ferocious, uncollared dog.

"C'mon in the house, Justin."

"Say goodbye to your friend, Fin."

"Bye, Juss. Hit me up lata."

Justin nodded then dropped his head and entered his house.

"Lata."

"You have a good day, Sir. Treat those wounds."

Big Fin pointed at his face and moved his finger in a circular motion. Andrew became enraged.

"KISS MY ASS!"

Andrew slammed the door. Big Fin and Fin stood there for a moment. Big Fin's eyes pierced the door as if he wished they could shoot lasers. Fin's eyes stayed on Big Fin. His father's arms were so tensed, Fin thought he was going to punch the door of its hinges with a single blow.

"Dad..."

fin

big fin

"DAD!"

"Let's go, son."

As they rode back to the house, Big Fin gathered himself. His trembling subsided, his quickened heart rate slowed to a normal pace. Fin though, grew angrier and angrier. He began to bounce his leg, frown his face and shake his head as he looked out of the window. Big Fin recognized the physiological changes occurring in his son, traits he was all too familiar with. When they pulled into the driveway, he turned the ignition off and they sat there in silence.

"Son, I..."

"You shoulda did it, Dad."

"Did what?"

"Punched him in his damn face!"

Big Fin let the curse slide, he knew his son was experiencing a rage he had probably never experienced before.

"Yeah? And then what?"

"He woulda been punched in the face! Let him see what it's like to get beat on."

"And I would've went to jail, my career over, and Justin would still be there. We would have accomplished nothing."

"So, we just gonna leave him like that?"

"For now, we have to. I will be making some calls. I have some good friends who are police and deal with child protective services as part of my job. We are gonna get him some help, Fin. We just have to go about it the right way."

fin

big fin

Fin didn't want to hear that answer. He remembered what Justin had told him: *The cops didn't help!*

"They not gonna help! His daddy used to be a cop!"

"I thought he looked familiar! I remember that piece of shit now! He got fired some years back for excessive force. It was all over the news!"

Fin started to calm down. He knew that there wasn't much he could do, more importantly, he trusted Big Fin. He knew his father never made a promise he couldn't keep. Big Fin was truly a man of his word. "A man can take anything from you son; your money, your car, your clothes, your left arm, your life. He can't take your integrity, however. That, you have to give up willfully." Fin never forgot the first time his father told him that when he caught him lying. It has stayed with him and strengthens him in this moment. *If Dad says we are gonna do something, we are gonna do it.* There was another burning question in his mind though, one he had to ask.

"Dad?"

"Yes?"

"I have never seen you like that before. All mad and scary like that."

Big Fin sighed. He felt ashamed that Fin got a glimpse of the old him, the man he had outgrown.

"Fin, I wasn't always Command Master Chief. Before I joined the Navy, I did some things and ran with some folks that I shouldn't have. I started getting into trouble and figured I could run from my problems, so I joined the Navy. I discovered I may have changed my surroundings, but I never changed myself. Wasn't too long before I started making mistakes up here too. I did a lot of things I still regret.

I am not that person anymore, but that old man almost came out today. I am sorry you saw that side of me."

"Things with Mr. Cooper?"

Big Fin's head snapped back in shock. *How does he know Coop?!!?*

"Cooper?!? You talking about Cooper Morton??!"

Fin nodded his head.

"Fin, how do you know him?!"

"I go to school with his son."

"Listen to me, Fin. You stay away from them. Stay far away from them. They are trouble!"

"He said y'all were close once. Said y'all even promised to look out for each other's kids."

"That was a promise between two young punks! I would NEVER let him do anything for you! Now I'm gonna say this once, and once only, you stay away from Cooper Morton and his people. You hear me, boy?!"

Big Fin rarely raised his voice at Fin. Fin could count on one hand in his fifteen years of life how many times he had. Thing was, this time, no matter how much Big Fin yelled, he knew he was going to disobey him. Stacks was his friend.

"Yes, Sir."

"I'M SERIOUS, FIN! YOU STAY AWAY!"

"James!"

fin

big fin

Both Finley men looked over and saw Rose standing on the porch. The concerned look on her face upset them both.

"Stay away from them, son. Promise me."

Fin gulped hard, then lied. "I promise."

Fin opened the car door, got out and slammed it shut. He walked as if he was going to the house, then made a sharp turn towards the street.

"FIN!" cried Rose.

"Let him be, Rose. He needs to clear his head. I'll talk to him some more when he gets back."

"What was that about?"

"Ghosts from the past."

Fin walked fast, leaning forward, his momentum almost pulling him. He was furious and frustrated. Helplessness is not a feeling he liked to sit in, but today he had no choice. He couldn't help Justin. He was mad Big Fin didn't hurt Andrew. He was hurt Big Fin told him to stay away from Stacks. Mostly, he was mad he lied to his father. He knew full well he wasn't going to stay away from Stacks, his subconscious mind knew it too. Fin was just walking and thinking, but when he looked up and became cognizant of where he was, he was on First Street, across the street from Brevoit Projects.

Stacks was sitting outside his apartment, leaning back in the white, plastic chair that was a fixture outside his front door. Gray Boy, stood to Stacks' right, rubbing his hands together, cautiously checking their surroundings. It looked as if Gray was expecting something to happen at any moment. As Gray looked around, he noticed Fin approaching and tapped Stacks' on the shoulder. Stacks looked up at Gray Boy, who then motioned his head forward. That's when Stacks saw Fin. He sat the chair back on all fours and shook his head. As Fin got close, Stacks stood up. Today was not the day for Fin to pop in unexpectedly.

"What up, Fin? You good?"

"Yeah….*FUCK NO!* I ain't good!"

"Oh, you mad?"

Gray Boy mixed in hard stares at Fin over Stacks' shoulder in between his continued watchful glances of the entrances to the Brevoit courtyard.

"Yeah, I'm fucking mad!"

"Well look, Bruh. I'mma need you to be mad somewhere else. This is a bad time, right now,"

Stacks suggestively looked over at the apartment then back at Fin.

"Man, I saw what you did last night."

Stacks looked away, annoyed that Fin was bringing anything he wasn't a part of up.

"Whatchu talking about Fin?

He figured Fin must have seen Andrew's face and put two and two together. His annoyance was he couldn't believe Fin was bringing it up. Up until this moment, Stacks saw Fin as someone that knew when to keep their mouth shut, knew when some things should remain unspoken. For the first time, he questioned this belief.

"I'm just saying…"

"Yeah, but you shouldn't!"

fin

big fin

"Shouldn't what?"

"Be saying shit!"

Fin figured out his mistake and looked away, his anger growing by the second.

"Look, Fin. Now ain't the time for this. I need you to get the fuck outta here!"

"Fine! Fuck it!"

Fin turned and began to walk away. Stacks didn't move, he watched him storm off. He wanted to talk with him but now was not the time. As he watched, another unexpected visitor entered into the Brevoit Homes.

"What the fuck you runnin', Stacks? A fucking community outreach center?!"

Stacks turned and looked at Gray. "The fuck you say??!"

"Look!" Gray exclaimed as he pointed to his right.

"WHAT THE FUCK?!?!"

Fin barely made it thirty feet away when he heard Stacks yell. He snapped his head around and saw what caused it. He immediately ran back to where Stacks was standing. Justin was running, barely. His eye was black and closed. His nose appeared broken. His bottom lip looked as if his teeth had gone through it from a punch. His shirt torn and covered in blood.

"JUSSS!!"

part two

stacks

chapter eight

family business

The evening before Fin's first day at Eastwood High School, Stacks was in the living room with Coop, Shan, Gray Boy, and his uncle, Big Tony. The Morton family business was in turmoil. Someone in the organization sold them out causing significant losses of both manpower and merchandise. A few weeks ago, one of the main gun stashes was raided by a rival crew. Sixteen crates of choice merchandise were gone, the three men guarding them were dead, and the warehouse out in Franklin was burned to the ground. The police have been questioning Coop and Big Tony, as well as other members of their organization, but Stacks and Gray Boy were off-limits, as both were technically still minors. Surveillance had increased on everyone. The police were expecting some sort of retaliation. Though Coop wanted to retaliate, his decrease in manpower and financial capital were a stumbling block. He needed a quick influx of cash to stabilize the business while he plotted his next move. He had a buyer lined up, willing to buy a shipment from his reserves of AR-15s, but it needed to be done quickly. The issue? Who he would choose to run point on it. Big Tony gave the first assessment of the situation.

"How we gonna make that drop? Heat is on us right now."

Shan, the ever eager yet insecure one, spoke up.

"I'll do that shit."

"Didn't yo' ass just get stopped over on Twelfth?" challenged Big Tony. "They know yo' ass! Ya' car too!"

Shan ignored his uncle's sound reasoning. "I can do it, Pop."

Stacks sat silently as he did at most of these quorums. He didn't want to be here, in *this*. Truth is, he hated guns, but was no stranger on how to use one. Only thing he hated more than guns was the family business. He knew Coop had been looking to get him more involve, but he wanted none of it. He wanted out. Coop felt this was the family's calling and the Mortons had been successful at selling guns for over one hundred years, more or less. Though Shan was next in line for succession, he wanted to hear from his desired successor, Stacks.

"Whatchu think, Chris?"

"I think this is a move we shouldn't make right now. Everyone is hot and we don't need extra eyes on us."

"Hmmppp, so what? We jus' supposed to not make money? To lose our foothold?"

"No, but if we..."

"If we don't do this then that's exactly what's gonna happen. Moment mafuckas 'round here think we can't get them that iron, they gonna go run to them white boys. I ain't giving them shit over me."

fin

family business

"All I'm saying is…."

"All you saying is shit I don't wanna hear. How 'bout this - YOU make the drop. Take Gray Boy whitcha."

Gray Boy nodded. Though he wasn't family, his loyalty to the Mortons was unquestioned. Gray Boy and Stacks grew up together in this crazy world they existed in. His father used to be Coop's number one, even over Coop's blood brother, Big Tony, but he was killed in prison while facing a twenty-year bid for gun trafficking. When he went in, Coop promised him he would look after Gray Boy no matter what. Involving him in illegal gun running was his way of "taking care of him." Big Tony didn't like the decision to include Gray Boy, however.

"Gray probably just as hot as the rest of us. Anyone snapping pictures see him all out in front."

Coop nodded and rubbed his face. "Good point."

Shan still wanted to show he had the chops to make the tough call.

"Let him take Dee with him. It'll just look like he's picking up his kid brother."

Coop hated the idea! He glared disapprovingly at Shan for his eagerness to include the youngest Morton. Dee was just a kid, but he knew they were in a bind and they needed to make this move. Still, he rolled his eyes at Shan for even bringing it up.

"Hate to agree to this, but we may have no choice."

Stacks was simultaneously dumbfounded and enraged. *How could y'all even think about including Dee in this shit!* This plan would not do.

117

fin

family business

"NO! I'll find some square at school tomorrow to give me cover. I ain't putting Dee in this shit."

"You gonna carry some punk mafucka whitchu one this?!?! Pop, he *trippin'*! Let me do this."

"You got someone in mind, Chris?"

"Yeah. I got someone."

Truth was, he didn't. He had no clue who he was going take with him as cover - he just wasn't taking Dee. He swore long ago to never let Dee get caught up in this life. Dee was the only reason he didn't take the money he had stashed at Shayla's, pack her up and got them all the fuck out of Norfolk. He stayed to shield Dee from what he should have been shielded from. He stayed to give Dee something that was taken from him long ago, a chance.

"Ok, boy. This is on you. But you fuck this up, we done! Everything we built is done!"

"I know, Pop. I got this."

Stacks rose, resigned to the fact he needed to handle this but had no earthly idea how he would. He walked through the living room, out the door and into the night. There was a humid, stagnant air lingering in Brevoit that night. The courtyard was dimly lit by the old, Victorian styled porchlights that hung to the left of every door except for theirs. Coop had removed it years ago. There was the buzz of older people talking as they sat on chairs, stools and crates just outside their doors everywhere. Some young boys played football in the courtyard grass, using the two large green communications boxes as endzone markers. He looked around at his neighborhood but kept coming back to the boys at play. He remembered when he and Gray Boy played like that, not a care in the world, neither wanting to accept the future they didn't see any way out of. The sound of the door opening then closing

118

behind him broke his trip down memory lane. It was Gray Boy. He waited until the door was closed behind him before he asked what had been burning in his mind.

"The fuck you tell yo' daddy you got someone in mind for?"

"I dunno."

"Man, how you gonna do this shit? Most mafuckas at that school terrified of you."

"Yeah I know. That's where you come in."

"How so?"

"Need you to help me pick someone out. You know every damn body."

There was a long pause as the two young men stared at the courtyard football game. Though they both were only seventeen, life had aged them far beyond their years. They should be looking at college applications, thinking of who they were going to take to the prom, or hanging with friends. Neither should have such weight on their shoulders. Neither had to comment on it, though. They both could feel the sense of sadness in the other. Stacks stared at the game a moment longer before he spoke.

"You got me?"

"Of course. Say less."

Stacks extended his hand. Gray Boy returned the handshake.

"Aight. I'mma catch you tomorrow."

"No doubt. Watch ya'self out there."

"Always."

fin

family business

Stacks watched Gray Boy walk to his silver Cadillac and drive off. He lingered a few moments before turning around to leave the darkness of the courtyard and into another darkness behind his own front door. As he navigated his way down the hallway, he stopped to check on Dee. He was already asleep. He walked in, kissed his cheek, then pulled the covers back over him which Dee had thrown off in his sleep.

"Night lil' man."

The next day Stacks rose with a sense of purpose. *Who the fuck am I gonna snag to ride wit' me?* His situation plagued his mind as he rode to school. As he arrived at the school, the street Eastwood High was on was busy with hormonal teenagers as usual. Boys and girls in small groups laughing, ribbing each other with jokes, young lovers holding hands, the quiet, non-descript kids attempting to blend in and avoid the bullies. All in their own worlds, that was, until he arrived. He slowly drove down the street, his eyes ever forward as the ones who thought they were cool enough shouted his name out. But as he drove down the street, all foot traffic stopped, some jumping out of his car's way. Not for some fear of being struck, but out of respect. He pulled up to his usual spot, which had been deemed off-limits to the entire student body. Though he had never been violent, his six-foot three frame intimidated most; his family name terrified the rest. He turned the engine off and sat there, leaned his head back on the head rest and closed his eyes. That's when Shayla approached.

"Hey, you."

Stacks looked over at his girlfriend and smiled. He needed to see her beautiful face smiling at him, feel her energy shine down on him as he sat.

"What up, baby?"

family business

Stacks watched as she walked around the front of the car. He loved watching her. Shayla was five foot five, though she would argue she was every bit of five seven. She had near shoulder length dreadlocks pulled into a ponytail today to display the necklace and locket he had given her the day before. Her green long-sleeved shirt matched her eyes. Her light brown skin was the color of raw shea butter. She always had a bounce to her step that excited him. As she approached the front, she ran her fingers across the hood and stared at Stacks, her eyes giving a sexual energy that he knew all too well. When she drew near the passenger door, he leaned over and opened it for her. She threw her bag on the floor and climbed in, slamming the door behind her.

"You mad at my door?"

"Boy, bye," she retorted playfully as she leaned back into the seat. "Thought you were coming over last night?"

Stacks looked away and out of the rolled down window. Part of it was because his mind wouldn't let him forget his tasking. The other part was, he hated breaking his promise to her.

"I got caught up with Coop. That fool was tripping last night."

She laughed and rolled her eyes upward.

"When is Coop *not* tripping?!"

Stacks snapped his head around to see her laugh. He loved how her eyes squinted and she leaned ever so forward when she laughed. Her bright white teeth and passion pink gums always made him smile.

"Oh, that's funny to you?"

Something in his eyes and tone concerned her.

fin

family business

"You aight, Bae? You seem off today."

"I'm good, baby. Just got a lot on my mind."

"Whatchu need, Bae? You need Shayla to make it better?"

The thought of being intimate with her, holding her, laying with her in her bedroom excited him, but it also distracted him. He couldn't have that right now. She reached over and rubbed the back of his neck. He closed his eyes again, her soft warm hands soothing his weary mind. In an instant, he turned to her, leaned and reached across her body, grabbed her waist and pulled her close to him. Their faces now inches apart, he stared deep into her eyes. She was gripped with lust; his aggressive move turned her on, but the struggle she saw in his eyes concerned her. Her eyes darted back and forth, looking into his.

"Baaaeee, what is i..."

He kissed her, deeper and harder than ever before. Her lips were his release. Her smell was comforting like the aroma of warm biscuits. Her taste sweet and intoxicating. She moaned as she felt every ounce of her concern wash away. His lips pulled away softly as he leaned his forehead in to meet hers.

"I'm ok, baby. I promise. C'mon, let's go."

Her eyes remained closed a moment longer.

"Mmmpphh. Okay, Bae." She wanted him.

Stacks exited the car, closed the door behind him, walked around the car to her door and opened it for her, grabbing her hand as she exited. Shayla was too strong a woman to need him to do anything for her. She did, however, love when he did little things like this. It made her feel regal. He closed her door behind her, placed his arm around her and they began walking to the building. As they approached the main hallway of Eastwood High, they embraced one last time. Their schedules didn't offer another chance meeting until after lunch, so this was their morning goodbye. He often thought they could be doing this in a few years, kissing each other goodbye as they left for their workdays. As much as Dee is an integral part of him wanting to get out of Norfolk, he didn't see that happening without Shayla.

"Text me?" she asked as if she had to. He smiled.

"You need to be concentrating in biology. Don't you got a 'C' in that class?"

"Whatever, punk! Text me!"

Shayla glowed and wiggled her fingers goodbye as she turned to head to biology class. She walked just a little extra sexy knowing he was still watching. Then she pulled out her phone and texted him.

Shayla: Stop looking at my ass fool! LOL

Stacks: Stop switchin it so hard!

Shayla: U like it tho so......

*Shayla: ttyl :**

"Hope that ain't who you taking."

It was Gray Boy, standing behind him, disrupting his morning fantasy.

"Fool, that girl would *kill* me if I even tried to. Besides, you know the rules."

"So, who you looking at taking?"

"Maaaannnnn, I don't even know. Needs to be a nobody."

"How the fuck you gonna get a nobody to just get in the car with you?"

"Oh, they *gon'* get in the car. Believe that."

"Aight, killa."

Gray Boy extended his hand. Stacks returned the handshake.

"Holla at you at lunch."

After an uneventful morning, Stacks sat in his American History class, his last class before lunch, upset as usual. An avid reader, he felt the version of history that was presented to the students did not match what *actually* happened, and often led to heated discourse between him and the teacher, Mr. Milley. Mr. Milley lectured, presenting his truncated, whitewashed version of the Reconstruction Era. Stacks, who would normally pounce like a cat on a mouse, sat silently. *I hope Gray Boy comes through on this.* He didn't pay too much attention to people, at least not in the psychological way Gray Boy did. In another world, Gray Boy would be a psychologist, a social economist or philosopher, anything but a soldier in a dying illegal organization.

BZZZZZZZZZZZZZZZZZZZZZZZZZZZZZ!

He pulled his cellphone from his front pocket and opened it.

Gray Boy: Get at me before lunch. I got someone.

Stacks: Bet!

He felt a moment of relief. Gray Boy never failed him. Failure was a sore subject for Gray Boy, it reminded Gray of his father. Gray

fin

family business

had been virtually on his own since he was twelve. He was an only child, his father murdered while incarcerated and his mother long gone - lost to the streets. The ever condescending Mr. Milley noticed his complete lack of attention to the lecture he was giving.

"Mr. Morton, do you agree with this assessment, or may I continue?"

"Man, you gonna teach what you teach. They can either choose to believe you or validate whatever this bullshit is you're slinging."

"Thank you, Mr. Morton. You just earned yourself detention!" Mr. Milley felt he achieved some sort of victory. He looked down at his desk and began writing a detention slip.

"Please, come and get your..."

The sound of the door closing paused his train of thought. Stacks was gone. He had had enough of Mr. Milley's passive-aggressiveness. The daily back and forth (as if a victory for Mr. Milley over a seventeen year old kid was some sort of upliftment for his version of history) was old. Truth was, he had no illusions of ever changing Milley's view of things. He challenged him daily in hopes of educating his classmates and sparking them to challenge the spoon-feeding they received in school. *Think for your fucking selves!* he would often think. Right now though, he had to think about *himself*, so he headed over to Gray Boy's class to meet him. As the bell rang, Gray Boy exited the math classroon fast and immediately spotted Stacks standing about ten feet down the hallway from the class door. Gray Boy calmly walked by him.

"Walk with me."

"You got somebody?"

family business

"Yeah, just walk though. New kid. Real quiet mafucka. Type a cat that just blends in."

Stacks spun his head around. "Who?"

"Walk. Show you in the cafeteria."

Stacks nodded and they made their way to the cafeteria. They chose a table close to the lunch line. Normally the science nerds sat there as it allowed them easy access into the cafeteria, and a quick escape, should things get crazy. It was also visible enough to observe any teacher or security guard that had lunch duty that day. As Stacks sat, Gray Boy remained standing.

"Chill here. I'mma go get us some wings."

Stacks looked around the cafeteria. Almost all of the kids he saw were either wanna be gangsters, or so polarly opposite to him and Gray Boy, no one would believe they would associate. Either way, it would be unnecessary attention. *He better be right, whoever the fuck he got!* Gray Boy returned with a stack of greasy, breaded chicken wings. As they began to devour their feast, Gray Boy tapped Stacks' foot with his and nodded his head slightly for Stacks to look over his shoulder at the cafeteria entrance. It was in this moment that he first saw Fin.

His initial impression of Fin wasn't much. He was tall and lanky, seemed socially awkward and almost as if he was scared to embrace his size. Unsure of this selection, Stacks looked back at Gray Boy, his expression spoke without saying a word. *Him??? You sure?* Gray Boy simply nodded. To Gray Boy, he was perfect because he was new and unassuming. He looked like he could be from the neighborhood, had enough size on him to make someone think twice, but was passable enough and unknown as not to draw attention. In their world, he blended in perfectly, or at least long enough to serve his purpose. Stacks, however, still wasn't sure. Then he saw Fin's interaction with LaTrell. Where at first he underestimated Fin, now he was convinced Fin might be more. *Dude got heart!* After Stacks and Gray Boy witnessed Fin punk LaTrell and then watched as he sat at a table alone before being joined by Justin, Stacks looked at Gray Boy and smiled. As the smile crept onto his face, and a fondness for Fin grew in his mind, it dissipated just as fast when he realized Gray Boy wasn't smiling. Gray Boy was displeased. He didn't like outsiders. As he watched Stacks look at Fin, he knew Stacks well enough to know Stacks would want to keep him around more. Gray Boy stared at him as if he could read his mind. Stacks noticed his uneasy glare. *Is he jealous right now?* He felt he might be, and much like the previous night in the courtyard, no words needed to be said.

chapter nine

promises

As Stacks finished telling Fin his family legacy, he watched for Fin's reaction. As much as Fin was learning about Stacks, Stacks was learning about him. He watched what books Fin grabbed as he marveled at his collection, as well as how Fin reacted to being in Brevoit; as if he was unmoved, his demeanor always stoic, nothing seemed to rattle him either way. Stacks had just brought him to one of the roughest projects in Norfolk, explained that he was in the home of one of Norfolk's most notorious gunrunners. Fin moved through Stacks' personal library as if he were in the Library of Congress, his spirit at peace - like he belonged around here. That's what intrigued Stacks the most. He knew Fin didn't grow up around here, but the reveal from Coop that he knew Fin's father, made Stacks want to know more. He watched as Fin thumbed through James Baldwin's *The Fire Next Time*.

"You ever read that?"

"Naaaaa. I always wanted to though. My dad has this book."

fin

promises

"Ya' Pops a smart dude. Whatchu know about my dude Baldwin?"

"Not much," Fin shamefully admitted. "I know he ain't have no problem calling mafuckas out though."

Stacks was impressed by Fin's answer. "HA! Take it witcha. Just don't tear up my shit."

"Never that. Good lookin' out."

Stacks rose from his bed, grabbed a 9mm from under the mattress, stuck it into his waist, then bloused his shirt over top of it.

"Make this run with me?"

Stacks normally would have made a demand and not given Fin an option, but he liked him. Fin stared at him for a moment, then down at the old, tattered cover of James Baldwin's seminal work. Fin looked back up at Stacks with a firmness, a resolve that broke through Stacks exterior. Fin nodded.

"Cool."

Stacks smiled, tapped Fin on the chest with the back of his hand, a gesture he would do often, and then led him back down the hallway. They both shouted "Lata Dee," as they passed the youngest Morton's room. When they entered the living room, Stacks found Coop sitting on the couch, sipping cognac.

"We 'bout to make that move, Pop."

"Fin, right?"

"Yes, Sir."

"Yes, Sir? Yeah, you definitely Big Fin's boy. Wait outside fo' me. Need to rap wit Chris here."

130

fin

promises

Stacks nodded his head towards the door. "Gimme a sec."

Fin could tell Coop's polite demeanor hid a fierceness and a simmering anger that was probably going to be directed Stacks' way. Fin wasn't a gangster by any stretch, but he knew enough to know that Stacks' had violated some sort of protocol. Shan grilled him as he walked out. Fin merely looked at him as resolute as he had Gray Boy earlier and LaTrell before that, as he departed.

"Nice meeting y'all."

Coop merely smiled and waved. Shan never moved. Once outside, Gray Boy who was now sitting in a cheap, plastic chair similar to the chair he and Curt sat in a few days earlier, stopped leaning against the wall adjacent to the door and brought all four legs to rest on the ground. He looked up and stared at Fin, the glare of the afternoon sun causing him to squint a bit. Fin had reached his limit with him.

"Fuck is your problem, man? You don't even fuckin' know me, Bruh."

Gray Boy hopped up out of the chair, flinging it into the grass as he did, and got right in Fin's face. He snarled, spitting as he spoke.

"I should bitch slap yo' ass for coming at me like that, Bruh. Fuck you think this is?"

Fin leaned right into the challenge, pressing his forehead against Gray Boy's. "Yeah? Like to see you try."

With a forceful and quick move, Gray Boy shoved Fin with his forearm, sending him stumbling back two feet. Fin quickly regained his balance, planting his left leg behind him, then using it to spring into action. He lunged at Gray Boy, shoving both hands into Gray Boy's chest. Gray Boy immediately realized he had not only underestimated

131

promises

Fin's heart but his strength when he landed down on his ass. A crowd started to gather, pointing at the two boys scuffling. Gray Boy knew he could not allow this blatant disrespect in *his* courtyard to stand. He stood, measured his shot and swung at Fin.

Inside the house, once Fin had exited through the front door, and the sound of the bolt engaging into the lock could be heard, Coop laid into Stacks.

"Fuck is yo' problem, boy? Bringin' that lil' mafucka up in here?!"

"Told you let me handle that shit, Pop! He too fucking soft for this shit! He ain't built for this shit!"

Shan rose as he said the last part. Ever the bully, Shan always thought that by exhibiting dominance over Stacks he would somehow curry favor with Coop. Stacks moved closer to Shan.

"Didn't I tell you to sit yo' drunk ass down?"

"ENOUGH!" Coop's eyes darted between his two sons. "Get this shit done boy!"

Stacks had recently learned two important factors that swung the pendulum in his and Shan's relationship; Shan drank too much and his own strength had surpassed that of Shan's. For years Shan had bullied and abused him. He knew it was jealousy. Coop always treated Stacks differently. In his mind, Coop had accepted long ago that Shan was a man that was trapped in the Brevoit mentality. He thought it broke Coop's heart too. Coop looked at Stacks as if he knew he was going to make it out of here if given the chance, but he also saw an heir, a Morton that could take their business to new heights. Thing was though, Shan saw it too and he took every opportunity he could to punish him for it. That was until Shan went to Deerfield for three years. In that span, Stacks had grown eight inches, gained forty pounds of muscle, and had enough fights to not only toughen his resolve, but hone his fighting skills to the point he no longer feared Shan. Shan knew that as well.

"Yeah take care of that shit, lil' bitch! And when its done, know this shit ain't!"

Stacks didn't even respond. Shan was huffing and puffing but truth was, he knew that not only did Shan not want to fight, but he would probably be too drunk to put up much of a contest anyway. His train of thought was quickly broken though. The sound of a growing mob cheering caught all three of them off guard. He quickly made it to the front door, Shan wasn't too far behind. Coop didn't run. He walked slowly, yet angrily, to see what the commotion was about. Stacks swung the door open and saw Gray Boy on the ground, Fin standing over top of him, a massive haymaker of a punch at the ready, its delivery imminent.

"FIN! WHAT THE FUCK?!"

Stacks grabbed Fin from behind by the torso, lifting him up so the punch wouldn't connect. Gray Boy landed a kick to Fin's leg as Stacks yanked him away. Shan, who was behind Stacks and Fin, saw Gray down on the floor, and went to sucker punch Fin. He cocked his fist back, his eyes wide as he homed in on his target, but was stopped by Coop. When Coop grabbed his forearm, the sound of the skin on skin contact let out a large slap. Coop barked in a furious yet low tone:

"YOU MUTHAFUCKAS IS FIGHTIN'?!?!? OUTSIDE MY HOUSE?!?!?"

All the boys paused. Fin wrestled himself free of Stacks. Gray Boy hopped to his feet. Neither boy was seriously harmed as the shoving match hadn't escalated into a full-blown brawl. Gray never thought to pull his weapon. He wanted to handle Fin brutally, painfully, and establish his dominance. He made the mistake of underestimating Fin. Shan yanked his arm free of his father. The Brevoit courtyard was at a standstill. The crowd that gathered watched as Coop exerted his will on the situation. Coop stared at Shan disapprovingly before getting right in Stacks' face. He needed to make sure only Stacks heard what he was about to say.

"Now we got all these mafuckas gunning for us. The police. Them white boys. Seventeenth Street. And whatchu do? You bring this unruly mafucka!" chastising him as he pointed behind himself at Fin. "Up in here fighting! He a fucking nobody!"

Stacks stared back defiantly. He never wanted to be in this position in the first place, the onus of the business, a business he wanted no parts of, on his shoulders. Coop's eyes squinted at Stacks' defiant stare.

"You might wanna back down, boy! Don't get embarrassed out here front o' everybody."

Stacks turned his upper lip up, and then looked away, trying to remain calm. He knew he could take Coop. Stacks had become the strongest person in the family, making light work of Coop would be easy. But Coop was his father, and for some reason, he still found himself respecting him. He stepped away and looked over to Gray Boy. Gray stared back at him with fury and hurt in his eyes. *You took that mafucka's side over me??!* Gray felt had the situation been reversed, he would have laid Fin out, no questions asked. Shan approached Fin huffing and puffing.

"Get this bitch ass mafucka outta here Stacks before for I end him!"

"You'll do no such thing, boy!" Coop ordered, his eyes still on Stacks.

promises

Coop now turned himself to Fin. Fin had no clue what Coop was about to say. He dared not challenge Coop the way he did LaTrell or Gray. He had too much respect for his elders in that manner. Coop slowly walked over to Fin.

"Now son, I know ya' daddy. Know ol' Big Fin very well. Know the kinda man he is. Kinda man that wouldn't want his son 'round hea'!"

Though Fin's head was down, his eyes were looking up at Coop.

"Yo' daddy left this shit behind a long time ago nah. But he and I had a pact. Said if something ever happened to me, he would look out fo' my boys. You wasn't even a thought enough to make his dick jump yet, but I promised if he ever had kids, I'd do the same. Now look atcha! Up here in the projects, acting like you a bad man. Yo' daddy? Now *that* was a bad man. Hard as they come. You? Hmmp! They'd eat your scrawny, untested ass like meat off the bone. So I'mma *keep* my word and look after Big Fin's boy.....carry yo' narrah, black ass from 'round here and dontcha come back, ya' hea'?"

Fin stared a moment longer, absorbing everything he just heard about his father. He dared not ask any questions, explain what happened between him and Gray Boy, nor protest his banishment. Fin accepted Coop's rendering and left.

"Nice meeting you, Sir. Sorry about fighting."

"Well, carry ya' sorry ass on."

Coop then turned to the remnants of the crowd still around them. "Fuck y'all looking at?"

promises

Fin walked through the crowd towards Stacks' car. Coop watched him for a moment, remembering when Big Fin left under similar circumstances. He turned to Stacks.

"Take care of what you need to take care of...and don't do that shit wit' that boy neither! Gray, ride wit' him!"

Gray nodded then looked at Stacks, waiting for him to say something. Stacks looked at Gray, then at Fin, and headed to his car. Fin reached the car and grabbed his book bag through the rolled down passenger window. As he turned, he saw Gray and Stacks approaching. Gray seemed to be looking for a reason to punch Fin. Stacks sensed Gray's intentions and grabbed him under his arm.

"Wait here."

Gray Boy watched furiously as Stacks walked over to Fin.

"You know how to make a fuckin' entrance, don't you? You gonna have to walk home from here, Socrates. Sorry I got you in this shit."

Fin peered over Stacks' shoulder to look at Gray Boy who was staring right back at him.

"Ain't *your* fault!"

"Y'all gonna have to work this shit out! Look, fuck what Coop say! Old mafucka paranoid and shit. You can come around here, ain't no one fuckin' wit you. Ain't that right, Gray?"

Gray sucked his teeth in disapproval.

"That means yes," Stacks replied with a half-smile. "Lemme go handle this shit. You don't need to be caught up in this BS. I'll get at you tomorrow."

"Aight."

fin

promises

They exchanged fist bumps. Stacks and Gray Boy watched Fin walk off then Stacks tapped Gray Boy on his chest.

"Let's ride."

Once the two were in the car, both put on their business personas. The emotions from earlier events were put to the side. That could be addressed later. Their minds became sharp and observant. Stacks would often play out business exchanges in his head, accounting for every possible scenario and his decided course of action. He had been thinking about today's meeting since last night. He likened it to playing chess; the anticipation of an opponent's move long before they even thought to make it. Gray too, played out scenarios in his mind, but more from a tactical aspect. He knew the players that would be at the meeting, the layout of the meeting place, expected artillery that may be present, everything. Gray was a true wartime lieutenant and took his role seriously. The meeting place was an old chop shop down near the shipping piers in Portsmouth. The drop was simple. Deliver the requested assault rifles to P-Town Mafia, a local gang in the midst of a turf war, get the money and leave. The chop shop was in the heart of P-Town Mafia turf, but Stacks and Gray not only knew it well, they had connections within Portsmouth that guaranteed their safety. At least they would in normal times. Their major shipment being raided a while back has left them without a bulk of product and down in manpower, which meant to the streets, they were vulnerable. Stacks knew something would be up.

"Get Lil' Rick and Hoop on the phone. Have them meet us there five minutes after we arrive."

Gray was confused by Stacks' order. "Thought Coop said he wanted us to handle it? Not a large show of force?"

"Look man, Pops is in panic mode right now. He ain't thinking straight. Why the fuck would he send us into the middle of P-Town unprotected? He was gonna have me show up with Dee, remember? Fuck was I supposed to do? Leave him in the car by himself while I drop off guns? Or maybe take him with me to a gun deal? Fuck outta here wit' that!"

"So, what's the play?"

"If these mafuckas is on the up and up, we will be in and out in ten minutes and Lil' Rick and Hoop will get there right as we leavin'. If these mafuckas is playing games though, they see us by ourselves and wanna try some fuck shit, they gonna stall. Try and get us comfortable. Then they gon' try and rob us. They ain't gonna shoot us. They damn sure don't need that heat. But they gonna try and come up."

Gray nodded his head while reaching for his cellphone. "On it."

They arrived at the chop shop, an old auto body repair shop that was a front for all kinds of illegal activity. They honked the horn as planned to signal their arrival. Seconds later they heard the mechanical gate begin to roll up. They glanced at each other, their eyes ensuring the other's preparedness, then they slowly drove into the garage. Gray spotted four men: one was at the top of the open, metal staircase leading to the upstairs office, holding a 9mm pistol; two other men leaned against a car to their left; the last man, the man they were set to meet, was straight in front of them, Badu. Badu was originally from West Baltimore and moved here when he was young. Wasn't long after that he was recruited into the street life. A fast riser, he assumed control of the P-Town Mafia at age twenty. Badu bore a deceptively grim smile. He took a welcoming posture, spreading his arms wide before slapping and rubbing his hands together.

"Yeah! There they go! Been waiting on y'all."

fin

promises

Stacks stopped the car just short of pulling it all the way in, leaving about three feet of the trunk in the rolldown path of the metal gate. He got out the car, then walked and greeted Badu, Gray Boy right behind him.

"What up, Badu?"

"Oh shit! What up, Stacks!! Thought I'd see Gray here, but I was expecting Shan. He on the way or somethin'?"

"I'm here. Let's do this."

"Damn! You all in a rush and we trying to conduct business."

Gray Boy never liked Badu. Thought he was too clownish to be trusted. "Mr. Stacks said we need to get this done."

Badu looked at Gray, then at the two men leaning against the car and smiled.

"Mr. Stacks?!!? Hahahahaha!"

The other three P-Town Mafia members laughed heartily. Stacks and Gray Boy didn't move. They gave zero reaction, their stoic faces quickly causing Badu and his crew to stop laughing as well.

"Aight, Mr. Stacks! Fuck it then! Business you want, business you get. You got what I need?"

"Yeah, we got it. You got my money?"

"C'mon now, Stacks. You ain't new to this shit right here! Fuck I look like pulling my money out first to mafuckas notorious for having every gun known to man! Mafuckas probably got some space age laser guns and shit!"

139

Again, Badu and his men laughed. Stacks and Gray shot each other a quick glance that needed no words; Badu was a clown. He was also stalling.

"Mr. Stacks, would you like me to go and get their delivery?"

"Please."

Gray Boy walked to the back of the car, scoping the garage as he did. He hadn't noticed it from his seated position in the car as they entered, but the car the two men were leaning on had its back, driver side door open. Gray knew why he would have that door open. It would be a perfect place to stash guns and have them at the ready, besides, an open car door in a garage can easily be overlooked. Gray got to the back of the car and popped the trunk. With the trunk popped, he was shielded from the view of Badu and company. He reached in his waistline and gently slid the safety off his weapon. He saw a car flash its lights towards him from up the block. It was Lil' Rick and Hoop, two of the best, and last, soldiers working for Coop. Gray nodded, signaling to Lil' Rick and Hoop that their presence was required. While Gray was at the car, Badu kept talking.

"Man, I'm glad to see y'all still up! Word was out y'all got hit hard. Didn't know if y'all would be able to supply my needs."

"Show me my money and we can talk about your needs then."

Badu sucked his teeth. "Man, get this mafucka his money! Damn!! Can't even be sociable wit' a mafucka no mo'!"

Stacks was fed up with his shenanigans. "We ain't friends, Badu. This is business."

Stacks looked over to his left, past the men leaning against the car. There was a side door leading outside. The door had a large glass pane in it, and through it, he could see Lil' Rick peering in.

fin

promises

"Y'all brought everything I needed though right, Mr. Stacks?"

Stacks nodded his head while he still made eye contact with Lil' Rick. Badu thought it was in response to his question. He was really signaling Lil' Rick that he was about to make his move.

"So, tell me Badu, how were you planning on getting away with it?"

"Whatchu talking about, boy?"

"Mr. Stacks is no boy, Badu." Gray had just arrived back next to Stacks, duffel bag in tow.

"Robbing us. I mean that is what's gonna happen, right? That skinny one pops up, shotty in hand he is gonna grab from the back of that car. He is gonna pull out on us, right?"

Gray smiled. Stacks had picked up on the same thing he had. For all of their differences in approach, Stacks and Gray Boy together were a lethal combination of intellect, strategy, and action. Badu smiled.

"You got me, *Mr.* Stacks. Fuck I look like paying full price to some mafuckas who ain't got no muscle?"

Badu reached for his gun. "See *I* prefer free-ninety-nine!"

Stacks was too fast, however. He pulled his weapon and stuck it under the chin of Badu. Gray drew his weapon just as fast and trained it on the gunman at the top of the metal staircase. Lil' Rick burst through the side door, surprising the two men near the car, his gun pointed at the one near the open car door. What Badu and his men hadn't realized was Gray Boy had removed one of the rifles from the bag and loaded a clip in it. He left it in the trunk which was still open for Hoop to grab. Hoop popped up from behind the car and pointed it at the gunman as well.

promises

"You 'bout a stupid mafucka! How you think we been able to run guns all these years? We study military tactics while y'all mafuckas outchea chasin' skirts. Frankly, Badu, I'm insulted. You feel insulted, Gray?"

"If I had pearls, I'd clutch 'em."

"You hear that, Badu? If he had pearls..."

"Wait, wait. Okay, hold up."

Gray smiled at Badu as he pleaded for mercy. The tables were now turned.

"I ain't gon' kill you, fool. There will be a fine to pay, however. Gray, see what they got in that car over there. Office too."

Gray walked over to the car and pistol whipped the man by the door. A sawed-off shotgun rested on the seat. Gray picked it up, hit the barrel release switch and emptied the shells from the gun, dumping them on the floor. Stacks eyes flared in rage.

"Tell ya' boy at the top of them stairs to throw that gun he holdin' down, and come join us."

Badu acquiesced. "Throw it down."

"Now you gonna make us tear this shithole apart looking for it or you gonna tell us where the money is? I know you had to have it here. You had no idea how heavy we was rollin' up. You took your shot, it failed."

"It's in the office."

Stacks looked at Gray Boy who nodded then headed up the stairs, passing the gunman, striking him in the back of the head with his gun as he did. He swung the door open and saw a small, black gym bag sitting on the desk. He opened it, saw the rolled bundles of cash, zipped it closed and returned to Stacks' side.

"We good?"

Badu looked over at Gray Boy, hoping he returned a favorable answer. Gray nodded.

"So, y'all just gon' rob us?"

This time, Stacks and his crew did the laughing. Stacks stopped laughing abruptly.

"Badu, your Norfolk privileges have been revoked. Your gun supply is cut off."

"I still need them guns, Stacks. We 'bout to be sitting ducks!"

"Tell you what. You still want them guns? The price just doubled. I'll take this cash. It is all there, right?"

Badu nervously shook his head in the affirmative. "Yeah, it's all there."

"Aight then, half the guns. Consider this a parting gift...that and the fact I don't redecorate this entire fuckin' building wit' yo' brain right now. Deal?"

Badu hurriedly nodded.

"Mr. Stacks asked you a question."

There was no laughter.

"Deal."

Stacks yelled over his shoulder at Hoop. "Get they shit!"

"On it!"

Hoop retrieved half of the guns, throwing them on the floor at Badu's feet. Stacks and company cautiously backed out. Gray jumped in the driver's seat and started the car. He slowly backed the car out as Stacks walked backwards in front of it, his gun still pointed at Badu.

"Badu, let this be the last time I see you. Next time, there won't be any deals. Won't be any words. Just my gun clapping. Understood?"

Badu stared at Stacks, his anger now rising, anger he didn't dare show moments earlier. Once the car was fully out of the garage and on the street, Stacks slapped the button on the automatic control for the gate, causing it to lower, ran to the car, then Stacks and his crew peeled out. Gray glanced over at Stacks.

"How'd you know they was gonna rob us?"

"It's what I would've done."

It suddenly occurred to Gray that Stacks never had any intentions of bringing Fin along with him. He knew Stacks to be the thinker, the strategist among the Morton family. He didn't just come up with this plan on the fly.

"You never had any intention of bringing that kid witchu, huh?"

Stacks chuckled and kept looking forward.

"Needed Pops to think I would go along with his paranoia. Fin was just gonna be a show for him and Shan. I was dropping him somewhere as soon as we left."

"Then what?"

"You were gonna get a call to meet me there, bring the hitters. All Pops did was change the batting order, not the starting players."

fin

promises

Gray chuckled and kept driving, thoroughly impressed by Stacks' plan. Stacks tapped him on the arm.

"You see that mafucka's face when that barrel hit his chin?"

They both let out a hearty laugh and returned home.

chapter ten

three dope boys in a cadillac

The day Justin showed up to school with his face bruised started a string of events that would change the three boys lives forever. When he first entered the cafeteria, Stacks saw his face. He always thought Justin was just a shit-talking, little punk that couldn't back it up. Stacks never felt sorry for Justin when he would get bullied or beat up in school. In Stacks' mind he probably deserved it. When Fin went to go check on Justin, he was madder at Fin for constantly trying to protect him. *Let that dude be a man! Baby him too damn much!*

Normally he could care less what happened to Justin, but the bruises on his face were pretty bad. So instead of ignoring them, he watched them. He watched as Justin seemed to not want Fin, his "knight in shining armor", to even be near him. He tried not to be concerned but he found himself repeatedly looking over his shoulder. He told himself it was because of Fin, but he knew it was really because of Justin. When Fin came back to the table and told him how Justin

147

got the bruises, a rage he had fought so long to suppress came bubbling up.

"Ya' boy aight? He talk shit to the wrong person, I bet."

"Yeah, his father."

"His *daddy* did that shit to him??!?"

"He the one always giving him them bruises."

Stacks looked over his shoulder at Justin. In that moment he realized he had more in common with Justin then he liked to admit. He had a father that didn't value him either. Stacks believed that to Coop, he was nothing more than an asset, a tool he could use for his own agenda, the way he did Shan. The way he would eventually want to do with Dee. Coop had already cost him his oldest brother, Mike, who was killed during a gun deal gone wrong. Stacks will never forget the exact moment he knew his father didn't love him or anyone else not named Cooper Morton.

He was ten years old and they had just left the burial site after laying Mike in the ground. Coop walked about six feet ahead of Shan and him, carrying Dee in his arms. When he arrived at the limo, he stood there with an annoyed look on his face as Dee fidgeted in his arms. Shan walked with a scowl on his face. Stacks never remembered a day when Shan wasn't angry.

"Hurry up and take this boy!"

Stacks jogged over to him and took Dee to soothe him. Coop just opened the limo door and climbed in. Shan shoved him out of the way so he could get in next. The shove caused him to stumble a bit and he almost dropped Dee. He stood there, shaking his head. He had been scared to cry over Mike. The oldest brother of the four, Mike had been his protector, the one who always made sure he did his homework and had snacks after school. He talked to him, laughed with him, took him to watch high school football games and would tell him about when he was the starting wide receiver for Eastwood. He wanted to be like Mike. He hadn't noticed he drifted off, thinking nostalgically about his big brother. Coop, however, noticed.

"Get in the damn car, boy!"

He climbed in and held Dee tight. *Why didn't he just let Ma take him! Why do I always have to watch him?* As they sat in the limo, Coop looked at the remaining Morton boys and spoke.

"They trying to end us! They trying to wipe out the Morton name! Y'all my legacy……WE gotta tighten up! Gotta take what's ours!"

Stacks, still with his innocence and confused by what his father was referring to, and still hurting from losing his big brother Mike, began to cry. Seventeen-year-old Shan was having none of it.

"Fuck you crying fo'? Stop being a bitch and man up dammit!"

Coop stared at Stacks as if he wanted to pierce his heart. "Now ain't the time fo' tears boy! All y'all gotta be ready to step up."

He then turned his attention to Shan.

"You ready? You ready to step up and fill ya' brother's shoes?"

Shan nodded his head, his face scowled. Shan would do anything for Coop's approval.

"Ya' brother is dead because he got caught slipping. He was careless. Stupid. Y'all gotta be smarter than he was or you gonna be dead in that ground with him."

Coop turned and stared out the window at the burial plot. The words he had said shattered Stacks' heart. The look on Coop's face however, turned his heart cold towards Coop. It wasn't a look of grief; it was a look of disappointment. As the tears continued to stream down his face, he had a single thought: *You got my brother into all of this shit and got him killed and you are disappointed in him!? It was HIS fault? Now you trying to get Shan to do it too?? FUCK YOU, MAN!! You ain't no better than the mafuckas that shot him!!!* His thoughts were broken by Dee crying in his arms.

"Shut him up," Coop snapped without taking his eyes off the window.

Stacks wiped his eyes with his suit sleeve and reached in the baby bag on the floor and found a bottle. Dee took it happily. As he sat there, looking between his father, Shan and Dee, he made a promise to himself. *I ain't NEVA gonna be like you! Shan neither! Y'all ain't shit! I'll die before I let you get Dee, too!* Coop looked at Stacks who was staring back at him. They stared at each other for what seemed like an eternity. Stacks stared at Coop, mourning the physical loss of his eldest brother and the metaphorical loss of his father, his innocence forever stripped before he even got to explore it. Coop looking at him with disgust and disappointment for showing weakness even here in the solitude of the limo. Coop rolled his eyes then looked at Shan.

"You ready, huh?"

"Fuck yeah I'm ready. Whatchu need me to do?"

Coop just nodded his head, then gave a slight grin before turning back to the window. He reached back with his hand and tapped the glass partition with his knuckles twice.

TAP! TAP!

"Get me the fuck outta here."

Stacks never forgot that moment, that feeling. The feeling when he realized his father didn't see him as a son; he saw him as a pawn to be moved around in service of the king. As far as he was

three dope boys in a cadillac

concerned, Coop might as well have fired the damn bullet that killed Mike himself. Now, and for the first time, he empathized with Justin. When a child lives in an environment where they aren't safe, they lose their innocence. Stacks lost his years ago. In that moment, he wondered if Justin ever had any. Fin became concerned as to where Stacks' mind was.

"*You* aight?"

"I'mma catch you lata."

Stacks got up and walked out, leaving his tray on the table. As he exited the cafeteria, he caught Shayla's eye. She knew something was wrong. She left the table she shared with her girlfriends immediately.

"I'll be back. Watch my stuff."

She ran behind him and caught him in the hallway.

"Bae?"

He heard her but kept walking.

"Bae!"

This time he stopped and turned to her. His eyes were looking past her. She walked up to him and placed her hand on his cheek. Her brow and eyes were scrunched with concern.

"Bae, what is it?"

"I don't wanna talk right now, Shay."

"You gonna tell me where you going at least? You just walked out."

"Shay, I gotta go."

"Chris, you're scaring me."

three dope boys in a cadillac

Shayla *never* called him Chris outside of the confines of her house or his. It was either Bae or Stacks. For her to call him Chris so openly let him know he was really scaring her.

"I'm fine, Shay. I just..."

"You just what?"

"I just need to go. Clear my mind."

"You still coming by tonight?"

He looked down at her and kissed her.

"I'll call you later, ok?"

She knew not to question him any further. Whatever was bothering him, she loved and understood him enough to give him the space he needed.

"Ok, Bae."

As he turned to walk away, her heart ached. She ran up in front of him and hugged him.

"I love you, Chris. Remember that. I'll be right here when you're ready."

He looked down at her, the one person that was normally his peace. He didn't know how to tell her that for the first time, she couldn't give him that. There was only one thing that could satisfy the urges he was feeling.

"I know, my baby. I'll be ok. I'll call you later."

She nodded as he pulled away, holding his hand as he walked by her for as long as she could until she couldn't anymore. He walked outside of the school and to his car. He drove around for hours until school had let out. Once he picked up Fin, they found Justin.

"Justin......get in."

fin

three dope boys in a cadillac

As the three boys drove away from Eastwood High, Fin couldn't help but wonder what Stacks was planning. Fin just wanted to make sure Justin was safe and planned to invite him over to his place until he could talk to Big Fin. It seems Stacks had another course of action he wanted to take.

"Where does ya' daddy like to hang at?"

"Why you wanna know that, Bruh?" asked Fin.

Stacks ignored him however and continued darting his eyes between the road in front of him and his visual of Justin in the rearview mirror.

"Justin. Where ya' daddy's drinking spot?"

"Pullman's."

"The cop bar?!?! Ya' daddy is a cop??!"

"He was. Beat up some old lady and got fired."

Stacks' feelings about Andrew were now confirmed. He was and always will be a bully. He leaned back into his seat, his elbow on the door's armrest, his hand covering his mouth. He was furious. He could neither understand nor accept a man that didn't take care of his kids. He had zero respect for a man that beat his kids. He had even *less* respect for cops. He had never met a cop that didn't either want some sort of payoff from his dad or harass him just because of his last name. Until the day he met Fin, he had never sold a single gun. Didn't matter though. He was a Morton. The boys rode in relative silence as Stacks drove across town to the edges of the Norfolk-Portsmouth border to Pullman's. Every now and then Fin would look back at Justin in the backseat. Justin was fast asleep. They arrived at Pullman's and parked. Pullman's was a small bar in the warehouse district. There was an auto body shop, a plumbing store, and a masonry lot surrounding the bar on its side of the street, an industrial park across from it. Stacks parked across the street at the industrial park amongst

three dope boys in a cadillac

a slew of cars, trucks and company vans. He parked with the trunk facing Pullman's while ensuring he could see the bar through the rearview mirror. Fin looked over his shoulder at the bar, then down at Justin who was slowly waking up.

"What are we doing here, Bruh?"

Stacks kept his eyes affixed on Pullman's. "Waiting."

Fin shook his head and reached for his Blackberry. He knew Stacks wasn't budging from this spot until he saw Justin's dad. Neither Fin nor Stacks had ever seen the man, so they had to rely on Justin. He figured since he had time to kill, he would shoot Curt an email. It would be early Saturday morning there and this was their normal time to work on their project. Though they were thousands of miles apart, technology allowed them to stay in contact with each other. He had written what he thought was an excellent line of code the night prior, which was an improvement upon the application they were developing, and he wanted to see if Curt had had a chance to check it out. After he sent the email to Curt, he took out his notebook and began writing with a purpose. Suddenly, his creative juices were flowing. Stacks looked over at Fin, curious as to what he was doing. Justin leaned forward, placing his hands on the back of the seats in front of him, and poked his frowned, curious face over Fin's shoulder. Stacks and Justin stared intently, trying to decipher the lines of code and flow diagrams Fin was writing at a hectic pace. Curiosity finally got the best of them.

"What is that, Socrates?"

"Yeah, Bro. What is that?"

Fin had been completely oblivious to Stacks and Justin staring at him. Upon hearing them both speaking to him, he snapped out of his laser focus induced trance and sat up.

"Huh?"

fin

three dope boys in a cadillac

"Whatchu doin', Socrates?"

"This? This is code."

Stacks frowned from confusion. "Code? Like sending secret messages and shit?"

"Naaaa. Computer code. Like for programs and stuff."

This bit of news excited Justin. "Yo, Fin! You know how to make video games and stuff?"

"Well, in theory. Yeah, I guess I could."

"That's dope! You could make video games and be rich!"

Now Stacks' confusion turned to curiosity. "Well if that ain't for a game, what is it for? I have seen you writing in that book before but always thought you was tryna be a rapper or some corny shit."

"A RAPPER?!?! HAHAHAHA! Naaaa man, my boy in Japan and I used to write little programs and stuff. Small little games...we once made a program that helped us write our midterm papers. Found all the key points in a story. We both got 'A's' too."

Stacks was genuinely impressed. He knew Fin was smart, there was no questioning that, but he had no idea he was *this* smart. Justin was equally impressed and curious.

"So, what is it? Has to be a game or something? What's all them squares and bubbles you drawing?"

"That's a flow chart. It's for an idea my boy Curt and I have for sneakers. Like how to trade 'em amongst sneaker heads."

Stacks smiled and nodded his head before turning his attention back to the rearview mirror. "Now *that* is something I could get into!"

"Me too!" exclaimed Justin.

three dope boys in a cadillac

Stacks and Fin looked at each other, then simultaneously they both turned around and looked at Justin, then down at his old, beat up sneakers, then at each other again, then burst out into laughter.

"What?"

"Nothing, Valebrook," replied a still laughing Stacks.

The boys sat there for hours, intermingling conversation, questions about Fin's project, life in Japan, and even Justin displaying his "dope rap flow" as he described it. It was in the middle of one of his "dope" freestyles that the mood changed. Stacks and Fin were nodding their heads and laughing as Justin rapped.

"Dope clothes, I'm a dope boy,

Dope hoes, take notes boy,

Guns real, ain't got no to...."

Without warning, Justin fell silent.

Stacks could barely contain his laughter. "What happened, Valebrook? You ran out of bars?"

"Yeah, Juss. Keep going!"

Stacks and Fin looked back at Justin who was no longer bopping. His energy drained, his face somber, his eyes staring straight ahead at the rearview mirror. Stacks adjusted his position to see what he was staring at. Fin spun around and looked out of the rear window. It was Andrew. Though neither of them had seen him before, from Justin's reaction alone they knew it.

"That him?"

"Yeah, that's him."

fin

three dope boys in a cadillac

Stacks' anger had reached the boiling point. Over the last few hours, Justin had grown on him, and the fonder he felt for Justin, the angrier he got at Andrew. The boys watched as Andrew made his way from the car, across the parking lot and into Pullman's. Andrew looked as if he had been drinking already, he could barely walk a straight line. Stacks stared at him, then looked around the area. Not many cars were there but from where they were positioned, the car looked inconspicuous enough. All the boys remained silent, watching Andrew as he entered the bar until Stacks broke the silence.

"Justin, where do you want me to take you?"

Once Stacks had dropped Fin and Justin off, he knew he needed to find Gray Boy. No way was he going to do what he needed to do alone, but there was also no way he could tell Gray what they were doing. He pulled up to the Brevoit Projects. The courtyard was buzzing with people, typical for a Friday night. Stacks walked quickly through the courtyard and didn't respond to the many greetings thrown his way. Not tonight. Tonight, he needed to focus. Shan had plans with one of his many women and wouldn't be home. Stacks knew he needed to go in, check on Dee, then find out where Gray was. He was hoping to avoid Coop but that turned out to be a false hope. As he entered, Coop grabbed the remote to turn the television volume down.

"Fuck ya' been, boy?"

"I was out with my friends."

"What friends? What I tell you about hanging with mafuckas we don't know?"

"I do know 'em."

"Ohhh......You was hanging with Fin's boy again, wasn't ya'? Didn't I tell you leave that boy outta this? His type of trouble ain't whatcha want."

fin

three dope boys in a cadillac

Trouble? What's he mean trouble? "How is Fin trouble?"

"Look here, Big Fin may be a Navy man, but he is real. Hard dude that coulda been somethin' round here. That mafucka walked away from it. Found out he was a heavy down in Florida, joined the Navy to get out the life but fell right back in it when we met. Then one day he up and decided to get out for good, got married and had that boy. You met him, but you wasn't nothing but a baby then."

Stacks had never heard Coop sound fearful of any man. He had seen Big Fin once, Fin's first day at Eastwood. He was in the hallway, having left early from his first class. Big Fin was walking alone, heading towards the exit after just finishing Fin's registration. Stacks is a large specimen of a man himself, and even he thought Big Fin was a mountain of a man. He thought he was just another Navy dude trying to get young kids to join the military. It wasn't until he saw Fin that he realized who he was. Fin looked just like his father, only smaller and thinner. Now he is hearing genuine fear and respect in Coop's voice. That gave him joy.

"Where's Dee?"

"You hear what I said Chris? Stay away from that boy! Last thing I need is that big mafucka rememberin' his old ways and comin' 'round here tryna start some shit over his kid. Now stay away from that boy!"

"Yeah I hear you. Dee in the room?"

"Fuck else he gonna be?"

Coop cranked the volume back up on the television. Stacks left the living room and entered the hallway. He poked his head into Dee's room, but the eight-year-old was sleep, laid diagonally across his bed, action figures in hand. He hated that he left Dee alone all day, stuck in this room to entertain himself. Normally, he is right there when Dee gets off the bus. They walk and talk about each other's day,

158

three dope boys in a cadillac

they get snacks, then after he is done with homework, they head to the park or go for a ride. Anything to get Dee out of Brevoit and away from Coop, Shan, Big Tony, even Gray Boy. Now that he was two weeks from turning eighteen, and school was ending, all he wanted to do was save up just enough money to get Dee, Shayla and himself out of Brevoit, out of Norfolk, the life, all of it. He wanted to go somewhere far away, forget the family business, the bullshit legacy, and start fresh.

Stacks walked over to his baby brother and kissed his forehead, removed the action figures from his hands, lifted his little legs and placed them under the covers. He leaned in and whispered *"I love you"* into Dee's sleeping ear, hoping it would echo in his dreams, then turned the lights off and shut the door as he left. He walked to his room, reached under his mattress and grabbed his 9mm. He dressed it in his front waist band and slung his t-shirt over top of it. He never carried it to school and truly felt naked being this long without it. He then made his way back to the front room. Coop never took his eyes off the television but knew he was there.

"Dee sleep?"

"Yeah. He eat?"

"Yeah, he had some burgers and shit."

"Seen Gray?"

"You 'bout an inquisitive mother fucker tonight, ain't cha?"

"C'mon, man. Have you seen Gray?"

Stacks' patience was running thin and his window to catch Andrew may be closing. He had no idea how long he was going to be in that bar but knew he needed to get back to Pullman's soon.

"Last I seen him, he was talking about heading to the court."

"Aight. Thanks."

fin

three dope boys in a cadillac

Stacks headed for the door.

"Fuck you going?"

It was too late though. Stacks had conveniently not heard his father and slammed the door behind him as he left. He needed to find Gray. Stacks hopped in his car and made his way over to the basketball courts two blocks away. He pulled up and saw Gray doing what Gray does. Gray was a monster on the court. He could have easily started at shooting guard for Eastwood High, and probably would have been recruited to a major college program, found a different way out of Valebrook, except Gray didn't want to do that. He felt sorry for Gray in that he dreamt so small, and his vision was so narrow. He hopped out of the car, the engine still running and walked along the chain-link fence toward the far court Gray was playing on.

Gray's team had just got a defensive rebound and swung the ball out to him on the left wing. He started dribbling up court, towards Stacks. A defender stepped in front of him that Gray easily dribbled by. The defenders were in a scramble to try and stop the inevitable.

"GET HIM! GET HIM!!"

"STOP BALL!"

Stacks saw Gray smile. Two defenders leapt in front of him. Gray dribbled behind his back, evading one, before throwing the ball through the other's legs causing him to fall as he reached for the ball. Stacks giggled, as he knew that was going to happen almost as soon as Gray saw the opportunity. The last two defenders hesitated and that was all Gray needed. He made one hard dribble to his left, leaving the defender as if he were a statue, and when he recovered, Gray stepped back and drained a three pointer right in his face. The crowd of onlookers went crazy.

"GRAY!"

fin

three dope boys in a cadillac

Gray Boy's head looked towards Stacks and he immediately ran to the fence.

"What up?"

"Take a ride with me."

"Say less."

Gray walked off the court as if the game wasn't even being played, much to the dismay of his teammates. He walked over to his girlfriend Trish, who was sitting on one of the metal bleachers surrounding the court. He leaned in and whispered in her ear, prompting her to reach into her purse and hand him his gun. Gray, dressed in jeans and a gray t-shirt, tucked it into his belt the same way Stacks had. He jogged around to the opening in the fence and met Stacks at his car. Stacks was already in the car waiting. Gray Boy hopped in and the two were off.

"What's up? We gotta handle something for Coop?"

Stacks pondered lying to him and just letting him believe that was the case. He respected him too much to do that though.

"Naaaa. Just need you to have my back on something."

Gray tapped his waist where he had placed his gun. "We need..."

"Shouldn't. But keep it handy just in case."

Gray didn't ask any further questions. He sat in silence, gathering his mind for a potential gunfight. He was a soldier and always ready for war. Stacks felt like a hypocrite. He often bashed Coop for treating him as if he were a tool, and now, he was doing the same to Gray. He started to drop Gray off and tell him nevermind, but he knew they were past that point. Gray would never get out of the

three dope boys in a cadillac

car. They drove to the other side of town where Pullman's was. They parked the car a few blocks away then Stacks got out, Gray cautiously following him. Earlier, Stacks had noticed an old abandoned, warehouse across the street from Pullman's, about five buildings down. He figured they could get into the building and scope out Pullman's in relative safety. Once they were in, Stacks set up near one of the large bay windows, covered in dirt, grime, and mold from years of neglect. It was then that Gray realized what their purpose in the building was. Stacks wanted to watch Pullman's.

"Why you scoping a cop bar?"

"Need to have a chat with someone."

"You need to talk to a fucking cop!!"

"Calm down, mafucka! I ain't no snitch!"

"The fuck you need to talk to a cop for then?!?!" an agitated and hostile Gray said.

Stacks walked away from the window and got in Gray's face.

"Like I said, I *need* to talk to the mafucka. Now if you wanna go, there's the door. Here, take my keys!"

Stacks tossed his keys at Gray as he walked away. Gray caught the keys but knew he had no need for them. Whatever Stacks needed to do, as much as he hated it, he was in. Stacks reassumed his position by the window. Gray soon joined him.

"Well at least tell me who we looking for."

"Short, drunk, white mafucka."

Gray shot Stacks a look.

"Bruh, this is Pullman's. You just described ninety-nine percent of the mafuckas in there."

162

fin

three dope boys in a cadillac

Stacks offered no reply. He continued watching Pullman's front door. They stared out that window, in silence for hours. Frustration was setting in with Gray Boy, however. Gray's cellphone kept vibrating, causing him to check the number calling, shake his head and it began to annoy Stacks. Stacks stayed focused on Pullman's.

"You need to be somewhere?"

"Supposed to be at Trish's house about two hours ago. How much longer this gonna take?"

"Not long at all."

"How the fuck you know? We been here for hours staring at a goddamn door for a white cop to come out of a bar full of white cops."

"I never said he was a cop."

Gray Boy snapped his head in Stacks' direction, but before he could speak, Stacks nodded his head towards Pullman's. Gray looked back at Pullman's and noticed Andrew, the only person that wasn't there when last he looked.

"Who? That short, dirty looking mafucka?"

"Let's move."

Stacks made his way downstairs and out the door, remaining in the vestibule out of sight of the patrons exiting Pullman's. Since Gray still had the keys, he told him to go get the car. Andrew was being loud and obnoxious to another man that was standing outside Pullman's. The man tried repeatedly to shoo Andrew away only to have Andrew jump in his face again.

"You want some of this, you *pussy*?!" he shouted, slurring his words, swaying back and forth.

The man feigned hitting him and Andrew jumped back about three feet and fell down. Stacks shook his head. *Typical bully.* Andrew

three dope boys in a cadillac

recovered from his fall only to be kicked in his ass by the man he was challenging. He stumbled a few feet further, gathered himself, then turned and shouted.

"FUCK YOU MOTHERFUCKER!"

Stacks continued watching Andrew as he made it to his car in the center of the parking lot. Andrew fumbled with his keys before unlocking the door, getting in and starting the engine. Just as Andrew began to back out, Gray Boy pulled up. Without losing sight of Andrew, Stacks quickly made it to the car and got in, then pointed to Andrew's car as Gray engaged the gears into drive and pulled forward. They slowly rolled by Pullman's, their eyes on Andrew. There was another set of eyes watching. Officer Delaine had also exited the bar and thought it odd two black men were cruising down the street past a reputed police bar with zero worries, as if the group of men standing outside weren't made up of cops and former cops. He saw Gray Boy's profile well and knew he had seen him before. Officer Delaine watched them as they drove down the street, turning at the corner.

Stacks and Gray had turned just a few car lengths after Andrew did. Gray knew how to follow someone and kept just enough distance between them as not to attract Andrew's attention. They followed Andrew and both seemed genuinely impressed by how straight and sober his driving appeared to be. When they made a right on to Tenth Avenue, Stacks remembered dropping Justin off not too far up this very street. He knew Andrew would be making a right turn pretty soon.

"He gonna turn on Cresthill. Get closer. When he does, jump in front of him and cut him off in the middle of the block."

Gray Boy simply nodded. They knew Valebrook like they knew their own faces, Cresthill would be completely dark save for an occasional porch light. Gray also wondered why Stacks knew exactly where Andrew would turn. As Andrew turned on Cresthill, Gray

three dope boys in a cadillac

followed as instructed, then made his follow-on move to cut in front of Andrew's car. Andrew slammed on his breaks.

"THE FUCK YOU DOING YOU FUCKING ASSHOLE?!"

Stacks and Gray exited their vehicle. Gray walked over to Andrew's car and opened the driver side door and removed him forcibly from the car.

"THE FUCK YOU DOING, MAN?! GET THE FUCK OFFA ME!!!"

"Mr. Stacks would like to have a word with you, Sir."

"WHO THE FUCK IS MR. STACKS?!"

Gray punched Andrew in the stomach. Not hard enough to make him evacuate its contents, but enough to force him to catch his breath and shut up.

"That was very rude of me. I apologize. Let me start again. My name is Mr. Mother-Fucker-You-Don't-Want-To-Piss-Off. *This* is Mr. Stacks. Mr. Stacks would like to have a word with you."

Gray stepped aside as Stacks approached.

"WHO THE FUCK ARE YOU?!" demanded Andrew.

"What kind of father are you?"

"What???!?"

"I said, *What. Kind. Of. Father. Are. You?*"

"Fuck you! I ain't about to let some...."

SLAP!

Andrew never saw it coming. He didn't even know what hit him. The warm sensation of blood filled his mouth.

fin

three dope boys in a cadillac

"Mr. Stacks asked you a question," said Gray Boy in an assertive, threatening tone.

Andrew's mouth was full of blood and whiskey laced saliva.

"FUCK YOU!"

SLAP!!

Stacks became enraged. "HIT ME! C'MON! YOU LIKE TO HIT KIDS! HIT ME!"

SLAP!!! SLAP!!!

"Please........."

Andrew's cries sounded like that of a child, Gray thought.

SLAP!!!!

SLAP!!!!

"Is that how *he* begs when you beating on him?"

Gray watched Stacks grow angrier and angrier. He had no idea where the rage bubbling to the surface was coming from.

SLAP!!!!!

SLAP!!!!!

Each progressive hit was more thunderous and brutal than the last one. Gray Boy began looking up and down the dark street to see if any neighbors decided to be nosy and see what was going on. Stacks reached down and grabbed Andrew by the back of the neck, the way one would a small puppy, lifting a now cowering, crying Andrew off of the asphalt. He turned him around and choke slammed him into the car. Stacks leaned over and gave his neck a tight squeeze. The stench of sweat, alcohol and fear were all over him. Then, he whispered into Andrew's ear.

fin

three dope boys in a cadillac

"You ain't no man. *You're. A. Bitch!*"

He released Andrew allowing him to gasp for deep gulps of air. Andrew gagged and coughed, spitting blood and saliva onto the pavement. He sobbed like a baby.

"LOOK AT ME!"

Andrew fearfully looked up. Stacks stared down into his terrified, tear filled eyes. "Remember my face."

Stacks then walked to his car. Gray Boy had never seen Stacks so enraged, so brutal. Andrew's face was red and bruised from the beating. One of his eyes was rapidly closing. His nose bloodied and leaking from both nostrils. Gray Boy wasn't exactly sure who this white man was or why Stacks gave a damn about him abusing his kids, but something about Andrew touched a sore spot for Stacks Gray didn't know existed. Gray looked down at Andrew, now bent over still gasping for air.

"You have a great rest of your evening."

Gray Boy returned to the vehicle. Stacks paused before he entered the car, looked at a battered and terrified Andrew, and then spoke:

"If you touch him again, I'll kill you."

chapter eleven

the beginning

When Stacks returned home after his rendezvous with Andrew, he entered the apartment to find two large crates made of heavy, industrial grade plastic in the room that should have been a dining room. He stood there, staring at them in disbelief. Big Tony sat on the couch. He saw Stacks' reaction to the crates, a reaction generated by a distrust in Coop's recent decisions. Stacks knew what the containers held, guns. Heavy artillery, military grade perhaps. Yet another misstep by Coop. *Why the fuck is he keepin' that shit here?! Pop is fuckin' slippin'!* He shook his head and looked at his uncle. Big Tony read Stacks' face. He agreed with his displeasure, though they never said a word. He pursed his lips, shrugged his shoulders and returned to watching the game on TV.

"Where the fuck is he, Unc?"

"Ya' father don't report to me, nephew. Left here about an hour ago when you didn't come back. Asked me to watch ya' brother."

fin

the beginning

Stacks felt sick to his stomach. "Dee see this *shit*?"

"Naaa, lil' man was sleep when they brought that shit in here."

"The *fuck*!"

Stacks pulled his phone out and texted Shayla.

Stacks: Hey baby. U up?

It was one in the morning so he knew she might not answer. He had half a mind to scoop Dee out of bed and take him to her place. When Shayla didn't answer, he was resigned to the fact they were trapped there for the night with enough weapons to lock everyone in the house up for a long time.

Stacks: Nite baby. Sorry I broke my promise...again. 😞 *I love u*

He slid his phone back in his pocket and walked towards the hallway.

"I'm going to bed."

"Mmmm-hmmmm."

Stacks went to his room, it was dark save for the streetlamp's halo of light poking out from around the side of the building and through his window. He took his gun out of his waist, laid it on the end table next to his bed, removed his shirt and pants, then crawled into bed. As he stared up at the ceiling, his eyes adjusting to the darkness, he recalled the night's events. He kept hearing Andrew's cries, the glorious sound of his hand making contact with Andrew's face. His satisfaction soon turned to rage as he thought of his own father, endangering the life of his brother and himself. He wished he and Justin both had a father like Fin, caring, loving, present. Three fathers, three men that couldn't be more different. One abusive, one careless, one loving. One intoxicated by alcohol, one intoxicated by power, one intoxicated by family. As he drifted off to sleep, his mind went back and forth, jumping from dream to nightmare as he thought of their different upbringings. He wondered what they were doing over at Fin's, the night they had. He wished he could've joined them. The last thought that he was able to hold on before sleep won him over was that of Dee. He would make sure he had the father he deserved.

The next morning, right around the time Fin and his father returned from taking Justin home, Stacks was also spending time with his father. The two father-son interactions couldn't have been more different. Stacks showered, popped his head in on Dee who was still sleeping, his usual on Saturdays, then entered the main room. Big Tony and Shan were inventorying the contents of the crates. Coop was on the phone. Coop looked over his shoulder and noticed Stacks' entrance.

"Get here soon, ya' hea'!"

He closed his phone then turned to Stacks. "I'mma need you sharp today, boy. Post up outside wit' Gray, while we finish this shit."

"Why we got these guns in the house? Thought we don't shit where we eat?"

Coop didn't take kindly to being questioned, especially in his own home about *his* business. He stood and approached Stacks.

"Oh. I guess you runnin' this family now."

Big Tony and Shan stopped what they were doing and watched the interaction. Big Tony wanted to be ready to diffuse any potential fireworks. Shan wanted Coop to slap Stacks.

"I'm saying, Pops. Dee right in the next room! You puttin' him in da....."

fin

the beginning

"DON'TCHU RAISE YO FUCKIN' VOICE IN MY HOUSE MAFUCKA! I RUN THIS SHIT HEA'!"

For a moment, a brief instant, Stacks almost beat his father the way he did Andrew the night before. His eyes tightened, his fists balled up, his breathing quickened. Coop pressed his chest up against Stacks, his face so close Stacks smelled the menthol cigarettes and cognac on his breath. Coop spoke his next words so calmly and mellow, everyone in the room was unnerved.

"When you think you ready for the crown boy, come take it. You betta come hard and true. 'Cause son or no son, you miss ya' shot, I'll *kill* yo' ass myself."

Stacks didn't want to fight his father. He didn't want to kill him no matter how much he secretly wished it was Coop that had died and not Mike. Stacks took a step back from Coop. Not out of fear nor respect. He stepped away from the confrontation for Dee. He didn't want him to wake up to the sounds of him pummeling their father. Shan smiled and returned back to his work.

"COOP! We ain't got time for this shit. We gotta move this shit up outta here!"

Coop kept his eyes locked with Stacks.

"Mmmm-hmmm. I'm just talking with my son, Tony. He is gonna do like his father told him and shut the fuck up about it, ain't he?"

Stacks walked to the door, grabbed the knob and paused. *I gotta get Dee outta this shit!* Coop wanted to assert his perceived authority a bit more.

"We got a problem?"

fin

the beginning

Stacks didn't reply. He looked over at Coop, opened the door and walked out. Gray Boy was already posted outside the door, leaning against the wall. Stacks extended his closed fist to which Gray pounded with his in return.

"This shit is fucked! He endangering Dee, man."

Gray Boy nodded his head. "I know, Bruh. Weak move. Fuck is up wit' Coop?"

Stacks shook his head in disgust and disappointment.

"He feel this shit slipping away. Seventeenth on our ass. Cops scoping us, tryna raid our shit, and this mafucka stashing merchandise in our fucking crib!"

"Never around women and children."

Stacks sat in the empty, white plastic chair that was always outside their door.

"Where's Lil' Rick and Hoop?"

"Coop sent them somewhere this morning. Fuck if I know for what tho'."

"So, we the only muscle. This shit is fucked."

Stacks needed something to make him smile. He pulled out his phone and sent Shayla a message.

Stacks: *Good morning my beautiful Shay*

Shayla: *Morning handsome. Sorry I missed your text. I was knocked out.*

Stacks: *It's all good baby. We still on for lata?*

Shayla: *We better be! You promised me some shoes!*

fin

the beginning

Stacks: Yeah yeah....C U in a couple hours

Shayla: Ok. You bringing my little boyfriend?

Stacks: Yeah and he can buy them damn shoes for you!

Shayla: Bye fool! Love U! Don't have me waiting all day either!

Stacks: I won't. Luv U 2

While Fin and Big Fin were leaving Justin's, and Stacks was in his living room nose to nose with Coop, Justin was about to have a father-son interaction of his own.

"You have a good day, Sir. Treat those wounds."

"KISS MY ASS!"

Andrew waited by the door, peering out through the peephole to watch Big Fin and Fin. Even behind the closed, heavy, wooden door he was terrified of Big Fin who was still standing on the porch, staring. Andrew, gripped in fear and paranoia, thought Big Fin could actually see him through the door. Andrew's heart was beating out of his chest.

"Dad....." pleaded Fin.

"*DAD!*"

"Let's go, son."

Andrew watched as they made their way down the stairs. *Git yo' fuckin' ass off my damn property!* When Big Fin and Fin finally drove off, Andrew staggered into the kitchen. His head was still pounding from a long night of drinking and the whooping he received at the hand of Stacks. He needed a drink to take the edge off, numb

fin

the beginning

the pain and help him focus. He grabbed his half-empty bottle of Old Jack's whiskey and a glass. He poured it half-full and downed it in mere seconds. Elaine had just made her way into the kitchen.

"I am going to call around some more. See if I can find Justin."

"No need to. He's in his goddamn room! Some black fella and his kid brought him back. He was with them all night."

Elaine sprinted out of the kitchen, into the living room, and turned down the hall towards Justin's room. She needed to see him. She needed to know he was safe. When he never returned home, she was a wreck. Andrew yelled and screamed, even blamed her for Justin "runnin' away," but he didn't lay a hand on her. Elaine thought Andrew figured missing a child was all the pain she could handle, at least that's what she hoped he thought. Andrew poured another glass of whiskey, this one more than the drink previous. He was tired, battered, embarrassed, and fed up with Elaine and Justin.

"Never shoulda married that fuckin' woman! Ain't been nothing but trouble."

Though his words slurred, and he was already way too drunk for any time of day, let alone this early in the morning, he finished the rest of his whiskey in one smooth gulp. Elaine swung the door open to see Justin sitting on his bed. He looked up and thought she saw a smile on his face, a smile from either of them was a rare occasion when Andrew was home. She frantically ran to him and embraced him, squeezing him harder and harder.

"Hey, Ma."

"Oh my GOD! WHERE WERE YOU?!?!"

"I was at Fin's house."

"The new boy? Why didn't you tell us where you were?

175

fin

the beginning

When Andrew screamed from the kitchen, they both jumped.

"HE THINKS HE CAN COME AND GO AS HE FUCKIN' PLEASES, THAT'S WHY!"

Elaine and Justin exchanged a glance, bracing themselves for what could turn really bad, really fast.

"I just needed to get away, Ma. We could, you know. Get away."

Elaine had dreamed of running more times than she could count. But where would she go? Andrew controlled the money, the car, and barely let her out the house. She dreaded the day her child would ask her to run. She knew she wouldn't have an answer.

"C'mon, Ma...let's just go. Please."

"Yeah, Ma!" slurred Andrew. "Let's just go."

Neither had noticed Andrew was now standing in the threshold of the door. They were so swept up in each other, they hadn't heard him drunkenly walking down the hall. Elaine looked up, and tears immediately began to stream down her face. Justin, however, didn't turn. He didn't have a chance. The first blow from Andrew's closed fist hit him so hard, he lost consciousness for a moment. He came to after a few seconds as Andrew beat him with a leather belt. Elaine screamed, pleading for him to stop, jumping on his back to slow down the abuse.

"NOOOO!! NOOOOOOOOOOOO!!!!"

Full of rage and alcohol, Andrew discarded her small body like she was a child. Justin was going to pay for making him worry last night, for making him care about where he was. Justin had to pay for him having to hear Elaine cry all night. Justin had to pay for Stacks' beating and emasculating him. Justin had to suffer for Big Fin

fin

the beginning

embarrassing him, threatening him. Justin had to pay for him losing his job. Justin had to pay for the public humiliation of his firing from the police force. Justin. Had. To. Pay.

And so, Andrew beat him. And beat him. Swing after swing of the belt. Blow after blow from his free hand which alternated between closed fist and open palm. Justin did the best he could to cover himself, protect himself from the barrage of cow leather, skin and bone being hurled his way. He almost lost consciousness again when the blows suddenly stopped.

CRASH!!!!

Andrew dropped to the floor, his hair full of broken glass and whiskey from the liquor bottle Elaine had just struck him with. She turned to Justin and screamed. Screamed the word she couldn't empower herself to do. With all of her soul, with the last scrap of motherly love she had left, she did what she knew she should have done a long time ago. She freed him from this hell.

"RUUUUUNNNNNN!!!!!!"

"RRRRUUUUUUUUUUUUUUUUUUUUNNNNNNNNNNN!!!!!"

Justin staggered to get up, finally making it to his feet.

Dazed and drunk, Andrew hastily reached for Justin's arm.

"WHERE YOU GOIN'?"

Justin shook free of Andrew's grasp and stumbled to the living room, bumping into the hallway walls, still attempting to regain his balance. He made it to the couch only to hear Andrew scream.

"GET THE FUCK BACK HERE!"

Elaine cried out. "Leave him alo…"

fin

the beginning

SLAP!!

"THIS IS YOUR GODDAMN FAULT!"

Andrew pulled himself off of the floor, as whiskey and broken glass rolled down his face. Elaine reached for his ankle to impede his progress. He kicked loose of her grip then staggered towards the living room. Justin's adrenaline kicked in, granting him a moment of clarity and composure. With one eye rapidly closing and growing cloudy, the other welling with tears, he found the front door, unlocked it and ran. He ran up the block towards Ninth Street. He ran past neighbors that were out in their front yards, mowing grass, tending to flower beds, or enjoying the morning's warmth. He needed to get to Fin, more importantly, Big Fin. His heart was broken when he finally made it to Fin's house. The car was gone. He ran up the stairs anyway. He had to try.

BANG! BANG! BANG! BANG!

"Please be home..."

BANG! BANG! BANG! BANG!

"MR. JAAAAAMES!"

BANG! BANG! BANG! BANG!

"FIN! MRS. FIN'S MOM!"

BANG! BANG! BANG! BANG!

"They ain't there!"

Justin turned to see an older, black lady, broom in hand on her porch. He began to panic. *What am I gonna do? No. NO! They GOTTA be here!!* He turned back to the house.

BANG! BANG! BANG! BANG!

178

fin

the beginning

"FIIIIIINNNNNNNNN!"

"I SAID, THEY AIN'T THERE!! Baby, you alright?!"

Justin didn't respond. He knew where he needed to go next. He jumped off the porch, hurting his ankle as he landed, and took off running, limping as he did. He ran and ran, ignoring the flashing "don't walk" signs at every corner. He didn't care. He was headed for Brevoit. When he made it to the corner of First Avenue and Portland Avenue, across the street from the Brevoit Projects, he darted across the street. He was completely oblivious to the police cruiser waiting at the stop light. Officer Delaine and his partner, Officer Christensen, were mid conversation when Justin passed them.

"So, you think you passed the Sergeant's exam?"

"Don't matter. Done took the damn thing seven times and still ain't promoted. Just ain't meant...."

Officer Delaine's response and train of thought was broken by Justin's battered and bruised body limping across the street in hysterics. He turned to his partner.

"Follow him!"

Back in Brevoit, Stacks was sitting outside leaning back in the white, plastic chair that was a fixture outside his front door. Gray Boy, to Stacks' right, stood rubbing his hands together, cautiously looking to his left and to his right. As Gray looked around, he noticed Fin approaching and tapped Stacks. Stacks looked up at Gray Boy, then in the direction he indicated and saw Fin.

"What up, Fin? You good?"

"Yeah...*FUCK NO!* I ain't good!"

"Oh, you mad?"

fin

the beginning

"Yeah, I'm fucking mad!"

"Well look, Bruh. I'mma need you to be mad somewhere else. This is a bad time right now."

"Man, I saw what you did last night."

"Whatchu talking about, Fin?"

"I'm just saying."

"Yeah, but you shouldn't!"

"Shouldn't what?"

"Be saying shit!"

Fin figured out his mistake and looked away, his anger growing by the second.

"Look Fin, now ain't the time for this. I need you to get the fuck outta here!"

"Fine! Fuck it!"

Fin turned and began to walk away. Stacks didn't move, he watched Fin storm off. He wanted to talk with him but now was not the time.

"What the fuck you runnin', Stacks? A fucking community outreach center?!"

Stacks turned and looked at Gray Boy. "The fuck you say??!"

"Look!"

Gray Boy pointed to his right.

"WHAT THE FUCK?!?!"

fin

the beginning

Fin barely made it thirty feet away when he heard Stacks yell. He snapped his head around and saw what he was yelling at. He immediately ran back to where Stacks was standing. Justin was running, barely. His eye was black and closed. His nose appeared broken. His bottom lip looked as if his teeth had gone through it from a punch. His shirt torn and covered in blood.

"JUSSS!!"

Stacks couldn't believe the shape Justin was in. "What the fuck happened? That mafucka hit you AGAIN?!"

Gray Boy now knew who the man was that Stacks viciously punished last night. He was none too pleased.

"YOU HAD ME OUT SCOPING A COP BAR FOR THIS MAFUCKA??!"

Before Stacks could respond, before Fin could tend to Justin, before Justin could even say a word, the wail of the police siren and flashing lights halted them all. Justin saw the cops and panicked.

"He sent them for me!! He knows all of them!"

"OH SHIT!" exclaimed Gray.

Gray turned and ran into the house, slamming the door behind him. Officer Delaine saw Gray Boy's face as he turned.

"That one...the one that just ran in the house....I saw him last night over by Pullman's!"

Both officers exited the vehicle. Officer Christiansen reached up for the walkie-talkie extension on his shoulder and called in what they had seen as they approached. Officer Delaine took in the surroundings, counting the number of people in the courtyard, his hand on his weapon. He spotted Stacks, Fin and Justin, all three in a

181

fin

the beginning

prone position, startled from fear, the way a group of cats pause for a split second before scurrying in different directions.

"Hey! Stop right there!"

Justin turned to Stacks and pleaded. "DON'T LET THEM TAKE ME BACK!!"

"FIN! Get him and get the FUCK OUTTA HERE!!"

Fin was frozen. The sight of Justin's battered face and body, the cops approaching and Stacks screaming, his body locked up, his brain couldn't focus. Stacks knew they were running out of time. He couldn't have Fin anywhere near Brevoit.

"FIN!"

"DON'T ANY OF YOU MOVE!" shouted Officer Christiansen as he and Officer Delaine drew closer.

"C'mon, Juss! We gotta go!"

"NOOOO!"

Suddenly, Justin shocked both Fin and Stacks. He ran. He didn't run away though, he ran into the house where Gray Boy was explaining everything to Coop, Shan and Big Tony.

"SOME WHITE KID ROLLED UP, ALL FUCKED UP AND SHIT, BEGGING STACKS TO SAVE HIM AND THE FUCKIN' COPS POPPED OUTTA..."

BOOM!

Justin burst into the house. The door hit the inner wall with a loud bang. Stacks couldn't believe it, but at least he could save Fin. He pushed Fin in his chest.

fin

the beginning

"OH SHIT! GO, FIN! RUN!!"

Officer Delaine quickened his pace, unsnapped the securing strap on his holster and drew his weapon keeping it at his side.

"DON'T DO IT!! DON'T FUCKING DO IT, KID!!"

Officer Christiansen drew his weapon as well. Stacks looked at the cops, a mere twenty feet away and closing, grabbed Fin who was still frozen, and drug him into the house, slamming the door behind him. Coop, Shan, Big Tony and Gray stood there in shock by what just happened. Fin and Justin met their shocked looks in kind. They saw guns everywhere. Fin knew he had made a huge mistake. *Why didn't I fucking run? Why did I even come over here?!*

BANG! BANG! BANG! BANG!

"POLICE!! OPEN UP!!"

Coop was furious. He darted to the door, shoving Stacks and Fin out of the way. He peered through the peep hole and saw the two police officers standing there, guns drawn. He shot a fierce glance at Stacks.

"You gots to be the *dumbest* mafucka I know! Can't *believe* yo' ass came from me!"

Shan set the assault rifle he was loading into the crate down and drew a .357 Magnum from his lower back. Gray drew his weapon. Coop already had his .357 in hand as he leaned into the peephole.

"Daddy, what's going on?"

Everyone turned to the hallway entrance to see Dee standing there, wiping sleep from his eyes. Stacks' worst fear was unfolding in front of him. He had tried so hard all of Dee's life to never have him in a situation like this. It was bad enough that Coop was housing so many

fin

the beginning

illegal weapons in the house, Dee would be a grandfather before any of their first parole hearings. But now, they had a beat-up Justin, enough weaponry to arm a small militia, plus two cops at the door and Dee was right in the middle of it. Coop dropped his head, shaking it in disbelief before leaning his shoulder against the door. He pressed the barrel of the .357 up against the door. He mustered the best polite demeanor he could, though its falseness could not be hidden.

"Can I help you, officers?"

Officer Delaine could hear how close the voice was to the door. He took a few steps back, waving Officer Christensen to do the same. The nervous officers raised their weapons and pointed them at the door.

"I need you to open the door, Sir!"

"Can I ask for what, officer?"

"OPEN THE DOOR, SIR!"

Stacks ran to Dee and scooped him up, carrying him back into his room. He didn't want Dee to fully wake up and take in what he was seeing. Once they were in the room, he set him down, squatted and looked Dee in his eyes.

"Baby boy, need you to stay right here. Okay?"

"What's going on? Why are the police here?"

"Oh, they got the wrong door, baby Bruh. Don't worry. Daddy is gonna handle it. But stay here."

Stacks stood up and went to the door. Dee ran up to him before he could close it.

"Chris..."

fin

the beginning

"No, Dee. You gotta listen to me, man. Please! Stay here! If you hear anything that sounds scary, you get under your bed, okay?"

Dee nodded and went to his bed and began to cry. Outside, the officers didn't know what to expect. They wanted Coop to open the door so they could figure out why the battered, white boy just ran inside. Brevoit was an all-Black housing project. Everyone knew it. Justin's presence didn't fit.

"SIR, OPEN THIS DOOR NOW OR WE WILL BE FORCED TO ENTER!"

"On what grounds? With what warrant?"

"SIR, THIS IS YOUR LAST WARNING!! OPEN THE DOOR!"

Coop needed Stacks' counsel, but right at that moment, he didn't trust him. Stacks was methodical, strategic, and never rattled. Coop couldn't believe Stacks allowed Fin and Justin anywhere near the Morton home, and of all days, today! *How the fuck you gonna run this shit and you making mistakes like this!* With Stacks' judgement clouded, Coop quickly realized that he would have to figure out how to diffuse this situation. His mind raced as he frantically thought of what he could say, what he could do. Shan wasn't up for diplomacy, however. Coop always knew he was the wild card; reckless, impulsive, always drunk and with little control of his emotions. It should have been to no one's surprise what happened next.

"FUCK YOU, PIGS!"

BANG! BANG! BANG!

Shan shot through the thin project walls to where he assumed one of the officers would be. Coop stood in horror, he raised his weapon to the door, grasping it with both hands in anticipation of a gun fight.

185

fin

the beginning

Oh shit! Gray Boy raised his weapon.

This mafucka is crazy! Big Tony picked up one of the rifles from the crate and loaded it.

Oh God! Fin dove onto the floor.

Justin cried and curled up into a ball.

What the fuck! Stacks stood up. "Stay right here!"

Dee cried.

Everyone had taken cover, everyone except Shan. Shan still had his gun raised, pointed at the officers on the other side of the wall. Coop backed away from the door and approached Shan.

"WHAT THE FUCK IS WRONG WITH YOU?!?"

"FUCK THEM PIGS!"

Stacks quickly reentered the room just as Shan stopped shouting. He ran over and knocked his gun hand down which was still pointed at the wall. Coop crouched down and stared at Shan and Stacks in pure disbelief by what his sons were doing this morning. Dee screamed from his room. Stacks turned to Fin.

"Go watch Dee, Bruh. Anything happens, you take care of him!"

Fin nodded, picked himself and Justin up off of the floor and made their way as quickly as they could to Dee's room, slamming the door behind him. Dee was crying loudly. He knew he needed to comfort him.

"Hey, lil' man. Remember me?"

"I waaaant Chrriiiisss!"

186

fin

the beginning

Officer Delaine and Christensen dropped low at the shots that ripped through the wall, about two feet to the left of Officer Delaine. Shan had watched way too many movies. He assumed each officer would be leaning against the wall on either side of the door. They quickly fell back, and Officer Christiansen began shouting into his radio.

"SHOTS FIRED! SHOTS FIRED IN THE BREVOIT HOUSING PROJECTS! OFFICER REQUESTS BACKUP! PORTLAND AND FIRST! AT LEAST FOUR MALES, THREE BLACK, ONE WHITE! WHITE MALE IS BADLY BEATEN!"

Big Tony had taken position at the window in the dining room, peering out from behind the old, patterned curtains. He kept looking to Coop for a queue as to what to do. Coop, assessed the room and saw Dee was gone, so too were Fin and Justin. Stacks could hear the officers calling for backup.

"We gotta get outta here, Pop!"

"And go where?! You don't even know how many of them mafuckas is out there?!!?"

Stacks stood and looked at Shan with a disgust and hatred that was indescribable.

"If something happens to Dee, I swear I'mma kill you!"

Shan turned to Stacks, both men with guns in their hands, each trying to look deep into the other's soul. At the sight of the standoff, Big Tony had reached his limit.

"WE AIN'T GOT TIME FO' YALL SHIT! THEY COMIN' IN HERE WHETHER WE LIKE IT OR NOT! BES' GET READY FOR IT!"

Outside, Officer's Delaine and Christensen were back at their vehicle, arming their bodies with Kevlar vests, and assessing the situation. Two more patrol cars arrived, one on the other side of the Brevoit courtyard, one right behind them. Officer Collins, already in body armor and gun drawn, ran in a crouching stance behind the cover of the two adjacent vehicles, arriving next to Officer Christensen to get a debrief of the situation.

"What we got?"

"Saw a white male, about five foot five inches, about one hundred and twenty pounds running down First Street and entered the homes. He was badly beaten and bruised. We followed him in here and saw him confronted by three black males in front of apartment one nineteen. When we approached to ascertain the health of the white male, they all ran inside. Repeated requests to open the door were denied then three shots rang out, ripping through the wall."

"MOTHERFUCKERS ALMOST SHOT ME!!" snapped Officer Delaine.

Officer Collins, a fifteen-year veteran of the Norfolk Police Department, was very familiar with Valebrook and the Brevoit Projects.

"Wait...apartment one nineteen? Which building?"

Officer Delaine pointed towards the Morton residence. "That one there, the first one to the right. One nineteen."

Officer Collins felt a knot grow in his stomach.

"That's Cooper Morton's house."

Officer Delaine turned in his prone position behind the open car door.

fin

the beginning

"*The* Cooper Morton??! Like Cooper Morton as in *Coop the gun dealer*?!"

"Yeah! Call for back up. This ain't gonna end pretty."

chapter twelve

smoke

It wasn't long before Brevoit was a circus. Within an hour of Shan shooting through the wall, Valebrook became something one would see in a movie. As more police arrived, sectioning off the surrounding streets, halting car traffic in both directions for two blocks either way, a crowd of on-lookers gathered, jockeying for position to maintain a line of sight to the Brevoit Projects best they could. Brevoit's residents were told to get into their homes and stay there save for the evacuated residents of the seven other apartments adjacent on either side of the Morton's apartment. Norfolk's Tactical Police Operations Unit, called TACOPS, was in route. Two paramedic units and a fire engine were on standby. Three local news stations were on scene reporting as the events were unfolding.

Reporter on scene: "Thanks, Carmen. We are live in the Valebrook section of Norfolk at the Brevoit Housing projects. What we know is this: according to a police spokesperson, two officers were shot at while trying to ascertain the health of a white male, described to be five foot five inches tall. What unfolded as the officers approached is something out of a crime drama….."

Rose had been watching an old movie on television when the channel broke in with breaking news coverage. She couldn't believe what she was hearing.

"James. Come look at this."

Witness: "All I know is, we were all just sitting outside and some little white boy come runnin' up in here, then the cops came and the boy ran in them people's house. The police was bangin' on they door then all of a sudden - Bang! Bang! They started shooting at the cops!"

Reporter: "A Police spokesperson stated neither responding officer was hurt. They know at least three black males entered the apartment with the young boy. Police have not…….."

Big Fin had arrived in time to hear the witness account on the television. His heart began to race.

"Where did they say this was, baby?"

"Right here in Valebrook. Brevoit! That's like eight blocks away!!"

"Rose, call Fin! NOW!!"

Big Fin ran down the hallway. Rose watched him dart back to the bedroom.

fin

smoke

"Why, James? Why would he even be over there?"

Big Fin ran into the bedroom, grabbed his keys then frantically headed towards the front door.

"Call him, Rose! C'mon! I'll explain on the way!"

As he sat on the living room sectional sofa, his .357 resting on his lap, Coop tried to make sense of how that morning escalated so quickly. He was resigned to the fact that he would either be going to jail or the morgue. He looked at Big Tony, Big Tony's eyes told him that he had accepted his fate as well. Shan was up, pacing, letting out indecipherable grumbles. Coop looked at Stacks with such disappointment and anger. Gray Boy guarded the window adjacent to the front door. Stacks sat on the other end of the sectional, numb to the situation. He needed to let Shayla know what was going on.

Stacks: Baby, we got a problem

Shayla: You ain't comin? You serious right now???

Stacks: We trapped in the house wit' the cops outside!

Shayla: You ain't gotta lie! Damn Chris!

Stacks: Why the fuck would I lie about that?

Stacks: You remember what we talked about? The emergency plan?

Shayla: Wait...ur serious???????

Stacks: Go get that money and call the lawyer. For Gray too!

Shayla: Chris...ur scaring me!

Stacks: I'm scared too baby.

Shayla: Where's Dee???

193

Before he could respond to her, Shan's voice rang out loud and clear.

"This shit is all yo' fault!"

"My fault, huh? 'Cause I'm the one bustin' off at the cops, right?"

"They wouldn't have even been here if wasn't for you and them two little bitches in the other room! And why they still here any goddamn way!?!"

Gray glanced over at Stacks with a look of disgust, agreeing with Shan's statement. Coop wanted to know the answer to that question as well.

"That's a great question, Chris. Why *are* they here? I told ya' about Big Fin's boy...and who the fuck is that white boy in there?"

Again, Gray looked at Stacks. This time, Stacks looked at Gray as well. He knew Gray wouldn't say a word about the night before. He began to feel the weight of his actions, his beating of Andrew, his empathy for Justin, his rage towards a terrible father instead of *his* terrible father, all were catalysts for this situation. He never thought Andrew would ever touch Justin again nor that Justin would run to the projects looking for help if he did. Coop noticed Gray Boy staring at Stacks.

"Somethin' you wanna say, Gray?"

Gray turned back to his post and stared out of the window.

"Naaaa."

Coop got off of the couch and walked over to Gray Boy.

"Yeaaah. You got somethin' to say. Whatchu know 'bout this white boy? Who is he?"

smoke

Gray looked over his shoulder at Coop who was now standing behind him, his mouth right by his ear. He was just as mad and confused as Coop was, but he would never betray Stacks. Never.

"Who is he, Gray? Why that fucked up lil' white boy up in my house?"

"Mafucka from school. That's it. I don't know why he's here."

Coop didn't believe him. "Mafucka from school, huh? That's all you know, huh?"

Coop returned to the couch, sat his gun down on the small coffee table and looked at Stacks.

"You let me down, boy. Never really questioned your judgement before. So, who is he?"

In the bedroom, Fin sat on the edge of Dee's bed, trying to figure out how this day got so crazy, a sentiment that was going around. His arm was around Dee's shoulder who was still crying. Justin, his eye now fully closed, was panicking.

"We gotta get outta here, Fin! Ain't no other way out?"

"Look at the window, Juss. There's bars on the windows."

Justin walked to the window and sized up the bars. "I could fit. I could get through that."

"I can't...and I ain't sending Dee out there with you."

"I'mma go! I gotta go!"

Justin's cries of panic and terror laced in every word, angered Fin. He sprung off the bed and got into Justin's face.

"You just gonna run?! You gonna leave me and Stacks up in here??!! Mafucka this shit all started because of you! Fuck you come over here for anyway?!"

Fin was furious. He knew Justin was scared. He knew Justin had been through a hell he could never imagine. He didn't care in that moment though. He couldn't stand cowardice almost as much as he despised bullies. He didn't care that he was up in Justin's face, glaring down at him as he spoke. It wasn't until he really looked at him that he calmed down. Justin stood there trembling. Fin had always been kind to him, his protector. In that moment, Justin was triggered. The anger and disappointment in Fin's voice, his physical presence in his space, reminded him of Andrew.

"I didn't know where else to go."

Fin took in Justin's reaction fully and tried to calm himself down.

"Look, this is gonna work out. They gotta know there are kids up in here. They not gonna come in here shootin' or they would have already."

His words offered Justin no comfort. "...I guess."

BZZZZZZZZZZZZ!

BZZZZZZZZZZZZ!

Fin looked down at his phone, it was Rose.

"Hey, Mama."

"Fin? Where are you?"

"I'm at a friend's house."

"What friend's house?"

fin

smoke

Big Fin snatched the phone from Rose as he drove furiously over to Brevoit.

"WHERE ARE YOU, BOY?! YOU UP IN THAT SHIT IN BREVOIT?"

"...yes sir."

Big Fin looked at Rose. "He is there. You ok, son?"

"Yeah, Dad. I'm sorry."

"Stay low, Fin. Stay low and find cover. We are on our way!"

A few seconds later, Big Fin and Rose parked just behind a crowd that had formed on Second Street. They hastily exited the car and ran to the first police officer they saw.

"Sir, I need you to move that vehicle."

Rose didn't care. "My son is in that house!"

"Ok, Ma'am. But I need that vehicle moved."

Big Fin became irate. "Sir, my fifteen year old son is right now trapped in that house! Y'all out here with a SWAT unit!!! You think I'm worried about where I parked?!"

The officer realized that Big Fin and Rose were not going to move until they got some answers. He pulled out his radio and called for a supervisor to explain the situation. Soon, a sergeant approached and took control of the conversation.

"Hello, I am Sergeant Mabry. Officer Barker tells me you know one of the suspects in the home?"

Rose took none too kindly to the description of Fin. "HE ISN'T A SUSPECT! HE IS A FIFTEEN-YEAR-OLD BOY WHO HAS NEVER BEEN IN TROUBLE!"

"Ma'am, I need you to calm down."

"We will calm down once you tell us what's going on with our boy!" replied Big Fin.

"If you calm down, I can take you to the On-scene Commander. I can't tell you what I don't know."

Big Fin grabbed Rose around her shoulder to calm her down, he took a deep breath, looked the sergeant square in his eyes and spoke, trying to remain humble and calm though his fear and concern for Fin made it unbearable.

"Sir....Sergeant, our son is in the house. Please, he is just a boy. Help us."

The Sergeant realized they were struggling. "Come with me."

Back in the room, Fin sat looking at the floor. He knew he had disappointed Big Fin. He was never one to disobey his parents, but his teenage hubris got the best of him. The fear he imagined his parents must be experiencing at that moment hurt him to his core. He quickly wiped the tears forming in his eyes. Stacks walked into the room, trying to avoid further interrogation from Coop. He walked over and picked up Dee, holding him tight while looking down at Fin. He didn't say anything to anyone. He just wanted to comfort his little brother; something Coop never thought to do. Stacks remembered what it was like to be small, vulnerable and scared and not have Coop or Shan to comfort him. Fear was a sign of weakness in the Morton family. Stacks always had to be hard, had to be tough. It stripped him of his innocence. He wasn't going to let that happen to Dee. Justin now sat on the floor underneath the window. He was exhausted, in tremendous pain and inside, he was dying, slowly giving up. It seemed no matter what he did, where he went, trouble followed. Then they heard the police.

"THIS IS THE NORFOLK POLICE! COME OUT WITH YOUR HANDS UP! WE DON'T WANT TO HURT YOU! FAILURE TO COMPLY WILL NECESSITATE US TO USE DEADLY FORCE!

Justin looked up at Fin. "They really gonna come in here shooting?"

"I don't know."

Coop *was* worried about Dee though. He was worried about all of his boys. He got up and proceeded down the hallway with the intention of going into Dee's room. As he reached for the door he paused. He couldn't go in there at that moment. Not when he himself was scared, unsure of how this would all play out. He placed his open palm on the door, rationalizing that Stacks was taking care of his baby brother as he always did. He wanted to tell him sorry, he wanted to tell all of them he was sorry, and he failed them. He lowered his head, dropped his hand and walked further down the hallway into his bedroom. He decided he needed to make a call, what he knew very well could be his last phone call for a while, quite possibly ever. The phone rang and rang. It had been a long time since he had dialed that number, but if he knew Big Fin, it hadn't changed. Big Fin saw a number he didn't recognize and stepped away from Rose to answer.

"Hello?"

"Long time. Sorry it had to be like this."

"Coop?"

"Didn't know this shit would happen, Fin. Never wanted your boy around here."

fin

smoke

Big Fin was trying to keep his anger in check. "Coop, is my boy okay?"

"He's fine. Them shots were Shan's stupid ass. Don't know where I went wrong wit' that boy...."

"Coop, they're coming in there! They got the damn TACOPS out here! Get my son outta there!!"

"Brother, I don't..."

"I *ain't* ya goddamn brother, Coop!"

"Yeah, well, in any event, here the fuck we are! You wanna argue over old shit or you wanna figure how the fuck we get ya' boy outta here?!"

Big Fin let out an exasperated breath. Rose looked over at him wondering who he could possibly be talking to at a time like this. The look on her face broke his heart.

"Coop, if I ever was your brother, if you ever gave a fuck about me, then you know you have my world in that house with you."

"Yeah, I hear ya'.....and you right, you were my brother.....I know what I need to do."

Coop hung up the phone.

"Coop? Coop?? COOP!"

The silence on the other end was the loudest thing Big Fin had ever heard. Coop flung his phone on his bed and entered the hallway just as Stacks was leaving Dee's room. He looked at his son, walked up to him and put his arm around him, escorting him back into the living room. Stacks, Shan, Gray and Big Tony had heard the police

smoke

declaration earlier. They all looked to Coop for answers. He had only one to give. Big Tony was still armed with one of the assault rifles they had been planning to sell. He ejected the magazine, checked it one last time, then re-inserted it into the rifle, pulling the lever to ready it. Gray, though visibly nervous, was steeling what resolve he could, preparing for a gun fight. Coop sat down on the couch and looked at his boys. Shan the reckless one that wanted the crown, Stacks the one that could easily take it but wanted none of it. For the first time in his life, Coop felt guilty about putting his boys in the gun business. He didn't have to, but some twisted sense of family legacy had always driven him. *This is all I know. All I've ever known! They didn't have to though. Shoulda let they mama take them when she had the chance.* His regrets meant nothing in this moment. Now, with their lives on the line because of his choices, his insistence that they be like him, could cause him to lose them all. In the bedroom, he had decided to do something he realized he had never done; protect them. He looked up at Shan.

"Get me one of them rifles. Might as well see if they work."

Shan became excited. "We blasting at these fools?"

"No. You, your brother and Gray gonna kick one of them back windows out, take them kids and get the fuck outta here. Tony and I got this. Y'all never shoulda been here in the first place."

The shame and acceptance in Coop's voice was a revelation to them all. Big Tony nodded in agreement as he handed him a rifle. Stacks couldn't believe what he was hearing. Shan's whole world shattered in that moment. He understood what Coop was saying, he just didn't want too. He and Big Tony would take the fall so they could be free...or they would die so that he and his brothers could live.

"WHAT?!?! NAAAA! WE MORTONS! WE GONNA...."

"YOU GONNA DO WHAT I TELL YOU TO DO!"

Shan became emotional. He began to tremble, his voice cracked as he spoke.

"I ain't losing you 'cause a no white boy! We gonna fight! I can't lose you."

Shan started sobbing like a baby. Coop got up from the couch, approached Shan and placed his hand on his shoulder.

"No, son. You're not. Now go. Don't defy no mo'!"

Shan, placed his gun in his waist, dropped his head onto Coop's shoulder and began to cry. Coop hugged him as a father for the first time.

"I love you, Shannon. I love all of ya'. I'm sorry I failed you."

In that moment, Stacks saw Shan differently. Shan was still a little boy trying to please his father, who would do anything for a pat on the head from Coop. Stacks always saw Shan as a wannabe. Now, he saw what Shan wanted to be, a loved son. He stood, walked over to his father and brother, feeling a newfound sense of compassion for Shan. He attempted to comfort Shan by touching his shoulder. Shan forcefully shrugged him off.

"YOUR FUCKIN' FAULT WE IN THIS SHIT!"

Shan stormed towards the hallway.

"THIS IS THE NORFOLK POLICE! COME OUT WITH YOUR HANDS UP! WE DON'T WANT TO HURT YOU! FAILURE TO COMPLY WILL NECESSITATE US TO USE DEADLY FORCE! THIS IS YOUR FINAL WARNING!"

Rose became frightened. "James! Do something!"

He turned to the On-scene Commander. "OFFICER! OFFICER! THERE ARE CHILDREN IN THERE!"

The On-scene Commander didn't acknowledge him. He continued looking at the Morton's apartment through his binoculars. A lieutenant, dressed in Kevlar, leaned into the On-scene Commander and asked about the children.

"True there's kids in there?"

"Did you see any children in there?"

"No, but..."

"Other than these people out here, did any intel come in saying that there are children in there?"

"No, Sir."

"Then as far as we know it's three suspects, possibly more, more than likely heavily armed in the house of a known illegal gun dealer!"

He dropped his binoculars and raised his radio.

"ALPHA team...move into position."

Justin stared at the floor. "I'm scared, Bro."

"Me too. Dee, get under the bed, okay?"

Dee hurriedly dropped to the floor and shimmied underneath the bed. Just then the door swung open and Shan stormed in. Fin stood up out of shock, inadvertently blocking Shan's path. Shan pushed Fin to the side, grabbed Justin off the floor and slammed him against the wall, holding Justin there as his feet dangled in the air. His eyes were bloodthirsty. His arms were bulging, his veins full of blood from rage.

"THIS SHIT ON YOU!"

He threw Justin down.

"GET OFF HIM!"

Fin charged at Shan but Shan easily repelled him and began kicking Justin. Fin landed on the bed, then the floor, whacking his head squarely on the hard tile. Dee began to cry, screaming Stacks' name from under the bed. Coop and Stacks heard the commotion and headed towards the bedroom. Before Fin could fully recover, Shan picked Justin up again by his neck and began choking him, lifting him off his feet once again. Shan's eyes bulged, he let out cries akin to screams, spit flying from his mouth. Justin kicked and flailed his arms, trying to get Shan to drop him. Fin got to his feet, came behind Shan and tried to get him to drop Justin. He punched him in the face. Shan didn't move, he was rooted in that spot. Justin began to black out. Fin screamed.

"LET HIM GO, MOTHER FUCKER!"

BANG!

"SHOTS FIRED! I GOT SHOTS FIRED!" screamed the ALPHA team point man.

Fin paused, in shock. Dee screamed even louder. Outside, Rose screamed and buried her face in Big Fin's chest.

"GET DOWN, SON!" Big Fin screamed, praying Fin could hear him.

fin

smoke

Outside, the seven-member Tactical Operations team held their positions and awaited the order to move in. Inside, Justin fell to the ground. Fin looked at Justin, gasping for air, Shan's .357 in his hand. Shan crumpled to the ground. Coop burst into the door, Stacks behind him. He looked and saw Shan laying on the floor, bleeding out, his hand reaching towards the bed. Dee's little hand reached out to hold Shan's soon to be lifeless finger. Coop looked over and saw Justin holding the gun. Justin looked up, his psyche completely broken. Coop pointed the assault rifle at him.

"MOTHER FUCKER!"

Fin leaped in front of Justin, trembling in absolute fear. He had to try to get Coop to hear reason through the shock and tremendous loss he knew he was feeling.

"WAIT! WAIT!!! YOU DON'T UNDERSTAND, MR. COOP!"

"FIN! For the sake of yo' daddy, move!"

"No, you don't understand! Shan was trying to kill him! It was self-defense!"

"I'mma say this one more time..."

He cocked the rifle, loading a bullet in the chamber.

"...MOVE!"

Big Tony screamed from the front window. "THEY COMIN'!!!"

The Tactical Team had their orders to move in and breach. Gray ran back to his position. Coop raised the barrel of his gun towards Fin's chest. He placed his finger on the trigger.

"Fuck it!"

fin

smoke

"NOOOOOOO!!!!"

BANG!!!

Coop turned in stunned disbelief and saw his son standing there holding a gun. Stacks was shaking, his hand could barely stay up, he was pointing the .357 that Coop left on the table. Tears were streaming down his face. *Why you make me do that? Why you couldn't just be my father?* Coop was completely heartbroken. The bullet had ripped into his upper arm almost shattering the bone. Coop attempted to raise the arm, still holding the rifle.

BANG!!!

Coop's body fell back on to the floor as the bullet hit him square in the chest. Fin only saw Coop get shot then fall back, but he knew who did it. As the ALPHA Team approached, Big Tony and Gray started shooting, exchanging gunfire with the police. The sounds of glass from the windowpane shattering, bullets striking the walls as they whistled through the apartment was deafening. A hail of gunfire ensued. Rose screamed her son's name. Big Fin held her back as she tried to break the police barricade and run to Fin. Stacks ran into Dee's room, wiped the gun clean with his shirt, and placed the gun he shot Coop with into Shan's hand. He grabbed Shan's gun from Justin, wiped it clean, ducked as he went into the hallway to stage it in Coop's hand, then returned to the bedroom. Fin was worried Stacks might get caught in the crossfire. He reached up and grabbed Stacks' shirt.

"GET DOWN!"

Stacks laid on the floor at the foot of the bed and called to Dee.

206

fin

smoke

"Baby boy! Look at me! It's gonna be alright!"

Big Tony knew what he and Coop had agreed on. This was their problem, not the boys. He shot at the approaching officers trying to keep them at bay.

"GRAY! GET IN THE BACK!"

Gray looked at Big Tony knowing if he left, Big Tony was dead.

"NOW, GODDAMIT!"

Gray shook his head reluctantly, but still ran for the hallway and dove onto the floor. As he laid on the floor, he looked down the dark hallway and saw the bottoms of Coops shoes, his body laying motionless, illuminated by the light coming from Dee's room. Seconds before the front door was breeched, Stacks yelled out to Gray Boy.

"THEY SHOT EACH OTHER, GRAY! THEY SHOT EACH OTHER!"

Gray hadn't seen Stacks shoot Coop so he didn't know what happened, but Stacks' comment left him confused. Stacks turned to Fin and Justin, both laying on the floor and whispered.

"...they shot each other."

With Gray Boy safely in the hallway and out of the line of fire, Big Tony stopped firing. He had to get the kids out of this horror.

"Aight! We surrender!"

The sound of the smoke grenade breaking the glass jolted him. The hissing sound of smoke played in the background like the soundtrack of a bad movie.

BOOM!

smoke

The door swung open. Big Tony was already throwing his weapon down when the point man entered.

"FREEZE! DROP IT!"

Big Tony threw his weapon to the floor and dropped to his knees. An officer ran up to him and hit him with the butt of his rifle, splitting his eye open and knocking him flat on his stomach. The team moved through the apartment, the red from their laser scopes dancing off the whips of smoke in the air. The boys all started coughing and gagging as the smoke made its way down the hall and into the room. Their eyes began to burn and water. Their lungs felt heavy. It was hard to breathe. They all wanted to flail, wanted to cover their mouths and pound their chests, hoping to knock the noxious gases out of them. But they dared not move. The sounds of the officers' boots rapidly moving on the apartment floor said otherwise. Move and get shot. Dee didn't understand this, however. Stacks had to help him. He grabbed his collar and lifted it over his mouth.

"Close your eyes and cover your mouth with your shirt, Dee! Like this!"

"DON'T YOU FUCKING MOVE!"

Stacks spread his arms out, placing his hands parallel to his head. He kept his eyes on Dee.

"THERE'S A KID UNDER THERE! UNDER THE BED!"

"SHUT THE FUCK UP! SAY ONE MORE WORD!"

Officer Robinson pressed the barrel of his rifle against the back of Stacks' head. Fin knew Stacks was right. Dee was innocent and had already seen enough.

"THERE'S A BABY UNDER THERE, MAN!"

He glanced at Fin, then the bed. He shouted for another officer to come in and verify their claims. The second officer entered as the rest of ALPHA team swept the house giving calls of "CLEAR" as they did. The officer came in and flipped the mattress over to find Dee, balled up in a fetal position, his shirt over his face, crying though no sound came out.

Outside, Big Fin and Rose were besides themselves in fear. Big Fin had to know what was going on with his son.

"OFFICER! OFFICER! MY SON!! IS HE...?"

"Sir, I am waiting for a report!"

"James, our baby!"

Just then, a call came in from inside the apartment. The On-scene Commander answered.

"ALPHA ONE TO ON-SCENE!"

"On-scene to Alpha One. Talk to me."

"FIVE MALE SUSPECTS, FOUR BLACK, ONE WHITE. I GOT ONE MALE CHILD, BLACK. ALL IN CUSTODY. I HAVE TWO BLACK MALES DOWN. BOTH DECEASED WHEN WE ENTERED. THINK THOSE WERE THE SHOTS WE HEARD BEFORE THE BREACH. IDENTITY OF FIRST DECEASED MALE IS COOPER MORTON. APPEARS HE TOOK TWO SHOTS, ONE TO THE ARM, THE OTHER THE CHEST. SECOND DECEASED MALE IS UNIDENTIFIED. CAN'T SEE THE ENTRY WOUND. NEED THE WAGON. WE ARE GONNA CUFF 'EM BRING OUT!"

"TEN-FOUR. Is the white male victim still in the house?"

"YES. HE'S BADLY BEATEN BUT HE IS ALIVE. I'M GETTING SOMEONE TO BRING THE KID OUT. LOOKS NO MORE THAN SEVEN OR EIGHT. NEED THE PARAMEDICS READY TO RECEIVE."

"TEN-FOUR."

Big Fin and Rose were being tortured. Was the unidentified deceased male their Fin? Stacks laid motionless on the floor, relieved Dee wasn't harmed, when a sense of dread covered him. *They 'bout to take Dee!* He had no idea when or if he would see him again. He watched as a member of the tactical team approached the now empty bedframe, looking through the metal springs at Dee. The officer looked at the cowering child then surveyed the room.

"What's his name?"

"Demarcus, but we call him Dee."

The officer removed his helmet. "Dee, my name is Officer Trotter. Are you hurt?"

Dee didn't reply. He was catatonic, crippled by shock and fear. Stacks knew he'd answer him.

"Dee. You okay, baby boy?"

Dee nodded his head, his arms around his knees, his t-shirt over his mouth and nose as Stacks told him, his eyes staring straight ahead into Shan's eyes as they stared back at him. Officer Trotter finally realized what Dee was looking at. *Damn! Poor kid!* He repositioned himself so that his feet blocked Shan's face from view.

"Dee, I am gonna have an officer lift this bed then I am gonna pick you up, okay?"

smoke

Stacks was appreciative that in all the hell they had just endured, someone was showing kindness to Dee. He didn't care what happened to him next, only that Dee was going to be safe, whatever that would or could be given the circumstances.

"Dee. I want you to go with the policeman, okay?"

Dee straightened out immediately and began to scoot out from under the bed screaming for his big brother.

"NOOO! CHRIS I WANNA STAY WITH YOU!"

As soon as Dee's upper torso was accessible, Officer Robinson gave Officer Trotter his command.

"Grab him."

Dee screamed, kicking and flailing his legs. Stacks tried to reassure him, his voice cracking from heartache. Officer Robinson straddled over Stacks and grabbed his hands, the sound of the cuffs clicking around his wrists intermingling with Dee's cries. Fin laid his forehead against the floor, he too, was being cuffed by another officer. Once Stacks and Fin were cuffed, Justin was helped to his feet. They asked Justin if the bruises he received occurred in the Morton's home. They put their arm around him. They escorted him from the apartment. Justin was never cuffed. He was treated as a victim. As he was escorted from the room, stepping oved Shan's corpse, over Stacks and Fin to exit the room, any sense of empathy or brotherhood Stacks may have once felt for Justin was obliterated. The person whose presence set off the events that led to Coop and Shan's death was treated as a victim. The person that killed his brother in front of Dee was treated with care. The person that Fin risked his life for, that forced Stacks to shoot his father, was innocent. In that moment, Stacks hated Justin.

smoke

The officers continued circling through the apartment, looking at the crates of automatic rifles, finding the stashes of personal weaponry scattered throughout the home, standing over them talking, as if they were throw rugs on the floor. Finally, the word was given to move them out. As Fin, Gray and Stacks were finally escorted out of the apartment in cuffs, Rose and Big Fin became instantly joyous yet still worried. Rose's relief poured out of her.

"FIIINNN! Oh my God! Baby, are you ok?"

"We are here son!" Big Fin echoed.

Fin looked at his parents, relieved he was alive, ashamed he didn't listen to his father, ashamed he had put them in this situation, scared because he didn't know if the story Stacks had concocted would work. Big Fin stormed over to an officer close to them.

"Where are they taking them?!"

"The Valebrook station."

"Come on, Rose. We need to be there when they bring him in"

Rose nodded as she wiped her eyes.

The van loaded with Fin, Stacks, Gray Boy and Big Tony pulled off. Fin's stomach was turning with anxiety. Stacks tapped Fin's foot with his to get his attention. Fin looked up at Stacks and saw him motion his head up. Stacks didn't want to see Fin with his head down. In Stacks' eyes, he was forever grateful to Fin. Fin protected Dee, looked after him when he couldn't, as if Dee was his own blood. Fin understood the non-verbal communication and leaned his head back against the metal walls of the large van. Gray sat there looking at Fin, then at Stacks, then finally at Big Tony. The temporary bandage the paramedics placed on his busted eye was bleeding through. Big Tony sat at the end of the bench closest to the door.

"Y'all look at me. Them was my guns. Y'all never touched 'em. What happened in that room...whatever happened in that room, had to happen."

An officer in the front passenger seat of the van opened the sliding, metal window before closing it just as fast.

"SHUT UP BACK THERE!"

"YA' HERE ME! THEM WAS MY GUNS!!! LEAVE THESE BOYS OUT OF IT!"

The van rumbled for a few more miles before coming to a halt. Big Tony and the boys could hear both the driver and passenger doors open and a gaggle of voices outside. The door swung open and a group of police officers waited to remove them. As they pulled Big Tony from the van, he locked eyes with his nephew.

"Y'ALL DON'T SAY SHIT! I DID THIS SHIT! IT WAS ME AND COOP! THEM WAS OUR GUNS!!"

As they drug Big Tony away, Stacks wondered if his uncle saw him shoot Coop. He wondered if he watched as he shot his father and understood why. He saw the look in Big Tony's eyes, his willingness to take the fall for it all, willing to sacrifice the rest of his life, his freedom so that he, Gray and Fin could go free. Stacks dropped his head and wept silently. The officers began to remove them one by one. Stacks saw Big Fin and Rose first, him being first to exit the van, pressed against the closed gate separating the street from the prisoner loading area. Stacks knew no one would be there for him, so he thought.

"I'M HERE, BABY!!!"

fin

smoke

Stacks turned and saw Shayla, crying, slapping her hands against the fence causing it to rattle.

"I'M RIGHT HERE, BABY! DON'T SAY SHIT!"

He exhaled.

As Fin was removed, his eyes darted around looking for his parents. When he heard their voices, shouting, in contest with Shayla's cries, he spun his head around and found them. His eyes welled as fear truly took hold of his spirit for the first time, a fear he had never felt before. He avoided being shot, but death might have been a more compassionate verdict if their story didn't hold up. Gray kept his head high, a snarl on his face. Gray knew he had fired at the police officers but didn't know if they knew. In the midst of the firefight and subsequent breach, so much confusion occurred he could only hope they didn't want to pursue this any further than accepting they all were in the house and let the blame fall on the adults.

As they made their way up the ramp, through the locked sliding doors that required electronic access coupled with a loud buzzing sound, they were filed into the staging area, one after the other. Big Tony had already been pushed through and taken to the adult holding area. Gray and Stacks were still seventeen, though both were only weeks away from being legally adults. Fin was still fifteen, thus, they all had to be treated as juveniles. The boys were sat down and chained to a wooden bench as they awaited processing. The next few hours would define their lives, all of them in their heads wondering what would happen. All except Stacks. Stacks' thoughts went back to his father. For a moment, for a brief moment, Stacks finally had the father he always wanted. Compassionate. Protective. Willing to sacrifice his own life for that of his sons. Then, moments before he shot and killed him, his father left. Coop came back, and Stacks knew he had to make him go away once and for all.

chapter thirteen

three rooms

Big Fin, Rose and Shayla all hastily made their way into the precinct's front doors. Big Fin leaned into the glass window to address the Intake Officer.

"I need to see my son!"

The Intake Officer was indifferent. He had seen countless people storm into the station, demanding to know the whereabouts of friends and loved ones. He never looked up.

"Detainee's name?"

"James Finley."

The officer began to type, still not making eye contact with Big Fin. The rapid clicking of keystrokes, followed by momentary pauses, then more keystrokes was driving Rose crazy.

"JAMES FINLEY! Y'ALL JUST BROUGHT HIM IN HERE!"

fin

three rooms

The Intake Officer paused his computer search. He stared at the computer momentarily before looking up at Big Fin and Rose huddled around the three by three, double-paned, bulletproof window. He was tired, annoyed and more worried about his fellow officers at the Brevoit scene than the four mopes that were just brought in. He was in no rush to be of service. The Intake Officer had no idea that Big Fin and Rose were looking for someone from the Brevoit Standoff. He knew what had occurred in the Brevoit Projects, the whole station had been listening to the entire incident play out on the police scanner. It was then that he deduced that their son must have been one of the four said mopes.

"Ma'am, yelling will get you nowhere. Please have a seat and I will let you know when he has finished processing."

Rose became unhinged. "HAVE A SEAT? HAVE A SEAT?!?!"

The Intake Officer had reached his limit. "MA'AM!! HAVE A SEAT AND I WILL LET YOU KNOW WHEN HE HAS FINISHED PROCESSING!"

Big Fin knew he needed to intervene. "HEY! No need to get nasty, Sir. We are just looking for our fifteen-year-old son!"

He turned to his bride. "Rose, we gotta let them finish the intake process. I am going to call our lawyer."

Rose looked up at Big Fin with tears and anger in her eyes. *Who are you? Why aren't you as pissed off as I am? Would you stand for this if it was one of your Sailors? Where is my baby?!?!* She couldn't understand how the man that protects Sailors he doesn't even know was now bowing down to an asshole cop that is keeping them from Fin. Truth was Big Fin was furious, but he had been in enough police stations, retrieving drunken or disorderly Sailors, that he knew the drill. Confrontation would get them no closer to Fin, it would only give

216

the police motivation to delay their reunion all the more. Big Fin pulled her close and wrapped his enormous arms around her.

"I'm just as mad as you, baby. We are gonna get him back."

"Y'ALL DONE?!?!"

Shayla had been standing there, arms folded, her leg shaking, angry and terrified that Stacks was going to get blamed for everything. She didn't know what happened. She didn't know where Coop or Shan were. Once she saw Stacks being brought out of the apartment after Dee, she ran to her car and raced over to the station. Big Fin looked up over Rose's shoulder and saw Shayla. She was a beautiful young lady that seemed just as scared as they were. He saw her a few feet away from them at the gate by the loading area and saw Stacks turn when he recognized her voice. He instantly knew who she was to Stacks. *If this girl goes off the way Rose just did, we are never gonna see them.*

"They haven't finish processing them, young lady."

"You don't know that!"

She shoved her way in between Big Fin and Rose and the Intake Officer's window, pushing them out of the way.

"EXCUSE ME! I NEED TO KNOW WHERE CHRISTOPHER MORTON IS!"

The Intake Officer was at his wits end. He stood from his chair; his brow revealed the stoic demeaner he had before was replaced with anger. He pointed at Shayla, his voice began to escalate as he spoke.

"Ma'am, I'll tell you like I told them. Whomever you are looking for will be available when they are done processing, not a second before! Now, all of you: SIT DOWN!"

fin

three rooms

"YOU'RE GONNA TELL ME SOMETHING! WHERE IS MY CHRIS??!"

Big Fin saw Shayla was hurting, was scared, just as he and Rose were. *Little Chris. Been years since I laid eyes on that boy. He had to be about three, maybe four-years-old.* He remembered how smart and inquisitive Stacks was as a child. He also remembered what Fin reminded him of in the car that morning, his promise.

"Excuse me, I am Fin's father. This is his mother, Rose. You can wait with us if you like. Yelling isn't gonna get us anywhere."

Shayla stared at Big Fin her eyes raging the way Rose's were moments ago. Her light-skinned complexion flush with blood. She didn't want to hear anything that didn't concern Stacks. She glanced over her shoulder at Rose. Something in Rose's eyes touched her. *Ok, she gets it!* While Big Fin tried to display a stoic, calm, commanding demeanor, Rose's emotions were raw like hers. Rose sensed a subtle shift in Shayla. She saw the raw emotion pouring out in anger, a defense mechanism that hid a growing fear that someone she loved was almost hurt and could still be hurt if she didn't get him free. After seeing Shayla, Rose realized what she must've looked like to her husband moments before. She tilted her head a bit. Her eyes softened.

"Come sit with us, honey. We will find out what's happening together."

Stacks, Fin and Gray sat in a temporary holding cell, none of them saying anything. The cell was painted a faded yellow, with chipped paint and graffiti scratched into the brick. There were two benches that ran parallel to the bars in front of them, they too marred with graffiti. There was a dank smell of urine emanating from a metal commode on the back wall, and years of sweat and must soaked into the benches and floor. Stacks rested his head against the wall as if he were staring at the ceiling. His eyes were closed however, and he seemed remarkably calm to Fin, an emotion he misread. Stacks was wrestling between denial of what he had done and accepting it, rationalizing it. His mind danced back and forth as a loud battle only he could hear raged in his head. Gray was hunched over, his elbows on his knees, his face aching from frowning so much. His mind was on Big Tony. Though he was Stacks' uncle, Gray looked up to him. Gray saw how he served Coop as his number one, his most trusted ally, a role he wanted to serve as for Stacks. In Gray's mind, he would do what Big Tony did and ensure nothing fell on the king's head. While Stacks and Gray Boy were lost in their thoughts, Fin's mind evoked a different reaction to their situation. Anxiety gripped him and he couldn't keep still. He would get up, pace, then sit back down. He felt ill, his palms were soaked, and his breathing was growing shallow. The stench of the cell didn't help matters. His anxiety was reaching new levels. Thoughts of his life flashing before his eyes when Coop had the gun pointed at him, the death of Shan and Coop before his eyes, and the growing pressure of trying to keep his story straight so as not to implicate Stacks, was driving him crazy. His body was merely responding as an involuntary physical response to his emotions. It began to wear on both Stacks and Gray. Stacks never opened his eyes, he simply patted the bench next to him.

"Sit, Fin."

"I can't, man...what we gonna do??"

Stacks opened his eyes and looked at him and raised his finger to his mouth, tapping his lips to signal Fin to stop talking. He patted the bench again. Gray Boy understood this was new for Fin. While he didn't particularly care for him, he knew what he was going through.

"Need to stop talking and listen for a change, Fin."

three rooms

Gray Boy pointed to the open space next to Stacks. Fin reluctantly went at sat down. Stacks closed his eyes and reached out and patted Fin's knee. Fin was still wrestling with his fears. *What am I gonna say to these cops? How is Stacks' plan gonna work? They gonna know I am lying. Where the fuck is Justin? Is he gonna stick to the story? I'm going to jail.* In the midst of his panic, while his mind was in overdrive, two uniformed officers came to the holding cell. They spoke one after the other.

"Morton! Let's go."

"OPEN THE TANK!"

A loud buzz was followed by the metal bolt unlocking the cell door. Stacks stood and looked at Fin, then gave him a slight grin before nodding to Gray. He walked out of the cell and was escorted to an interrogation room. Moments later, more officers came and removed Fin, placing him in his own interrogation room. Gray Boy was left alone.

On the other side of the station, Justin sat in the Station Chief's office, Chief Warren. Chief Warren was a twenty-nine-year veteran of the force. His office had a huge window that overlooked the precinct floor. His desk was immaculate, not a pen or paper out of place. The walls were decorated with citations, copies of his degrees, and pictures of him with influential people throughout the city and a few celebrities. There were two upholstered sofa chairs in front of his dark, mahogany desk and a small couch that rested underneath the window. He had been the Station Chief in Valebrook for the last seven years. Chief Warren recognized Justin's name and knew who his father was.

"Justin, are you okay, son?"

"I guess."

fin

three rooms

"Justin, where is your mother?"

"Home, I guess."

"And your father?"

Justin shrugged his shoulders. He knew where he was just as sure as he knew his world was on fire, Pullman's. Chief Warren knew it too and had already sent two officers to retrieve him. Pullman's wasn't your typical bar. Though city ordinances demanded that bars close by two in the morning and not open until noon, Pullman's never had to worry about such limitations. Pullman's stayed open well into the early, dark hours of the morning, often closing at sunrise for an hour or two to allow for a quick cleaning and restocking of alcohol, washing of mugs and changing out of beer kegs. Police officers loved to drink after a shift. Pullman's was the place most of the white officers came to do it at. Normally, Pullman's would have a pretty robust crowd at this time of morning on a Saturday. The Brevoit Standoff had pulled many of them back to the station for auxiliary support. The bar was dark, and the jukebox played softly in the background. The L-shaped bar extended from the back hallway leading to the bathrooms all the way to the front, save for about six feet of space in between the end of the bar and the large window. The window's glass panes were all painted black except for the top three panes which allowed in sunlight, the one signal to Pullman's regular crowd of the passage of time. Andrew sat on a bar stool closest the front door. He was already five beers in. Officers King and Madden entered the bar and spotted Andrew immediately.

"Andrew," shouted Officer Madden as they approached, "need you to come with us."

"That *bitch* called you guys on me? Ha! Figures she'd do that."

Officer King shook his head, expecting that type of reply from Andrew. "Orders of Warren."

fin

three rooms

"Fuck Warren! Son of a bitch don't run me no more!"

"C'mon, Drew. Don't make this a thing."

Andrew took a swig of his beer. "I ain't makin' shit anything, and I *ain't* goin' nowhere!" He took another swig of beer.

"It's about Justin. There's been a shooting."

Andrew slammed the beer down and stared at the mirror behind the bar, making eye contact with the officers. Andrew didn't much like Justin, thought he was a mistake the moment Elaine told him she was pregnant.

"What shooting? Fuck that boy do?"

"It's the thing on TV. Come with us."

"Is he dead?"

"Just come with us, Drew."

Andrew had been watching the events at Brevoit on TV. The sound was down so he could only go off of the banner that scrolled across the bottom of the screen. When he first saw it, he wasn't surprised. *Whadya expect from them people?* Never did he think his boy was involved. He slammed a twenty on the bar, slid off his bar stool and followed the officers out of Pullman's.

Detective Patricia Tanner was assigned as the lead detective on this case. A seventeen-year veteran of the Norfolk Police Force, with the last seven being on Homicide, Chief Warren couldn't think of any other person he wanted to head this case up. She made a name for herself a few years back, when she cracked the Apology Killer case. Though she was only on patrol duty at the time, she immersed herself in the case. She didn't make many friends in doing so, but her notoriety became more than any naysayers could overcome. Wasn't long before she was fast tracked to Detective. She had just closed a major triple homicide a week ago and was supposed to be out of the rotation. This, however, was a special situation. Detective Tanner was a fit woman with a complexion that rivaled lightly milked coffee. She had eyes that could almost see through a person but knew when to make them flash compassion. She was as good as Chief Warren had, good as the department had the way Warren saw it. He often thought it was a matter of time before she would be promoted to Captain, then Chief and run her own station. Her partner, Detective Timothy "Tim" Arrington, a twenty-seven-year veteran himself, was winding down and looking forward to retirement. He had no problem allowing Detective Tanner to take the lead and ride her drive to a high case completion rate.

Having seen Justin through the window in Captain Warren's office door, Stacks and Fin on the camera feed from their interrogation rooms, and passing Gray still sitting in holding, Detective Tanner's experience and intuition told her Fin was the one she should question first. He didn't seem jaded or hardened by the street life like Stacks and Gray, nor abused like Justin. He looked like a good kid caught in the wrong situation. Detective Tanner entered into the main lobby where Big Fin, Rose and Shayla impatiently waited. She understood that save for Big Tony, all other parties involved where juveniles and she couldn't question them without a parent, guardian or lawyer present. When the door swung open, Big Fin, Rose and Shayla all sat up.

"Who is here for James Finley?"

Rose and Big Fin stood and spoke in unison.

"We are."

"Hello, I am Detective Tanner. I am heading this investigation up. Can you both come with me please?"

fin

three rooms

Shayla felt ignored. "What about Christopher Morton?"

"Are you his parent or guardian? You look a bit too young to be his lawyer."

"No, I'm his..."

"Then Ma'am, unless you are a witness, his parent, guardian or lawyer, I am not going to be able to say anything to you at this time."

"WHERE IS DEE??! Y'ALL TOOK HIM!"

"You're referring to the child. He is safe with Child Services. Mr. and Mrs. Finley, please follow me."

"THIS IS BULLSHIT!"

Detective Tanner shot Shayla a glance that immediately made her pause and sit back down, then she escorted Big Fin and Rose into the back of the station.

As the door closed, Shayla rolled her eyes and angrily folded her arms.

"Bitch!"

Fin sat in Interrogation Room Three, his left hand cuffed to a gray, metal desk. The room was well lit by the overhead fluorescent lights that revealed the chipped, white paint on the cinder-block walls. He looked around, taking in his surroundings but his focus kept returning to the small, dirty window in the door leading to the hallway he was just brought down. Fin was caught off guard by the appearance of the room. He figured it would be dark with a hanging light over a table, shadowing the officers' face that would be interrogating him, much like he saw on TV. He was cold, tired as he crashed from his earlier adrenaline rush, and scared. All he wanted was his dad.

fin

three rooms

Detective Tanner led the Finleys down a hallway and stopped just before they reached the room holding Fin.

"Mr. and Mrs. Finley, so before we go in there, can you give me some background? What was your son doing in the Brevoit Homes?"

Big Fin and Rose looked at each other. They really didn't know how to respond because they had no idea until that morning that Fin knew anyone over there.

"We - we really don't know," explained Rose.

Big Fin put his arm around her. "Didn't even realize he was hanging over there until this morning. Told me this morning that he goes to school with Christopher Morton."

"Hmmmm. I see. Look, I am gonna level with you. This doesn't look good for any of the boys involved. Not only was there a gun fight with police, but..."

"My boy didn't shoot at any cops!"

"Mr. Finley, I don't think he did. But he was there and knows who did. There were also two crates of some heavy, military grade weapons."

Rose could not believe what she was hearing. "WHAT?!"

"I understand your shock, but there's more. From what we can tell, there appears to have been a shootout inside the house. Two men are dead. A Shannon Morton and Cooper Morton. Those two were known gun runners, both with sheets on them. I need your son to be honest with me. He can't hide anything."

Rose looked at Big Fin. "I think we need a lawyer."

225

fin

three rooms

Big Fin was crying on the inside. He always believed Coop would end up dead or in jail, but hearing it, that he actually *was* dead, and that Shan was dead as well, was a shock. He spoke to Coop just moments before the shooting started, now he was gone. He also heard Big Tony screaming that the guns were his. He knew Big Tony from the days he, Coop and Big Tony ran the streets of Norfolk, long before he met Rose. Big Tony was loyal to Coop, but even more loyal to Coop's sons. If he was trying to take the fall for those guns, and was screaming it for God and country to hear, the gun charge wasn't going to stick on Fin. Big Fin deduced that what Detective Tanner wanted to really find out was who killed Coop and Shan. He needed to talk to Fin.

"Can we have a moment with our son, Detective?"

"Of course."

Detective Arrington didn't like it and showed his displeasure all over his face, but he trusted Detective Tanner's judgement. Though he was far more senior to her, he knew Detective Tanner had unparalleled instincts when it came to investigations, so he would roll with this breach of protocol. He looked at her.

"We can start with the Morton kid."

As Detective Arrington opened the door to the interrogation room, Fin looked up and saw his father standing behind him. His eyes welled up. He had never been so happy to see Big Fin. When the door opened, Rose rushed in and hugged Fin. With his free hand, he wrapped his arm around her waist and buried his face in her stomach. Big Fin rushed to the other side and placed his hand on his shoulder, then bent down and kissed the crown of his head. Detective Tanner waited until Big Fin looked up at her.

"We'll give you a minute."

226

fin

three rooms

Stacks sat in Interrogation Room One. When he taxed Badu the day he met Fin, he took all of Badu's money and only gave him half of the guns. When he returned to Coop however, he gave him half the guns back and only half the money. He took some of that score and paid Gray, Lil' Rick, and Hoop. The rest he gave to the one person he knew he could trust with holding it, Shayla. He told her that money was to be used for one of three things; savings to move Shayla, Dee and he out of Norfolk, money for a lawyer, or to take care of Dee should something happen to him. In the following months, he added to that pot of money, had secretly placed a lawyer on retainer, and was making plans to disappear once and for all. Though he had been detained by the police before, he had never been charged with anything. This is the first time he had been in a room such as this. Stacks wasn't going to answer a single question about what happened in his home that morning without his lawyer present. His plan would work as long as everyone stuck to the story. When the detectives entered, he slouched down in his seat and began feigning sucking something out of his teeth.

"Afternoon, Mr. Morton. My name is Detective Tanner, this is Detective Arrington. We need to ask you a few questions."

"Lawyer."

Detective Tanner and her partner sat down.

"Your lawyer will be here soon enough, I'm sure. You're almost eighteen correct? Couple of weeks from what I understand."

"Lawyer."

"Let me ask you this then, Mr. Lawyer...I mean Mr. Morton. Why was Mr. Bell in the Brevoit Projects this morning?"

"Law. Yer."

fin

three rooms

Detective Arrington didn't care for Stacks. He didn't care for any of the Mortons. He had been waiting for years to get something on one of them. He wanted Coop. He wanted Big Tony. He really wanted the notoriously violent and intimidating Shan. He'd settle for Stacks.

"How'd he get the bruises? You beat him?"

That question got Stacks attention. He looked up at them, leaned in and spoke.

"Why don't you ask his daddy?"

While this peaked the detectives' interest, the rumors of Andrew Bell's violent home behavior weren't foreign to the detectives. They both looked at each other with a look of disgust, disgust that Andrew Bell was ever associated with good police. Detective Tanner was looking for a way in, an angle she could leverage into a hole in whatever story she would receive from Stacks, Gray, Fin and Justin. She just got her first clue.

"You mean Andrew Bell, Justin's father? You're saying Mr. Bell did that to Justin?"

"Short, drunk, white mafucka? Yeah. He one of y'all ain't he?"

More than the Mortons, Detective Arrington hated Andrew Bell.

"He ain't no cop!"

Now it was Stacks probing, looking for a way to rattle the detectives and get them looking in one direction instead of the one they should be looking.

"Well, no one in my house did that. Dude showed up that way."

fin

three rooms

"Let's get back to that, why did he come to the Brevoit Homes? Officeerrrr..."

Detective Tanner stalled as she looked at the preliminary police report and notes from the Dispatch Sergeant that monitored all of the radio traffic.

"...Delaine. Officer Delaine said he saw Justin Bell running into the projects. He also states that he saw a vehicle, matching your registered vehicle, the night previous outside of Pullman's. Wanna tell us about that?"

"Lawyer."

"Of course, Mr. Morton. One last question, who shot your father?"

Stacks looked away from the detectives when the question was posed. Detective Tanner saw interrogations like a boxing match. She would often throw off-topic, unexpected questions at a suspect only to hit them with a real pertinent one to gauge their reaction. Soft jabs, as she saw them. One of her jabs just landed. *Got him.* Before any further questioning could happen, the phone in the room rang. Detective Arrington answered it. Detective Tanner kept her eyes on Stacks. The nature of Coop's death was a soft spot she planned to exploit. She figured the phone call was about his lawyer. She would use this break in the questioning to watch Stacks. She watched his brow wrinkle, his refusal to make eye contact. She could feel the vibrations of his leg bouncing a bit underneath the table. When he finally glanced over, he composed himself. She smirked. *Too late, Mr. Lawyer. Your father's death is a soft spot. I'll start there with your friend, Mr. Finley.* When Detective Arrington returned to the table, he leaned into Detective Tanner and whispered in her ear, confirming her suspicion about the nature of the phone call. Her smirk grew to a full-on smile.

fin

three rooms

"Seems that lawyer is here, Mr. Morton. Sure you don't wanna answer my last question?"

Stacks smiled.

"Sounds like another question to me."

"Not to worry, there will be more."

She closed her file and readied herself to head down the hall, to interrogate Fin. Detectives Tanner and Arrington entered the hallway and started towards Interrogation Room Three. When they were outside of Interrogation Room Two, in between Stacks and Fin and outside of their earshot, Detective Arrington stopped Detective Tanner.

"What are you doing, Patricia?"

"Fishing."

"You know anything that Morton kid says is inadmissible."

"I never thought he would tell me anything. But the kid's father was just killed, his brother too. See his reaction when I asked about it?"

"Yeah, I saw."

"Had we killed him, he would've screamed to all holy hell and blamed us. Hell, even if we didn't do it, the smart play would've been to blame our guys. Why didn't he? Now I am gonna ask this Finley kid the same question. If he looks away, doesn't try assigning blame, then we know we are on to something."

Detective Arrington didn't see it in that context until it was pointed out to him. *Damn, she is too damn smart! Glad she ain't my wife!* He nodded then began walking. Detective Tanner hated when everyone questioned her motives and reasoning. Her track record of

fin

three rooms

successful case closures should have garnered her the benefit of the doubt, yet she always felt there was someone ready to pull the rug out from underneath her. She felt that is why Detective Arrington was assigned as her partner. To Detective Tanner, the department viewed him not as her partner but as her handler. When the detectives entered Fin's room, the Finleys all looked up in unison. She decided to seize on this moment of unease the Finley's were experiencing.

"Sorry to keep you waiting. Mr. and Mrs. Finley, you seem like good people, and from everything I can tell about James here, he seems like a good kid. I hope you're willing to work with me, to allow James help me figure out who killed Cooper Morton."

Detective Tanner watched as Fin shifted in his seat and dropped his head. She lowered her head over the table to try and establish eye contact with Fin.

"James, I am Detective Tanner. Do you know something about who killed Cooper Morton?"

"I think we should wait for our lawyer to arrive. I have already called one," responded Big Fin.

"I understand and you're only doing what's best for James. Its just - "

Fin looked up at Detective Tanner's intentional pause.

"See, I have been at this a long time, James. I have seen good kids like you get used by more street savvy guys like Mr. Morton, or what is he called on the street, Tim?"

"Stacker, I think."

"Stacks," Fin corrected.

"That's it, Stacks. You have a nickname?"

fin

three rooms

"Fin."

"Ok, Fin. See I don't want someone like Stacks to take advantage of you and leave you holding the blame for this. We see it all the time."

"Blame for what?"

"I don't think you had anything to do with the guns in the home. I just want to know who killed Cooper Morton. Do you know what Mr. Morton, or Coop as he was known, do you know what he did? Who he was?"

Fin shook his head no.

"He is...well he *was* one of the largest traffickers of illegal guns in the state. The whole family was and have been for decades. Was this a deal gone bad? Who killed Coop and his son? What was his name, Tim?"

"Shan," answered Fin.

"See, you seem to know a lot about these people."

Detective Tanner looked at Big Fin and Rose. Rose looked over at Big Fin in absolute shock. *Illegal guns???* She could tell by the way Big Fin didn't budge that that information wasn't new to him. Rose felt betrayed. *You knew about this? I don't know either of you, do I?* She needed to know Detective Tanner's endgame.

"What do you want from our son?"

"Well, Mrs. Finley, we would like it if Fin helped as to who shot Coop. And who shot Shan for that matter. Think you can do that?"

Fin nodded. Detective Arrington leaned back in his chair, folded his arms and smirked. He always marveled how Tanner could do that, completely disarm a person with relative ease.

232

three rooms

"Tell me Fin, who shot Coop?"

Fin lowered his head.

"How about this; let's start from the beginning. Why did you go over to the Brevoit Homes?"

"I was looking for Stacks."

"Why?"

"I was mad."

"About what?"

Big Fin looked down at his son. "Tell the truth, son."

There was a pause, Fin looked at his father, then lowered his head and sighed.

"I was mad about Justin. We had to take him back."

"We? Take him back where?"

"Justin stayed with us last night, Detective," interjected Rose. "Fin brought him home late last night and he was badly beaten. Fin told us his father beats him. We know it was wrong, but we couldn't send him back there. The child had wondered the streets the night before after running away from home."

"And that made you mad, Fin? Taking him back home?"

Fin nodded.

Big Fin scolded him. "Use your words, Fin."

"Yes."

"Why run to Mr. Morton afterwards?"

fin

three rooms

"We were all hanging out the day before, then Stacks needed to drop us off."

"Is that when you were hanging outside of Pullman's?"

Fin looked up in shock then quickly looked down. *So, you were all at Pullman's. Interesting. But today started with the Bell kid arriving in the Brevoit Homes. But why would a kid like Morton hang out with Bell? Or even this boy for that matter?* The way Detective Tanner figured it, the only link between Stacks and Justin, was Fin. She took a shot in the dark about Fin being in the car the night before. Fin's reaction led her to believe she was right. Now she needed to figure out why and what caused the standoff that followed.

"Were you and Mr. Morton looking for his father?"

"WE DIDN'T DO NOTHIN' WRONG!"

Rose was embarrassed by Fin's outburst. "JAMES FINLEY!"

"It's ok, Mrs. Finley. No one said you did anything wrong, Fin. We just need to understand why Justin came to the Brevoit Homes. So, you were there with Mr. Morton this morning?"

"Yes."

"When did Mr. Bell show up?"

"Right when I was leaving."

"How did he look?"

"Pretty bad."

"Had he been there before?"

"I don't think so."

fin

three rooms

"So why did he run into the apartment? Officers Delaine and Christensen say that as they approached and told you all to halt, Mr. Bell ran into the apartment, followed by Mr. Morton who pulled you in."

"He was scared."

"Scared of what? The police?"

"Yeah. His daddy was one of y'all. He said his daddy is always beating on him and his mom. Said every time the police were called, nothing happened. He thought they were trying to take him back over there."

"I see."

Detective Tanner *hated* the Blue Wall mantra, especially when it is applied to a lowlife, degenerate, alcoholic, sociopath like Andrew Bell.

"Tell me, what did you see when you entered the Morton's home?"

"Nothing. Stacks pulled me into his little brother's room."

Fin saw what she was trying to do, to get him to admit he saw something illegal. Once again, he could hear Big Tony screaming "THEM WAS MY GUNS!" Fin knew the detective couldn't prove what he did or didn't see. He wasn't saying anything about guns or shooting anyone.

"So, you saw nothing? Even though we found two crates of automatic weapons, and a literal armory throughout the house, you saw nothing?"

fin

three rooms

"I was scared and confused. Stacks wanted me to watch Dee. He was scared for his little brother. So, Dee, Justin and I sat in his room. Then everything went crazy."

"Did you try and escape?"

"There are bars on the windows."

"Did you call for help?"

Big Fin had enough. "Hold on now, Detective. Are you trying to say my son did something wrong here? Because we can end this right now!"

Whenever she spoke to Big Fin and Rose, her eyes remained on Fin.

"Mr. Finley, I am just trying to find out what happened. So, you didn't try and escape. When did the shooting start?"

"I don't know. We was in there a long time. I heard the cops calling, the people outside, we were in the room with the door closed. We heard arguing, then I heard three shots. Next thing I know Shan stumbled in bleeding. Mr. Coop was on the floor, then Stacks ran into make sure Dee was safe."

He looked up at Detective Tanner. "Then y'all came in with the gas, shooting."

"Where was Justin during all of this?"

"We were on the floor, Ma'am."

"I think that's enough, Detective," demanded Big Fin. "Anything else you will need to ask when our lawyer is here!"

"I understand, Mr. Finley. I think we have enough for now."

236

fin

three rooms

Detective Tanner stood and looked down at Fin. She knew he wasn't telling her the truth. Up until that point, everything told her he was in the wrong place, at the wrong time, and now is looking to protect his friend. She didn't want to treat him like a criminal. She wanted to give him the benefit of the doubt, however Fin was leaving her little room to do otherwise. Detectives Tanner and Arrington exited the interrogation room and were met by Chief Warren in the hallway. By the look on his face, they could tell he had something to tell them.

"Andrew Bell is here."

"Where?" asked Detective Tanner.

"I stashed him in the compliance office. He reeks, been drunk since God knows when. Funny thing though. He's pretty beat up too."

That last tidbit of information intrigued both detectives causing them to look at each other.

"The kid's mother ever show?" asked Detective Arrington.

"She's in my office with the kid. You get anything outta these two?"

"The Morton kid lawyered up quick. Wasn't giving us anything other than Drew beat his kid pretty bad," answered Detective Arrington.

"What about the Finley boy? His father is a Master Chief for a three-star Admiral, ya' know?"

"You are just full of surprises today, aren't you Chief?" a sarcastic Detective Tanner replied. "The Finley boy knows something. Too scared to talk. Makes sense now why the father wanted to cut that short, seeing who he is and all."

fin

three rooms

"You talk to Little yet?"

"Darius Little aka Gray Boy. No priors, still got him in the tank. He is street like Morton, he ain't gonna talk. Think Finley and Bell are the ones who may crack, give us some leverage."

"Give Andrew's kid a run. I gotta go get ready for a press conference," the Chief said before he made his way down the hall.

"Why are you doing a press conference already? We barely even talked to them!"

"Wasn't my call. It's an election year, Detective. Have to show the good voters of Norfolk that our lovely Mayor has a grip on the situation. Deputy Ops is already in the briefing room which means *I'm* in the briefing room."

Chief Warren adjusted the combination cover on his head. "Now, how do I look?"

"Like a man that's about to sling some bullshit!" quipped Detective Arrington.

"Well, get me something to spray perfume on that shit. Talk to Bell's kid and wife. Oh yeah! The wife, Elaine, she's pretty banged up too."

Detective Tanner had never met Andrew Bell. He was fired before she transferred into the Valebrook station. She was never one for Pullman's either. It wasn't exactly a Black or woman friendly establishment regardless of the shield. Her bar of choice was The Decatur Lounge, not too far from the Navy piers. Even there, Andrew Bell's name rang out though. Needless to say, she wasn't a fan. They walked through the precinct floor, which was still buzzing from the morning's events. One of the officers from the scene saw them leave the hallway stemming from the interrogation room.

fin

three rooms

"Here y'all got one of them Morton fucks in holding!"

The detectives ignored them. While they had different styles of approach to cracking a case, spilling unnecessary information wasn't something either would readily do. They arrived outside Chief Warren's door and saw Justin and Elaine through the partially opened slats of the blinds. Elaine's arm was wrapped around him. Detective Arrington shook his head and rolled his eyes at the sight of the bruises on Elaine and Justin. He looked over his shoulder towards the compliance office where Andrew was being held. *I have half a mind to beat that fucker to a pulp!* The ever-observant Detective Tanner saw her partner's growing anger.

"Not now, Tim. Bell will get his. Let's focus on getting the Chief some answers."

"Perfume. Got it."

She nudged him with her elbow. He nodded.

"I'll handle the questioning, ok?"

"You always do, partner."

They entered the office. Elaine turned in her chair to see the detectives. Justin's head remained down. His arms were folded across his knee, his forehead on his forearms.

"Good afternoon, Mrs. Bell. My name is Detective Tanner, and this is my partner, Detective Arrington."

"Hello."

The Detectives looked at Elaine for a moment, taking in her frail, waif-like frame. Her eyes were sunken in and she looked older than her years. She was slurring her words. Life had been hard on her.

"You must be Justin, right?"

239

fin

three rooms

"Yes, Ma'am."

"Hi, Justin. Do you mind if we ask you a few questions?"

Justin nodded his head while it remained on his forearms.

"Can you look at me? Please?"

Justin slowly raised his head. The detectives tried their hardest to not react to the sight of Justin's face, riddled with bruises. The image, in conjunction with Elaine's bruises, were a bit too much. Detective Tanner walked in front of Justin and leaned against the desk.

"I'm sorry this happened to you, Justin. I want to help you."

The look Justin gave to the detectives showed his complete lack of trust in the police. Detective Tanner knew she couldn't play the same cat and mouse game she had with Fin and Stacks. This one needed to be handled delicately.

"Justin, walk me through this morning. What happened after the Finleys dropped you off?"

Justin remained silent and lowered his head back down to his knees. Detective Tanner dropped into a crouched position. She stared at Justin's arms, dotted with bruises, his face was so beaten and swollen, she could hardly fight back tears. His shirt fell on his body in a way that it revealed how malnourished he was. Detective Arrington was just as disturbed, his anger rising the more he looked at Justin and Elaine.

"Justin, can you look at me?"

Justin's head remained at rest, but he tilted his head up slightly, allowing his eyes to peek over his forearms.

fin

three rooms

"Justin, I can only imagine the hell you have been through today. Your friend told me you don't trust the police. From what we hear, we have given you zero reason to trust us."

Justin's eyes fell again. Detective Tanner gently placed her hand on his back.

"Justin, please look at me."

He raised his head slightly off of his arms. She placed her left index finger under his chin, lifting his head up. With her right hand, she grabbed his.

"I'm not those cops. Neither is my partner. We don't turn a blind eye to shit like this."

"Goddamn right!" affirmed Detective Arrington.

"So, when *we* say you can trust us with the truth, you can trust us. Okay?"

Justin nodded and wiped tears from his eyes.

"Now, what happened when the Finleys dropped you off?"

Justin began to tell them the events of the morning in vivid detail. Detective Arrington and Tanner listened in horror. Elaine dropped her head in shame, crying as Justin spoke. They asked Justin about two nights prior to that morning, the night that caused him to spend last night with the Finleys. They found out about Justin, Stacks and Fin all hanging out near Pullman's. They realized that Justin was looking for Fin the morning of the Brevoit Standoff, and when he didn't find him at home, he ran to Stacks. Detectives Tanner and Arrington tried to bottle up their rage as they listened, Detective Tanner often having to look away, her head up attempting to defy gravity pulling her tears down. As Justin detailed the beatings, she could see the corresponding bruise that proved it. Detective Arrington couldn't take

fin

three rooms

another word. He stormed out of the office, slamming the door behind him. The action startled both Justin and Elaine.

"Sorry about that, like I said, we don't like to hear about these types of things. Thank you for sharing that with me, Justin. You're a very brave young man. Justin, I need you to be a little braver for me. What happened in the Morton's home? Did you see anything strange?"

Justin shook his head, lowering it as he did.

"You're doing great, Justin. Did you see anyone shooting?"

Justin knew Shan fired the first shots at the cops. He knew Stacks killed Coop. It was his killing of Shan that ate at him. Like Fin before him, Justin heard a voice too; Stacks'.

"...they shot each other."

"I didn't see anything, I just heard it. They was yelling, Stacks' little brother was crying, I was scared. Fin looked after us in the room."

"Then what, Justin?"

"Then - BANG! BANG! BANG!"

"From inside the house?"

"I think so."

"Then what happened next?"

"The guy in the white t-shirt came in the room. He was bleeding."

"You're referring to Shannon Morton?"

"Yeah, I guess. I didn't know his name."

fin

three rooms

"So, who shot Cooper Morton, Shannon and Stacks' father?"

"I don't know. I just saw the other guy bleeding and he came at me."

"Is that how that blood got on your shirt and hands?"

Justin hadn't really noticed it until that moment. He had been in shock, the early stages of PTSD were setting in. His hands and shirt were covered in blood splatter.

"Umm..."

"Justin, you've been doing great until now. I need you to tell me the truth. How did that blood get on your hands and shirt?"

"I...I...I didn't do...."

The loud commotion of furniture moving, scraping across the linoleum floor, and screams interrupted the interview. Detective Tanner, Elaine and Justin all looked up through the half open blinds of the window to the main floor of the precinct and saw numerous officers running towards an office. Detective Tanner knew what it was instantly. *Fuck!*

"Stay here!"

She darted to the compliance office. Detective Arrington was in full throat. He had locked the door and was giving Andrew Bell a beating like he had never had, but the one he deserved. Andrew screamed for mercy, begging officers outside of the room for help. He screamed he was sorry and would never touch Elaine or Justin again. Chief Warren ran from the briefing room, still in his dress uniform. He saw what was unfolding, grabbed a fire extinguisher off of the wall and slammed down on the doorknob to the office until it broke. Once the door opened, three officers ran in and restrained Detective Arrington.

fin

three rooms

His normally pale, white face was flushed with blood, he was spitting as he screamed at him.

"YOU AIN'T NO FUCKING COP! YOU AIN'T NEVER BEEN ONE OF US YA' PIECE OF SHIT!"

The officers struggled to control Detective Arrington. Detective Tanner rushed over to Andrew, though barely conscious he still managed to be indignant even after such a beating.

"FUCK YOU, TIM! I'M GONNA SUE YOUR FUCKING ASS OFF! YOU GONNA OWE ME YOUR WHOLE DAMN PENSION WHEN I'M DONE WITH YA'!"

Blood sprayed from Andrew's mouth as he shouted. Detective Tanner had had enough.

"ANDREW BELL, YOU ARE UNDER ARREST FOR ASSAULT OF A MINOR, RECKLESS ENDANGERMENT OF A MINOR, DOMESTIC ASSAULT AND ANY FUCKING THING ELSE I CAN THINK OF YOU PIECE OF SHIT!" as she flipped him over and slapped cuffs on him.

"What are you doing, Tanner?!??!" demanded Chief Warren.

"What should have been done years ago! Getting this asshole off the street!"

chapter fourteen

my brother's keeper

Chief Warren sent Detectives Tanner and Arrington into Captain MacCollough's office, his second in command.

"GET IN THERE!"

They both looked at each other and walked over to the office. Detective Tanner was pissed, but she was also worried about Elaine and Justin. Detective Arrington felt no regrets. *Yell all you want, I'd do that shit again!* Chief Warren watched his detectives enter then turned to the floor.

"Get this cleaned up!"

He walked over to the office and slammed the door shut. Detectives Tanner and Arrington were already seated.

"WHAT IN THE ENTIRE FUCK WAS THAT?!"

fin

my brother's keeper

"It's on me, Sir. I lost my cool. But, you see what he did to his kid?!"

"Yeah, I saw it. We *all* did! Andrew Bell was born a piece of shit, will always be a piece of shit and will die a dried up, piece of shit, and now thanks to *you*, the motherfucker is gonna have a grievance against us! Of *all* days, when I need you to give me something, I can feed up line on this Brevoit fiasco, you go and beat him into a bloody mess!"

Detective Tanner tried to reason. "Chief, he was already pretty banged up when he got here."

"You think that shit is gonna play out like that? You think the department needs the moral shit stain that is Andrew Bell to rear its ugly, fucking head??!?! DO YOU?!?!!"

The detectives fell silent. They knew they needed to let the Chief blow off this steam then they could give him what they had.

"At least tell me you got some new info on this shooting. Something more than the bowl of dog-shit clichés I just gave the media!"

Detective Tanner looked at her partner, her eyes raised, gave a shake of her head then proceeded to read from her notes. She detailed the excessive beatings Andrew gave Justin. That it was one such beating this morning that prompted Justin to go to the Brevoit Homes looking for Stacks and Fin. She even explained that neither Fin nor Justin admit to seeing who shot Coop or Shan.

"So, what you're telling me is you got nothing!"

"Think the Morton kid has something, but he lawyered up before I could work him."

246

fin

my brother's keeper

Chief Warren shook his head. He was counting on Tanner to bring him something, anything he could dangle in front of the upper brass to appease their need for a deflective sound bite. Prior to Detective Arrington's beating of Andrew, the Chief was told that preliminary findings from the scene were coming in.

"Well, give the Morton kid another go, *with* his lawyer this time. This might help; initial gun residue swabs on the deceased's hands are positive for Shannon Morton. They are negative for Cooper Morton."

Detectives Tanner and Arrington looked at each other, surprised by what they had just heard. They both knew there were multiple shots fired in the home, both Fin and Justin had admitted as much. The question was who fired them. They made their way back down to the interrogation room that held Stacks. They looked into the window and saw Stacks in conference with his lawyer. They knocked on the door then entered. Detective Arrington recognized Stacks' lawyer. He beat him on a drug possession case a few years ago, when Detective Arrington had the guy dead to rights. *This fucking asshole again.*

"Counselor."

"Detective Arrington. Good to see you again."

"Still representing shitbags, I see."

"You know this man, Tim?"

"Norman Taylor. Beat me on the Diaz case. Bullshit technicality."

Mr. Taylor smiled. Stacks gave Detective Arrington a triumphant glance.

my brother's keeper

"I'll be representing Mr. Morton and Mr. Little. What are the charges against my clients?"

Detective Tanner decided to seize control of the conversation.

"Right now, nothing, Mr. Taylor. We are merely having a conversation with the young man. On that note, Mr. Morton, if you're not yet eighteen, how did you legally retain counsel so fast? You have no legal guardian, with your father and brother deceased and uncle in custody."

"Let's not play games, Detective. My client is thirteen days away from being considered an adult. Child Services wouldn't even have time to print the forms to take him in before the that whole charade would be a moot point. Now, we can stall this for thirteen days if you like, hell I prefer it. Or you can tell us what you want."

"I wanna know who shot your father? Who shot your brother? Who killed them, Mr. Morton? According to your friends, they were in the room with the door closed and didn't see a thing. Let me guess, you were in the broom closet and didn't see anything either?"

"The *fuck* is a broom closet?" asked Stacks before bursting into laughter.

His lawyer shot him a glance that told him to pipe down. Stacks looked at his lawyer, his eyes asking if he could talk. Norman nodded.

"I don't know who shot who. I was in the living room with Gray and Uncle Tony. I ain't see shit! Maybe y'all shot 'em!"

"Well no, you see, we know that three shots rang out before the police opened fire. Hell, all of Norfolk knows that. You were on the news today, Mr. Morton! What we don't know is who shot those first three shots. Walk me through what happened."

my brother's keeper

"Look, all I know is I was chillin' outside with Gray, my man Fin came up, then the white boy all beat the fuck up, then the cops showed up! Shit was cool until they got there."

"Yeah, especially with all those guns," said Detective Arrington.

"Yes, let's talk about the guns, Mr. Morton. Whose guns were they? Your father's? Shan's maybe?"

"I don't know shit about no guns!"

"Oh, come on, Mr. Morton. We saw the house. There were guns in every nook and cranny of that house. You're telling us we won't find your prints on any of them?"

"The guns were his father's. My client is a juvenile, with no priors and was just present for the horrific deaths of his father and brother. Unless you have some pretty strong evidence to the contrary that proves my client committed a crime, I think we are done here."

Stacks sat back in his chair and smiled at both detectives. Detectives Tanner and Arrington knew they had nothing on Stacks, at least not yet. Detective Tanner also knew that they all were hiding something.

"Well, I'll let him stew in holding for a bit while we await the final report from the scene. Pretty sure some of that strong evidence will turn up by then."

Detective Tanner motioned to her partner for him to cuff Stacks. Detective Arrington got up, unlocked the cuff bonding Stacks to the table, then instructed him to stand. Mr. Taylor protested and instructed Stacks that him and Gray were to remain calm and say nothing, words he didn't have to utter. Detective Tanner unlocked the door, stepped into the hallway and held the door for Detective

Arrington to bring Stacks and lead him back to the holding cell with Gray. As they made it to the threshold of the door, they paused. Another officer was leading Andrew down the hall in cuffs.   When Stacks saw him, he felt a sense of accomplishment, his retribution was just validated. He smiled at Andrew. Not the sarcastic grin he was giving the detectives, a smile of true happiness. Andrew looked up and saw Stacks, then turned his head forward, keeping it high out of some false sense of pride. Detective Tanner noticed the exchange.

"Friend of yours?"

"Never seen that dude before in my life."

Another officer opened Interrogation Room Three, two doors down, where Big Fin, Rose and Fin were held. Detective Arrington began walking Stacks back to holding, away from the Finleys, when Big Fin called out to him.

"Christopher!"

Detective Arrington paused, halting Stacks. Big Fin looked at Detective Tanner as he approached Stacks.

"Can I have a word with the boy?"

Detective Tanner looked at her partner, then at Big Fin and nodded. Big Fin walked to Stacks, stopping just short of him to allow him to turn around. Big Fin saw Coop's eyes staring back at him.

"I'm sorry about your father."

"I'm not. Never gave a fuck about us."

"That's not true. I knew him, met you when you were just a baby. He loved you."

my brother's keeper

"Mr. Finley, the Coop you knew and the Coop I knew were two different people. Maybe your Coop gave a fuck. Wish I could have met him."

The words hurt both men as soon as they left Stacks' mouth. As they stared at each other, Big Fin saw years of pain and neglect in Stacks' eyes, the same that he used to see in Coop's. It was part of the reason he walked away from Coop all those years ago. Those eyes reflected his own pain growing up, an absent father, whether physically there as Coop's father was in his, as Coop was in Stacks', or a memory, a dream like Big Fin's father was to him. A void that offered no love and guidance, no protection, no lessons of manhood. A void that allowed the street to swallow them all whole.

"My daddy said he knew you. Said you made him a promise. That true?"

"Yes, yes, it is."

"Then be a better man than he was. Keep your word. Be a man and keep your word."

"Son, ain't much I can do for you?"

"Not me. Dee. Don't let him get caught in the system. He deserves a better life than what my father gave us."

"Dee?"

"His baby brother, Dad."

Big Fin looked over his shoulder at Fin, before returning his eyes to Stacks. He took a deep, long breath. He knew Stacks was right. He didn't know how he would do it, but he was going to fight to get Dee. His heart already ached for one boy he had sent back into a horrible situation this morning, a move he stood there in that moment

251

and regretted. *If I would have kept him with us, none of this shit would have happened.* Now he had a chance to save another little lost boy.

"I'll do everything I can. I promise."

Stacks nodded then looked over Big Fin's shoulder at Fin. The two boys locked eyes for what seemed an eternity, their eyes having a conversation that need not be said. Fin nodded at Stacks. Stacks nodded back then turned to walk away. Fin wanted to cry, rage cry. He knew all of them were put in a horrific situation. He too began regretting choices he made. Big Fin watched Stacks walk away and around the corner. He took another deep breath then turned to Detective Tanner.

"Where is the boy?"

"Mr. Finley, I really don't think you......"

"WHERE...is the boy?"

Detective Tanner relented. "Child services."

Big Fin walked over to Fin and Rose, placed his arm around his son, and led them out of the station. Detective Tanner went to find Chief Warren. Chief Warren sat at his desk, reading the preliminary findings from the Brevoit Standoff, as the press had dubbed it.

"Chief, they know something."

Chief Warren didn't look up at Detective Tanner, he kept thumbing through the preliminary report.

"And what do you think they know?"

"Finley and Bell claim they didn't see anything, only Shannon Morton stumbling in shot. The Morton kid says they shot each other."

"But you don't believe them."

my brother's keeper

"They're hiding something. Is that the preliminary report?"

"It is."

Detective Tanner couldn't understand why the Chief was being so nonchalant, almost evasive.

"Can I see it?"

Chief Warren closed the file, placed it on his desk, then folded his hands placing them on top of the file. He looked at his detective, his best! When he assigned her to the case, he did so knowing she would get answers quickly, answers he could give the top brass to show they had a grip on the investigation. It wasn't until he saw Fin's name, James Finley, that he knew he was premature in assigning Detective Tanner. He didn't need quick answers. He needed a slow burn. He needed this to drag out as long as possible. He remembered the name, James Finley, not for Fin, but for Big Fin. He took special care to avoid being seen by Big Fin. The two had history, a history that if Detective Tanner continued to dig up would be bad. Bad for himself and for some of the very people that were demanding answers. Back when Big Fin and then Detective Warren first met, Big Fin was just another local Sailor getting into trouble. That trouble involved Cooper Morton. Now, he was Command Master Chief James Finley, the senior Enlisted leader for a three-star Admiral. Now, Big Fin had enough political clout to make any investigation into his son, an ugly, drawn out affair, an investigation that would lead to questions about Coop, Big Tony, and the prison death of D-Ray, Gray Boy's father. It would lead to scandal.

"What do you really have, Detective?"

Detective Tanner was thrown for a loop by the Chief's tone. *Why is he making it seem like I didn't do my job? Or is he hiding something?* Her curiosity grew in lock step with her dissolving trust of her Chief.

fin

my brother's keeper

"What am I missing?"

Chief Warren leaned back in his chair. His hands gripped the armrests. He let out a long, exasperated breath. *How do I tell this woman to let this go? She gets a case and it's like a dog trying to find a bone. She ain't gonna like this.* Detective Tanner became visibly frustrated.

"I have four kids, three that I have spoken to, that are hiding what really happened. I am going to get the ballistics reports, dust those boys' for gun powder residue, canvas…"

"What you're gonna do is accept that in one day, we got two of the biggest and longest standing traffickers of illegal guns off the board."

"But…."

"*And* we finally got enough evidence to lock up that piece of shit Andrew Bell that disgraced this department! This very station you're sitting in. And we did it without a police officer killing a citizen, a poor, Black citizen."

Detective Tanner could not believe what she was hearing. She had half a mind to take this to Internal Affairs. *Why is he stonewalling me? What was in that preliminary report from the scene? What is he hiding?*

"Chief, I am trying to wrap my head around this. Are you telling me to write this up as a double homicide? A domestic dispute gone wrong?"

"I am telling you that you have inconclusive evidence and a lack of motive to go hard at four teenage boys for possible murder wraps on two known criminals. I'm telling you that you have a child now in the system that will need counseling for years to come. You

my brother's keeper

wanna be the one they label monster for making him relive it? Because that's what they'll do. I am telling you that you have a man in custody willing to cop to possession of all the guns on scene. *If* ballistics comes back and you can prove one of those boys shot at a cop, take it. Let the media speculate about who killed Cooper Morton. From what you're telling me, if the shots were fired prior to our breach, we didn't kill Cooper or his son. Let it play the way it is."

Detective Tanner stood up, completely disillusioned by what she was hearing, by what was happening. She didn't want to drag Fin or Justin into the web of criminality the Morton family weaved. She also didn't like letting a murderer walk free. She didn't know who shot either Coop or Shan. What she did know was that the stories she got had more holes than a sieve. She stormed out of Captain Warren's office, stormed to her desk, grabbed her keys and headed for the door. Detective Arrington entered into the squad room, having returned from holding.

"Where are you going, Tanner?"

"To get some air. It fucking stinks in here."

Later that evening, the day shift was already gone, and the night shift was out on patrol, Detective Tanner sat at her desk still upset about what she was being directed to do; to lie. Once again, her back was pressed firmly against the Blue Wall. She tried to type the lies they wanted her to, but her fingers were unwilling to cooperate, her subconscious telling her no, her pride telling her brain don't. Chief Warren had watched his detective through his office window throughout the day. He reached into his desk side drawer and retrieved a file. *Tried to keep this from you, Tanner. But you won't let this go.* He slowly got up, knowing that his next actions would more than likely break one of the best police officers he had ever seen. He walked out onto the squad room floor. Detective Tanner was leaning back in her chair, staring at her computer.

fin

my brother's keeper

"Detective."

She was furious. She couldn't even look at him, her respect for him and the shield he wore were all but gone.

"I know you don't like this, neither do I."

"Yeah, but you're willing to eat some of that shit you were slinging earlier. I ain't got the stomach for it."

"Then you'll never make Captain. Never make Chief. You're hellbent on always doing what's right but you never think about the fallout, who could get hurt."

"You think I give a fuck about dirty cops?"

Chief Warren held his tongue and looked down at her as she looked up at him, her eyes of betrayal piercing him. The file he had hoped he didn't have to share with her became heavy in his hands, as if the truth was weighing him down. He hoped she would try to find the silver lining in the situation. *Dog with a bone. She's got her teeth in this one. She ain't letting it go.* He took a deep breath, sighed then laid the file on her desk.

"What's this?"

"A little light reading, Detective," he said as he walked away. "Good night."

Detective Tanner looked at the brown file he placed on her desk. The white label on the tab was crisp and she could tell that this file wasn't kept in archive. The department no longer kept old case files in these types of folders. This was from someone's personal archive. She looked at the name on the file.

"Donald Raymond Little?"

fin

my brother's keeper

She sat back in disbelief once she realized the connection. *D-Ray? Gray Boy's father? What does this have to...* She opened the file and began to read. The file contained surveillance reports, D-Ray's arrest record, notes from police and District Attorney interviews, and the subsequent trial. Donald Little tried to implicate numerous police officers in a subversive scheme to supply confiscated weapons, surplus riot gear and protective equipment to Cooper Morton, and his father Ezekiel Morton before him, a plot that according to his testimony, went back for decades. She scanned down at some of the names.......two of them stuck out; Detective Carlton Warren, the now Chief of the Valebrook station, and the current Assistant Deputy of Tactical Operations, the then Detective Frank Tanner, her husband. Detective Tanner's hands began to tremble, her heart almost jumped out of her chest. *Frank?* Her anger and confusion turned to heartbreak. When this happened, she was just a patrol officer. Frank was her original partner and the two fell in love long before his promotion. After his promotion to Detective, they married and never served together again. She closed the file, locked it in her desk, grabbed her keys and stormed off towards the door. She needed to get home.

Just as Chief Warren predicted, the case played out as a domestic incident gone terribly wrong. The media released the final report which read that Coop and Shan shot each other in a fight, most likely triggered by the police's presence and the gun found in Coop's dead hand was matched to the three slugs that pierced the wall when Shan shot at Officers Delaine and Christensen. Big Tony pled guilty to multiple felony gun possession charges with intent to distribute. With two prior convictions on his ledger, he received a twenty-nine years to life sentence, eligible for parole in fifteen. Ballistics came back proving a gun with Gray's prints was used to fire at police. He received five years solely because he was a minor and their lawyer argued that both *my brother's keeper*

he and Stacks were influenced by Coop, Big Tony and Shan. He served seventeen months. Stacks received fifteen months of house arrest for possession of illegal firearms. Not for the crates of automatic weapons but for his personal stash of weapons in his room. At Shayla's suggestion, Mr. Norman convinced the judge to allow Stacks to serve his house arrest at the home of Everett and Denise Lawson, Shayla's parents. Because both Stacks and Gray were minors at the time of the crime, Mr. Norman was able to get their records sealed as juvenile offenders. Fin was treated as an innocent witness caught in the wrong place, at the wrong time, and no charges were brought against him.

It was the treatment of Justin, however, that drew the ire of Stacks. As the press was fed information about the standoff, Justin became the unwitting catalyst for the horrific events of the "Shootout at Brevoit", and its most sympathetic victim. The press jumped at the chance to rehash all of Andrew Bell's wrongdoings, his dismissal from the force and his abuse of Justin and Elaine. The outpouring of sympathy from citizens was sickening to Stacks. It wasn't that any of what the press said about Andrew or what Justin endured was false, it was that in all of the victims, they never mentioned the most innocent victim of them all, Dee.

Dee, the eight-year-old boy, that lived in a world where his last name meant he was a target, viewed as a problem before he woke up in the morning. Where simply being in public with his father could endanger his life. The little boy that was in the room when his drunken, violent, callous older brother was killed, and a mere three feet from where his power hungry, indifferent, cold-hearted father was killed. That hid under a bed, in a room with two strangers, in the midst of a gunfight. That little boy, the most innocent person in the home, was forgotten. He was never mentioned at all, as if he didn't exist. The mere thought of it moved Stacks to such uncontrollable anger and sadness he would bury his head into a pillow and scream. Luckily though, there was someone that knew the horror he endured, that didn't forget him. Someone finally kept a promise to protect him - Big Fin.

Leveraging his political connections in the Navy and with the help of a few community leaders, Big Fin and Rose got temporary custody of Dee. While Stacks was serving his house arrest, Fin would bring Dee over to Shayla's house every day after school. Stacks and Dee would talk about everything from homework, to Dee trying out for the local little league football team, cartoons, even a little girl Dee liked in his class. Sometimes, Dee would get really sad and tell Stacks he missed Coop. Stacks would scoop his little brother up, sit him on his lap, and relay some of the very few good moments he shared with Coop. Even though Coop was never a father to him, Shan or Mike, Stacks never disparaged Coop to Dee. He wanted the image of Coop to be far greater than the man himself.

The sad irony was, Stacks knew he was being a hypocrite. While he hated Coop and wanted to do better for Dee, Stacks began following in his father's footsteps. With Coop out of the picture, there was a void in the gun distribution business in Norfolk. Stacks knew where all the gun caches were, the secret stashes of cash Coop, Big Tony and Shan had, the connections to the importers and distributers, the secret deals made at gun shows and the less than scrupulous military members willing to smuggle top-notch, military grade weaponry for a price. With the help of Lil' Rick and Hoop, he kept the Morton name alive, becoming almost a mythical figure. Mr. Stacks, the invisible man pulling the strings. When his house arrest was up, he bought a small warehouse, miles out of the city, to serve as the Morton Organization base of operations. Business was always done in private, face to face meetings, and never around anyone they loved. Once Gray was released on parole, it wasn't long before the two built one of the most powerful, lucrative and secretive organizations in the city. Mr. Stacks was almost never seen and would only surface for the most important of clients, or to handle a problem in a way that only

fin

my brother's keeper

he and Gray could. To the outside world, he had left the business behind. He would spend most of his time with Shayla, Dee and her parents. The Lawsons eventually took over custody of Dee, providing him a loving and nurturing home. Dee and Shayla already had a strong bond before that fateful day at the Brevoit Homes. Shayla always said their relationship gave her the little brother she never had. When Shayla became pregnant, it only seemed right that Dee be close to Stacks, Shayla, his "big sister," and eventually, his nephew little Chris, Jr. Stacks and Shayla bought a house close to her parents, a three bedroom, just to make sure Dee had his own space.

Stacks' relationship with Fin stayed strong. Fin was like a brother to him. Justin however, he wanted nothing to do with. Stacks knew Fin and Justin still kept in contact with each other, since they were still in school at Eastwood. Fin tried to explain to Stacks that it wasn't his fault the way it all played out. He would share with him that that female detective would come around and check on Justin and Elaine. Every time Fin would bring up Justin, Stacks would snap.

"Bruh, I told you I don't wanna hear about that mafucka! *Fuck* him!"

Fin could never understand his animosity towards Justin, after all, the night before everything went to hell, Stacks tried to help Justin. Save for the last time they were all together in the police precinct, the three hadn't been in the same place together until after Fin and Justin graduated high school. That wasn't an occasion any of them wanted. It was after the death of Big Fin.

After Big Fin's sudden and tragic death, Stacks found he needed to check on Fin, be there for his brother the way Fin was there for Dee. Fin became despondent and depressed. He had dropped out of college, had given up on his computer programming dreams, and was working odd jobs here and there. It broke Stacks' heart to watch Fin give up on himself. He used to have dreams, goals. He wanted to

260

develop computer programs, teach kids in their very own Valebrook how to code. Now, he worked at Brown's Stop-N-Go, a convenience store close to the school he once studied at. Stacks decided that today was the day he was going to convince his brother to get on with his life. Stacks pulled up in front of Fin's grandparents' home early one morning. After Big Fin's death, Fin and Rose moved back in with Patrick and Odella. Rose couldn't handle being in the home she and Big Fin purchased any longer. Everything reminded her of her late husband. That morning, Fin was sitting on the porch, in his grandfather's wicker chair. Stacks climbed out of his dark blue, candy painted Cadillac DeVille. He smiled and opened his arms wide.

"What up, Socrates?"

"What up, Chris?"

"Think you cute, huh?"

He strolled up to the porch, climbed the steps and gave Fin a hard, loud handshake.

"What brings you around here, Mr. Stacks?"

"You fool! Came to see how my boy is doing!"

"I'm doing, I guess," Fin said as his voice trailed off.

"Better question, what are you doing?"

"Whatchu mean?"

"Fin, you know I got love for you, right?"

"Should I go get some tissues, man? Shayla got you watching Lifetime movies again?"

"Fuck you, Bruh!"

fin

my brother's keeper

The two old friends laughed loudly.

"Naaaa, I'm just saying. Look, you know how I feel about you and your family man. Y'all were there for me in a way that I can never repay. What you did for Dee…"

"Stop! You don't ever have to thank us for that. That was all my Dad though."

"I know, and that's why I wanted to rap with you. Your dad was a man, a *real* man. Good dude. You know, I went up to see my uncle not too long after he went in."

"How is Big Tony?"

"Living day to day, that's all you can do up in there."

Stacks paused as he gathered his thoughts. He wanted to tell Fin how he really felt but the words were running from him. Fin grew confused and curious.

"What, Bruh?

"Big Tony told me about your dad. Told me he used to run with my dad, him, even Gray's dad, D-Ray. Said he was one of the biggest, scariest, most vicious dudes he'd ever seen. Said the first time he and my dad met Big Fin, said there was a brawl and yo' daddy was knocking fools out left and right. He had never seen anything like it! Now you know how big that mafucka is, if *he* is impressed by yo' daddy, yo' daddy must've been THAT DUDE!"

Fin thought back to one of Big Fin and his last conversations before he died. Big Fin knew his time was limited and in that moment he confessed he had done some things in his life he regretted, including his time running with Coop, however he never told him any of what he was hearing in that moment.

262

fin

my brother's keeper

"What are you telling me?"

"I'm telling you your daddy knew when the life he was leading, the path he was going down was getting him nowhere. Yo' daddy wanted to be more, knew he could be more, so the man did somethin' about it. He walked away from all that shit my daddy and them was doing. Yo' daddy made something of himself."

Stacks scooted his chair closer to Fin.

"He *showed* you how to be a man. Why you sitting here, scared to live? Why you ain't doing something with the computer thing? And when you going back to school?"

Fin didn't have an answer, yet he knew Stacks was right. Big Fin would be disappointed in what he had been doing, which was nothing. He realized he owed it to the legacy of the best man he ever knew to snap out of it and live his life.

"You're right. But let me ask, what's your excuse?"

"Whatchu talking about?"

"Man, I used to always hear you talk about getting outta here, getting you and Dee away from Coop, from Shan and the life. You had a chance and you fucked it up. When you going to do what you were mad at Coop for not doing?"

"Hold up nah, Fin. I take damn good care of Dee. Fuck you talkin' about, Bruh?"

"Yeah, but what about little Chris? How are you setting a better example for him than Coop did for you?"

Stacks knew exactly what Fin was alluding to, he just didn't want to hear it. Of late, he had been wrestling with the thought that this life was what he was meant to do, that maybe the family business

263

fin

my brother's keeper

was a destiny he ran from but should learn to accept. With a few words, Fin had just challenged that rationalization.

"You gotta be the smartest person I know, but you too damn stupid to get out of this shit? You spend time with Dee and Chris, provide for them, but at what cost? You still endangering them man, just like Coop did you."

Stacks hated hearing it, and the spoonful of truth Fin just shoved down his throat tasted sour, but his soul needed it.

"You right, man. Here I am comin' over here to drop some knowledge on you and you schooling me!"

"Not everything that is faced can be changed."

Stacks was impressed. He looked over at Fin.

"But nothing can be changed until it is faced. You really just hit me with Baldwin, Bruh?"

Fin smiled. "Still got your book ya' know!"

"Yeah, I know. The Fire Next Time! Still my favorite."

"Make me a promise: I'll get off my ass and get back to school, if you get off your ass and get out of the life."

Stacks leaned back into the wicker chair he sat in. He shook his head as a loving grin crept on his face. He came here to help his brother find himself again, and in the process, his brother found him.

"Promise."

part three

cori

chapter fifteen

the bench

As Cori sat in her last tutoring session, she couldn't help but look at the clock. She only hoped her excitement and anxiousness didn't read on her face. She had picked up a few tutoring sessions to make extra cash as she desperately wanted to get out of her parents' house. Nicholas and Ann Porter were good people, and even better parents. After retiring from the Navy, the former Master Chief Nicholas Porter became the regional manager for a string of supermarkets. Ann ran her own accounting business from home after retiring from her twenty-five-year job as a bank manager. The Porters only had one child, their beloved Corianne Naomi. They doted over Cori, they made sure she was taught not only in school, but a more comprehensive curriculum at home that exposed her to literature, fine art, music, dance, and history from a Black American perspective. Cori was always the smartest student in class, was captain of the debate team, a star track athlete and a National Honor Society award winner. She had her choice of colleges around the country. Needless to say, both Nicholas and Ann Porter were disappointed when she decided to forego her numerous Ivy League scholarships and stay at home to attend Tidewater State University, a historically Black university.

While the Porters thought the credibility of a medical degree from an Ivy League school would set her up for life, Cori saw bringing a student of her stature to an HBCU would signal to the rest of America that HBCUs are just as prestigious as any other school. While her parents exposed her to Black American contributions to America, they didn't have her vision. To Cori, choosing Tidewater State over an Ivy League school was just as significant a contribution. She had big dreams for her life: graduate from Tidewater State University in three years, get accepted to Tidewater's medical program, run the 4x200 and 4x400 and qualify for the Olympic team, become a doctor, then open her own practice right here at home. She wanted to make a difference, wanted to be an example.

But for all her dreams, there was one she has had since she was thirteen; find the tall, cute, shy boy she only saw once all those years ago. Imagine her surprise when he walked into her College Algebra class. She almost couldn't believe it! She had not too long ago ended a two-year relationship with her high school sweetheart, Julius, after she caught him cheating. He had been calling and texting her non-stop ever since she walked into the local skating rink and saw him pressed up against Keya McCoy. She stood there, staring as tears rolled down her face. He didn't see her, but Keya did. When Keya noticed her there, she devilishly smiled then turned to Julius and kissed him deeply. Cori stormed out and hasn't talked to him since other than to tell him they were over. Right now, she was still on an emotional high from seeing Fin again after all these years. Her mind wasn't on this tutoring session. It was on Fin.

"So, I use the distributive principle then factor for f?"

Cori was so lost in her thoughts of Fin she nearly forgot the young lady was sitting across from her. She snapped out of her daydream and stared at the textbook that the young student slid in front of her.

"Oh! Ummmm, yes. I am so sorry, but can we end today's session a little early?"

The student was a bit taken aback but tried to sound in agreement. "Oh! Sure!! I think I got this!"

"Great. I am so sorry, but I just realized I am late for something."

Cori hurriedly stuffed her textbook and laptop into her bag. She really didn't care in that moment if her tutee understood it or not. It was four nineteen and it was at least a ten-minute dash across campus to go meet up with Fin. She slung her large leather tote that doubled as a purse, navigated through the circular tables of the study hall, and exited into the main hallway. The rubber soles of her shoes squeaked loudly against the tile flooring as she briskly walked towards the main entrance. Normally she would be more self-conscious about it, but today she didn't even care. She swung the main door to the library open and almost knocked another student clean out as she exited the building.

"Sorry!"

fin

the bench

Fin was anxiously waiting in the hallway at the exact spot Cori had left him, leaning against the wall, wondering if she would really show up. He had left his last class before the professor had finished speaking just so he could arrive ten minutes early. He tried to read the particle board covered with announcements, fliers for available apartments or people looking for roommates, anything to distract the anxiety that was causing his stomach to dance. If his stomach was dancing, his mind was in a frenzy of convulsions. *How does she know me??! God she is beautiful! I probably looked like a fool earlier. Calm down man......you got this. She remembered YOU!*

Just then he heard her voice and all of his anxiety washed away. There she was, standing gloriously in front of him, her smiling beaming like the early morning sun.

"Hello, Mr. Finley."

"Hey. You really came."

They stood there for a moment, admiring each other. Cori, finally getting her chance with the boy she saw all those years ago. Fin was stunned a woman as smart and as beautiful as her wanted to talk to him. He never had much luck when it came to dating. He was usually too tongue-tied to adequately express himself in the early stages of a relationship. When the relationship was plutonic however, he was a fountain of words. He felt awkward talking to women, engaging with women he was interested in. That was until this moment. This felt right to him and he didn't know why.

"I said I was coming, didn't I? I'm just glad you didn't run off like you did after Algebra!"

She was still a bit out of breath from her mad dash across campus.

fin

the bench

"Looks like you were the one running just now, not me."

Fin didn't know where that came from or how it would be received. Her sassy frown and reluctant smile put him at ease.

"Oh, we got jokes huh?"

They both chuckled.

"C'mon boy, let's go eat that lunch."

Cori grabbed his arm and turned Fin around, leading him where she wanted him to go. They walked in silence for a few moments. She would look up at him and smile, to which, he would smile and shy away.

"You have such a pretty smile you know. Just like you did all those years ago."

"Okay, you gotta tell me. How do you know me?"

Cori reveled in keeping him in suspense. She smiled wide like a kid with a secret. She finally decided to let him in on it.

"Wellllll. The first time I saw you, you were pretty sad. You were sitting in that chair, pouting. You looked up briefly and I thought you saw me. I was with my parents. We were new there and didn't know anybody yet and I thought 'He's cute. Maybe I can talk to him.'"

The suspense was driving him insane. "New where?!?! What chair?!?"

Cori didn't relent, she was going to tell her story *her* way and see if he could figure it out.

fin

the bench

"Then all of a sudden your eyes lit up. I thought it was because of me but it wasn't. It was because big head ol' Curt walked in."

Fin stopped in his tracks. Cori took a few steps more before he grabbed her gently on the arm and turned her around. She willingly allowed him to do so. He stared at her, his face frowning as he tried to remember. *She knows Curt??? That would mean she was in Japan!* She shyly smiled and dropped her head. Fin reached out, he placed his pointer and middle finger under her chin and lifted her beautiful face. Her smile slowly faded. *Please, Fin! Please remember me!*

"Japan!"

Her smile returned bigger and brighter than ever! *HE REMEBERED! HE DID SEE ME THAT DAY!* Her mind filled with excitement and relief.

"You were the cute girl at the going away BBQ! The new girl! The day of my dad's going away!! That was you???!"

She nodded and bit her lip, trying to contain her smile. Fin was still in shock that the pretty, little, chocolate girl he saw all those years ago was standing in front of him.

"I remember you!"

As Fin lowered his hand from her chin, Cori reached out for it. She clutched his hand affectionately, tenderly and stared for a second more before speaking.

"That day, I was so nervous. My dad had just gotten stationed there and I really didn't want to go to some stupid BBQ. I was mad and wanted to be back here, in the States. But when I saw you, I

fin

the bench

watched you and Curt talking. I watched y'all talking about sneakers and laughing. I giggled the whole time."

"You giggled??"

She looked up, slightly embarrassed that she told him about her infatuation that day.

"Yeah, y'all were cute! But it was really you I was looking at."

Her forwardness was something Fin appreciated. He admired any person that could just say what was on their mind, even in moments like this, when new emotions often clouded judgement. He began to notice the soft strength in her grip of his hand, the smoothness of her skin as his thumb rubbed the back of her hand. Something magical was happening and he prayed it would never end.

"C'mon, Mr. Finley. Let's go eat. I want to take you to one of my favorite places."

Like his father before him when he met Rose, Fin knew he would follow Cori anywhere. They walked slowly, allowing the setting sun and warm breeze to engulf them in a moment. The noise of cars, passersby chatting, birds singing their evening songs all faded into the background. One would catch the other allow their glance to linger a moment extra prompting them both to giggle. As they walked, Fin listened to Cori as she filled him in on the last seven years; where she had been, the things she had seen, her goals of being a doctor. Her ambition excited him. It reminded him of his dreams. She stopped walking in front of a large building. He couldn't take his eyes off of her in that moment. She longingly looked forward at the building.

"A doctor?"

the bench

"Yes. I have wanted to be a doctor since I could remember. Its why I brought you here."

He finally looked at the building. They were in front of the Dr. Rebecca Lee Crumpler building. Fin had seen it numerous times but never paid much attention to the name above. They sat down on a bench directly across from the cement stairs leading up to the entrance. As she sat down, she gently grabbed his hand, pulling at it for him to sit closer her. Fin, enamored with the beauty and majesty of the building, looked over his shoulder at a sitting Cori. He placed his bookbag on the ground in between his legs and rested his lunch bag on his lap. He didn't feel much like eating. He was completely and utterly overwhelmed by her in that moment, the way his father was for Rose all those years ago. All he wanted to do was talk with her, listen to her, understand her. He looked back at the name over the building.

"Who is Doctor Rebecca Lee Crumpler?"

"First Black female physician in America. In 1864, a year before slavery ended, *she* became a doctor! Learned about her when I was like nine years old, what she went through. I could only imagine how hard it was for her back then."

He watched her as she spoke, hanging off of every word, listening to the way she admired this woman. She asked him his story, what he had been up to in the past seven years since he left Japan. Fin detailed the best parts of his life; enrolling at Eastwood and meeting Stacks and Justin, writing computer code, wanting to provide computer coding classes to the residents of Valebrook (which she was impressed by as much as he was with her dreams), even his continued friendship with Curt to which she was surprised by. They talked and talked for what seemed like hours, neither was cognizant of the passage of time. Laughter switched to philosophical debate, smoothly transitioning to political ideologies, then back to laughter. The two even mused what may have happened had Fin stayed in Japan longer.

"What if you had stayed in Japan after I got there?"

"I dunno. You probably would have stalked me or something!"

"Mr. Finley! Are we full of ourselves now?"

She scooted away from him, trying to hide a smile.

"I'm saying, you popping up with a brother's lunch bag and all. You know you would have been alllll over me."

He burst into laughter as he reached for her to pull her back close to him. She playfully protested; her head turned away.

"Nope. Nope. Do something nice and look!"

He slid closer to her. "I'm sorry. What can I do to make it up to you?"

She looked at him, gazing into his eyes. *Him and those big, brown, puppy dog eyes are gonna be a problem.* She realized she would never be able to stay mad at him. She playfully rolled her eyes then gave him a side-eye and smiled. He smiled back.

"Can I ask you something? You don't have to answer if you don't want to."

"Sure. Ask me anything."

"What happened that day? Like, what really happened that day you were in the projects?"

Fin, once again, was shocked she knew so much about him. She didn't have to expound on her question. Fin knew what she was referring to; the day Justin killed Shan and the day Stacks killed Coop. It was a topic he never really discussed, not since the interrogation room with the police. If anyone up until this point asked him about it, he would have normally said he didn't want to talk about it. Not with Cori though. He knew, for the first time, he could be himself, he could be honest, he could be open. The feeling of comfort and trust was foreign to him. Where anxiety would have normally filled his mind, taken over his physiological responses, with her, it was ease and peace.

"What do you want to know?"

"Well, I remember hearing about it in Japan. All everyone talked about was that Master Chief Finley's son was in a shootout. I remembered his name from the BBQ and instantly I was heartbroken. I thought something had happened to you. I kept asking my mom and dad if they had heard anything. If you were alright. My mother finally told me you weren't hurt."

Fin watched her as she spoke. It was as if she was experiencing hearing the news all over again. Cori became visibly agitated. Her beautiful skin wrinkled on her brow. Her hands became fidgety. He reached out and placed his hand on top of hers.

"Hey, relax. I am ok."

"Were you scared? Did anyone try and hurt you? What happened?"

Fin let out a sigh. He wanted to tell her and knew one day he would, just not now. He didn't want the worst memory, the worst experience of his life after the death of Big Fin, to mar the best day of it so far. He knew though he needed to tell her something.

"Cori, I am fine. Was I scared? Of course. No one tried to hurt me."

He knew that last part wasn't entirely true.

"It was all the craziest set of circumstances that I promise, one day, I will tell you about in full detail if you like. But right now, I don't want to go there, to that place. Right now, I want to be here. Right here with you, in this moment."

He let out a slight chuckle to which Cori seemed bothered by.

"No, you don't understand. I almost didn't come here today. I had dropped out for nearly two years after my dad died. Watching him deteriorate physically and my mother's spirit with him, was hard. I was lost, not knowing what to do. But now, I'm here. I'm here, on this bench with you. I just want to enjoy it, okay?"

She nodded, accepting his reluctance to discuss Brevoit. She leaned into him, rubbing on his knee to signal her acceptance of his feelings.

"What made you come back?"

"A friend. A friend who was there with me in that moment you were asking about, that day in Brevoit. After my dad died, I was lost. I didn't have much in the way of motivation. My dad was my North star, my example. Right when I needed him most, he died. My family tried to snap me out of it, but it took my boy...my brother, to put his boot in my ass. Today, he sat on my porch and told me I was wasting my life and needed to get *off* my ass and get back into school. He actually dropped me off here today."

He chuckled in amazement and shook his head in disbelief.

"I raced into the Registrar's office and Algebra was one of the only classes that was available. Crazy circumstances."

Cori smiled. "And now, you're here with me."

"Yeah, now I'm here with you."

Neither knew what was happening to them. Neither wanted to know. They didn't want to let their brains get in the way of what their hearts and spirits were telling them. This was meant to be.

"Thank you for sharing that with me, Fin."

He placed his hand on her thigh just above her knee. Cori scooted closer to him and leaned on his shoulder. One would have thought these two were lifelong lovers by their intimacy. She popped up and looked at him.

"Take a picture with me. Let's make new moments."

Before he could answer, she reached into her bag and pulled out her cellphone. She scooted closer to him, opened her camera app on her phone, held it out in front of them as he placed his arm around her. As she positioned herself for the picture, he turned his head towards her, breathing in the scent of shea butter on her skin, hemp oil in her hair.

"Smile."

fin

the bench

CLICK!

She examined the picture on her phone and realized he never looked at the camera. She turned and looked at him as he longingly stared at her. His deep, chocolate skin glowed under the sun's radiance. She raised her hand and gently caressed his cheek. She began tracing his mustache and lips with her fingertips. With the back of his fingers. He tickled the nape of her neck, moving them in a circular motion. They were lost in each other's eyes for what seemed an eternity. As she closed her eyes, he leaned in and kissed her softly on her lips.

chapter sixteen

meet the family

Fin and Cori fell in love that day on the bench. They found ways in between classes to steal moments with each other. Sometimes he would exit class to see Cori standing there, her beautiful smile lighting up his otherwise drab day. Other times, she would receive a text message telling her to look to the porthole window in her classroom door, only for her to look up and see his face either smiling or blowing her a kiss or making a funny face that would cause her to burst out in laughter and her professor stare at her. They made sure to eat dinner together every night, no matter what. After a few months of dating, the ever-intuitive Rose began to sense something was different about Fin. One day, he was at his grandparents' home, sitting on the couch and texting Cori.

fin

meet the family

"Alright, who is she?"

Fin was caught off-guard. "Huh?"

"Don't 'huh' me. The young woman that has you over there smiling and texting. You haven't said more than three words to me since you got here."

His sheepish grin confirmed her suspicion. She was genuinely happy he had found someone to love. She had also seen that look before. The glimmer in his eye, the smile on his face, even the way he hugged her was different. She had seen that look before. It was how she felt when she and Big Fin first met. Fin relented, knowing that Rose wouldn't stop prodding until he gave her something.

"Her name is Cori, Ma."

"Cori, huh? Tell me about her."

"Well, she is about five-foot nine, brown ski..."

"BOY! I don't care what she looks like! Tell me about *her*! What kind of woman is she?"

Rose half expected Fin to pause at the question given its new context. She was pleasantly surprised when he didn't.

"Ma, she is amazing. Smart, strong, her mind is like...I don't know, deep seems too small of a word. She is going to be a doctor. Wants to open a practice right here in Valebrook."

"Is she from here?"

meet the family

"No, she is from the other side of Norfolk, Park View. Her parents seem nice."

"Wait, you've met her parents and I haven't met her yet??!?"

Fin knew instantaneously he was in trouble. It's not that he didn't want Rose to meet her, he just didn't want to rush and have Rose tell him she didn't like Cori. The thought of Rose rejecting Cori broke his heart.

"You're right, Mama. I'm sorry."

"Well, invite her over to dinner on Sunday."

"Wait. Here? To GrandMa and GrandPa's house? For dinner?"

"Yeah, unless you think you two aren't ready for that."

Fin thought for a moment. He knew how he felt about Cori, and he also knew that she could more than handle her own under the scrutiny of the Murphy Clan. Since he was the only grandchild, they were extra protective. He also knew that he loved her and would defend her to the end, regardless of what anyone said. Rose however, had no intentions of driving Cori away. She merely wanted to see how serious Fin was.

"Okay then. Sunday it is."

Rose had a huge smile on her face. "Come a little early. She can help Mama and I cook,"

"Mama! Be nice!"

fin

meet the family

"What? She can cook, can't she?"

"Of course, she can!"

Fin and Rose shared a few more moments before he left. As he hopped on his bike to head back to campus to meet up with Cori, he had one thought: *Sweet Geezus I hope this woman can cook!* They, being college students, only ever ate fast food or in the campus cafeteria. Before he started pedaling, he reached in his pocket and pulled out his phone.

Fin: Hey you

Cori: Hey baby. OMG I can't wait for this class to end!

Fin: Baby, if you had to cook me one meal, what would it be?

Cori: Ummmm Mr. Finley, are you low key trying to get me to cook for u

Fin: I'm just saying IF you had to what would you cook?

Cori: Well, I make a mean pot of greens

Fin: WHAAAATTTTT????

Cori: For real!! I always make the greens on holidays!

Fin: Can you make some for me on Sunday?

Cori: Where am I supposed to do that at?

fin

meet the family

Fin: *My grandparents' house. Sunday. We have been*
         invited for dinner and my Mama wants us there early
         so you can help in the kitchen with my grandma and
         her

Fin grimaced as he sent that last text. Then the text messages that were coming in rapid fire, all of a sudden stopped. He sat there a moment. He could only imagine her face. Rose peered at her son through the upstairs window, giggling as she watched him knowing he was relaying the news of Sunday dinner. He got a bit anxious then decided to just head to the campus. He placed his phone in his pocket and began to ride off. He barely made it fifteen feet when his phone began to ring.

RIIIIIIINNNNGGGGGGG!!

RIIIIIIINNNNGGGGGGG!!

He applied the bike's brakes immediately and prepared for what he expected to be an earful. He tried to preemptively calm Cori down to no avail.

"Heeeeyyyyy baby!"

"Really?!? Fin!"

"Are you mad?"

"GOD NO!!! You are taking me to meet your Mama and Grandparents?? Baaaabbbyyyyyy..."

He was shocked and relieved. He assumed the thought of being in the kitchen with Rose and Odella would intimidate her. Hell, they were his people and he dare not venture into that kitchen! He also realized, in that precise moment, his love for Cori would never be in question again. She was embracing the opportunity to bond with his mother and grandmother. She was excited to get to know him at a deeper level.

"I thought you would be mad."

"WHHHYYYY??? You must think I can't cook for real!"

"Well, we are gonna see!"

"James Finley, get yourself over to this campus and kiss me!"

"Okay, baby. See you in a few."

As she hung up, Cori was completely giddy. When she saw his text, much like she did to the student she was tutoring, she dropped what she was doing and bolted out of her last class. She had been waiting for Fin to feel comfortable enough to invite her to meet Rose. She knew that the respect he had shown her thus far, was not just because of her beauty, was not just because she was a woman, but it was because of who she was *as* a woman, and that could only come from having a strong, powerful woman in his life to teach him to view women that way. He talked about Rose so much, she had been dying to meet her.

When Sunday rolled around, Cori could hardly wait. She hopped in the car her parents handed down to her, and stopped at the store to grab the ingredients for her world-famous greens, before swinging by Stacks' house to pick up Fin. She never really liked Stacks. She understood the bond he and Fin shared; she knew their history as Fin had told her. It was his lifestyle she disagreed with. She couldn't understand why Stacks *chose* to stay involved with guns and thought the "family business" rationale was a weak excuse, a cop out. Their interactions were usually kept to few words, save for the one time they had a heated debate over the social validity of Booker T. Washington's separatist ideology versus that of W.E.B. DuBois. It was at the end of that debate that she despised him even more. Not because he opposed her views, but because he was intelligent enough and eloquent enough to argue his point. She thought he was wasting his life. Fin did too, but he always seemed to give him a pass. As she pulled up to the home Stacks shared with Shayla, Fin and Stacks were sitting on the steps leading to the porch. Stacks noticed Cori's car pulling up.

"Ain't that ya' lady?"

"Yeah, that's her."

"She had better be ready for Rose Finley."

Stacks was being half sarcastic and half serious.

"She'll be good. I ain't worried about her on that front."

"Aight, love bird," Stacks poked back as he let out a laugh.

"Whatever, Bruh!"

Fin leaned into the screen door. "Lata, Shayla!"

Shayla approached the door with little Chris in her arm.

"Bye, lil' bro! Say bye to Uncle Fin, Chris."

Fin reached out for Chris's hand as the child smiled and laid his head on Shayla's shoulder. Shayla saw Cori's car now parked in front of the house. She smiled and waved to which Cori smiled and waved

meet the family

in return. Cori's eyes then turned to Stacks who was waving as well, a devilish, half-hearted grin on his face. Stacks liked Cori, more importantly, he liked Cori for Fin. Like Rose before him, he saw the change in Fin since the two of them met. Cori waved at Stacks, but if *"I really don't like you but I'm gonna be nice for the sake of Fin"* had a hand gesture and matching face, Cori had just delivered it to Stacks. As Fin descended the stairs, Stacks couldn't resist the opportunity to poke at Fin one last time.

"That woman just don't like me."

"Man, you trippin'." Fin stated though he knew it to be true.

Stacks tilted his head, raised his eyebrow and looked at him.

"Bruh."

The two locked eyes for a moment. Stacks staring at him as if to ask what world he had been living in. Fin trying to act naive before finally relenting.

"Nah. She don't like yo' ass at all!"

The two men laughed, dapped each other, and then Fin jumped in the car, leaning over to kiss Cori as he did.

"Why do you hang out with that fool?"

"Hi, baby!"

"Hey, baby. I'm sorry. It's just..."

"It's just we gonna be late to my grands' house if you don't *stop worrying about Stacks and drive.*"

fin

meet the family

She leaned back against the driver side door.

"Bossy much, Mr. Finley?"

He mocked her gesture, leaning against the passenger door.

"Triggered lately, Ms. Porter?"

Stacks and Shayla watched the entire exchange and laughed. Shayla thought Cori and Fin were cute. Stacks just enjoyed seeing Fin give Cori as much sass as she could handle. Cori and Fin heard them laughing.

"What's he laughing at?"

"Will you drive, woman?"

"At least that baby is cute. *Thank God* he looks like Shayla!"

She started the car and engaged the gears. Fin looked at Stacks and Shayla, shook his head and smiled in a welcomed frustration, then waved at his two longtime friends as Cori drove off. As they made their way to Sunday dinner, the setting sun dancing inside the car as they wound through the Norfolk roads, Cori's confidence slowly began to fade. For every block they drove, a million questions popped into her head. A few blocks away from their destination, she began to ask them of Fin in rapid succession.

"What's your grandparents' names again?"

"What I'm wearing is fine, right?"

"I got collards. Your grandma likes collards and not mustards, right?"

fin

meet the family

"You think your mom is gonna like me?"

"Is this dress ok? Wait...did I ask you that already?"

"Patrick and Odellia...no! Patrick and ODELLA! Right?"

"Should I just call them Mr. and Mrs. Murphy or Sir and Ma'am?"

Fin let her go for a bit and calmly answered all of her questions. He had learned enough to know that she needed to talk out her nervous energy. He only stopped her when her natural questions started to turn into self-doubt.

"Fin, I don't wanna mess this up."

He reached out and grabbed her hand.

"Baby, pull over."

"What? We *can't,* Fin! We are gonna be late."

"It's okay. Pull over."

Cori sighed.

"For me. Just pull the car over."

She pulled over and parked alongside the curb. They were on Dorian Street, a block away from Patrick and Odella's. The tree canopied street allowed for hints of sunlight to poke through. It was a warm day, but a gentle breeze greeted him as he got out of the car and walked around to her door. He opened it and extended for her hand. A nervous Cori acquiesced and exited the vehicle.

fin

meet the family

"Baby, what are you doing?"

He didn't reply. Instead, he reached into the car, turned the engine off and removed the keys from the ignition. He took her hand, led her to the back of the car, then scooped her up and sat her on the trunk. The move caught Cori completely off guard, but before she could make a sound, Fin said something that caused her to melt.

"My mother, my grandma and grandpa, they are gonna love you. They are gonna love you because I love you. I knew I was gonna love you from the moment you were standing there with my lunch bag. I would have met you anywhere, anytime you asked me to. I knew I was in love with you when we sat on that bench. Looking at you, seeing your determination, your vision, hearing your passion. I knew I was madly in love with you when I told you about this dinner and you were excited, not mad or scared, but excited. Excited that you want to get to know me, my family, and my history. And right now? I'm even more in love with you. I think it's both beautiful and hilarious that you truly think somehow you could mess this up. You aren't on trial at this dinner. You're not auditioning for a part. Baby, you have nothing to prove. You won my heart a long time ago. Tonight, my family isn't meeting my new girlfriend. Tonight, they are meeting a new member of the family for the first time...and you're meeting your new family. Okay?"

The tears could not stop flowing down Cori's face. Her deep brown eyes staring at the man in front of her. She knew she loved him, she hoped he felt the same. In her head she was screaming *I LOVE YOU TOO, BABY!* Her mouth was open, but no sound came from it. All she could do was nod. He gently wiped her eyes.

"Now, are you ready to fix me some of these famous greens you been bragging on?"

fin

meet the family

She burst into a nervous, happy laughter. "YES!"

Fin smiled seeing her worries wash away. He placed both hands on her cheeks and leaned into her.

"I love you, Cori."

"I love you too, Fin."

He helped her down from the car and escorted her to the passenger side. He opened the door and stepped aside to allow her to enter. The ever-strong-willed Cori realized he wasn't going to let her drive. *He thinks he's slick!*

"I can drive, you know?"

"I know," he replied as he closed the door behind her.

Moments later they arrived at Patrick and Odella's. Patrick was sitting on the porch smoking a cigar.

"Odella! Rose! Fin and his….."

Patrick was taken aback when Cori exited the car.

"…BEAUTIFUL young lady are here!"

Cori blushed as she looked over the roof of the car at Fin, who smiled back at her matter-of-factly, his smile saying, *I told you they are gonna love you!* Fin reached in the back seat and grabbed the groceries as Rose and Odella made it to the porch, the squeaky screen door announcing their arrival. Prior to Fin and Cori's arrival, Patrick and Odella were pleasantly surprised when Rose explained Fin would be bringing his new girlfriend. Patrick couldn't have been happier at the news.

"Finally found him a woman, huh?"

"Ya' met her yet?"

"No, Mama, but the way he lights up when he talks about her is all I need to know. Haven't felt this much joy in his spirit in years."

Odella returned to rinsing her black-eyed peas in the sink.

"Well, he get that from you, I suppose."

"From *me*?"

"Mmmmmmm-hmmmm. I remember your spirit changed when you saw his daddy for the first time. Then when he finally took you out, I'd half to climb to the roof just to talk to ya', ya' head was so far up in them clouds."

Patrick was tickled as he recalled his daughter's early days with Big Fin.

"Hahahaha! Ol' Fin was a good man...a good man."

His voice trailed off as he became melancholy, thoughts of losing the only son he ever had still pained him. Now, Fin and Cori where there and his heart filled with joy. When Rose and Odella heard that they had arrived, they could hardly get out of each other's way trying to get to the door. Cori was amazed, and a bit intimidated by seeing Patrick, Odella, and Rose standing on the porch, waiting to greet them, like a royal court welcoming guests to their kingdom. When Cori saw Rose, she was awe struck by her beauty, just as she was years before. Rose stared back at her, her smile beaming as she took Cori in. Odella thought she was absolutely radiant.

"Fin. Bring that pretty thang up in heya', child!"

Fin extended for Cori's hand to escort her to the house.

"I think they like you already."

He opened the gate for her and allowed her to enter. She looked up at Rose, Patrick, and Odella as they gazed at her, all of them anxious to meet one and other. When Fin grabbed her hand again after closing the gate, Patrick and Odella glanced at each other, their hearts full.

"Hey, Mama. Hey, Grandma and Grandpa."

Patrick rose from his chair to greet them.

"Now boy, what an ol' big head boy like you doing with a lovely woman like this??!"

Odella waved him off and made her way to the top of the stairs.

"Hush, fool! Let these babies come in heya' befo' you start with yo' foolishness!"

Patrick's face frowned as he shot Odella a glance then returned to smiling as he looked at Cori. Cori let out such a chuckle that caused all of them to smile. Instantaneously, all her nervousness washed away. She could feel the love and admiration this family shared. Finally, Rose, who had not moved or spoken up to this point, greeted her son and his love.

fin

meet the family

"Hello, baby," Rose said as she hugged him before releasing him to greet Cori.

"Hey, Mama. Mama. Grandma. Grandpa. This is *my* Cori. Baby, this is my family."

Odella smiled and wrestled her hands. "Baby, huh?! Alright nah!"

Cori blushed. "Hello."

"Oh, Fin. You didn't do this woman any justice. She is glorious!"

Rose reached out to hug Cori. Cori could not stop smiling. She couldn't remember ever feeling so beautiful, so accepted, so secure as she did right there on the Murphy family porch, in Rose's embrace. Patrick reached out for a hug himself.

"Cute as a bug, I tell ya'!"

Rose giggled. "Yes! Cute as a bug. Think that's what I'm gonna call you, Cori; Little Bug."

Cori chuckled. She thought the nickname was cute.

"C'mon heya' child and hug me! I'm Odella, that fool there is Patrick, but you call us Grandma and Grandpa ya' heya'?"

As she hugged Odella, Cori and Fin locked eyes for a moment before she settled into Odella's embrace. Patrick put his arm around Fin. The firmness of his grasp told Fin he had done well. Rose took the grocery bags from Fin and opened the door.

fin

meet the family

"I hear you are making some greens?"

"Yes, Ma'am. If that's ok?"

Patrick's chest poked out. "Gotchu a Southern gal, Fin!"

Odella grabbed Cori's hand and escorted her into the house.

"Well, c'mon. Let's get supper on the table, baby."

Fin watched as Cori and Odella entered the home. Rose lingered back for a moment to look at Fin. She smiled at her son and placed her hand on her heart. Words need not be said. Fin knew that Cori had won Rose over in an instant, the way she had won his heart over. The rest of the evening was a dream and a blur to Cori. She laughed and talked with Odella and Rose, answered all of their questions, and even asked a few of her own. Odella shared her secret to fresh buttermilk biscuits, a must with black eyed peas, greens and smothered pork chops, at least according to Odella. Rose admired how eloquent, intelligent and respectful Cori was. Cori really won them both over when Odella asked if she wanted some lemonade. She said yes, but first wanted to see if Patrick and Fin wanted some as well. As Cori left the kitchen to inquire, Odella looked to Rose.

"Think she gonna fit in just fine around heya'."

"I like her too, Mama."

Dinner that night was a rousing success. Cori's greens were a hit, and she could not get over how good Odella and Rose's cooking was.

fin

meet the family

"Well I know two things; I need to come over here and get some more cooking lessons and I am gonna pick up some pounds doing it too!"

The table laughed as they all enjoyed each other's company. After dinner, Cori and Fin began to clear down the table when Odella stopped them.

"Y'all don't need to worry 'bout them dishes. Y'all got school in the morning don'tcha?"

"No. Grandma. We can help," said Fin.

"We can do it, Grandma. We have time," echoed Cori.

"Nah, I said I got it. Y'all need to go get some rest."

Fin raised both hands in the air, surrendering to his grandmother's will. He gave Cori a look. *Don't argue.* Cori simply smiled, acknowledging Fin's non-verbal communication, then transitioned into their exit.

"Well, we should get on the road then. Thank you all so much for having me in your home."

"Well, you are more than welcome to come back anytime, honey," said Odella.

Patrick slid his chair back, stood up and walked over to Cori. He reached down and placed her soft, delicate hands in his. Cori thought her hands looked like that of a child in Patrick's large, strong hands.

fin

meet the family

"Young Lady, I just wanna say what his grandmama and mama are feeling. Thank you for bringing the life back in our Fin's eyes. It's been a hard time around here since his daddy passed, but you……." he took a deep breath before continuing, "you in just a wee bit a time, done brought life and energy back to him, and in doing so, to us."

Oh my, God! Cori couldn't believe he was saying this to her. She spent but an evening with them and already they are embracing her as if she was born into the family. It was in this moment that she truly understood why Fin loved so hard and so purposefully; he knew no other way. She let out a chuckle as she wiped the tears forming in her eyes.

"Y'all gonna make me cry."

Patrick pulled her in close.

"Nah, don't go and do that. Just promise me you gonna come back and make them greens again."

"I promise. Thank you."

She leaned in and hugged Patrick. Odella stood up and walked around the table to get her hug too. Rose had already made her way to the front door, standing patiently to say goodbye to her son and Cori. Fin looked at his grandparents with love and admiration, then embraced each of them individually before leading Cori to the front door as Patrick and Odella followed. Rose's arms were open, a motherly smile on her face.

"Come here, my Lil' Bug."

Cori hugged Rose hard.

fin
meet the family

"You make sure you keep Fin in line. He likes to skip meals so fatten him up for me."

"I will."

Patrick had his arm around Odella, her arm around his waist.

"Fin, need to get ya' own place so we can come eat yo' food!"

"I gotcha, Grandpa."

He leaned in and hugged Rose. "I'll be home in a bit. Just need to make sure she gets home safely."

"Be careful, baby."

"I will, Mama."

The two waved at Rose, Patrick and Odella as they made their way into the warm night air and to the car. After Cori was safely in the car, Fin hopped in the driver's seat, started the engine, and pulled off, honking the horn to signal one last goodbye.

"Oh my God, Fin!! They are amazing! You are so lucky to have family like that!"

"Yeah, I am. I knew they would love you."

"And your Grandma is something else!"

"Yeah, Grams don't play nor hold her tongue. Grandpa is pretty smart too."

"He shocked me as we were leaving. When he started tal......"

fin

meet the family

"Move in with me."

Cori was floored. Her head snapped around and stared at him.

"What?"

"Move in with me."

"You're serious, aren't you?"

"Never been more serious about anything in my life."

"You think we are ready for that, baby? That's a big step."

"I'm ready for my life with you Cori. You wanna wait, we can wait. You wanna do it, we can go looking at places tomorrow. But we are gonna be together. So whene......"

"Yes."

Fin needed assurance he understood what she was saying yes to.

"Yes?"

"Yes. Let's move in together."

As they reached a red light, he leaned across the seat and kissed her. As the light turned green, he straightened up, grabbed her hand and they drove to Cori's house, both overjoyed and swimming in their love.

chapter seventeen

the night before

Fin and Cori found a small studio apartment about twelve blocks from campus. Fin still worked at Brown's, and Cori had started working in the Cafeteria of Norfolk General Hospital. He'd wanted to move closer to the hospital for the sake of Cori's job, but she insisted on being near Tidewater State. Their apartment didn't have much, but it was more than enough for them. A queen-sized bed, a small futon at the foot of the bed, a desk that doubled as an entertainment stand and held the TV and Fin's computer were his only contributions to the decor design. The lamps, rug, picture frames, and fresh flowers were all Cori. The two made it a home. Oftentimes, she would wake up in the middle of the night to find him typing away on the computer. He would wake up at one or two in the morning so he could instant message Curt. Curt stayed in Japan and is currently attending university there, but the thirteen-hour time difference made their communication difficult. So usually they shared information, ideas, strings of code, and updates on their daily lives via email. Fin enjoyed their instant message sessions however, even if it meant waking up in the middle of the night. Cori thought he needed to get out and meet more people. As far as she knew, he had three friends; Curt, who was still in Japan, Stacks, who she really didn't like, and Justin, who they had over for dinner to celebrate his completion of Basic Training. Justin seemed nice in Cori's eyes.

They had been living together for just over eight months now and had developed a routine that they grew to love. No matter how busy their schedules were though, they still made time to have their moments with each other. They took turns sharing all the chores, save for cooking. Cori handled that, though in the last week Fin had been the exclusive chef of the household. He wanted to take some pressure off of her, her being pre-med and all. Cori didn't have the heart to tell him his cooking was horrible. *How did that man grow up around Mama Rose and Grandma Odella and cook* this *bad?* For the last few days, she ended up feeling nauseous and would go to bed early. Yesterday morning she woke up vomiting.

But they loved their routine as they navigated how to love and support each other. Sometimes, Cori would wake up to see Fin at the computer working and would just get up, curl up on the futon with a textbook and study. Anything so they could be present in the moment together. This night however, Cori awoke and saw that Fin wasn't in the bed. Normally she would look for the glow from the computer screen or the light emanating from under the bathroom door to signal his location. Tonight, it was pitch black in the apartment. She rolled over to look at the alarm clock on the nightstand: one forty-five in the morning.

"Fin?"

All she heard in reply were sniffles and muffled sighs. She sat up, and saw he was on the futon which rested at the foot of the bed.

fin

the night before

"Baby......."

He didn't reply. He sat there, his elbows resting on his knees, his head hanging low into his hands. He was crying. She got out of bed and walked over to join him, to comfort him. She sat down next to him.

"Baby, what's wrong?"

He simply leaned into her, laying his head on her lap. She began to stroke the crown of his head, letting her fingers play in the fullness of his hair, her fingertips gently massaging his scalp. In all their time together, she had never seen him cry. This was an unsettling feeling for her. The always prepared Cori didn't know what was wrong nor how to comfort him.

"I never told you what happened to my dad. Why I dropped out of school."

"No, baby. I just figured you would when you were ready."

Fin let out another deep sigh, wiped the tears from his face and then began to speak.

"When I was eighteen, in the middle of my freshman year here, my dad and I had a horrible argument. I don't even remember what started it, but I do remember I was mad he was almost never there, and when he was, he was always sleeping. I remember us yelling at each other, me almost walking out the house, my mama begging us to stop. She kept saying, 'Fin, you don't understand.' My dad finally had enough, left the room, and went to their bedroom. As he slammed the door shut, I heard him say, 'I can't take this with my health!' All I remember was thinking was, *Wait - his health? What does he mean?* I tried to calm down. I wasn't angry anymore. I was scared."

"What did you do?"

"I slowly walked into their bedroom. My mama was crying as she followed me in there. Baby, I swear that was the longest walk of my life."

In the midst of Fin sharing the story with Cori, he suddenly felt himself drifting into a sort of dream state. He was no longer in the room with Cori, but transported back in time, to that very bedroom. It all became real again.

When Fin entered the bedroom that day, Big Fin was sitting on the edge of the bed. Rose sat down next to Big Fin on the edge of the bed. It wasn't until that moment that Fin really saw his father's weight loss. His face was sunken in, his eyes glassed over a bit. His once massive frame had withered over the last few months. Big Fin, a tall, muscular man, who in his prime, weighed a solid two-hundred and forty plus pounds, was easily down to about two hundred, if that. His muscles that once caused his clothes to stretch every fiber, now draped over his smallish frame. Fin knew something was wrong. He had suspected so for weeks. He wasn't ready for what he was about to hear. Rose placed her arm around Big Fin.

"What do you mean, your health?"

"Fin, I'm sick."

"Sick? How sick? What's wrong with you?"

fin

the night before

"We have to tell him, James. He needs to know."

"Tell me what?"

Big Fin heard his son's voice cracking. The fear in his eyes hurt him. He dreaded what he was about to tell him. He knew it would hurt him all the more.

"I'm sick, Fin, and all this arguing and stress is killing me."

Fin felt like he was going to vomit. His heart was pounding.

"Dad, what's wrong with you? Tell me."

Rose wanted to calm him down. His hands trembled at his side. His brow frowned with fear and anger. She knew he was scared. She was too.

"Fin..."

"TELL ME!"

"I'm dying, Fin. I have cancer."

Fin's world was turned upside down. He had seen him lay in bed all day a few times, complaining of massive headaches and stomach pain. He had noticed Rose and Big Fin coming in the house together and his father heading straight to bed. He never thought Big Fin was sick. He figured he was just tired from work, the weight of his position heavy on him. *CANCER?? How? When??!!* He began to weep, stammering in between his sobs.

"What......are you......talking about?"

fin

the night before

Big Fin didn't have the strength or courage to say anything else. Rose gripped his hand and he hers.

"Your father has stage four pancreatic cancer, Fin."

"Why didn't you tell me?"

Big Fin looked up at his son. "I wanted you to focus on school."

"So, y'all LIED TO ME?? HID IT?!?!"

Rose quickly stood and walked over to Fin.

"Baby, your father and I didn't want you to worry. We need you to focus on school, baby."

"BULLSHIT!"

"Watch your mouth, boy!" an angered Big Fin chastised.

Rose now began to cry. Fin was fuming. He felt betrayed. He felt disrespected. *I'm a grown man! I could have handled it! How y'all hide something like this from me!* Then he realized they were right. He wasn't handling it well, not at all. He stormed out.

"Fuck this!"

"FIN! BABY, WAIT!"

Big Fin reached up and grabbed Rose by the hand, stopping her from pursuing Fin.

"Let him go, Rose. Let him process this."

fin

the night before

Cori was stunned by this revelation. Fin never talked about his father's death. Whenever they were around his family, the mere mention of his name would bring a sadness to the whole room. She suspected it was an illness, but she never thought he reacted the way he was telling her. Not the way with the loving reverence he normally spoke of his father.

"Oh my God, baby. You left?"

"Yeah. I was young and stupid and didn't know what else to do."

"Where did you go?"

"Stacks."

After he left his parents' room, he stormed into his room, packed a bag, and walked over to Stacks' house. Stacks stayed not too far from Brevoit projects. When he arrived, Stacks could see something was wrong.

"The fuck is wrong with you?"

"Can I crash here for a few days?"

"Moms kicked yo' ass out, huh?"

He didn't respond. He didn't budge. His head was down, trying to hide the angry tears flowing down his face. Stacks became agitated.

"Fuck you crying fo'?"

fin

the night before

"Dad has cancer."

Stacks stepped away from the threshold of the door and allowed Fin into the house, placing his arm around him to provide comfort. Though for completely different reasons, Stacks understood completely what losing your father meant. He didn't press the issue, not that night. He knew what Big Fin meant to Fin. Truth was that the news was hitting him hard too. Stacks had the utmost respect for Big Fin, the man that kept his promise. Stacks gave Fin space to process the news. After a few days, he knew he needed to talk to him. He hoped in his car and drove to the corner store. He grabbed two cold forty-ounce beers and returned home. When he arrived, he shot Fin a text.

Stacks: Come outside

Fin: Aight

Fin had been laying down in Dee's room. He threw his sneakers and coat on and went outside. Stacks stood there, a cold beer in each hand.

"Come rap wit' me, Bruh."

Fin reluctantly walked down the stairs and out the front gate. It was a cold night. It had snowed earlier that day and now the air was still. The once soft, untouched snow had been packed down by foot traffic. Even in the dead of winter, the streets were buzzing as usual, a typical Valebrook evening. He walked over and grabbed one of the beers Stacks was extending to him. They twisted the tops off, clinked the glass bottles and poured a bit of the beers out into the snow. Fin leaned up against the car and took a long swig.

fin

the night before

"Bruh, have you called home?"

"Naaaa. Not yet."

"Don't you think you should?"

"How could they hide it from me?"

"Fin, let me tell you something. You see Dee in there? That boy is twelve and since the day he was born, I loved him like he was my son, like I made him. I thought I knew the feeling that a father should have. But he is only my brother. When little Chris was born, I truly knew what it meant to be a father, and let me tell you, I don't know how I would be able to look at either of them and explain to them I was going to die. That there was nothing they, or I, could do about it. Cancer is a mafucka, Fin. That shit don't care if you rich, poor, black, white, man, woman or child. It just comes, and steals, and destroys. How do you tell your son there is something you can't beat? How do you tell your son their Superman is going to die?"

Fin cried. He was so caught up in his feelings, he never thought how his father must be feeling, what must be going through his mind. Stacks set his beer on the roof of the car and put his arm around his brother.

"You should go home, Bruh. Go be with your family.

Fin nodded and then fell into his brother's arms.

Cori now understood why Fin was so beholden to Stacks. It wasn't just because of that day in Brevoit, it was because in his darkest moment, that was who Fin turned to.

309

fin

the night before

"How long had you been there?"

"Only a few days. The next morning, I went home."

Fin slowly ascended the snow-covered stairs to his front porch and sat on one of the wicker chairs, the one Big Fin normally sat in when he and Rose sat out front, reading or just enjoying each other's company. It was an early February morning, a Sunday, and bitterly cold outside. Just by the look of the house, Fin knew his dad was sick. Snow covered the walkway leading to the porch, the stairs and had blocked both cars in the driveway. Big Fin was meticulous about keeping the house presentable. It snowed the day Fin stormed out and the grounds hadn't been tended to in the three days since he had been gone. Seeing both cars were there let him know both of his parents were home. As he sat there, taking in the scene and realizing he would need to do more around the house, the front door swung open. Big Fin slowly made his way out onto the porch. He saw Fin coming up through the living room window. He watched him as he sat down, confused and mad. Big Fin knew his son had questions that rightfully deserved answers. Fin looked up and saw Big Fin laboring a bit to walk. He stood and helped his father, sitting him in the seat he had just vacated.

"Thank you, son."

As Fin sat down, his eyes welled up.

"I know you have lots of questions, Fin. Hell, I do too. First one I asked of God was 'Why me?' They say the Lord has a plan, and damn, I wish I knew what the hell it was."

"How long have you known?"

fin

the night before

"Your mother and I found out about four months ago. We didn't wanna tell you at first. Wanted to see what treatment options we could take….I could take."

"So, what they got you on?"

"Chemo. That's why I am so tired and sick all the time."

Fin's heart dropped at the word chemo. He knew if that's what Big Fin was enduring, this was bad.

"Ya' mama wanted to tell you. I told her let's wait until we were sure."

"Y'all was wrong for that. I'm part of this family too. This affects me just as much. Y'all was wrong."

"I know, son, and I am sorry. We just wanted you to focus on school and the rest of your life. One day you'll understand when you have kids of your own."

Fin realized that whenever that day came, Big Fin wouldn't be there to see them.

"How long?"

"How long for what, Fin?"

Fin stared at Big Fin, his eyes begging his father not to make him say the words.

"Oh, *that* how long. We honestly don't know, son. The Navy doctors are trying everything. They have me seeing a private

311

oncologist as well. Truth is, with pancreatic cancer, you just don't know."

"How did this happen? I mean, why didn't they catch it before?"

"That's the thing with pancreatic cancer; they usually don't find it until it's too late."

Fin didn't respond. He was trying to process everything. Rose, now looking at her son and husband through the living room window, was crying herself. It was early in the morning and the still of the neighborhood hadn't been disturbed, so she could hear them talking.

"I'mma help out more around here. Get a job to help pay for your treatments."

"You'll do no such thing, Fin. Look at me, son."

Fin's head remained down.

"Fin. Look at me."

Fin looked up. He didn't think he had any tears left, as many as he had cried over the last few days, but now there were more than ever.

"You will *not* let this stop you, Fin. When my daddy died, I was no older than seventeen. I was a defensive captain on the football team, one of the best D-tackles in the state of Florida. I had schools drooling over me too. But I had to walk away from it. I dropped out of school because I had to. I had four brothers and sisters that I had to look after. My mama was a shell of herself when Daddy died. Stopped working, going to church, talking to people. Someone had to provide, so I dropped out and got a job. Eventually, I started running with the wrong crowds, doing shit I wasn't supposed to."

Big Fin never talked about his family much. Fin had only ever seen his grandmother, aunts and uncle a few times in his life. In fact, Fin knew very little about Miami, Florida or any of his relatives there.

"You will not have to do that. Your mother and I made sure you were provided for, and that you will continue to be provided for. So, you don't worry your head about that."

Big Fin stared off into the air.

"You know that day you went into Brevoit, I was so mad at you. Not mad you disobeyed me and went over there after I said not to. I was mad because I thought your life may be over before it even began."

Fin's sobs grew in intensity.

"There is a part of me that you don't know, a part that I don't like to talk about. Maybe it's time I should, time you understand who I was then and why I am the way I am now.'

Cori thought she was going to be sick. She wanted to stay there though. She fought her uneasy stomach, wiped the sweat from her brow and let out a long, deep breath.

"What did he tell you?"

fin

the night before

Cori always heard the reverence in which Fin, Rose, Patrick and Odella spoke of Big Fin. Even Stacks and Justin made note to mention him in their first meetings with her.

"He told me everything. He told me about how he grew up in Miami, his dad being killed, my grandma's struggle with drugs and how he had to take jobs he didn't like in order to provide for his sisters and brothers. He told me about him and Coop and what they used to do, how he almost got caught up, ruined his life. I'm in shock now just thinking about it. That wasn't the man I knew."

Cori listened as Fin bared his soul, his most intimate of moments. She wanted to be a comfort for Fin, his peace. She also wanted to allow him the space to get it out.

"What else did he say, baby?"

"Son," Big Fin continued, "you have so much potential. You can be anything you want in this life. It kills me that I may not be here to see you reach your glory."

Still listening, Rose's heart couldn't take much more. She walked away from the window, went into the bathroom and sobbed hard and unabashedly, muffling her cries and screams by biting a towel. The last thing she wanted to do was ruin this moment, this necessary conversation Big Fin and Fin needed to have.

Fin slumped out of his chair and knelt in front of his father.

"Dad........."

fin

the night before

Big Fin reached out to his boy, cradling his head in his arms as Fin wrapped his arms around his father. From the moment Big Fin found out about the cancer and its severity, he had no concerns for his own life. He cared only about Rose and Fin and how they would handle this. Rose was with him when he found out and he saw the terror in her eyes. He didn't want to see the same heartbreak in Fin's eyes, but he knew it was inevitable. Now, he needed to muster the strength to comfort his son, much the way he did when he was just a boy.

"I need you to be strong, son. Not for me, but for your mama. She's gonna need you."

Fin cried uncontrollably, his sobs echoing in the still silent winter air. A car rolled past and muffled Fin's wailing only to allow them full throat seconds later.

"NOOOOOOOOOOOOOOOOOOOOOOO! WHYYYYYYYYY!?!?!"

"I know, son. I know. You go on ahead and cry."

Big Fin now allowed his emotions to flow as well, knowing this may well be some of their last moments together.

"C'mon, son. Let's go inside."

Though weak, Big Fin found a bit of strength left in his fatherly reserves to lift his son, hug him, hold him, give him that safe space to gather himself.

"I love you, Fin."

Fin whispered. "I love you too, Dad."

315

fin

the night before

"Baby..." said Cori, now in tears. "I am so sorry."

Fin wiped his eyes and tried to collect himself. The reliving of that moment took him back to emotions he has long fought to suppress.

"Is that why you dropped out of school?"

"Not quite. I stayed in school like he asked me to. Then one day, a few months later, I was in class and got a call from Mama."

After Big Fin and Rose revealed to Fin the true nature of Big Fin's health, Big Fin began to deteriorate rapidly. He had been hospitalized only a week ago and the doctors told them all, that at this point, there was nothing more they could do other than try to provide him peace and dignity in his last days. Fin was supposed to go see Big Fin the day before, but called him because he had to study for an Algebra exam, the class he was sitting in. Fin was in the midst of his Algebra exam, trying his best to focus. That morning as he left for school, Big Fin and Rose were heading to the hospital for a routine visit. He called to check on him. Rose told him his father didn't look good that morning and didn't touch his breakfast. He wanted to go with them, but she wouldn't allow it. Then, as he looked down at the exam on his desk, his phone rang.

"Fin, baby, you need to come to the hospital."

"Ok, Mama. I'm leaving class now."

The irony wasn't missed on him as he walked out of the door; he was going to fail that test regardless. He called Stacks who dropped everything and raced him over to the hospital. When he arrived in Big

fin

the night before

Fin's hospital room, Patrick and Odella were already there, along with his father's mother, Shirley, and his sister, Colleen aka Aunt Leenie. Rose was in the chair adjacent to Big Fin's bed. Shirley looked over at Fin as he entered.

"Oh, my word! Fin, if you don't look like your daddy! Come here and give Grandma a hug!"

"Hey, Grandma. Hey, Aunt Leenie."

Big Fin was sleeping with help from heavy medication for the pain. Rose leaned into Big Fin's ear.

"James. Fin is here."

"He made it. He made it," cried out Big Fin through the pain and narcotics as he awoke.

Fin looked at his father, a shell of himself, now down to one hundred and eighty pounds. The skin on his face draped over his skull the way a towel would over a lamp; loose while still revealing the sharp structures of the lamp shade. He began to wonder when his grandmother and aunt had arrived from Florida.

"When did y'all get here?"

Leenie, Big Fin's youngest sister looked at Fin. She saw the rage in his eyes. She had seen it before in her eldest brother.

"We got here this morning, baby. Drove all night after ya' mama called us."

Fin returned his attention to his father, took his hand, and kissed his forehead.

317

fin

the night before

"Hi, Dad. I'm here."

"You made it, son. You made it."

Fin didn't want Big Fin to see him crying, so he tried to hold it in. The finality of this moment, as well as the anger for his family from out of town was too much for him to bare. *Where the fuck have y'all been all this time?* He tried hard to stifle the pain in his voice.

"Yeah, Dad. I made it."

The family began to say what they all knew would be their final goodbyes. Odella went first, her handkerchief in hand, wiping her eyes and nose as she approached.

"Fin, now you hear me, son and you hear me well. Not many men on this planet like you. No, Sir! God sent us a blessing when you came into our lives. You just know that *you* were and always will be a blessing in our life. I love you, son......love ya' like I raised ya'. You go on and rest ya' heya'. We gon' be just fine."

Then she kissed his cheek and stepped aside so Patrick could speak.

"James, as a man...a father, I couldn't have asked for a better man to marry my Rose. You inspired me to be a better husband. The strength and wisdom and love......I....I......"

Odella comforted her husband, her hands on his aged arm, the other around his back.

"I love you too, Patrick. Always have," Big Fin feebly replied.

318

fin

the night before

Patrick leaned in and hugged him. Patrick had never kissed another man, but in that moment, he kissed his son.

"I love you, James. I love you more than you'll *ever* know."

Leenie didn't speak. She walked over to the side of the bed that Rose was on, leaned in and kissed her eldest brother, and cried on his chest. Big Fin reached up and stroked her hair.

"Take care of Ma," he whispered, "Tell Mickey and Joshua I love them....and I'm sorry."

Leenie nodded her head against his chest, picked her head up to look at Big Fin. He feebly smiled at her, trying to reassure her it was ok.

"I love you."

"I love you too, James."

Shirley was the last to say her goodbyes. She approached the bed, touched his face, then leaned in and kissed him.

"I love you, James. I love you my baby."

He wrapped his arms around his mother. She became hysterical.

"MY BABY! MY BABY! OH LORD!! MY BABY!!"

Big Fin looked over his weeping mother's shoulder and nodded at his sister. Leenie came over and pulled Shirley up. She wept fiercely as Leenie escorted her out the hospital room screaming, stifling her own pain to console Shirley. Patrick and Odella came over

319

fin

the night before

to say goodbye to Rose, then to Fin. Patrick said a prayer as the four all laid hands on Big Fin. Then Patrick and Odella kissed Rose and Fin and left. Alone finally, the Finley family sat; Rose on one side of the bed, Fin on the other. James looked at his wife and son.

"I love you two with every fiber of my being. I have never loved anything the way I do the two of you. I am sorry I am leaving you. Sorry about the pain this is gonna cause. Just know that no matter where you are, where you go, I am right there with you. Both of you. Always and forever."

Rose got up from the chair, lifted the hospital blanket off Big Fin, moved the numerous tubes connected to his body out of the way, and crawled in bed with her husband. As she laid her head on his chest for the final time, she cried. Big Fin kissed the crown of her head. He inhaled her smell, her essence as if it gave him life itself. Fin scooted closer to the bed and laid his head on Big Fin's lap.

Cori didn't know how much more she could take.

"Fiiinnnnnnn..."

Fin was barely able to keep talking as he told her his father's final moments, but he knew he needed to get it out, a pain he had been holding onto for far too long. A pain he had never spoken aloud. Fin loved Cori with all his heart, the way Big Fin loved Rose. He hated Cori never got to meet him. He hated that his father wouldn't be there at his wedding. He wouldn't see him graduate college. He would never hold his grandchildren. Fin was angry and hurt, longing for his father. Cori was the only person he could share all of these emotions with.

fin

the night before

"So, you were right there when he died?"

He looked at her pitifully. "Yes..."

As Fin laid his head on his father's lap, Big Fin placed his hand on his head and began stroking his hair. Fin felt a release. In this one moment, their last moment with Big Fin, he didn't want to be sad, he wanted to enjoy this time with his father. He wanted to stay there forever. This peace, this release, caused him to close his eyes and drift off to sleep. Rose just looked at Big Fin as he comforted their son. When she was confident Fin was asleep, she spoke.

"James, look at me, my love."

"Always."

"James, I never knew what I wanted in a man or even needed in a man, until I met you. You have been everything to me. My lover, my best friend, my champion. You supported me in every way imaginable. My spirit is alive because of you. Thank you for being mine. Thank you for making me yours. Thank you for loving me."

Big Fin looked at his wife and smiled. He was ready to move on.

"Rose, the honor of you has been all mine. I loved you from the moment we met. You have been my peace and strength from day one. Thank you. I love you."

The two kissed, softly, passionately, a kiss they never wanted to end. Then Rose drifted off to sleep. Big Fin looked at his wife and son resting for a moment.

fin

the night before

"I love you, both. I'll see you in your dreams."

Big Fin closed his eyes and drifted off to sleep. He was at peace. The Finleys slept in that hospital room for hours. Suddenly, Fin was awoken to the sound of the room door swinging open and nurses rushing in. He wasn't sure how long he had been asleep. He looked up and saw Rose just as confused. Then it hit them both simultaneously. One of the sounds they were hearing was ominous, the sound no family wants to hear.

BEEEEEEEEEEEEEEEEEEEEEEEEEEEEEEEEEEEEEEEEEEEEEEEEEEEEEEEEEEE EEEEEEEEEEEEEEEEEEEEEEEEEEEEEEEEEEEEEEEEEEEEEEEEEEEEEEEEEEEEE EEEEEEEEEEEEEEEEEEEEEEEEEEEEEEEEEEEEEEEEEEEEEEEEEEEEEEEEEEP

"JAMES!"

"Ma'am, please step aside so we can help him."

"DAD!! DAD!!!"

The room was suddenly fool of doctors and nurses, pushing them aside as they tended to Command Master Chief James Finley's lifeless body.

"I don't have a pulse," said one of the doctors.

The other doctor went over to Big Fin, opened his eyelids and shined a penlight into his eyes hoping for pupil dilation. A nurse checked the machines. Then one of the doctors spoke the words Fin would never forget.

"I am going to call this."

"Noooooooooo......JAMES WAKE UP BABY!"

fin

the night before

"DAD!! DAD!!!!!"

The doctor looked at Rose somberly.

"Ma'am, I am very sorry."

Rose collapsed on the floor. Fin knelt next to her and the two wept as they stared at James. The doctors and nurses left to allow them a moment to grieve. Fin helped Rose to her feet, and she walked over to James with his support. He had a peaceful look on his face. Rose laid her head on his chest, then crawled in the bed with him. She reached back and turned the fluorescent light behind them off. Fin kissed his father, then his mother, then left the room.

"That was September 25th, 2010. I was nineteen years old and my life was never the same again."

Cori's nausea got the best of her. She darted to the bathroom.

"Baby, are you okay?"

She began to vomit almost immediately and barely made it to the toilet. Fin rushed in behind her and rubbed her back. When her stomach had finally stopped ejecting its contents, she turned to Fin who was kneeling by her side and cried.

"Baby, are you ok? You have been throwing up a lot the past few days."

Cori didn't care about how she felt. Her heart was broken for Fin.

fin

the night before

"I am so sorry, baby."

"For throwing up?"

"No, that you lost your dad!

"You didn't give him cancer, Cori."

He sat down, placing his back against the bathtub and pulled her in between his legs. She leaned her back against his chest as they sat on the cold bathroom tile. The bathroom light was still off and the only light was that of the streetlamps outside, peeking through the window.

"I am sorry you had to go through that. Now I get why you dropped out. I would have, too. I can't even begin to imagine if I had to watch my daddy die like that."

"It actually wasn't because of that. It was my mama. When dad died, she went into such a depression. She stopped going to work and almost never left her room. I took the rest of that semester off to be with her. Eventually, I had been out for so long, I just decided to get a job and work on my programming on my own."

"What made you come back?"

"Like I told you the day we met, a friend. He came over, I was sitting on the porch in Dad's chair, and he basically told me to snap out of it. Mama was doing better too. But my boy convinced me that I was wasting my talent. He dropped me off on campus and that same day I registered for class. Only classes they had left were Algebra and Philosophy."

Cori looked over her shoulder at Fin and smiled, realizing had

fin

the night before

it not been for that friend, and that conversation, they may never have reconnected. *Next time I see Stacks, I am gonna hug him. Still don't like him though.* Fin felt at peace, a peace he hadn't experienced for a long time. He looked down at the woman he loved and kissed the crown of her head.

"C'mon, my love. You have a big day tomorrow."

Fin motioned for her to adjust so he could stand and then help her up. Cori had almost forgotten that she did have an important meeting the next day, one she had been anxious over and dreading simultaneously.

"Oh my God, after tonight, and the way I have been feeling, I don't know if I can do it."

"You got this, baby. Tomorrow our dreams start coming true."

The two kissed then went to bed. Fin turned his back to her, to try feigning sleep.

"Fin?"

"Cori?"

Cori giggled, and gently shoved him in the back, causing him to smile and turn towards her.

"What made you think of all of that? What made you tell me that tonight?"

"That's simple. You."

"What do you mean, me?"

fin

the night before

"You were what my father wanted for me. You've been my inspiration to live again from the moment I laid eyes on you. I was trapped in that moment, the moment my father died, my head still laying on his lap, sleeping. The day I walked back on campus, I didn't wanna be there. Then I saw you. You changed my life. Tonight, I wasn't just sad he was gone. Tonight, I was more saddened because he would never get to meet you or you him. That you'd never know how special he was. I just miss my dad, is all."

Cori reached out and caressed his face.

"I love you, Mr. Finley."

"I love you too, Ms. Porter.

She cuddled up close, her back to him as he wrapped his arms around her. The two drifted off into a deep, peaceful sleep. Tomorrow was the day that would change their lives.

chapter eighteen

flashing lights

When Cori woke the next morning, she crept out of bed carefully as to not wake Fin. She was exhausted from the night before, but knew she had no time to rest. The day prior, she was informed she would have a meeting today at the School of Medicine Program Office. The meeting was to be with her counselor, and the Dean of the M.D. program, Dr. Finch. She had submitted her early entrant application to the program last year, and was denied, that denial was delivered at a similar impromptu meeting as well. She wasn't looking forward to this meeting, and the last thing she needed was another letdown, especially the way she had been feeling recently. She also received word that she would need to come into work tonight on what was supposed to be her first day off in over a week. After last night, she was mentally and physically exhausted. She walked into the bathroom. The door closing behind her woke Fin.

"Morning, baby."

fin

flashing lights

Cori reopened the bathroom door. "Hey. Did I wake you?"

"It's all good. You getting ready to go to campus?"

"Yeah. Might as well get this meeting over."

Fin got out of bed and walked over to the bathroom. He leaned into the open door.

"Now why are you thinking like that? They gonna tell you that you got it."

"I just can't take another disappointment, baby."

Fin entered the bathroom and wrapped his arms around her from behind. She rubbed her hands on his forearms as he kissed her neck. She closed her eyes.

"Cori, you are the smartest person I know. You've been wanting to be a doctor since you were a kid. Besides, did Dr. Crumpler give up when someone told her no?"

Her heart warmed. *He remembered. God, do I love this man!*

"How about I make you some breakfast?"

She looked at him over her shoulder.

"Oh, so you just gonna kill me now and put me out of my misery?"

"What did you say, punk?"

328

fin

flashing lights

She squealed as he began tickling her. She wrestled free and pushed him out of the bathroom.

"Go, fool! Let me get ready!"

She closed the door and turned to the mirror. *He is so damn silly!* She showered, hastily did her makeup, then got dressed. She walked back over to the bed where Fin was laying down, his face buried in his phone.

"Better not be talking to no one else!"

"Hedging my bets. In case you don't become a doctor, I got a pre-law student lined up."

She jumped on him, causing him to let out a howl as her weight landed on his stomach.

"Mr. Finley, don't get beat up."

"If you did, I'd have her sue you!"

She twisted the flesh on his bare chest as he laughed and gave in. He flipped her on to her side, restraining her hands.

"You know there is no one else, but you. You're all I need."

He let her hands go. She reached up and pulled his face close.

"Better be..."

They kissed as his hand ran down the side of her torso, settling on her thigh.

fin

flashing lights

"I love you, Ms. Porter."

"I love you, too."

"Now, go be smart!"

Cori loved when he said that to her. She grabbed the keys to the car, left their apartment then drove to campus. Her stomach began to grow uneasy as she parked. She took a deep breath, fighting her stomach's desire to throw up, then walked the long stretch across campus, nervously increasing her speed, although every step filled her with dread. As she approached her destination, she realized she had never noticed the number of stairs in the front of the building before. As she approached, her eyes quickly scanned their number. *Thirteen fucking stairs. Thirteen unlucky fucking stairs!*

Her legs felt heavy; each step felt like she was climbing a mountain. She was still feeling the heaviness of the night before, after hearing Fin's pain, and that feeling carried on throughout the morning. The anticipation of what she was going to be told, only made it worse! She reached the top, and swung the heavy mahogany door inlaid with glass panes that had the TSU crest laser etched on one pane, the image of Dr. Crumpler on the other. Dr. Crumpler's stern and powerful gaze still impacted Cori every time she saw her picture. She walked down the hallway lined with cream and gray marble flooring. Her sneakers gave off a slight squeak as she transited to Dr. Finch's office. Cori finally arrived at her destination, grabbed the antique doorknob and hesitantly knocked on the door as she entered. Dr. Finch had a standard knock then enter policy.

"Ms. Porter. Please, come in," proclaimed Dr. Finch in her deep, southern drawl.

fin

flashing lights

Dr. Finch was a tall, slender woman. Her honey toned skin always seemed to glow of regality. She was simultaneously captivating and intimidating, as if in the presence of royalty. Mr. Maddox, her student advisor, wore a slight grin though Cori hadn't really noticed

"Hey, Cori. Glad you could make it so fast."

Mr. Maddox had been Cori's student advisor since she arrived at TSU and was a fairly decent looking man from Detroit. Most of the female student body on campus would kill to have him as their S.A. If any of them got to know him the way Cori had, they'd know that a fleeting relationship isn't what he wanted, not since his wife's passing from breast cancer a few years back. He still carried the pain of her loss in his eyes.

"Good afternoon, Dr. Finch. Mr. Maddox."

Her normal, powerful, sassy voice was nowhere to be found, at the moment. She felt as if she was talking underwater with marbles in her mouth. Dr. Finch sensed Cori's unease. She waved her hand as if she was presenting the crown jewels,

"Please, have a seat. So, I am going to get right to it."

Right then, a gentle smile crept across both of their faces. She had been accepted into TSU's Medical Program. It was a much-needed boost to her day; hell - to her life! She couldn't wait to tell Fin, but she didn't want to tell him over the phone. She loved the way his big, brown eyes glowed as they looked at her whenever she shared good news. No one had ever looked at her like she was their everything until Fin. She didn't want to waste the magnitude of something this significant over the phone. Her day was a blur, all she could think of was that morning's meeting. Now that she was at work, she was excited to get off. She needed to feel his joy in her presence. She had been hinting and teasing him throughout their nightly, endless text messages about her news all evening.

> Cori: *7:06pm Wait 'til I get U home tonight. I am gonna blow ur mind.*
>
> Fin: *7:06pm Oh do tell.....>:)*
>
> Cori: *7:06pm Get your mind out the gutter! LOL WYD*
>
> Cori: *7:10pm Baby?????*
>
> Cori: *7:12pm Ummmm....hellooooooo?*
>
> Fin: *7:14pm Well I WAS talking to my Mama. Kinda hard to concentrate on Christian endeavors when ur talking about blowing things.*
>
> Cori: *7:15pm LOLOL C Y U always gotta be nasty?!?!*
>
> Fin: *7:16pm Why U gotta be so damn fine?*
>
> Cori: *7:16pm LOL Boy bye. Tell Mama Rose I said hello TTYL :**
>
> Fin: *7:18pm She says hi Little Bug. TTYL baby <3 U*
>
> Cori: *7:19pm I <3 U 2*

Fin was her everything. No one made her feel so secure and empowered the way he did. Now she gets to share this moment of perseverance and determination fulfilled with the love of her life. Her dream, *their* dreams were coming true. But first, she needed to get to him. She didn't mind her job in the cafeteria. She rationalized her position in the food service industry because she thoroughly enjoyed interacting with the doctors and nurses at Norfolk General. The times she was able to share a meal with one of them, and talk about their day-to-day, invigorated her. Tonight, wasn't one of those nights. The only thing that kept her spirits up was news of medical school, and her anticipation of sharing it with Fin.

It was 10:17pm, and by the time she counted her register, clocked out and got to the car, it should be around 10:45pm. That would give her plenty of time to get to Brown's and pick up Fin. Fin would just hang in the back room and study until she got there, as usual. She let out a little giggle as she secretly hoped Paulie was working tonight. She liked teasing Fin by feigning she liked Paulie's comments about her. Cori saw Paulie as an old, harmless man that was having fun in his later years. She truly liked him. She made speedy work of counting down her register, as she always kept a running total of what she took in mentally. *Two hundred ten dollars and twelve cents.* Her mental ledger matched the actual one. Cori gave her receipts and cash to the shift supervisor, and after a brief review, he signed them off without looking up.

"Goodnight, Ms. Porter."

"Night."

She almost skipped away with excitement. Cori went back to her register station, grabbed her purse, tote bag with her lunch and sweater (sometimes the cafeteria got a little chilly), slid her cellphone into her bag and waved goodbye to her fellow service workers.

"Nite y'all!"

fin

flashing lights

She was met with a chorus of "Byyyeeeee Cori."

She wound through the myriad of corridors to get to the front entrance, passing various orderlies, nurses, food service workers picking up empty trays, doctors, nurses, patients in robes on an evening stroll until finally she reached the security desk. She waved to the two security guards on duty that night.

"Night, Steve. Night, Jay."

They merely waved and smiled, as she briskly passed them by. The sounds of the set of automatic double doors as they opened were quickly drowned out by a simple thought: *Damn, it's kinda cold tonight!* When the unusually cold air whipped into the entrance of the hospital, she was reminded of her objections to Fin getting the heater fixed. She knew Fin would throw it in her face, but she wasn't going to let him know she was glad he did it, or that he was right. Once again, she giggled. Cori reached into her bag to grab her sweater and put it on before she went outside but paused when she noticed the white indicator light on her phone was blinking. She had missed a call. Her phone was still on vibrate as she isn't supposed to have her cellphone at her register, but all the girls do it. She tapped the screen and saw it was Fin. *I'll call him as soon as I get to the car.* She wouldn't be able to hear him over this wind anyway.

Cori pulled her sweater on, grabbed her keys out of her purse before throwing it and her tote over her shoulder, then made her way to the car. A few seconds later, Fin was calling again. She hit the button to answer but didn't hear anything.

"I'm coming, baby. Gimme a sec to get to the car, and I'll call you back."

334

fin

flashing lights

She didn't know if Fin could hear her, Lord knows she couldn't hear him. She hit the disable button for the alarm on the Caprice's key fob, opened the back door, threw her bags inside, jumped in the front seat, started the car and turned the heater on full blast. It was only 10:46pm. Cori saw she was a bit behind schedule. The three-minute ride to Brown's Stop-N-Go meant she would be to Fin in no time. As she pulled out of the parking lot, she called Fin.

RIIIINNNNGGGG!!!

RIIIINNNNGGGG!!!

RIIIINNNNGGGG!!!

He didn't answer.

"Hey, you've reached Fin. Leave me a message and I'll get back to you...or not."

BEEEEEEEEEEEEEEEEEEP

"How you gonna blow me up, then not answer when I call you back? You are something else, Mr. Finley! I'll be there in a few, baby. I have something to teeelllllll yooooouuuu!"

She blew a kiss before she hung up. Just hearing Fin's voice had her on cloud nine. She navigated the tree-canopied road of Greenwich Blvd towards the highway. She was only two exits away once she got on I-266 W and after passing the Westborough Blvd exit, she reached Ballentine Road. As she exited the highway using the corkscrewed exit ramp, she could see a police cruiser, with its sirens blaring and lights flashing, flying down Ballentine. She hated that Fin kept the job at Brown's, but knew it was a temporary peril for a long-term gain. Fin was one of the smartest, most articulate, most creative people she had ever met; her chocolate dreamer as she would tease him. She giggled once again.

She turned into the parking lot in front of Brown's, passing the two gas pumps out front. The row of fluorescent lights under the awning above the gas pumps flickered. *When is Brown gonna get that light fixed?* She made the sharp turn into the parking space in front of the entrance. The wheels let out a loud squeal. *Lord, this man is gonna have to get them brakes looked at! See?!! We could've used that heater money on these breaks!! That's what I am gonna say when he tries to bring up how cold it is tonight!* Cori reached for her phone to text Fin.

> Cori: Hey baby. I'm outside. Grab me a sweet tea on your way out pleeeeeaaaassseee?

No answer.

"Lord, this man got his ringer turned off again."

She shook her head and turned the car off so she could exit and go inside Brown's. The jingle of her keys echoed in the still night as she walked the six feet from the car to the entrance of Brown's. She remembered how Fin often teases her for having all of the unnecessary keys (as he calls them), club member cards and trinkets on her keychain. *I do sound like a damn janitor.* She approached Brown's and opened the door.

Ding-a-ling!

"Fin!"

336

fin

flashing lights

No one responded. Her cry met only by the door's chime announcing her entrance. She stepped into Brown's fully and the door closed behind her.

"FIN!"

Again, no answer.

Cori decided to walk in back and find him. The store seemed unmanned, but she figured his head was buried in one of his analytics books. *Now, he knows full well if Mr. Brown walked in, he..........*

An odd aroma broke her train of thought. While she couldn't place the smell, it was off putting to her nose. The scent of gunpowder and blood can do that to those unfamiliar with it. She began walking, passing the counter and was going to head in back where she assumed, he was. It was then that something in her peripheral vision caught her attention. *What was that behind the counter? Something isn't right...*

Her heart began to race. She approached the counter and register framed in plexiglass that allowed a large window for customer-clerk interaction. The plexiglass was decorated in state lottery scratch-offs, cigarettes, cigars, bootleg CDs and other items. Tears rolled down her face. She now knew what had caught her eye. Blood, bone and brain littered the back wall behind the register. Her once silent cry now turned into a full-on hysterical meltdown as she saw Paulie dead, heaped on his side, eyes gazing up at her.

"Oh my GOD!!!"

"FIIIIIIIIIIIIIIIIIIIINNNNNNNNNNNN!!!!!!!!!!!!!!!!!!!"

"FIIIIIIIIIIIIIIIIIIIINNNNNNNNNNNN!!!!!!!!!!!!!!!!!!!"

fin

flashing lights

Cori wanted him to come save her from this horror, but he was nowhere to be found. Panicked, she darted to the back of the store to head down the aisle leading to the back room and was greeted by the wreckage on the floor. Cleaning products, bottles of motor oil, packages of paper plates and toilet paper were everywhere, courtesy of the fleeing gunman. She navigated the trip hazards in long, leaping, panic-filled strides, and made it to the back room. The room was dark, the computer which was normally on was off. The only light besides the soft glow from two video monitors that displayed the front and inside of Brown's Stop-N-Go was the orange glow from the streetlamps creeping through the slightly ajar door that led to the dumpster out back. She burst through the doors and could see the officer, kneeling, his service weapon on the floor as his fist rested on top of his weapon. His head was down hiding his face. He seemed to be crying but whatever he was crying about couldn't be seen as the dumpster blocked her view. She took another step and saw Fin's head, face up next to the officer's knee.

"FIIIIIIIIIIIIIIIIIIIIIIIIIIIIIIIIIIIIIIIINNNNNNNNNNNNNNNN!!!!!!!!!!!!"

Cori flew over to Fin, pushing the officer onto his ass, scooped Fin's head up in her arms and cradled him.

"GET UP, FIN!"

"GET UP, BABY!!"

"NO! NO! NO! NO!! GET UP, FIN!!"

"..............Cori................"

"PLEASE, GOD, *NOOOOOOOOOOOOOOOOOOOOO!!*"

fin

flashing lights

Cori's cries could be heard for blocks and drowned out the voice speaking to her.

"FIN, BABY PLEEEEEEEEEEEEAAAAAAAAAASSSSSSSSEEEEEEE GET UP!!"

"Cori….."

Cori, blinded by her tears and pain, heard the voice calling her this time. It was a voice she knew. She looked down at her Fin; his motionless body, still cradled in her arms, his beautiful, brown lifeless eyes still moist from his tears, staring back at her. She thought her prayer had been answered, that her Fin, her chocolate dreamer, her everything was alive. But it wasn't him. It was the officer.

"Cori…I'm so sorry."

Cori snapped her head over to the voice. Her already broken heart was now completely obliterated.

"WHAT?!?!……………………NO…NO….NO…………YOU DID THIS! WHAT DID YOU DO!?!?!? NO….NOOOOOO…..noooooooo……"

Her voice trailed into uncontrollable crying, riddled in disbelief and a gut-wrenching pain that would never be healed. Just then, white headlights from the patrol car illuminated the back of Brown's. The red and blue lights on top of the car danced on Cori skin, on the officer and reflected in Fin's eyes. The officer's partner had given up chase of the other suspect upon hearing his partner's frantic radio call and returned to the scene. The senior officer had completely broken protocol by leaving him in the first place; he figured the kid wouldn't catch the other suspect anyway, but when he heard the call of shots fired, suspect down, his heart sank. The officer exited the vehicle, drew his weapon, and surveyed the scene. He saw his partner,

fin

flashing lights

kneeling, his dark hair drenched in sweat, his white skin pale from horror, his hands trembling and reaching out towards Cori, his cheeks moist from tears. He saw Cori, inconsolably weeping, cradling Fin's lifeless body. He knew how this would be spun. He knew that this would be controversial; a white cop killing an unarmed black man. He kept looking for a weapon but couldn't find one. The young officer kept repeating something over and over as he wept through pain and regret.

"I thought he had a gun...I didn't know it was him...Oh, my GOD..........."

Finally, the senior officer spoke.

"Justin...*what did you do?*"

chapter nineteen

my brother's keeper part two

"You right, man. Here I am comin' over here to drop some knowledge on you and you schooling me!" said Stacks.

"Not everything that is faced can be changed."

Stacks was impressed. He looked over at Fin.

"But nothing can be changed until it is faced. You really just hit me with Baldwin, Bruh?"

Fin smiled. "Still got your book ya' know!"

"Yeah, I know. The Fire Next Time! Still my favorite."

"Make me a promise: I'll get off my ass and get back to school, if you get off your ass and get out of the life."

fin

my brother's keeper part two

Stacks leaned back into the wicker chair he sat in. He shook his head as a loving grin crept on his face. He came here to help his brother find himself again, and in the process, his brother found him.

"Promise."

He extended his closed fist to Fin. Fin reciprocated. No further words needed to be said, not between brothers. But words interrupted their moment, though the words didn't come from either of them.

"What up, Fi......."

When he saw Stacks sitting on the porch, Justin's voice trailed off. He froze in his tracks. He had heard through Fin that Stacks had animosity towards him. He wanted to tell Stacks thank you. He wanted to tell him that his life was good now, that Andrew was out of it. He wanted to apologize. *I'm sorry, Stacks. I didn't know any of that would happen. I'm sorry...and thank you.* He wanted to say all the thoughts running through his mind, but he said nothing. Stacks and Fin looked at Justin. Fin quickly looked over at Stacks who kept his glare on Justin. Stacks had many words for Justin but kept them all to himself, he simply stared at him. Fin didn't dare attempt to orchestrate a reconciliation in this moment, he knew Stacks wasn't ready for it. Truth was, he may never be ready for it. Stacks was full of anger and hurt. He stood up from the chair and extended his fist one last time to Fin.

"I'mma go, Bruh."

As usual, Fin reciprocated. "Aight."

Stacks took his sunglasses out of his jacket, placed them on his face, then walked down the stairs, his head high looking past Justin.

fin

my brother's keeper part two

Justin had a rush of fear take over him, not knowing if Stacks would greet him, hit him or simply ignore him. Stacks made it to the gate and opened it, pausing to look down at Justin. Justin's nerves got the best of him.

"What up, Stacks?"

What's up? What's up is my daddy and brother are dead. What's up is my baby brother had to see all that shit!! All 'cause I was weak. I was stupid and fucked around with you! Like Justin before him however, Stacks remained silent. He simply closed the gate behind him, walked to his candy painted, dark blue Cadillac and drove away. Justin and Fin both watched him as he drove off before Justin opened the gate and walked up to the porch.

"He never gonna fuck with me again, huh?"

"I dunno...doubt it."

"That shit wasn't my fault, man!"

"Ain't how he sees it."

"Fuck, if he ain't whip my dad's ass, none of that shit woulda happened!"

"Oh, yo' daddy would've never hit you again, huh? Maybe you should go tell him that."

"Bro, I ain't tryna die!"

Justin made his way atop the porch and plopped down in the open chair.

"So, what you been up to, Bro? I haven't seen you around lately."

Fin gave a shoulder shrug. "I dunno. Living, I guess."

343

fin

my brother's keeper part two

"Living?!? That ain't the Fin I know, Bro. You gotta snap outta this shit!"

"So, what you got going on 'Mr. My Life Is Perfect'?"

"Oh, shit! CHECK IT OUT!!"

Justin stood up and removed his sweatshirt revealing a gray t-shirt that read NORFOLK POLICE DEPARTMENT CADET.

"A COP?!?!"

"Yeah! Dope, right?!"

"YOU??!?! A COP?!?!"

Fin burst out into laughter. Justin's face looked as if he was just told Santa Claus wasn't real. Fin tried to temper his amusement, covering his mouth and raising his hand towards Justin. He saw that Justin was offended. He stifled his laughter.

"You serious, huh? My bad, Bro. Fuck you wanna be a cop for?"

Justin sat down, disappointed by Fin's reaction.

"Thought you'd be proud of me, Bro."

"What made you think that? And you still ain't answered my question: the fuck you wanna be police for?"

Justin's head remained low; his hands now folded across is stomach.

"'Cause of you!"

"ME?!?!"

fin

my brother's keeper part two

"Yeah, you. You always protected me. You ain't even know me but you stood up for me, protected me from LaTrell, from Stacks when he would pick on me. You ain't have to do that."

Now Fin felt terrible. Though he never asked anything of Justin, this simple acknowledgement meant more to him than he ever thought it would. He dropped his head. Justin looked over at him and continued.

"I look up to you, Bro. I ain't smart like you with computers and shit, and I don't be reading all those books like Stacks, but I do know when people are hurtin' and need help, need protection. I'm gonna do that..."

Justin looked at Fin before he continued: "...like you did for me."

Fin looked over at his "other" brother. The boys had been through so much together. Though he, Justin and Stacks never hung out again the way they did that day in Stacks' Cadillac, Fin still had a fondness for both of them. When Big Fin died, both were there to comfort him. Stacks at the hospital right after Big Fin passed, Justin at the funeral. To hear that he inspired Justin to be a police officer, to want to protect and help people, a far cry from the environment Justin grew up in, touched him. He didn't see himself as a protector, he simply didn't like bullies. Justin had obviously thought long and hard about this. It was something that burned in his heart. Fin knew he had no right to mock that.

"You're really serious about this, ain't you?"

"Yeah, Bro. Besides, the Bell name ain't shit in these streets. Everybody remembers how fucked up my daddy was as a cop and as a human fucking being. I wanna be better."

fin

my brother's keeper part two

Fin nodded his head approvingly. He was proud of and happy for him. He couldn't miss an opportunity to taunt him though.

"They gonna give yo' crazy ass a gun?!"

"And a damn badge!

 Justin jumped up and made a gun with his fingers pointing it at Fin.

"I'mma be like 'FREEZE!! SHOW ME YOUR HANDS'!!"

Fin slapped his hands away. "Man, sit yo' trigger happy ass down!"

Then the two old friends burst out into laughter.

chapter twenty

broken

Patricia Tanner got the call about the shooting at Brown's at eleven-thirteen, right in the middle of her date night. She looked over to her husband with a look of dread as she listened to the details. Frank Tanner knew the drill. He got up, went to the bedroom, and readied her uniform, laying it flat on the bed. Frank had retired nine months ago, stepping down as the Norfolk Police Department's Deputy Operations Commander after thirty-five years on the force. He had taken many calls like the one his wife was handling in his day. Frank reentered the room and saw her on the phone.

"Trish, your uniform is on the bed."

Patricia pulled the phone away from her mouth and kissed him on the cheek.

"*This* is why I love you."

fin

broken

As the dispatch officer spoke, she took mental notes of the details as she hastily dressed. *Brown's, robbery, two dead, officer shooting, one in store, one behind store by dumpster, no officers hurt.*

"Who were the officers involved?"

"Officer Jimenez and Officer Bell.

"Bell? Justin Bell?"

"Yeah. He shot the suspect behind the store. That's why I called you personally."

"Fuck! Press on scene?"

"Not that I know of, but you know they will be."

"Tell the On-scene commander I'll be there in ten."

"Copy!"

She hurriedly got into uniform, grabbed her service weapon, and searched frantically for her keys.

"Fraaaaaaaank!"

Frank was standing at the door, her car keys in hand.

"This a bad one?"

"It's Justin. He shot a kid."

"I'll grab my jacket."

348

fin

broken

"No, Frank. I am the chief of this station. I have to be the lead on this. You show up, and everyone will turn to you, retired or not, when they should be turning to me."

"You're one hundred percent correct. I apologize."

"No, baby. I get it."

She kissed him. "I'll call you once I have all the particulars."

Patricia switched into Chief Tanner mode. She tried to focus her mind, reminding herself that she had to remain impartial, that she couldn't let her affinity for Justin impact her responsibility to make the correct call. She struggled with it though. When Justin first told her he wanted to be a police officer, she initially had reservations. She wasn't sure if after everything he had been through, he had the mental make-up to handle the streets, especially in Valebrook. When he completed Basic Training, she pulled some strings to have him assigned to a less dangerous area, Parker Heights. Her recent hit in manning though made her take whatever officers Downtown forced upon her. Justin Bell was one of those officers.

Within minutes, Chief Tanner arrived on scene. She switched her siren and lights off about a block away. She wanted to do a quick sweep around the area in relative anonymity. She saw a crowd gathering, and two local news stations were already there. *Damn vultures!* Yellow tape and uniformed officers quarantined the majority of the parking lot in front of Brown's. Two patrol cars were parked under the flickering lights of the gas pump awning. Detectives were crawling over the scene, at least three inside of Brown's, another two walking the area behind the building where a body laid covered in a white cloth, the signal that the person was deceased. The crowd seemed normal, neighborhood folk wanting to know what happened at Brown's. Across the street was an empty parking garage, save for one vehicle in the back corner that sat there with its headlights off. The vehicle looked to be occupied. Normally she would investigate but right now she had more important issues to tend to.

She grabbed her combination hat, covered in white cloth, its shield and fretting prominently displayed on top. She made her way across the street towards the crowd. An officer standing perimeter duty saw her approaching and notified the On-scene commander of her arrival. Lieutenant Devine began looking for which direction she approached from and made his way to her once he located her.

"Chief."

Chief Tanner slid on a pair of rubber gloves she retrieved from her pocket and they entered Brown's.

"What do we know?"

"Seems like this was a robbery gone bad. We ran the security footage and saw two men enter into Brown's around 10:42. One had a gun, pointed it at this man. So far, no name on him."

"We got an ID on the shooters?"

"Black, both wore masks, looked young. Only one had a gun from what we could see. Looked like he had dreads and some sort of tattoo on his right hand. Called in tech support to enhance the video, see if we have a match in the gang database."

"You think this is a gang related shooting?"

"Doubt it, but we will see if it turns anything up. Video shows some brief talking, you see headlights outside through the door. I am assuming that was Jimenez and Bell. Haven't talked to either yet. I know the need their PBA reps present."

Chief Tanner looked at the scene and knew this wasn't gang related. *Why would a gang rob Brown's?* She looked over the counter at Paulie, looking past the detective behind the counter taking notes.

"Why'd they shoot the clerk?"

"Can't say exactly. The guy gave up the money. The shooter even cracked him in the face with his gun to get him to do it."

She shook her head. "And they still killed him."

Chief Tanner walked to the back of the store and saw the mess of products on the floor in the back aisle leading to the back room. She turned back to the front to exit Brown's. The On-scene commander looked puzzled as to why she stopped.

"You don't wanna walk that?"

Chief Tanner turned to walk out of the door.

"Doesn't look like it's been worked yet. Get a team in here to dust everything on the floor and that shelf for prints."

The On-scene commander made a quick radio call to comply with Chief Tanner's orders. As she exited the store, she paused to look at the crowd. It had grown and a third news crew had arrived. She made her way over to the group of officers under the awning.

"Where's Bell?"

"Right there, Ma'am."

fin

broken

The junior officer pointed to a police cruiser with its door open. She approached the car and saw Justin, sitting there motionless, almost catatonic.

"Officer Bell."

Justin didn't move, he stayed silent, the same way he did all those years ago in what is now *her* office.

"Officer Bell!"

Again, he didn't respond.

"JUSTIN!" she shouted, startling him back to life. "What happened?"

Justin just started crying, mumbling something in audible under his breath.

"Officer Bell, look at me! LOOK AT ME!"

He snapped his head up and stared at her, his eyes red from weeping and glassed over.

"I need you to get it the fuck together! There are news crews here and if you're sitting here crying, you are as good as done in the court of public opinion. Now tell me what the fuck happened here?"

He started crying again.

"I didn't know it was him! I didn't knooooowwww.....I didn't knooooowwww....OH MY GOD.......I didn't knooooowww....."

"Who, Justin? Didn't know it was who?"

fin

broken

She looked over to the second crime scene behind the building.

"Who is that? Who did you shoot?"

"OOOHHH MYYY GOOOOODDDD..."

Chief Tanner left Justin in the car, closing the door to muffle the sound of his cries, and quickened her pace to the second scene. As she approached, two detectives, two of her best, were working it. Detective Dalton saw her walking towards them.

"Shit show here, Chief. We got a real shit show here on this one."

Chief Tanner crouched down by the body and removed the cloth from Fin's face. Her gasp was so loud, both detectives froze immediately and looked at her.

"You knew him?"

She was in disbelief. She looked back to the car where Justin sat only to see him looking back at her through the window.

"Yeah...James Finley. I knew him. So did Bell."

Both detectives looked at each other. "Damn!"

"This some personal beef?"

Chief Tanner felt numb and nauseated.

"No. Did we notify next of kin?"

fin

broken

"Not yet. His girlfriend is around the corner though."

"Where?"

Detective Dalton walked from behind the alley, followed by Chief Tanner, and pointed to another police cruiser where Cori was sitting.

"Get Bell out of here!"

Detective Dalton didn't move.

"NOW!"

Cori now sat in a patrol car, the door open, her feet firmly on the ground though she felt weightless. Her hands were between her legs. She wasn't cold but their placement was the only thing that kept them from shaking. She kept having uncontrollable bouts of crying followed by states of absolute shock. Shock doesn't adequately express her state of mind though. She couldn't stop seeing Fin staring back at her. She kept replaying the last hour or so over in her mind.

Why didn't I take my phone off of silent?

Why didn't I stop to talk to him?

Why didn't I call him before I left the building?

Why did my Fin have to die?

This can't be real.

fin

broken

Oh, my God.....Mama Rose.

Why, God? Why?

Cori didn't know how long Chief Tanner had been standing there, trying to get her attention.

"Ma'am."

Chief Tanner leaned into the car and touched Cori's shoulder.

"Ma'am."

Cori jumped. She didn't want to be touched. She didn't want to be held or consoled. She wanted her love back. Chief Tanner recoiled her hands, throwing them into the air to show she meant no harm.

"Ma'am, I am Chief Tanner. I need to ask you a few questions."

"Any of them gonna bring him back?"

The finality in her words tore her apart.

"Ma'am, I truly am sorry for your loss."

"Sorry? You're sorry?"

Chief Tanner had been in this situation before. Next to visiting the family of a fallen officer, talking to the family of a person that was just killed, especially when that person was killed by police, is the most difficult thing an officer has to do. She was prepared for Cori's righteous anger and wrath, but she needed to get more information.

355

fin

broken

"Ma'am, are you family of the deceased?"

"James."

Chief Tanner immediately knew her mistake and she knew she needed to correct it quickly.

"His name is…"

"James Finley."

Cori looked up at her, surprised that she rattled Fin's name off so quickly. For a brief moment, she went back to when she and Fin first met, and she did the same to him.

"I am sorry Misssss….."

"Porter. Cori Porter."

Normally, Cori would have been more polite and understanding. *Fuck being polite! Fuck her! Fuck Justin! Fuck all of 'em!*

"Ms. Porter, I am so sorry for your loss, but I need to ask you these difficult questions."

Cori checked out again, her mind reminiscing about their conversation that morning. She could hear Fin telling her he loved her, telling her to go be smart. She lamented the fact he didn't know she got accepted to the medical program. He didn't know how much she would miss him, how much she needed him, how the giant crater-sized hole in her heart felt empty and simultaneously filled with fire. She never heard any of the questions Chief Tanner was asking her. Her phone ringing broke her train of thought. She looked down to see who it was and immediately started crying. She answered it.

"Mama…"

"Lil' Bug, where's Fin? They said on the news there had been a shooting where he works and he isn't answering his phone! They said people were KILLED, Cori! PUT HIM ON THE PHONE! PLEEEEAAAASSSEE!!"

"Maaaamaaaa…"

"CORI!! WHERE IS FIN??!! PUT HIM ON THE PHONE, CORI!!"

"Mama he's…they…….Mama………Fin is……"

"No! NO!! PUT HIM ON THE PHOOooooooonnnnnee….."

Cori's world stopped spinning; she was frozen in a moment of pain and helplessness. As much as she wanted her own pain to stop, she wanted to stop Rose's all the more. Rose's heartbreaking, guttural cries were a sound she would never forget. Chief Tanner bent over close to Cori, who was now sobbing almost in chorus with Rose. She touched her gently on her shoulder and took the phone from Cori's limp hand. This time, Cori appreciated the touch. She couldn't have resisted her even if she wanted to.

"Hi, Mrs. Finley. My name is Chief Tanner. We met once before. I am so sorry for……"

Chief Tanner's voice trailed off as she walked away from the police cruiser, not that Cori was listening anyway. It was only then that Cori regained some semblance of awareness to her surroundings. Her eyes drifted off towards the alley where her love still laid. The busy scene didn't seem right. She hadn't noticed that local news stations had arrived and were interviewing witnesses. She couldn't understand why no one else was sad, no one else hurt, no one else seemed to care for her Fin. There were police officers standing just outside of the alley in Cori's view. Their jovial mood angered her. *MY FIN IS LAYING THERE DEAD, KILLED BY ONE OF YOU AND YOU BASTARDS ARE LAUGHING?!?!?* Her sorrowful mind turned into rage. Cori hadn't noticed she had gotten up. She didn't realize she was walking towards the officers. She didn't feel how heavy her breaths were. She didn't hear herself screaming. All she felt was rage, all she felt was pain and the sons of bitches laughing were going to feel it too. Chief Tanner noticed Cori had left the cruiser and was heading towards her officers. She screamed as she darted towards Cori.

"MS. PORTER! MS. PORTER!"

Chief Tanner looked around quickly and saw another officer standing perimeter near the news crew.

"OFFICER WILLIAMS! STOP HER!"

Officer Williams spun around and saw a raging Cori heading towards the other officers standing there, all of them now staring at Cori.

"I HATE YOU! I HATE YOOOOUUUU!!!"

Cori's rage flowed out like venom.

"YOU DID THIS! YOU MOTHERFUCKERS DID THIS TO MY FIN!!"

Officer Williams intercepted Cori before she got anywhere close to the officers. He held her tightly, the pin from his silver shield pressing into his chest as she raged. Then she fell limp in his arms and screamed. While she didn't make it to her targets, she now had a line of sight of the alley. The white sheet draped over his body was stained with two large red, bloody circles that had now merged at their edges. The small, numbered, orange cones on the floor marked where shell casings and Fin's cellphone were found. The yellow tape marked "CRIME SCENE DO NOT CROSS" were draped all around him. Two plain clothes detectives walked around Fin like a coffee table that was in their way. Their gloved hands manipulating Fin's pockets, searching for evidence.

Cori couldn't take it anymore. She fell to the floor and screamed until no sound came out. The crowd that gathered fell silent. The news reporters that were in the middle of live feeds all spun around, their camera operators following suit, aiming their lenses at Cori. Chief Tanner arrived moments later to give direction to Officer Williams to care for Cori, before storming off towards the once jovial but now stoic and fearful officers. Chief Tanner knew what set Cori off and she was having none of it. After thoroughly scolding the officers, Chief Tanner returned to Cori. Cori sat on her bottom, her legs folded out to her side, her right hand on the ground, her left gripping her chest hard as if it could hold the pieces of her heart together. Officer Williams knelt at her side, his arm around her. Chief Tanner knelt down next to them and placed her arm around Cori.

"Ms. Porter, let me take you home."

She and Officer Williams slowly helped Cori to her feet. They escorted her across the street, away from Brown's Stop-N-Go, and into Chief Tanner's cruiser. Once Cori was in, Chief Tanner closed the door and turned to give Officer Williams further instructions. She then walked around the front of the car to take the long, uncomfortable ride to wherever Cori needed to go. Again, she saw the car with its headlights off, sitting there. She entered her vehicle and stared at the

broken

car; it seemed vaguely familiar to her. Her concentration was broken by Cori's voice.

"You knew my Fin?"

"Yes, I did. We met once long ago."

Chief Tanner felt a rush of guilt. She should have persuaded Justin to do something else. Once again, when it came to Justin and Fin, she didn't trust her instincts and do what she knew she should have. She touched Cori's hand as sympathetically and gently as she possibly could.

"Where can I take you?"

"Take me to my Mama's house."

"Ok, where does she stay?"

Cori burst into tears for a moment before gathering herself, leaned her head against the cold window glass, and whimpered:

"On Dorian Street."

Chief Tanner knew by the street name, that she wanted her to take her to Rose. She had worked these streets long enough to know where someone was from. Cori was not a Valebrook product, and Dorian was mere blocks away from Brevoit. As she engaged the car in drive, curiosity got the best of her. She decided to take the back entrance out the parking lot so she could pass the mysterious car from a distance. As she approached the dark blue, candy painted Cadillac DeVille, she realized why she knew the vehicle and why it sat there, its sole occupant staring at Brown's.

fin

broken

She slowed down, her brakes slightly squeaking, and she looked over at Stacks. Stacks looked over at her briefly, the pain and rage she saw in his eyes, the tears streaming down his face, struck her soul. These three boys, Fin, Stacks, and Justin forever intertwined in tragedy, in violence, in grief. He looked away, back at Brown's. Chief Tanner allowed him to grieve and drove away.

chapter twenty-one

the return

Cori sat next to Rose in the hearse. They both sat in silence, hand-in-hand. Though many family members wanted to ride with them after the burial, Patrick ensured they both rode alone. Since Fin's murder, both Rose and Cori had been bombarded with phone calls from friends, family, reporters, lawyers, you name it. They barely had a chance to breathe, let alone process such a devastating loss. For the first time Patrick saw a window where his baby girl and Cori could have peace. He ensured they had it. As she watched Rose, Cori's heart broke all-the-more. The thought that the two most important parts of her life being buried up on that hill, both tragically taken, was unimaginable. Just then Rose turned to Cori, her eyes riddled with pain and grief.

"I love you, Lil' Bug. I loved you from the first day I met you. It was how my baby looked at you."

fin

the return

Tears flowed from Cori's eyes.

"I knew that he was in love with you and why. You brought life back to him. Thank you for giving my baby purpose again. After James died, he huddled around me. He said he was worried about me, but I knew what it was. My baby was lost without his daddy. Then he found you."

As she said that last sentence, Cori dropped her head. Rose, reached out and placed both hands on her cheeks, lifted Cori's head and leaned in closer to ensure their eyes met. Rose's eyes tightened as she stared into Cori's. Rose spoke with all the love and strength she could.

"You made him *so* happy. Y'all love was special baby,"

Cori, for the first time since the night Fin was murdered, broke. She cried hard. She cried loud. Rose pulled her close and laid her head on her bosom.

"You hold on to that love. That's how we keep him with us."

Cori could only nod her head as she wiped her nose. She knew she would never let go of Fin. Truth is, she and Fin found each other right when they needed each other the most. She felt nauseous as if she would vomit right there but she knew she needed to remain strong for Rose. That's what Fin would have done. She gathered herself, stifled her emotions, then sat up and looked at Rose.

"I love you, Mama."

"I love you too, Lil' Bug. More than you'll ever know."

fin

the return

Rose turned back to the window. She stared at that hill, staring at her husband and son's final resting place. Then she spoke into the glass.

"Tell the man I'm ready, Lil' Bug."

"Ok, Mama."

Cori leaned into the partition and gently tapped on the glass signaling to the driver they were ready. As the driver started the ignition and engaged the gears, Rose placed her open hand firmly on the glass and spoke in a soft, barely audible whisper.

"Mama loves you, baby......forever. Take care of our baby, James. I love you both with all my heart."

Rose's head turned to keep the hill in view as the car wound through the cemetery. When the hill could be seen no more, she gently leaned her head against the glass and reached out for Cori's hand. They sat there, hands locked in grief, bound by love and comfort, silently for the rest of the voyage back to Patrick and Odella's home.

Leaning against his blue Cadillac, Stacks watched Cori and Rose as they sat in the hearse. He didn't join everyone at the burial or funeral. He waited patiently until everyone had left, with Rose and Cori being the last remaining mourners. He knew Cori didn't like him, though he was fond of Rose. He hadn't been by to see either of them yet, but he would. First, he needed to be alone, alone with his brother. So, he patiently waited and watched as they sat in the hearse. When he heard the car's engine turn on he let out a deep sigh. As much as he wanted to talk to Fin, he wasn't looking forward to it. Seeing the grave would make it real. As the hearse turned the last bend, he slowly made his way towards the burial plot. He ascended the hill slowly, every step weighted with anguish. When he arrived at the summit, the finality of the moment rocked him.

"What up, Socrates?"

He felt lightheaded, fell to one knee and removed his sunglasses.

"Damn, Bruh. Can't believe your gone."

He looked around to ensure no one could see him in his moment of vulnerability. He didn't want to be Mr. Stacks right then. He needed to be Chris. He sat down next to the open grave and looked down at Fin's black casket adorned in chrome. He began to cry.

"Man, when Mike died, I was just a kid. Had *to be tough* though. Wasn't really allowed to cry about that shit. Coop wasn't having it. All I wanted to know was why my big brother was dead...and why no one seemed to be sad like I was. I know *now*, they were hurting too, just in a different way. Streets rob you of a lot of shit! Being vulnerable is definitely one of 'em.

"I ain't even wanna go to Coop's funeral. I couldn't. I was so fucking mad he made me do that shit. Hmmph! Probably woulda burned that fucking church to the ground if I had. Mafucka was never my father, I was never his son. I was just another Morton soldier in a long line of Morton soldiers. Shan? I felt bad about Shan, but he was never a brother to me, just a fucking bully. He was still my blood so, guess I had to feel something. But he too was just another Morton Soldier!"

He shook his head and wiped his eyes on his sleeve.

fin

the return

"I ain't gonna be that shit no more, Fin. I promise you that. I was already getting me, Shay, Dee and CJ outta here. I was gonna tell you next time I saw you. I was keeping that promise, Bruh."

He wrapped his arms around his knees. His heart began beating rapidly. He let long, angry breaths flow from his mouth.

"Why you, Fin? Why, man? You were smart. Like genius smart with your computers and stuff. You were supposed to make it outta here, make us all proud. Shit ain't right! This shit ain't fucking fair, man!"

He put his head in between his knees and cried. He cried for Fin. He cried for Mike. He cried for Shan. He even cried for Coop. Mostly though, he cried for himself. He had been carrying so much weight, had so many scars, many that had never healed and hurt as if they were fresh. He never allowed himself the space to cry. He felt he couldn't. Fin's death was the final wound on his battered soul, one that he knew if he didn't address, would fester and kill his spirit. So, for the first time, Mr. Stacks allowed Christopher Morton to cry. His audible sobs gave a slight echo high up on the hill, but he didn't care. This was his brother laying in that hole. He looked up at the sky and took in a long deep breath, holding it before exhaling then turning back to Fin.

"I'mma make sure CJ knows about his Uncle Fin. I promise you that. And even though we getting' the fuck outta Norfolk, I'mma always check in on ya' mama and ya' girl. Oh, I forgot something."

He rose to his feet and dusted himself off, then he reached into his inside jacket pocket and produced the tattered copy of James Baldwin's book he lent Fin all those years ago. He rubbed his fingers over the wrinkled and partially torn cover. He thumbed the edges of its pages, many of which had folded or damaged corners.

367

fin

the return

"You always did like this book. Take it with you, Bruh. When you get up there, tell Brother Baldwin I said what up."

He tossed the book into the dark grave. The sound of the thud of the book against the casket resonated throughout his body. He wiped a final tear from his eye.

"I love you, Fin. Be easy."

He placed his sunglasses back on, kissed his fingertips then tapped his heart. He gave the grave a final look, then turned to return to his car. It was then that he noticed Gray Boy leaning up against his Cadillac. *The fuck he doing here? He ain't even fuck with Fin like that! This ain't the day for no business shit!*

"What up, Gray?"

"Boss Man."

Gray walked over to meet Stacks as arrived at the bottom of the hill. He extended his hand, and when Stacks accepted it, he pulled him in closer and hugged him. Stacks wasn't prepared for the embrace, but he gladly responded in kind.

"I know you hurting, Bruh. He was a stand-up dude."

Stacks nodded his head, then they released one and other.

"Whatchu doing here, anyway?"

"One, to pay my respects. I didn't fuck wit' Fin too tough, but like I said, he was a stand-up dude. He had heart."

"Yeah. Remember how he punked LaTrell's ass?"

fin

the return

The two laughed.

"You said one. What's two?"

Gray Boy reached into his pocket and pulled out his cellphone. He unlocked the screen and open his video application. Stacks stared at him. *What the fuck is he doing?* Gray found what he was looking for and handed the phone to Stacks.

"The fuck is this?"

"Press play."

Stacks frowned, then looked down at the phone. When he pressed the button, all of his hurt turned into sheer rage. It was a copy of the surveillance video from Brown's.

"How'd you come by this?"

"A detective owed me one."

"You talking to cops now?"

"I use them for what their worth, information. It's how I got that. Keep watching."

Stacks looked at the video again. As he watched the ordeal unfold, he had a detailed aerial view of the counter from behind. He saw as the gunman threatened Paulie. He saw how his accomplice watched the door. Then he saw the gunman point the gun at Paulie's head. Something caught his eye. Gray had been waiting for Stacks to catch what he did.

"You see it, don't you?"

"Yeah. What the fuck is on his hand and wrist?"

"Some sort of tattoo. I'mma give it to Harp. He's good with computers. See if he can blow that up and get a line on these mafuckas."

Stacks looked at Gray as he handed the phone back. He didn't need to say it. He didn't even need to *think it*. Gray already knew what he wanted. Gray nodded and took the phone back from Stacks.

"Say less."

As the hearse carrying Rose and Cori turned on to Dorian Street, Cori saw a large gathering outside the Murphy home; well-wishers and neighborhood folk that didn't attend the funeral. It wasn't until the car got closer that she realized it was much more. People holding signs that read "NO JUSTICE! NO PEACE!" and "STOP KILLING US!" could be seen throughout. Others had t-shirts with Fin's face. They were angry, but their roars quieted as the limo came to a stop in front of the house. Patrick was there to protect them just as he was at the cemetery. As he opened the door, cries of "WE LOVE YOU, ROSE!" and "THEY AIN'T GONNA GET AWAY WITH THIS" broke up the uncomfortable silence. Patrick grabbed Rose's hand, lifted her from the vehicle and put his arm around her, then turned to the crowd. Cori immediately had a revelation. Cori always thought Fin's protective nature must've come from his father. She now knew he inherited that trait from Patrick as well. The crowd parted the way greasy water spreads out when one drops liquid soap into it. They walked up to the steps leading to the porch, Patrick and Rose in front, Cori only a few steps behind. Cori could feel the palpable anger flowing amongst the crowd, it let her know what she was feeling wasn't wrong. She wanted to join the crowd, march to Justin's house and kill him herself. She dared not do that though. Now wasn't the time. As they ascended the steps, Odella swung the screen door open to receive Rose and Cori. The crowd began to murmur, their vocal anger returning.

"Y'all c'mon in hea'. They just hurtin' like we are."

Patrick remained at the top step, right on the edge of the porch and watched as Rose and Cori entered the house. As she ushered Rose and Cori into safety, Odella gave Patrick a look that needed no words. Patrick nodded and waited until the screen door closed behind them, then he turned to the crowd. Cori turned and watched Patrick.

"Cori, baby. C'mon nah. Patrick gonna handle them."

"Lil' Bug....."

Cori didn't budge. She stared at the crowd, then again at Patrick as he began to speak in his deep, authoritative voice.

"Friends. Nah, I know y'all mad. We mad too! I know y'all hurtin'. We hurtin' too! But today *ain't* the day for this! I just buried my........my........only grandbaby. Let us grieve. Let us pray. Let us be in peace."

Patrick stood there, motionless. All that he had he gave in that speech. Cori thought this big, tree trunk of a man might pass out. Just then, there was motion from within the crowd. She could see someone was trying to make their way to the front. It was an older man, dressed in a gray suit, a white button up shirt and no tie. He didn't move fast but he did move with purpose and power. Cori thought he might be a church elder coming to be with the family. The man ascended the steps leading to the porch. When he arrived at the top, he extended both arms out and placed his hands onto Patrick's shoulders, a sympathetic look was in his eyes. The two men looked at each other before Patrick nodded.

"Brothers and Sisters. Family! Now I know we all are mad! Believe you me, we are mad too! Though we want, and WILL GET JUSTICE, today is not the day. Today is a day of mourning. Today begins the healing process. We *must* let this family heal. Now I beg of you, please, go home. Pray. Pray for strength. Pray for guidance. Pray that God, our Father, steels your will so that we may see this to its righteous conclusion. But today is not that day….so I say again, go home."

The man's sing-song like cadence confirmed Cori's suspicions. He turned to Patrick, placed his arms around him, hugging him fiercely as he spoke into his ear. She watched as Patrick slowly accepted this moment of comfort. Up until that moment, she had never seen Patrick grieve. As Patrick's arms slowly rose to return the embrace, the man continued to speak to him. Patrick's shoulders began to shake, the throws of sorrow taking hold of him. The crowd watched, as did Cori. Then, finally, the crowd began to disperse. She remained at the screen door; her eyes affixed on Patrick. Patrick, the man that greeted her so warmly on that very porch a little over a year ago, now fought to gather himself, both moments because of his love for Fin. He collected himself and said his goodbyes to the man, then turned and was shocked to see Cori there. She saw a rush of shame fall over his face, her having witnessed his breakdown. She decided she would return the gesture of love and acceptance he once gave her. She swung the screen door open and extended her hand to him. He smiled through the hurt and took her hand.

As Patrick and Cori made their way through the home, Cori took in the array of familiar and unfamiliar faces. Dee, who sat in a corner holding Little Chris, almost seemed to be in a daze as the two-year-old Chris fidgeted and whined in his lap. Shayla came over and hugged Cori, her eyes still red and her cheeks flushed with blood. The two had never been close, but Cori understood her love for Fin through Stacks. Stacks didn't appear to be in the house, or at least not where she could see him. Classmates of Fin, both past and present filled the home, eating food and talking. There was a circle of older women talking in the living room. The kitchen had members of the church, cleaning and cooking. Cori continued on to the screened-in porch in the back where Rose, Odella, and her parents, Nicholas and Ann, sat and talked. As she entered the room, Rose looked up and motioned for Cori to come sit beside her. Her voice raspy and hoarse as she spoke.

"Hey, Lil' Bug."

"Hey, Mama."

Her mother, Ann, came and sat on the other side of her, placing her hand on her knee.

"Corianne, have you eaten?"

"Not really."

Odella rocked back in her chair and propelled herself upwards. Cori didn't feel much like eating, but she knew the decision of whether she would eat or not had already been made.

"Ya' need to eat somethin' nah, baby."

She wanted to protest, but she saw Fin at the dining room table the first night she came here, his hands up telling her don't argue with Grandma. She simply nodded her head.

fin

the return

"Y'all c'mon in hea'. Let's get that baby somethin' to eat. My Rose too."

Odella's *I'm-not-really-asking-you* tone was heard by all. Nicholas and Ann picked up on the signal and followed Odella out of the room, much to the surprise of Cori. The two women sat there, much like they did in the limo, in silence, both spiritually, mentally, emotionally and physically exhausted. Though the murmur of the house grew louder in swells only to fall again to a dull hum, the sounds and sights of the backyard were tranquil. The two women stared out through the mesh screen wrapping around the back porch. It was dusk and the sun would soon set. Shade covered most of the backyard. They could hear the beginning sounds of crickets warming up for their evening chorus. The wind rustled the trees offering a cool relief to the warm, muggy air. Their tranquility was soon interrupted.

KNOCK

KNOCK

Cori and Rose were jolted out of their mental daze. Their heads turned to their left as they looked up behind them at the man poking his head out of the door.

"Mrs. Finley, may I come in?"

"Yes, baby. Do I know you?"

Cori stared at the man curiously as he approached. She saw him at the funeral and the burial ceremony. He was of even complexion, the color of light brown sugar, with a chiseled jaw line, well-manicured beard and wire-rimmed glasses. His eyes seemed warm, even in the sorrow of the day. He was of average height, but his suit appeared as if it was cut to fit his well-built, muscular frame.

She stared at him off and on throughout the day's events, unsure why he stood out to her so much, unsure if or how she knew him. As the man approached, Rose's face began to scrunch up, she too unsettled by the man. He bent down, dropping to one knee in front of her. Rose stared at him, then her eyes got big, her eyebrows raising in surprise. She reached out and placed her hands on either side of his face.

"Hi, Mama Rose."

Rose gasped as tears of joy welled up. She pulled him into her embrace.

"Curtis Davis! Oh, Curt!"

CURT! Cori hadn't seen him in years. He was a chubby, little teenager the last they saw each other. She instantaneously felt a rush of guilt. *Oh my God, I never called him!* She knew Curt and Fin spoke often, but in the midst of everything that happened, the rush of emotions, it simply never occurred to her to reach out to him. However he heard about Fin's death, it should have come from her. Rose hugged Curt as if her embrace could take her back to the last time she saw him, knowing her Fin would be there. Ironically, that is exactly where Curt's mind went. Curt silently cried, his tears dropping softly from his chin onto Rose's shoulder, dotting her sheer blouse. He leaned back and looked at her, Rose stared at him, then she pulled him into her bosom again.

"Curt, Curt, Curt, CURT! I cannot believe how handsome you are! It is so good to see you!"

Curt released Rose, and she smiled through a grimace, her brow frowning realizing he never got to see the man Fin had become. He turned to Cori.

fin

the return

"Hey, Big Head," then hugged her.

"Oh my God, Curt! I am so sorry I didn't call you!"

"It's good to see you, Cori, but you have absolutely nothing to apologize for."

"I just......."

"Cori, these last few days have seemed like a bad dream to me. I can only imagine what it's been like for you two. Stop apologizing. I feel zero offense. Besides, I'm here aren't I?"

She smiled at him, appreciative of him attempting to absolve her guilt.

"How are your parents, Curt? I haven't heard from them in years."

He sat down in the old, wooden chair adjacent to Rose.

"They are good, Mama Rose. Mom retired a few years back. Dad started his own practice. They live in California now."

"And you? What have you been up to?"

"I'm blessed. Married now with a little one on the way. I live in Japan now."

"Still in Japan?!?!"

"Yes, Ma'am. I love it there. Moved back after high school to attend university there. It's been a bit of an adjustment for my wife though."

He pulled out his phone and showed Cori and Rose pictures of his wife.

"Oh my, Curt. You have a beautiful family!"

Cori remained silent, still feeling guilty for not reaching out to him. He sensed Cori's guilt and Rose's longing for Fin. *I need to tell them now.* He reached out and touched her hand.

"Mama Rose, there is something I need to talk to you about."

Cori saw that as her queue to excuse herself. She figured Curt and Rose deserved to have a private moment, him being Fin's oldest friend after all. As she stood up to leave them be, he reached out and stopped her.

"No, Cori. Stay. You need to hear this too. I think what I want to share, if I know Fin…….."

He paused once he realized the tense of his words.

"If I knew Fin, and what he would have wanted, you have to stay."

Cori and Rose looked at each other perplexed, neither having any idea what he was about to reveal, and both hoping it wouldn't be the final straw that broke their spirits once and for all.

"Now, I know I haven't seen either of you for years. Hadn't seen Fin either. But he and I kept in contact. You know that. Cori."

Cori nodded her head. Rose seemed flabbergasted by that information.

"Wait, I didn't know that?"

"Mama, they were always working on some computer stuff. I used to wake up and see Fin on the computer all times of the night."

"Well, that's actually why I need to talk to you."

Curt sat back a bit, reached into his inside jacket pocket and retrieved an envelope. The white envelope was stuffed with tri-folded papers that he removed, unfolded and handed to Rose. Cori scooted closer to read over her shoulder. She looked up and saw him anxiously watching, his arms rested on his knees as one leg bounced in anticipating of her and Rose's reaction. She began reading.

Dear Mr. Davis,

After careful review by our computer science team of your and Mr. Finley's application code and customer input algorithm, we feel with some minor modifications, this is a project we feel could be extremely profitable for all parties involved.

Our Board of Directors here at Takahashi Investments has decided to go further and invest in your and Mr. Finley's business proposal for "BroBro" and "BroBro.com" for the purpose of selling, trading and promoting unique athletic footwear and apparel to the burgeoning footwear collector market. Takahashi Investments is prepared to offer a capital investment of $500,000, fifty percent of which will be paid in advance before the effective date of the enclosed agreement. Our standard rate of two percent annual profit on investment, and other financial expectations, can be found in the enclosed agreement.

We are saddened to hear about the untimely passing of Mr. Finley. Takahashi Investments offers you and Mr. Finley's family our

fin

the return

most heartfelt condolences. As such, you will need the executor of his estate to agree to allow us to use his portion of the code, as well as the "BroBro" name, before we can begin the capital investment process.

We look forward to hearing from you and are excited to be working with you.

Best Regards,

Satoro Takahashi

Chief Financial Officer

Takahashi Investments

As Rose read the letter, tears of joy and shock streamed down her face, her hands shook. Cori could barely believe it either. Rose looked up at him.

"Did he know?"

He gently wiped his eyes.

"I was meeting with them the day he died. It's a thirteen-hour time difference so it was still early in the day there. When I got out of the initial meeting with Takahashi, I called his phone, emailed, instant messaged and never got a response. It was only a few days later that I heard of the shooting on the news."

Curt dropped his head and wept.

fin

the return

"We had this idea when we were kids, and I never got to tell him we did it."

Cori leapt from her seat and hugged him, burying her face in his neck.

"He loved you, Curt. Thank you for making his dream come true, and trust me, he knows."

Rose, still in shock, turned her head, and rested it in her hand, which was now propped up on the arm of the sofa. She sat there thinking of all the possibilities stripped from her son, the good he could have done in the world. She finally gathered herself enough to speak.

"What do you need from us, Curt?"

Curt and Cori released each other. He took a moment to corral his emotions, looked up at Cori then over at Rose.

"All you have to do is sign the last document, Mama and Fin's portion of the company will become yours. I took the liberty of having my lawyer draft up a separate document, to indemnify you and the family of all legal responsibility and the day to day operations. You will be a silent partner. I take all the risk."

Rose looked at Curt long and hard, then down at the document.

"Do you have a pen?"

Curt reached into his jacket pocket once again and produced a beautiful wood grain fountain pen and extended it to Rose. She stared at his hand, then down at the documents, before finally turning her head up to Cori.

"Not for me, honey. For her."

Cori looked at Rose in utter shock.

"Mama. I can't."

"Nonsense. I don't have a doubt in my mind who you are, who you were meant to be. My boy was going to marry you. I know it like the air I breathe, Fin was going to marry you. What kind of mother would I be if I accepted this, when I see his wife is standing right here before me?"

Rose lovingly handed the documents to Cori. "Now sign it, Lil' Bug."

Cori began to tremble, still in disbelief by what she was hearing. The fact that Curt just dropped a bomb on them both was inconsequential at that moment. Rose just told her she knew Fin would marry her one day. She saw her as a daughter and always would.

"His father took damn good care of me; made sure Fin and I were provided for after he was gone. Fin is his father's son. He would have done the same for you. Now sign it, baby."

Just then, Odella and Ann returned with plates of food. Odella could see something had occurred but was confused by the different emotions of shock, sorrow, joy and love all wrapped into each of their faces.

"Y'all must really be hungry! Never seen people so happy to eat my food!"

fin

the return

Odella provided a much-needed relief of laughter for Rose, Cori, and Curt. She looked at Curt.

"And who are you, honey?"

"Curt, Ma'am. You must be Grandma Odella. I have heard so much about you."

"And it's all true! Now c'mon in hea' and get you some food!"

Once again, they all laughed. Cori took the pen from Curt as he left, sat down next to Rose, and set the documents down on the small coffee table in front of the sofa. Ann set Cori's plate down next to the documents. The plate had all of Fin's favorites: fried fish, greens, cornbread and lima beans salted with ham. As she leaned over to sign the documents, Ann's curiosity got the best of her.

"Cori, honey, what is that?"

"A gift from Fin."

chapter twenty-two

a kiss goodbye

The Murphy's home was finally winding down, as many of the family and friends that had gathered were filtering out. Cori found herself exhausted with the barrage of hugs and "thank you for coming" statements she had to say. It wasn't that she didn't appreciate everyone's support, she just wanted to be left alone. She managed to sneak outside, away from the last few people in the house besides Patrick, Odella and Rose. Her parents had left about an hour earlier, but her father promised he would come get her when she was ready to leave. She wasn't sure if she wanted to leave though.

She sat in Odella's seat to the far left of the porch. The front porch light was off, so the dark, humid night gave her a private space right out in the open. Shayla, Dee and Little Chris came out of the house. Little Chris looked more and more like Stacks by the day. As he laid sleep on Shayla's shoulder, Shayla came over and grabbed Cori's hand. Cori stood and looked at Little Chris resting, stroked his

fin

a kiss goodbye

back and kissed his little cheek. Shayla's free arm wrapped around Cori.

"Look girl, I know you and Chris don't get along, but you are always welcome at our house."

"Thank you, Shay. That means a lot."

Cori turned to Dee. Dee was now fifteen years old and was just as tall as Fin was. He wore short dreadlocked hair with faded sides, an earring, and though rail thin and young, Cori thought he was an extremely handsome young man. His light brown eyes and bright white smile always made her think he was going to be a heartbreaker one day. Today, though, his big, beautiful eyes were red from tears, his smile nowhere to be found.

"Hey, cutie! Come here."

Dee approached Cori, still saddened by the day, and hugged her.

"I know, sweetie. I miss him too."

Shayla watched as the two embraced, then they all turned to the front door as Stacks walked out. Stacks seemed scarce at the repass, at least that's what Cori thought. She actually understood and was a bit envious of Stacks' ability to become invisible today. She wished she was afforded the same opportunity. Stacks reached in his pocket, pulled out his keys and handed them to Shayla.

"Take lil' man and Dee home, baby. I need to talk to Cori for a sec."

"Okay, Bae. C'mon, Dee. Remember what I said, girl."

384

fin

a kiss goodbye

"Bye, Cori," Dee said somberly.

"Bye, y'all."

Stacks snapped his head over to Cori as Shayla walked down the porch stairs, her heels clicking loudly.

"What she say?"

"I said she should come over, and she don't need to worry about yo' punk ass!" Shayla shouted as she walked away.

Cori giggled. Stacks frowned at Shayla, then turned to Cori.

"Oh, that's funny to you?"

"Stacks, what do you want to talk to me about?"

She rolled her eyes at him. *I don't have time for his foolishness right now. Lord, give me strength!* Stacks responded by throwing his hands up in surrender.

"I'm here to talk Cori, not war. Not today, Sis. Can we sit? Please?"

Cori reluctantly sat down. Internally, she was torn. She really didn't like or respect Stacks, not for what he did or stood for. However, she appreciated him for who and what he was to Fin. She decided to listen. Stacks looked out into the street, staring at Valebrook, taking in all of its beauty and ugliness.

"Look, I get why you don't like me. Hell, Fin sat right here in this same seat I am sitting in and called me out, this was before he met you. Told me I was too smart to be doing this shit."

fin

a kiss goodbye

Stacks' head dropped in shame.

"And as usual, he was right. I made a promise to that man to get out. Get out the life, get out from under the cloud that is being a Morton, to get the fuck out of Norfolk. Since that conversation, it's all I have been trying to do."

Cori remembered how Fin would defend Stacks, saying he was getting out, an excuse she thought he gave to rationalize associating with a man that sold illegal guns.

"But what you don't understand, what no one understood was, how I felt about that man. My oldest brother Mike died when I was just a kid, younger than Dee. Shan, the brother over me, he was just as lost as I was. He took his anger out on me. We were never close. I am more like Dee's father than his brother. After that day in Brevoit, I had no one except for Shayla - Shayla and Fin. Fin was more than my friend; he was my brother. I loved that dude."

Cori listened as Stacks poured his heart out, tears slowly slipping down his face. She turned and looked at the view with Stacks, trying to reconcile the front he put up for the streets to that of the man that sat beside her.

"What happened that day in Brevoit? Fin never said anything about it."

"Not even to you?"

She shook her head. Stacks chuckled a bit and shook his head.

"He finally learned."

"Learned what?"

fin

a kiss goodbye

He smiled. "About sayin'."

"What?!"

Stacks knew it wasn't his place to tell Fin's version of the story, so he told his, the only version he chose to remember.

"What happened that day was, Fin showed the caliber of man he was going to be. He protected Dee, and literally put his life on the line, all because I asked him to. That day, he showed me what true love and brotherhood was. I can't ever repay him for that. None of us talked about it. Not me, not him, not even that mother fucker Jus....."

Stacks didn't even want to say his name. She never realized Justin was there that day, because Fin never spoke about it. She grew angry with herself for feeling a flash of sympathy for him. Stacks continued:

"You know, part of me, I mean as much as I hate that mother fucker, and have since that day in Brevoit, part of me feels sorry for him."

Cori held back everything she had not to slap the taste out of Stacks' mouth. *SORRY FOR HIM!* Stacks saw her, griping the arms of the wicker chair, the thin strips of wood cracking under her rage-filled grip. He reached out and grabbed her hand then looked forward again.

"Shit happened that day no kid should have to see. All of us found our own personal demons, our own piece of hell that day. Justin was living in hell long before then. I often wonder if I caused that whole string of events."

fin

a kiss goodbye

As he paused to reflect and wipe a tear with his other hand, Cori began to relax. She could tell this was all eating at Stacks in a way she couldn't fathom.

"I was there that night, at Brown's. I heard on the news there was a shooting there and I came to check on Fin. When I got there, I saw you."

Cori looked at him, her eyes welling up.

"You were there? Where?"

He gazed back into the night.

"I pulled up across the street. Saw you sitting in a cop car, the tape all around the store, and around what I realized was Fin. I saw Justin sitting in the car, crying like a baby. I knew what had happened. Mafucka never shoulda been a damn cop!

"I even watched as that female police, what's her name....Tanner? Yeah, she was just a detective back when we all met her, watched her deal with that shit. She is a fucking dog, don't take no bullshit."

Cori couldn't believe what she was hearing.

"Why didn't you......"

"When you screamed, when you charged at them......"

Cori could feel Stacks' hand shaking. She wondered if this moment was his first time crying as well. He wasn't at the funeral or burial. She stopped feeling animosity towards him, instead, she was awash in compassion. She turned her hand over from under Stacks'

fin

a kiss goodbye

grip and held his instead. She gave it a firm yet loving squeeze causing him to look at her.

"Wanna here something crazy?"

"Crazier than you and I sitting here crying together?"

Cori simply giggled then reached over to the table. She picked up the documents Curt had given her and handed them to Stacks. He frowned as she handed it to him, curious what it was. *People just handin' me stuff all day!* As he read, he slumped down when its contents revealed themselves, covering his mouth with his hand. Cori watched him, her love and respect growing as she saw the pride for his brother's accomplishment and regret that he would never know he did it.

"Wow. He did it. He fucking did it!"

"You knew about this?"

"That man talked about this shit since we was kids! I asked him, sitting right here, when he was gonna do something with it."

She always figured it was Stacks that dropped him off at school. This confirmed it for her.

"The day you took him to campus so he could register for school. That's the day we met."

Stacks looked at Cori confused.

"Cori, we talked about him going to school, but I never actually took him anywhere. I left because Jus......."

fin

a kiss goodbye

The two stared at each other, the realization of what Stacks never finished saying hit them like a haymaker. The moment didn't last long, however. Gray Boy appeared outside the gate.

"You ready, Boss Man?"

Cori and Stacks looked up and saw Gray. She had never met Gray before, so she looked at Stacks who gave her a nod of approval, signaling Gray was okay.

"Ms. Cori, I just wanted to offer my condolences. Fin was a good Brother."

"Give me a minute." He turned back to Cori. "If you ever need anything, I am a phone call away."

Stacks stood up, leaned over to Cori and kissed her on her forehead. Cori gave zero response. Stacks looked down at her one last time, laid the documents on her lap, then made his way down the porch steps. When he reached the bottom, she called out to him.

"Stacks! Wait!"

She leapt out of the chair, walked down the stairs, stopping at the bottom step so she and Stacks were eye to eye, and threw her arms around him.

"Thank you……Boss Man."

Stacks embraced her back and let out a deep, long sigh.

"Chris. To you Sis, its Chris."

fin

a kiss goodbye

Cori leaned back and smiled. Stacks let her go and walked out of the gate. When he arrived at the edge of the gate, he and Gray began to walk away. She watched them walk away then returned to sit down. Patrick and Odella had greeted the last of the guests and retired for the evening. Rose had long ago went to bed. Her body could take no more grieving that day. She sat in Patrick's chair, Fin's favorite chair. Patrick told her from the time Fin was just a baby, he would always want to sit in his Grandpa's wicker chair. She ran her hands along the armrests, thinking that Fin's hands once touched these very spaces. She leaned back into it, nestled into the high, woven back soften by years of wear and tear. She sniffed its old smell and imagined she caught a whiff of Fin's scent. She looked at the street, lined with cars and remembered the first night he brought her here. She could still see him getting out of the car and smiling at her in reaction to Patrick. She could hear his voice as she sat on the trunk of her car, telling her....

"They are gonna love you. They are gonna love you, because I love you."

She heard him say it over and over in her mind, in her heart.

"They are gonna love you, because I love you."

"Because I love you...."

"I love you..."

She remembered their last night in bed, after he bore his soul to her, his playfulness, turning away just so she could push him. She could see him turning over and smiling. She saw the way the moonlight that peeked through the window danced in his eyes, the way his dark skin glowed. She could see his big, beautiful smile looking at her.

fin

a kiss goodbye

"I love you, Ms. Porter."

His voice was so loud in her mind she swore the world could hear him. She was glad they couldn't though. Those were her moments. He was hers and she was his. She pulled out her phone and found the picture they took. Their first of many photos they would take but by far the most important. The picture on the bench, where they fell in love. She closed her eyes, and she could still feel his lips. She felt the warm breeze blow on her skin, just as it did that day on the bench as they kissed. She could still taste his lips, smell his skin, feel the warmth of his body as she leaned into him.

She stared at that photo. She kissed him. Her Fin. Her love. He spoke to her.

"I love you, Cori."

"I love you too, baby. Always."

epilogue

my brother's keeper part three

"I'mma be like 'FREEZE!! SHOW ME YOUR HANDS'!!"

Fin slapped Justin's hands away. "Man, sit yo' trigger happy ass down!"

The two old friends burst out into laughter.

"So, what about you, Bro? When you gonna go back to school and do your computer thing? I need them sweet sneaks!"

Fin chuckled and shook his head. "Sneaks, huh? I don't know, man. I know I need to go back."

"For real, Bro! I always be telling people 'my boy Fin gonna be rich selling sneakers and shit'!"

"Yeah, I know. Like that time you told Shanice McConnell if she went out with you, I was gonna get her some J's!"

fin

my brother's keeper part three

"All you had to do was talk to her friend and tell her you were gonna get her them J's!"

"*Who?!?! Vee??* That girl is a mud duck!"

Again, the boys shared a hearty laugh.

"Seriously though, Bro. When you gonna go back to school?"

"Why is everybody on me about this school thing?"

"'Cause, we know you smart, fool!"

Justin reached into his pocket and pulled out his cellphone. He typed quickly, his face deep in thought. Fin wondered what he was doing. After finding what he was looking for, he tossed Fin the phone.

"No time like the present!"

Fin looked at the phone and saw it open to the Tidewater State University homepage. The home screen had a banner that scrolled across it stating that it was the last day to register.

"Think you cute, huh?"

Justin simply smiled at him.

"C'mon, Bro. I'll give you a ride."

"You ain't got a car, Juss, and I ain't riding on the back of no bike."

"Naaaa, Bro. Check it out!"

Justin proudly pointed to an old, beat-up van parked two houses over.

Fin's face scrunched up. *I know he don't expect me to get into that!*

fin

my brother's keeper part three

"What. Is. That?? That thing looks like it has two right turns and one push of the brakes left before it falls apart."

"Don't talk about my baby, Fin. Just shut up and go get your book bag. I know you still got it."

Fin smiled; Justin knew him too well. He nodded, relenting to the pressure, walked into the house and grabbed his book bag, quickly threw a sandwich together and placed it in an old, gray lunch bag that was once Big Fin's, and headed out the door. Justin was already in the van. Fin walked around to the passenger side only to be stopped by Justin.

"Yeah, soooo...that door don't open. Gotta get in through the back door and climb over."

Fin shook his head and went around to the passenger side. "Ooohhhkaaayy."

He climbed into the van, making fun of how beat up it was, anything to mess with Justin. The two friends laughed all the way to the college campus. As Justin applied the brakes, a squeal let out that hurt Fin's ears.

"Did I say this thing had two right turns left? That was a lie!"

"Man, get out of my van!"

"Gladly!"

Fin climbed into the back of the van and exited the way he came in. He slammed the door shut then stepped forward to talk to Justin.

"Aight, Officer Bell. Proud of you, Bro!"

"Proud of you too, Bro. Now get in there and program some robots and shit!"

fin

my brother's keeper part three

"You funny! Seriously. Thanks, Bro. Means a lot. I think I needed a kick in the ass on this."

Fin looked around the campus.

"Hey, when I graduate Basic Training, we gotta celebrate!"

"No doubt!"

"Love you, Bro!"

Justin engaged the gears and drove away. Fin watched him leave. He smiled when the beat up, old van as it reached the corner and its brakes squealed.

"I love you too, Bro."

Fin looked at his watch, got his bearings, then made his way to the Registrar's Office. Fin registered for class and rushed to find the one currently in session, College Algebra. He heard the sound of the professor down the hallway. He quickened his pace and swung the door open causing all the students to turn, including Cori, and stare at him. The professor looked up at him.

"Can I help you?"

closure

As he walked out of that door, his last piece of business now complete, Stacks felt a huge weight lifted off of him. It's been three weeks since Fin's death, but he still had a promise to keep; to get out. Now that he had kept that promise, he wished he could tell him. For the first time in his life he was free, though his freedom took a heavy toll on his spirit and cost him so much. All he could think of was getting to Shayla's parents' house, picking up Shayla, Dee and little Chris, and getting on the road. He was finally leaving Norfolk, and the family business, breaking the generational curse that had plagued the Mortons for decades. He pulled his signature shades out of his jacket pocket and slipped them on his face. Just then, Gray pulled up in his silver Lexus ES 350. Stacks started to ask how he knew where he would be, but this was Gray, he always knew where everyone was. As the car pulled adjacent to Stacks' car, Stacks could hear the car being put in park and out hopped Gray. He walked over to meet Stacks now standing on the sidewalk.

"Boss Man."

closure

"That's you now, remember?"

"Not just yet. Got one more deal you need to close."

"Gray, I couldn't have been clearer. I'm done. I'm out!"

Gray removed his sunglasses.

"I know, but you still need to be with me for this one."

His stare conveyed to Stacks that this was serious. It wasn't often that Gray and Stacks actually came close to guns anymore. Their attendance at such meetings was reserved for the big deals and even then, only a sample was present and never any money. Stacks extended his hand for their ritualistic handshake.

"Say less."

"Follow me. I got a car for us."

Stacks followed Gray through the city, carefully avoiding highways and major streets where cameras could mark their path. They pulled up to an empty strip mall in a section of town where no one cared enough to monitor. They both parked their cars and exited. Stacks followed Gray to an old Crown Victoria that had seen better days. It was disposable, probably had more parts swapped out on it than one could count making it virtually untraceable. Stacks gave the car a cursory look. *Hope we don't gotta make a getaway in this shit!*

"Fuck you get this piece of shit?"

"Don't matter. Won't need it that long."

Gray turned the old V4 engine over. They cruised clear to the other side of Norfolk, near the shipping piers. The homes over there carried the scent of burning factories and despair. They were engulfed in power lines overtop that looked like a post-apocalyptic tapestry.

fin
closure

Gray knew Stacks was well-versed in every play they could encounter, so a briefing as to what they were going to see on the inside wasn't necessary. They finally stopped in front of an old, one story home that looked like it had been here since the dawn of time. Two doors down were a group of young men, drinking and talking loudly. Stacks recognized them to be part of the local gang, the Pier Street Boys, so named after the street on which they were established, just three blocks east from their present location. He didn't stare too long, as he didn't want to attract attention. They exited the car, Gray walked up the cement walkway and up the three old, wooden stairs, whose paint had chipped off long ago. He used his forearm to bang on the door. Stacks stayed at the bottom of the stairs, their typical tactical cover maneuver.

BANG! BANG! BANG!

Gray's cautious knock instantly put Stacks on alert. He made sure not to leave any prints on the door. Stacks could hear the mechanics of the locks, deadbolt and chains being manipulated. The door swung open only a few inches, stopped by the chain, as the suspicious eye of a young woman peeked out.

"Yeah."

"Hello, Ma'am. Is Wiwo home?"

Stacks had never head of Wiwo before, nor could he understand why he needed to be present for a no-name. Even more curious was why Gray needed to handle this deal himself. *This was a job for underlings! Fuck he got me here for?* Gray asked he be here so he would play his role. The woman looked Gray up and down, then over his shoulder at Stacks, sucked her teeth, and then closed the door to remove the chain and allow them entrance. When the door closed, Gray looked back at Stacks with a disapproving look on his face. Stacks knew what it was for; they never kept women or children in places they did business, let alone let them answer the door, lessons they learned all those years ago. Whomever they were here to see was a joke. The woman opened the door fully, stepping to the side.

"They in back."

Stacks thought she would have been beautiful if she was kept. Her frizzed hair was pulled back into a sloppy ponytail, the dark circles around her eyes looked costume like against her bright yellow skin. Gray slowly entered, Stacks a few deliberate paces behind him. Gray walked through the dark, dank smelling house. The scents of weed, cigarette smoke and body must were heavy. The only light besides what little crept through the shaded windows, came from the TV the woman had returned to watching and the light from the end of the hallway that Stacks assumed was the kitchen. As they made their way down the hallway, he began to hear indecipherable talking over the sounds of the TV.

"Gentlemen," Gray announced as he entered the kitchen, his voice echoing down the hallway.

"What up, Gray?"

Gray became irritated. "Y'all gonna stand up?"

"Hold up! Who you tal....." said Wiwo, his challenge interrupted by Stacks' entrance into the kitchen.

The word had gotten out that he was stepping down, but that did nothing to erode the reputation of Mr. Stacks. The man who was speaking, now sat awe struck by his presence. Both men popped tall upon seeing him.

"Allow me to introduce you to Mr. Stacks. Mr. Stacks, meet Wiwo and Tone."

"What up?" Wiwo asked.

fin

closure

"Now, Wiwo. Is that the way we address a man of Mr. Stacks' caliber?" Gray said in a mock, disappointing tone.

Gray had a way of giving direction by simply asking a question.

"My bad. Mr. Stacks. I'm Wiwo...this here is Tone."

"Hello, Mr. Stacks," said Tone.

Gray stared at Wiwo.

"Well? Shake his hand like a true gentleman."

Wiwo nervously extended his hand. He was smaller than Stacks, his thin, muscular physique clothed in a tank top and sagging jeans. Stacks looked at Gray, curious why he wanted this joke of a man to shake his hand and why he thought he should reciprocate. As he looked down at his hand, Stacks noticed what appeared to be a tattoo. He calmly extended his hand, grasped Wiwo's hand firmly then gently turned it over to reveal the markings. It was three bullets wrapped in a circular sentence that read THREE THE HARD WAY. Gray was right; he did have one last deal to close. Stacks looked at Gray who gave him a subtle nod.

"Soooooo.....I hear you gentleman want some guns?" asked Gray.

"Yeah, man. But you ain't have to bring the big man for this."

"It's my last day on the job," interjected Stacks. "You'll always know the last deal that Mr. Stacks ever closed, was with *you*. You'll be famous."

Wiwo and Tone looked at each other and smiled, the thought of the street cred that the last deal Mr. Stacks ever made was with them gave them excitement.

403

fin

closure

"Mr. Stacks, you want to go get them what they need?"

Stacks looked at Gray then the two men.

"Be right back."

He slowly walked back down the hallway towards the entrance, the rush of anger and the anticipation of revenge coursing through him. As he entered the front room, the woman never looked up from the show she was watching. *That's it. Keep watching that TV.* He got to the front door and stopped. He reached under the left side of his jacket and withdrew his weapon from his holster. He reached into his right inside pocket and withdrew the silencer. He slowly screwed the silencer into place. The woman finally noticed him standing there.

"You gonna leave or just stand there looking stupid?"

In one smooth motion, Stacks swung around and fired.

PEWNK! PEWNK!

Her lifeless eyes stared at the TV having been struck in the head and chest. Stacks walked over to the coffee table littered with empty beer bottles, overflowing ashtrays, and empty fast-food bags. He grabbed the remote and cranked the TV's volume up to maximum levels. The woman's eyes appeared to stare back at him, piercing his soul. He turned towards the hallway and began walking to complete his last job. He could see Gray had drawn his weapon and was pointing downward. As he reentered the kitchen, he saw Tone and Wiwo were on their knees, terrified yet protesting with as much bravado as they could muster.

"WHAT THE FUCK, GRAY BOY?" pleaded Wiwo.

"Y'ALL MAFUCKAS JUST GONNA COME IN HERE AND ROB US?" a pathetic sounding Tone shouted.

404

fin

closure

"Shhhhhhhhh......gentleman. Have some respect. Mr. Stacks would like to speak."

Gray looked at Stacks who hadn't taken his eyes of Wiwo. Stacks pulled one of the old, metal chairs from underneath the table, placed it so it faced the two men, then flipped the table over, sending it flying in between Tone and Wiwo who frantically dodged the projectile as food and drug paraphernalia scattered everywhere. Gray was even startled by the move but kept his eyes and gun trained on the two gunmen. He sat down calmly. As the men gathered what little bearings they had left, they returned their gaze to Stacks and Gray. Wiwo gave one last plea, his voice cracking, unwilling to accept his fate was inevitable.

"What's this about, man? We ain't DID *SHIT*!"

There was no escaping this predicament. Stacks never said a word. He stared at the two men, the two men that had caused the death of Fin, that caused so much pain....to Rose, to Cori, to him. He slowly sat down and exhaled, his hand holding the gun resting between his legs. His mouth was open as he fought back rage, his tongue rolling side to side inside of his bottom lip and over his teeth.

"*This*?"

The tears finally rolled down his eyes. "This is for my *Brother*."

PEWNK! PEWNK!

PEWNK! PEWNK!

hope

It's been eight years since Fin died and Cori has struggled every day since. She once heard someone say that with each passing day it got easier. *Whoever said that didn't know shit!* Today was her last day at Norfolk General Hospital. She once was a cashier working in the cafeteria, and now, eight years later, she just completed her second year of residency as an emergency room resident. Every time a patient was wheeled in with a bullet wound or a stab wound or even a heart attack, she would work to save them as if her life depended on it. In her mind, it wasn't some random patient on that hospital gurney, it was her Fin. *If only I knew then what I know now.*

Dr. C, as she was known around the hospital, was quite popular. Though a doctor, when most looked at the nurses, janitors, food service attendants, maintenance personnel, clerical workers and security guards as beneath them, Dr. C didn't. As far as she was concerned, she was still one of them. She made a point to enjoy every meal she ate in the cafeteria she once worked in, and whenever possible, she would sit with the cashiers and cafeteria workers and talk to them. She hoped that she could inspire them to reach for their dreams too. She never forgot her humble beginnings, that was something Fin taught her. Cori can still hear him explaining to her in one of their great, philosophical debates, as to the merits of staying in a poor community like Valebrook when emotionally, mentally, and financially a person has outgrown it. She remembers one exchange vividly.

"The bottom is my foundation, it's who I am. If a person forgets their feet and legs, acts if they never had them or they just don't exist, how do they expect to stand? To walk? To run?"

"But don't you fear the danger of jealousy rearing its head and coming for what you have?"

"Baby, the world is full of dangers. At least in the hood when they come to rob you, they come with a gun. In some places they rob you with a smile. But I also believe if you can teach the man or woman who has nothing how to get what you have, they will forever respect you because you didn't see them as less than you but as someone worthy to know what you know. Then, they can get it on their own, righteously and in good conscience."

Fin's belief in people, his empathy, his wisdom that was far beyond his years, always melted her. *I miss you, baby.* As she sat at her locker for what would be the final time, she reflected on her life these past nine years since she met Fin. The triumphs, the utter heartbreaks and devastation, the love, the hope, the pain, the misery. She felt she had lived a lifetime, but she wasn't done living. She owed it to herself, and to Fin, to see her part of their dream through. She slowly retrieved her belongings out of the locker, removing the old photo of her and Fin from the locker door last, pausing to remember that moment. His arms wrapped around her as they sat on the bench across from the Dr. Rebecca Lee Crumpler building. *Four thirty, Mr. Finley.* She smiled, kissed the photo and placed it in the cardboard box along with the rest of her stuff, then closed the locker. She reached for her keys and stood up. The keys jingled. She giggled. Then she heard a sad, sing-songy voice from behind.

"Hey, Girl! I am gonna miss YOU!"

It was Renee, a fellow intern. She and Cori had become close since she transferred in from St. Paul's Medical Center in Charlotte.

"I am gonna miss you too! All this means is you gotta come visit me!"

"Girl you know full and well I am *not* the flying type!"

"Trust me I know. I'm still mad you missed Vegas last year."

"They have casinos in Atlantic City, girl. I'm good!"

The two women laughed and quickly turned their smiles upside-down while poking out their bottom lips. Cori set her box of belongings down in a chair, turned to Renee and hugged her fiercely. Cori began to cry, her voice breaking as she spoke.

"I am really gonna miss you, Renee."

"Don't make me cry, C."

The women let out a nervous laugh, leaned slightly away from each other to take mental pictures of the other's face, embraced again, then reluctantly released.

"I'll call you as soon as I get settled."

"You better!"

"I love you, girl."

"I love you too, C. Now go before I change my mind and not let you leave!"

fin

hope

They laughed, wiped their eyes, then Cori picked up her box and walked out of the locker room. She walked down the corridor to a repetitive chorus of "Goodbye, Dr C," and "We are gonna miss you, Dr. C!" As she made her way to the nurse's station to tell her favorite nurse, RN Calloway, goodbye, she began to hear the audio from the TV in one of the many triage areas.

News Anchor: "Former Norfolk Police Officer Justin Bell was released today after six and a half years in prison for the accidental shooting death of James Finley. Finley, a student at Tidewater State University at the time, was getting off work when two masked gunmen entered into Brown's Stop-N-Go in Norfolk. They robbed the store, then shot and killed the clerk on duty, Ishmael "Paulie" Washington, before fleeing.

"Bell was a rookie police officer for the department at the time, and broke protocol by hopping out of his patrol car without the authority or back up of his partner, despite the more senior officer's objections. Bell, thinking James Finley was one of the gunmen, opened fire on Finley, striking him once in the arm and once in the stomach. Finley died at the scene. It was later discovered that Finley worked at the convenience store and was taking out the trash at the end of his shift.

"The tragic twist to this story was that Finley and Bell were childhood friends, both former students at Eastwood High School in Norfolk. Bell's plea agreement led to massive protests by the Black Lives Matter Movement with counter protests by the Hampton Roads Fraternal Order of Police.

"Bell's attorney refused to comment on his client's release, but did issue a statement saying that while Bell will never forgive himself for his horrific and tragic mistake, Bell's debt to society had been paid and he deserved a chance to recover his life."

She tuned out the rest of the news anchor's comments. She didn't know why she had stopped to listen to the report at all. She also hadn't noticed the tears rolling down her face. An orderly passing by became concerned as to why Norfolk General's favorite resident was crying.

"Dr. C, are you okay?"

Cori gathered herself and cleared her throat. "Oh, ummmm. I'm just a little emotional. Today is my last day."

"Oh noooooooo. Well you take care of yourself. We will miss your smile and energy around here."

She smiled, thanked the man, and then moved to the nurses' station. RN Calloway wasn't there at the moment. She looked down at her watch and saw she couldn't wait for her. She reached for a pen and pad, but she began to hear the news station once more. *I gotta get out of here!* She dropped the pen and pad and left the station. She walked briskly through the corridors waving and saying goodbye to everyone as she did until she finally made it through the glass double doors, into the parking lot and to her car. She set her box on the roof of the car and fumbled with her keys, her shaking hands made pressing the unlock button near impossible. She was an emotional wreck.

Jingle-jingle-jingle

She smiled. Once again, memories of her love made her smile right when she needed it most. She finally got into the car, loaded the box onto the front passenger seat, started her car, and drove away. She openly began to sob as she made her way through the Norfolk

fin

hope

streets. She knew there was only one thing that would put a smile on her face, one thing that would bring true joy and peace to her heart. She needed to go get the most important gift Fin ever gave her, because when she did, when she held that precious, precious gift in her hands, she truly felt loved and that Fin was right there with her. She looked at the time and began to drive a bit faster. She knew she needed to rush. She finally pulled into the parking lot. It was packed. Instead of jostling for position in the line of cars closest to the building, she found the first open spot she could. She had a brief moment to collect herself before…..

RRRRRRRIIIIIIIIIIIIIIIIIIIIIIIIIIIIIIIIINNNNNNNNNNNNNNNNNNNGGGGGG!!

She hopped out of the car and made her way towards her treasure. It was a warm day, though the sun wasn't really shining. The loud screams and laughter from children running to their parents, and purring engines of the waiting activity and school buses was deafening. *I couldn't deal with all this screaming every single day! I don't know how they do it.* Just then, she saw her baby. He was so tall he looked like a fourth grader, though he was only seven years old. She always thought his brown skin looked like warm syrup on pancakes. He had curly hair in a tight little afro that resembled a crown on his head. *That boy even walks like his daddy!* The thought always made her chuckle. As she watched him, she saw his head was down. She reasoned he must be sad about today being his last day, that, or *that damn Russy was talking trash again.* She waved her hand in the air and raised up on her tiptoes to get his attention.

"FIIIIINNNNNNNNN!"

fin

hope

Little Fin looked up and saw his Mama to his left near the basketball court. He turned sharply, artfully avoiding contact with darting children, fast-moving teachers, dutiful school administrators and searching parents. Cori watched as he cheerlessly walked over to her. *He is really taking his last day hard.* She frowned her brow and the corner of her mouth turned up. She walked towards him. Little Fin looked up and saw her approaching and quickened his pace. They met in the small patch of grass separating the incoming and outgoing traffic of the parking lot. He stopped just short of her and her outstretched arms. She, taken aback by him not rushing into her arms, stopped and cocked her head a bit.

"Hello, Mr. Finley. You mad so Mama can't get any love?"

He shrugged his shoulders and stuck his arm out towards her, presenting the dreaded note, his head held shamefully down. She retrieved the note from his trembling hand.

"What's this?"

She watched him as she opened it, waiting to see if he would clue her into its contents. When he didn't, she began to read.

Dear Dr. Porter-Finley,

I wanted to say congratulations on your new position. We couldn't be happier for you and all of your success. James is such a great child. His intellect, warmth, wit and strength made all of us better. He will be sorely missed. Please keep in touch and if there is ever anything I can do for either of you, please feel free to call me.

Hug my little protector Fin for me.

413

fin

hope

Sincerely,

Mrs. Graves

She looked down at her little man, his head still down, his hands gripping the straps on his bookbag. *Protector. You are more like your daddy than you realize, baby.* She grabbed his chin and pulled his face up so she could look into his eyes, his father's eyes before him. He kept them looking down at the ground, part out of shame, part out of sadness.

"James Buckley Finley, look at me."

He looked up at his mama with tears in his eyes. She saw Fin's deep brown eyes in their son every time she looked at him. Much like his father, the safety of resting in her embrace, gave their son peace and a safe space to release hurt, frustration and sadness. She would be that for him, but first he needed to hear her.

"Baby, you are such a special young man. Everyone who encounters you is left all the better for it. That, you get from your father. And I know you're sad baby, no one likes to leave their school or their home town, but there is a whole world out there waiting for you to see it. You'll make more friends. We will come back and see Grandma. We aren't leaving Norfolk forever baby."

"You promise?"

"Yes baby, Mama promises"

Then she lovingly grabbed her and Fin's son. She felt like she was holding Fin, *her* Big Fin, all over again and he was holding her. He gripped her waist hard and buried his face in her belly. They both cried

fin

hope

a bit. She kissed the crown of his head, breathed in the scent of coconut and aloe from his hair, then she leaned back. She placed his beautiful face in her hands as his arms remained around her waist and smiled at him. He smiled back.

"I ever tell you about when my daddy's job made us move to Japan when I was a little girl?"

"YOU LIVED IN JAPAN??"

"Yup. For three years. It's also where I met your father, but he didn't even notice me."

She slid her arm around his shoulder so they could walk to the car. He gave her a smile that melted her heart.

"Mama, you are the prettiest girl in the world. He noticed you."

"See, *you* are super smart. You get that from me!" a sassy Cori said as she pointed to herself which made both of them laugh.

"Mama..."

"Yes baby?"

"Did you know they make Lucumi Warriors in Japan??"

The life in his voice returned. That warmed Cori's heart.

"Really now?"

"Yup! And did you know......."

Cori and Little Fin walked to the car slowly, enjoying each other's presence and the warm afternoon air. They walked in laughter and conversation. Hope surrounded them. They walked in love.

415

book one

a story of love and hope

book two

big fin

a story of redemption

wasting talent

Summer, 1987

Big Fin was growing tired of working at daVinci's. The night club was full of would be gangsters, military members who told tales of their "pre-Navy gangster life", wild women looking for a good time, and drunkards. The job served a purpose though. The extra money he collected helped take care of his mother back in Florida. Big Fin left Miami to start over, to make a new life for himself, and to help provide for his family. The way he figured it, he was single with no kids, he didn't need the money for himself. His mother, Shirley, did. He owed her that.

Saturday nights were always the most rambunctious of nights at daVinci's, especially if it was a pay day weekend. It wasn't long before Big Fin had to display why he was hired. It was just prior to one in the morning, an hour before daVinci's closed. The commotion started just inside the door, but before Big Fin could step in to see what was going on, the fight spilled out into his lap.

BOOM!!!

The dark-tinted, double glass doors flung open. A full-on melee poured out of the club, men and women both fighting. Two other bouncers tried to break it up to no avail. Big Fin grabbed the closest fighting body to him and flung the man at least six feet like one would a rag doll. He stepped into the center of the brawl, and with one hand, picked up a man as the man swung at another patron, lifting him two feet off the ground. He too was flung to the side. By now the other brawlers stopped focusing on fighting and more on who this big, behemoth of a man would wrangle next, all except for one.

One man kept yelling and trash talking as he pummeled another man. Big Fin reached for the back of the man's shirt to pull him off of his victim. The man wildly swung as Big Fin's tug swung him around, striking Big Fin on the jaw. Big Fin's head snapped to the side, the metallic taste of blood swimming in his mouth. The man, once enraged, froze in his tracks, realizing he had made a catastrophic mistake. Big Fin turned and looked at him.

"Go."

The man however did not. The crowd, once in shock and awe by Big Fin's display, became bloodthirsty.

"FUCK THAT!! HIT HIS BIG ASS AGAIN!!" shouted one woman.

"PUNCH THAT BIG MAFUCKA! HE DON'T WANT IT!" yelled a drunken man.

"Walk away," Big Fin said, offering one last chance for the man to retreat before he turned and started towards the club entrance.

The man didn't walk away. He waited until Big Fin had turned his back, saw an empty beer bottle on the curb, picked it up and swung it Big Fin's head. His hand was stopped mid swing. Big Fin had turned around, tipped off by the low yet rising murmur of the crowd that could see behind him. With the man's wrist firmly in his massive hand, he grabbed the man's shirt, lifted him off of his feet and slung him into the glass doors of daVinci's. As the man laid there, unconscious and bloody, covered in broken glass, the club manager ran outside.

"WHAT THE FUCK?!! YOU PAYIN' FOR THIS SHIT!! YOU SUPPOSED TO STOP THEY ASSES FROM BREAKIN' SHIT, NOT BREAK IT YA' DAMN SELF!"

Big Fin looked down at the bloody, glass covered man, then up at the manager and made his decision. This job took him to a place he didn't want to go anymore, especially for what he was being paid.

"I quit."

"FUCK YOU MEAN YOU QUIT!"

Big Fin who had turned and started towards the parking lot stopped, he didn't look at the manager. He didn't need to. He knew his words would be enough.

"I said I quit. If you wanna discuss it further, come see me."

No one moved, not Big Fin, not the manager, not the onlookers, and definitely not the man laying through the broken frame of daVinci's doors, covered in glass. After a few moments of silence, save for the muffled sounds of the music emanating from the club, Big Fin walked towards the back of the parking lot to his car.

"You wastin' yo' time and talent up in there!" a voice yelled from the next aisle over.

Big Fin didn't want to deal with anymore foolishness, not tonight. He wanted to just go home, have a drink and rest.

"I said you wastin' yo' talent!"

Big Fin kept walking. Right before he made it to his car, he heard the sounds of an engine revving, and before he could react, the car was on top of him, blocking his path to his car. A man stepped out of the passenger seat of a dark blue, candy painted Cadillac DeVille. The man, who Big Fin thought was no older than he, wore a tight white t-shirt, underneath an unbuttoned plaid shirt. His khaki pants and Chuck Taylor sneakers let Big Fin know he was a gangster, not the kind that he dealt with in daVinci's, but a real gangster.

"I could use a man like you."

"I'm good."

"You good, alright. I ain't *neva'* seen nobody end some shit like that! I could use that in my organization. Pay real good too."

Big Fin could tell the man wasn't lying. It wasn't like he hadn't muscled before. Back then though it was small time. Whatever this man was into was serious.

"What's ya' name, Bruh?"

"They call me Big Fin."

"Yeah, yo' ass big alright! Coop. Let me holla at you a couple ticks!"

about the author

Born in Brooklyn, NY, and having spent many of his formative years in Miami, FL, Gamal Williams now resides in the Hampton Roads area of Virginia.

He joined the Navy in 1999 and became an Aviation Electronics Technician. He retired in 2019, after a successful twenty-year career at the rank of Senior Chief Petty Officer. He now spends his time writing and spending time with his children. A die-hard New York sports fan, music lover and avid reader, he ventured into writing as an outlet after a long battle with alcoholism. His first novel, "fin: a story of love and hope", started as a recurring dream he just could not shake.

"I never saw myself as a writer, definitely never saw myself writing a book. But we all have a hidden talent, a burning desire to do something, do or create something special, even if only for ourselves. Most times though, we are too scared to act on it. We only get one chance at this thing called life, why let fear stifle us? Why not see how great we can truly be? Go be great!"

 @authorgamalwilliams

www.authorgamalwilliams.com

(Background artwork by Amber Hightower. IG: theartofthevibe_arae)

fin: the playlist

prologue

the note

"Mama Knew Love" by Anthony Hamilton

fin

chapter 1   a night at brown's

"Girl" by the Internet feat. KAYTRANADA

"Living for The City" by Stevie Wonder

chapter 2   leaving bro bro

"Everybody Loves the Sunshine" by Roy Ayers Ubiquity

"You're All I Need" by Marvin Gaye and Tammy Terrell

chapter 3   eastwood high

"The Message" by Furious Five and Grandmaster Flash

chapter 4   brevoit

"1-900-HUSTLER (Instrumental)" by Jay-Z, Freeway, Memphis Bleek, and Beanie Siegel

chapter 5   bruises

"Runnin'" by the Pharcyde

chapter 6   the sleepover

"Home" by Stephanie Mills

chapter 7   big fin

"Uprising (Instrumental)" by Muse

stacks

chapter 8   family business

"C.R.E.A.M." by Wu-Tang Clan

chapter 9   promises

"The Watcher" by Dr. Dre

chapter 10   three dope boys

"Two Dope Boyz (in a Cadillac)" by Outkast

"Spot Rusherz" by Raekwon

chapter 11   the beginning

"Cell Therapy" by Goodie Mob

chapter 12   smoke

"Made You Look" by Nas

chapter 13   three rooms

"Ain't Nobody Worryin'" by Anthony Hamilton

chapter 14   my brother's keeper

"One Love" by Nas

I do not own the rights to any song listed above. They were simply inspirations for my writing. To the artists, thank you for touching my spirit.

fin: the playlist

cori

chapter 15   the bench

"A Long Walk" by Jill Scott

chapter 16   meet the family

"Anything for You" by Ledisi and PJ
Morton

chapter 17   the night before

"Dance with My Father" by Luther
Vandross

"Angel" by Lalah Hathaway

chapter 18   flashing lights

"You're All I Need" by Aretha Franklin

"Flashing Lights (Instrumental)" by
Kanye West

**chapter 19   my brother's keeper
part 2**

"Bad Boys (Instrumental)" by Inner
Circle

chapter 20   broken

"Far Away" by Marsha Ambrosious

chapter 21   the return

"Free Bird" by Lynyrd Skynard

chapter 22   a kiss goodbye

"Lay Me Down" by Sam Smith

epilogue

my brother's keeper part 3

"Count on Me" by Bruno Mars

closure

"In the Air Tonight" by Phil Collins

hope

"As" by Stevie Wonder

wasting talent

"I Ain't No Joke" by Eric B. and Rakim

*I do not own the rights to any song listed above. They were
simply inspirations for my writing. To the artists, thank you for
touching my spirit.*